THE SISTERS *of* LANCASTER COUNTY / BOOK ONE

—A—

PLAIN LEAVING

LESLIE GOULD

BETHANYHOUSE
a division of Baker Publishing Group
Minneapolis, Minnesota

© 2017 by Leslie Gould

Published by Bethany House Publishers
11400 Hampshire Avenue South
Bloomington, Minnesota 55438
www.bethanyhouse.com

Bethany House Publishers is a division of
Baker Publishing Group, Grand Rapids, Michigan

Printed in the United States of America

Library of Congress Control Number: 2017945294

ISBN 978-0-7642-1969-6 (trade paper)
ISBN 978-0-7642-3115-5 (cloth)

Scripture quotations are from the King James Version of the Bible.

This is a work of fiction. Names, characters, incidents, and dialogues are products of the author's imagination and are not to be construed as real. Any resemblance to actual events or persons, living or dead, is entirely coincidental.

Cover design by LOOK Design Studio

Cover photography by Mike Habermaan Photography, LLC

Author is represented by MacGregor Literary, Inc.

17 18 19 20 21 22 23   7 6 5 4 3 2 1

In memory of my father
Bruce Egger
1923–2017

The just man walketh in his integrity:
his children are blessed after him.

Proverbs 20:7

-1-

Jessica Bachmann

MARCH 2013

Tom Foster leaned toward me and extended the file. "You're the one to do the initial interview on this. With your background in Lancaster County, I'm counting on you." The case concerned an Old Order Amish family by the name of Stoltz and a contaminated well, possibly caused by fracking on their property.

It was an issue I had researched quite extensively in the last three years, out of fear of what my brother Arden wanted to do on our own family farm. My fear seemed to be unfounded, but it was still a topic I found fascinating, in a horrifying sort of way.

I steadied myself against my desk. "I'll do my best." As I took the file, Tom's hand brushed mine. My heart began to race, something it hadn't done in the last three years, not since Silas Kemp had kissed me for the very last time.

I swallowed hard, attempting to ward off the old familiar

hollowness that threatened to ruin my moment with Tom. There was no reason for me to think of Silas now.

"Is that your phone?" Tom nodded toward my desk. Something was buzzing. No one ever called me at work, not on my cell anyway.

"Probably." I patted the papers strewn across the top, retrieving my phone from under the farmers' markets file. My desk was usually perfectly organized. Embarrassed, I held it up as if in victory, but the buzzing had stopped.

He smiled. "Are we still on for lunch?"

"Definitely," I answered. "Eleven forty-five. I'll meet you in the parking lot."

I watched as he headed down the hall. Tom was thinner than Silas and not as tall. He looked like a man who worked *in* an office and worked *out* at a gym. On the other hand, Silas looked, or had looked, like a man who bucked hundred-pound bales of hay and wrestled a team of mules, starting when he was fourteen.

Silas hadn't tried to contact me, not once in the last three years. And why should he have? I made my choice. I knew what I was giving up. My parents. My remaining brother. My two sisters.

I sighed.

And Silas.

I concentrated on Tom, who glanced over his shoulder as he stepped into his own cubicle and smiled again. I waved, sure my face was turning red.

I slunk down into my chair and opened the file. I'd been dying to begin researching the case since Tom first mentioned it. Mentally, I zipped through the basics of fracking, which was actually slang for hydraulic fracturing. It consisted of drilling into the earth and directing a high-pressure mix of water, sand, and chemicals into rocks and creating fractures, which then released the gas inside. It was controversial for several reasons, including increased geological activity, including earthquakes in some areas. Depleted water tables due to the massive amounts of water needed to complete the process was another problem. Along with the spread of chemicals from the site of the fracking, which possibly caused contamination to ground and well water.

An energy bill, passed eight years before, exempted oil and gas industries from the Safe Drinking Water Act, which further complicated fracking cases.

Yes, I was looking forward to investigating the Stoltz case, but that needed to wait until I finished the list of all the farmers' markets for the Pennsylvania Department of Agriculture website, which was indicative of the sort of projects I was usually assigned as a clerical assistant. And whom could I blame? I had an eighth-grade education—and now a GED. Although I'd taken a few online classes at the community college, I was the least-educated person in the office.

I placed the Stoltz file to the side of my desk and glanced at the missed call on my phone. My heart lurched. Someone from home had called, from the phone in the office in the barn. Was it *Dat* calling? Had there been some sort of emergency? Hopefully he was just calling to let me know he planned to visit me soon. It had been several months since I'd seen him.

Just as I began to return the call, my phone buzzed again. Same number. Taking a raggedy breath, I pressed "accept" and put it to my ear, aiming to sound professional in case any of my colleagues were listening.

"Hello, this is Jessica," I said in English. "How may I help you?"

"Jess? Is it you?" Leisel, my youngest sister, asked.

I turned toward the wall, my voice low. "*Jah*, it's me." She'd never called me before. "Is everything all right?"

"No, it's not. It's Dat."

I fixated on a crack in the plaster. "What's wrong?"

"He passed this morning."

"Passed?" I choked on the word. What was Leisel saying? Dat was as strong as a workhorse.

"*Jah*, it all happened so quickly." Leisel stopped with the English. "I meant to call."

"What happened, exactly?" I managed to ask.

"He had a cough through the winter that he couldn't get rid of."

My legs began to shake as Leisel spoke, bumping my chair against the desk and making it rattle.

"He finally went to the doctor, but it was too late," she said.

I pressed down on my knees with my free hand, willing the shaking to stop.

"It was cancer. Lung cancer."

Lung cancer? He'd never smoked. "Did he die in the hospital?"

"No. At home. I took care of him." Leisel weighed maybe a hundred pounds and was all of nineteen. Dat weighed over two hundred pounds and was well over six feet tall. How could my baby sister have cared for him?

"Come home." Leisel's voice cracked.

"Does *Mamm* want me to?"

"Of course." Leisel's voice didn't sound convincing. I doubted my mother would ever forgive me for leaving, and I sincerely doubted if she wanted the stress of having me home.

"Come right now," Leisel added. "We need you."

"What about Marie?" She was our middle sister. "Does she want to see me?"

Leisel hesitated for a half second and then said, "Jah, of course."

"And Arden?" Our brother and I had clashed our entire lives, but our relationship had grown absolutely intolerable before I left.

"Don't worry about him," Leisel said. "Just come home."

I managed to stand, launching my chair backward as I did. "I'm on my way," I said. "Tell Mamm and Marie . . ." Tell them what? That I was coming home for a few hours? A few days? A week?

I told Leisel good-bye and that I'd see her soon.

I started down the hall to Tom's cubicle, taking the Stoltz file with me. He was on his phone, but when he saw me he excused himself and put his hand over the mouthpiece of his phone.

"Sorry." I stopped.

"It's fine," he answered, a concerned expression falling over his face. "What happened?"

"It's my Dat." I couldn't stop the tears.

He quickly ended his conversation, stood, and stepped toward me, coming around the side of his desk and wrapping his arm around me. "Is he ill?"

"No, he passed," I whispered, wanting to take back the words as soon as I said them. Perhaps I'd dreamt Leisel's call. I buried my head against his shoulder, but then quickly pulled away.

"Jessica." He always used my full name. "I'm so sorry. What happened?"

I gulped in a shallow breath of air. "Lung cancer."

"When was the last time he was here?"

"Before Christmas," I answered, as I tucked the file under my arm and swiped beneath my eyes with my index fingers. It was now mid-March. Every three or four months, Dat would hire a driver to bring him to Harrisburg to see me.

"What do you need?" Tom squeezed my shoulder.

"A few days off. I'll go talk with Deanna." She was our supervisor. I held up the file. "Do you want to take this over?"

He shook his head. "No, you're the best person for it."

I thanked him and hugged the file to my chest. I'd ask Deanna about the file and see what she said. I wouldn't be back to the office for several days, depending on when the service was held. She might want to take the Stoltz file back and assign it to Tom, regardless of what he just said—I knew how important it was to keep projects on schedule.

Tom took a step backward, releasing me. "Do you want me to go with you?"

I hesitated for a moment, imagining arriving at the farm with Tom by my side. I could see Mamm's raised eyebrows. Marie's frown. Arden's crossed arms. "No," I said. "But thank you."

"All right. But I'd like to attend the service."

"I'll call," I said. "Once I know the details." Tom had met Dat a few times, and there had been a mutual respect between the two, mostly based on a love of the land and farming in general, although for Tom it was mostly theory. A college degree in communications with a minor in ag, and then a job in the Pennsylvania Department of Agriculture, had given him a lot of head knowledge, although not much practice.

Before Tom drove down to Lancaster County, I'd need to fill him in on the details of an Amish funeral. The service would be conducted in Pennsylvania Dutch and High German, and because Dat was well respected and also a deacon, hundreds of people would be there. Tom might be the only *Englischer*, besides me. Unlike Dat, the rest of my family would not be as understanding.

Tom squeezed my shoulder again, a little awkwardly. We'd

been dating, taking it very slowly, for the last six months. However, we'd managed, mostly, to keep our relationship a secret at work.

"Thank you . . . for everything." I stepped away from him.

He smiled kindly. "Call as soon as you can."

"I will."

I slipped down the hall to Deanna's office. She was in her mid-fifties and a friendly and compassionate woman. After I told her what happened, she gave me a hug. "Take the whole week," she said. "Don't give work a second thought."

"Oh, I don't think I'll be gone that long," I said. "I'll most likely be in on Friday, maybe even on Thursday." I assumed the service would be held on Wednesday. I held up the file. "What about the Stoltz case? Tom just gave it to me."

"Keep it," she said. "I told him I wanted you to do it. A little bit of a delay won't matter."

I thanked her. After I placed all of my files in my top drawer, tidied the remaining papers on my desk, and logged out of my computer, I wiggled into my coat, then grabbed my purse, and hurried to my car—a gray 2005 Toyota Camry. To anyone else, it appeared to be a conservative, safe, economical car. To me, the ex-Amish girl, it was an absolute miracle. I thanked God for it every time I sat down behind the wheel. Thankfully I'd driven to work that day—I often walked.

I worked two miles from the Pennsylvania State Capitol and lived only two blocks from it. As I turned off Cameron Street to State Street, the capitol building came into view. Most days I marveled at the beauty of the building with its green dome and expansive wings, but today my troubled soul barely noticed it. I found a parking place, locked my car, and hurried the half block to my brick building.

My apartment was over the coffee shop where I'd worked when I first moved to Harrisburg. I quickly unlocked the door to the outside staircase and hurried up the steps to the third floor. My studio was at the back of the building, overlooking the courtyard. I had a pullout couch, a small table and two chairs, a dresser, and a desk with my laptop on it. The hardwood floors shone, thanks to my polishing them, and the place was decorated with old photographs and prints, all landscapes, that I'd found at secondhand stores.

The space had been my place of safety since I fled Lancaster. I'd first used my computer here. I explored the Internet, discovered Netflix, and watched my first movie. I'd Googled current events, pop culture, and fashion.

I soon learned all sorts of things about myself, starting with that I said *jah* far too often and in what others heard as an accent. In time, I'd been able to rid myself of it. My job at the coffee shop and the regular customer interaction helped cure me of my odd words and speech patterns. I also learned I held my knife and fork differently than the general population, that my hair was frizzy, that I didn't understand most Englisch jokes, and that I had no clue about Taylor Swift, Facebook, or Angry Birds—let alone politicians or world events.

Besides current events, I'd also Googled farming techniques, land development in Lancaster County, fracking, water rights, toxic chemicals, living off the grid, and hundreds of other topics. My thirst for knowledge was insatiable.

Practically everything I'd learned in the last three years came to me by surfing the Web, or from an Englisch co-worker or friend pointing out some new piece of information, usually with an amused look on his or her face. A year after I arrived in Harrisburg, I completed my GED courses and then started taking an online community college class nearly every semester. The apartment was my place of safety, but my computer was my window to the world. I'd changed beyond measure in the last three years.

I grabbed an overnight bag and filled it with my pajamas and two sets of clothes. I figured I'd wear the skirt and sweater set I had on to the service. Next I hurried into my closet-sized bathroom for my toothbrush and toiletries and placed them in the bag too.

I took a moment and peered out my window and down into the brick courtyard of the coffee shop. Last October, on the last warm Saturday morning, Tom and I had sat at one of the tables, potted plants surrounding us. It was the first time we'd talked about "us." Tom had told me I was the "kind of girl" he'd been hoping for his entire life. I'd warmed inside. He longed for someone sweet and caring, he'd said. Someone who knew how to run a home, but who also loved the outdoors. Funny thing was, out of all the girls I knew who grew up Amish, I was the worst at domestic chores, but I supposed—compared with the average Englisch girl—I did know my way around a kitchen, as well as doing the laundry and sewing. Laughably, my family never would have agreed with Tom. Most of them believed I would make the worst wife ever.

Of course, I couldn't tell Tom that he *wasn't* the type of man I'd been waiting for my entire life. For the first nineteen years of my life, I thought I'd marry an Amish man who could handle a team of mules, plow a field, break a horse, build a barn, and help raise eight or more children. That wouldn't be Tom. But since I left the Amish, he was exactly the sort of man I'd been waiting for. He was kind and dedicated to his church. He was a hard worker, in his own way, and a good leader both at work and among his friends. He loved his family. And he seemed to love me too.

I focused on the bare courtyard, which appeared to be ready for the upcoming spring days. I longed to sit there with Tom again. It was our spot, just as the old oak tree on the farm had been where Silas and I often retreated. *Silas.*

I grabbed the bag, locked my door behind me, descended the stairs as quickly as I could, and then hurried back to my car, the wind whipping my hair around my face. Was I brave enough for what was ahead of me? Leaving Lancaster County was one thing—returning was an entirely different proposition, especially when my father wouldn't be there to protect me.

Because I'd joined the church, once I left I had been thoroughly and irrevocably shunned. *Streng Meidung* was what was done by our district. The strong shunning. I'd been put under the *Bann* permanently. I'd absolutely expected it. Anyone who grew up Amish knew the verses that supported shunning. I remembered one in particular from Matthew: *"And if he shall neglect to hear them, tell it unto the church: but if he neglect to hear the church, let him be unto thee as an heathen man and a publican."*

I'd broken my vow of baptism. I'd disobeyed. And I'd refused to confess my sin.

I knew the Bann was out of love. Everyone in our community wanted me to return, to keep my vow. I received letters from family and friends, begging me to repent and return to the fold. Not only had I broken my vow to the Lord Jesus, but I'd broken my vow to them as well. The only way to preserve the Amish way of life was to shun those who left—it lent strength to the community, based on Christian principles. In the Englisch world, it would be called "tough love," although I didn't know of anyone in the general population who loved quite as toughly as the Amish.

I'd never dreamt I'd leave. The day I'd been baptized had been the happiest day of my life. I truly believed the second would be the day I married Silas. But then everything changed.

After I left, I stood firm. I read each letter and then put them in the trash.

Now, as I drove, I prepared myself for what the Bann would mean. I wouldn't be able to sit at the kitchen table with my family. I wouldn't be able to sleep in my old bed in the room I'd shared with my sisters. But at least I would be able to stay in my family home. And I would be able to attend my father's funeral.

A sob shook me. Jah, it was easy to try to ignore that I would live the rest of my life under the Bann when I was living in a completely different world, but going home I'd have to face it and deal with it as best I could and with as much grace as I could possibly muster.

During the hour-long drive south to our family farm, near the community of Leacock, I thought through what my shunning would look like in the next couple of days. I vacillated between denial and gut-wrenching grief. One minute I'd think my father's passing was a cruel joke intended to get me to come home, and the next minute I'd be wailing in despair.

Especially when I had no clear understanding what Arden's plan for the Bachmann land might be now that Dat was gone. Unfortunately I had a pretty good guess.

My heart lurched as I slowed, shifted down into fourth gear, and then turned down the Oak Road toward the historic Bachmann *Bavvahrei*.

I shivered. *Farm*. It had been a while since a Pennsylvania Dutch word had slipped through. Three years ago all my thoughts were in my mother tongue. It was amazing how quickly I'd adjusted to speaking English and thinking in it all the time.

I refocused on the landscape. The cold blustery days of March had always been Dat's favorite time of year. He said he felt an affinity with the unseen life growing under the decay of winter, despite the threat of hail, blizzards, and even tornados. I shared his sentiments. Even now I could make out new shoots of growth in the field between the rail fence and the windbreak of fir trees.

Generations of Bachmanns had farmed our land, beginning in 1752 with Walter Bachmann. Dat had mentioned him a few times, and I could imagine the joy Walter had felt when he acquired this particular piece of farmland.

Of all of Dat's five children, I loved the land with a passion like his, which I imagined matched someone from each genera-tion for the last 259 years. My half brother, Arden, lived with his family on the west side of the property and farmed with Dat, but he didn't love the land or the crops or the animals. His purpose was earning enough to support his family, which was a worthy cause in itself, but it still infuriated me. Of the many things that inspired me to leave the Amish, Arden's views toward the farm was one. Now I feared that with Dat gone, he might sell out to a gas company or a corporate farm, or overwork the land for a larger profit, or sell off a section to a developer.

I'd held on too tightly to my beliefs about the land back then, and finally realized my defeat and gave up altogether. *The Lord giveth and the Lord taketh away; blessed be the name of the Lord*. The words tumbled through my head—ones I'd surely hear over and over in the next few days. But God hadn't taken the farm from me. I had chosen to leave.

Regardless of the circumstances, my heart swelled invol-untarily at the thought of being back on the land. Nothing screamed *home* to me like our farm. I thought of the vast universe, the blue ball of Earth spinning in space, then North America, the state of Pennsylvania, Lancaster County, and finally our 140 acres. I imagined myself flying over it in a plane and seeing the way the green fields, bordered with strips of plowed earth and trees, would appear like a crazy quilt. I doubted there was anywhere on the planet as beautiful and fertile as Lancaster County.

The field gave way to pasture, spotted by Holstein cows. A group huddled together under the oak tree in the middle. One raised her head and stared at me. My heart lurched at the sight. I'd missed it all—the land, the animals, the crops, the oak tree, the woods on the far side near the highway. Even the mud, which this time of year covered nearly everything.

I shifted into third and rounded the corner. The old sprawling farmhouse with the wraparound front porch came into view. What was now the enclosed back porch of the farmhouse had once been part of the original log cabin. Of course the house had been added to many times over the years. One wing and then another. A second floor. A front porch. A sunroom. It spread out in every direction. It was so big we could have easily squeezed in Arden's family of seven, but it was better they had their own place on the other side of the farm. His kids were fine—it was Arden and his wife, Vi, who had made my life miserable, along with the new bishop. And then my sister Marie too.

Plus my mother, but that hadn't changed in any way. She'd been critical of me for as long as I could remember.

The memory made me cringe, and I slowed even more. I was visiting—not returning. My apartment, smaller than the farmhouse's back porch, was now home to me. It's what I'd chosen.

I focused on the land again. On the left side of the lane, bale tubes of silage covered the edge of the field. A sheltie I didn't recognize ran along the fence line, barking at my car. On the right side of the lane, cows and horses huddled near the oak tree. A colt bounded away from its mother.

How could Dat be gone? The pasture. The animals. The crops. All of them screamed *Dat* to me. He was the gentle farmer. The caretaker. God's steward.

A sob shook me, and I gripped the steering wheel tighter.

He was only sixty-seven. Much too young to die. I'd been sure he'd live another twenty years at least, providing plenty of time to sort out our differences.

I concentrated on the house again. The porch skirt above the foundation needed to be painted. Most likely the task was on the list of projects for summer. Along with pruning the trees along the side of the house. Beyond them, I could see that the barn roof needed to be repaired. In fact, overall, the property looked much shabbier than I remembered. I reminded myself that Dat had been ill for the last few months, but all of those jobs should have been done last fall. Perhaps he hadn't been feeling well even then, but if so, Arden should have taken charge.

Leisel, wearing a black dress and apron, stepped out onto the front porch. Already a collection of buggies was parked around the barn. I hadn't thought of the houseful of neighbors ready to help with meals and chores.

I parked my car at the edge of the driveway and dabbed at my tears. Leisel came down the steps, pulling a black shawl tight around her shoulders. She walked with what seemed like confidence mixed with fatigue. She'd always looked a little like a pixie—fair skin, blond hair, grayish eyes. And petite. Marie and I appeared to be giants next to her.

We had been the Bachmann sisters, the three of us born in

just three years. Loyal to each other above all, through thick and thin. Marie and Leisel had been my best friends all of my life, until things turned sour about five months before I left Lancaster. Up until then, we'd gone everywhere together. Singings. Outings. Volleyball games. We were protective of each other. Caring of others. And bound together as only sisters can be.

I opened the car door, grabbed my purse, and climbed out, patting my coat pocket to make sure my phone was still there. It was.

I took a step in the gravel, my low-heeled pumps rocking a little with the movement. Leisel tugged the shawl even tighter as she came toward me. At the sight of her red-rimmed eyes, another sob shook me. She was in my arms before I could control myself, and I patted her back reflexively as we both cried. "I'm so sorry," I whispered, my words slipping through as the intensity of my sadness grew.

She tightened her grip on me. Over her shoulder I could see our mother in the doorway, but then she turned and disappeared back into the house. I searched for Dat's sister, *Aenti* Suzanne, but I didn't see her. She would be my ally, I was sure. At least I hoped so.

Thankfully there was no sight of Arden. I'd count my blessings, no matter how small.

"Has anyone called Amos?" I whispered. He was Arden's identical twin, the first prodigal in the family to leave, sixteen years ago when I was just six.

"None of us knows his phone number," Leisel said.

"Dat didn't tell you?" I knew he kept in touch with Amos.

She shook her head. "He planned to. We talked about it. We all thought Dat would live another month, at least a few more weeks. But he went so quickly. Everything changed two days ago."

23

I could only hope someone had planned to let me know Dat was ill, so I could have come to say good-bye. But I wouldn't think of that now. Amos and I had both brought shame to Dat, although he never put that on us. Others certainly did though, doubly because Dat was a deacon.

"Maybe Amos's information is in Dat's desk." I pulled away from Leisel and started toward the house. "We can look."

Leisel nodded and fell into step beside me, taking hold of my arm. The wind whipped the skirt of her dress and the ties of her *Kapp*, tugging at her hair beneath it. We stepped together, entwined in the grief that connected us.

At first I thought the sound behind me was the wind. But the second time, I couldn't deny someone had spoken my name.

"Jessie."

And I knew who said it. He made my name sound like music. I turned.

Silas came toward me slowly, his straw hat in his hand, his dark hair a little long over his eyebrows. The sleeves of his forest green shirt were rolled up to his elbows, and he wore no coat or vest. His hazel eyes reflected kindness, even after the way I'd left him. "Jessie." He was the only one who called me that. "You're here."

I hesitated for a moment, remembering our past and then the clean scent of his Mamm's soap, mixed with the sweat of hard work on his skin. I remembered how I'd felt when he'd held me, when he'd kissed me under the oak tree.

"Jah, I *am* here," I finally answered as another sob overtook me.

– 2 –

Silas stared at me for a long moment. I couldn't help but notice the bones of his face appeared more chiseled and his shoulders wider than three years ago. Yet he was still lean and wiry.

I dropped my gaze, brushing away my tears as I did.

"How about some coffee?" Leisel proposed. "And a sticky bun? Marie and Gail made them." She gave Silas a pointed look that confused me. Gail was Marie's best friend. She was kind and gentle—and very beautiful with her thick dark hair. After her parents moved to Ohio, Dat had told me, she was staying at our house quite a bit. She'd moved in with her older sister, but she seemed to prefer staying with our family. I wasn't surprised. She'd fit in—much better than I had. She was the daughter Mamm had always wished I had been. Domestic. Compliant. Conscious of her appearance.

As Leisel steered me toward the steps, the curtain in the living room window fluttered a little. For a split second I could make out Marie's face, and I guessed Gail's too. I scanned the empty porch. Mamm and Dat's white rocking chairs were positioned in the exact spot they were when I left. I gulped at the sight of Dat's.

25

Beyond it was the picnic table where we often ate on summer evenings. I'd been told I'd learned to walk on the porch, Amos at my side. After those first steps, it was difficult to keep me inside. All I wanted was to be a *Bavvah*. That was before I understood that women weren't farmers, at least not in our community.

Silas stepped forward to open the front door, and Leisel led the way through it. It smelled the same as always. Lemon polish. Freshly baked bread. The faint scent of kerosene.

The open floor plan meant I could see into the dining area and then the kitchen from the living room. No one sat at the long oak table, but several women stood around the island in the kitchen. I hoped Aenti Suz was in the huddle, but after a moment I could see she wasn't.

My mother's back was to me. She was tall and thin with perfect posture and impossible not to spot. She turned toward me.

In a firm voice she said, "I can't believe you came."

"I called her," Leisel answered before I could.

Mamm inhaled, wrinkled her nose, and then turned her back toward me. She hadn't changed in three years—not in looks or behavior.

"Bethel . . ." I couldn't tell who spoke my mother's name.

My mother shrugged in response.

The speaker stepped forward and said, "Can I get you some coffee?" It was Silas's mother, Edith.

"Please." I could use a shot of caffeine.

A minute later I took the mug from Edith. She'd aged in the last three years, and her hair was completely gray now. She was much older than my Mamm. Silas was an unexpected baby, who arrived after his parents had given up all hope of ever having children. I was my mother's second child, born when she was in her late twenties.

Edith smiled at me warmly. I'd thought for years she would be my mother-in-law, and I'd always adored her.

Leisel stepped into the kitchen, but Silas stopped in the living room.

The coffee was too hot to drink so I couldn't busy myself with that. Finally I turned toward the table, deciding I would sit down. By myself.

As I did, I realized that Gail had stepped to Silas's side. The two were arm to arm, practically touching. She gazed up at him with loving eyes. As I stared, the mug slipped from my hand. In slow motion, I jumped back as the hot coffee splashed all around me, splattering the white wall. Next the mug hit the hardwood floor and shattered. The ceramic bounced and flew into smaller pieces and then settled on the floor with a clatter.

"Oh dear." Edith was already at my side, pulling a kitchen towel from her shoulder. "Are you burned?"

"No," I gasped. "Just embarrassed."

"I'm sorry," she whispered. I wasn't sure for what. The coffee spilling? That I was such a klutz? That her son was courting someone else?

What had I expected? It was three years since I left. He could easily have married in that time. Easily have been a father by now.

How self-centered of me to have expected life in Lancaster County to have frozen in time when I moved to Harrisburg. Had I thought I could come back and pick up where I'd left off?

Leisel approached with a rag. I took it from her and sank to my knees, mopping up the coffee as Edith picked up the bigger pieces of the mug. "Careful," she said. "We'll have to sweep."

I nodded, keeping my head down, avoiding eye contact with Silas or Gail. Edith retreated to the kitchen, leaving the towel on the floor. Someone approached, and then Silas knelt beside me and picked up the towel. Footsteps fell toward the front door. I raised my head to see Gail slip outside.

"Go after her," I said to Silas.

He shook his head and continued to work in silence, the muscles of his arm contracting as he picked up the smaller pieces. Now that he was close to me, in the house, I could make out the scent of the homemade soap on him—and something more. The spring wind? The warm soil? He loved the land as much as I did, yet his family only had ten acres. Part was in pasture, which allowed them to raise a few steers each year. His Mamm grew vegetables, herbs, and flowers that she sold during the summer and then dried more to sell throughout the year. Ten acres was not enough to make any kind of living, but they managed because Silas earned a good living by helping my family farm our land.

I ducked my head, surprised at how drawn I felt to him. Tears stung my eyes again, and I concentrated on the last of the pieces, picking them up and then dropping them in the bin Edith had positioned by my side. She stood poised with both a broom and mop to finish the job.

Once Silas and I finished, I headed into the kitchen and washed my hands at the sink. When I finished, Leisel handed me another cup of coffee. I tightened my grip on it as I heard my mother say, "We don't need this. You've been gone three years. Why would you come back now to stir up trouble?"

"That's not my intention. It was never my intention."

Mamm shook her head. "It was—it appeared to be from the start."

I winced. Her oldest child, also a girl, died the day after I was born. Mamm and I were still in the hospital when it happened. It seemed she'd never forgiven me for it. Dat always told me to ignore it as best I could. "Your Mamm's never gotten over her grief," he explained.

Mamm definitely had her favorites. Out of her two stepsons, she despised Amos and adored Arden. Just like she adored Marie. For a long time, even though she criticized me, it seemed perhaps she could tolerate me, until I brought her shame.

"Finish your coffee, then be on your way," Mamm said.

There was no way I'd leave so soon. I needed to find out what Dat's last wishes were and what Arden intended to do with the land. I needed to let Amos know Dat had passed. I needed, if possible, to mourn my father with my family. I left the kitchen without answering my mother and headed to Dat's study. The room was just as I remembered it. Meticulously organized business ledgers filled a bookcase on the left wall. On adjacent shelves were bottles of herbs, vitamins, and supplements that he dispensed to friends, relatives, and friends of friends. He was a self-taught healer. He only charged for the cost of the products, never for the knowledge he'd accumulated. Although I'd asked several times, he never told me how he knew so much about healing beyond that he'd read a lot of books through the years.

To my right was the large picture window that overlooked the side yard. I stopped in front of it. Gail and Marie were huddled together between the apple trees, my sister looking as if she was comforting her friend. It was the first I'd seen Marie. She'd grown even prettier since I'd left.

I expected Silas would join Marie and Gail soon enough. I continued on toward the desk, hoping neither of the girls saw me through the glass.

A knock fell on the door as I reached for the first drawer.

I turned and said, "Come in," expecting Leisel. But it was Silas.

He stepped into the room, leaving the door ajar. "Your Mamm's upset."

I nodded, annoyed with him now. I wasn't obtuse. I turned back toward the desk. "I need to find Dat's address book." I opened the top right drawer of the old roll-top and searched quickly, then opened the next drawer down.

"Jessie," Silas said.

I shook my head without turning around, willing him not to call me that again.

"You need to listen," he said. When had he grown so patronizing? Perhaps he'd taken lessons from Arden.

Ignoring him, I opened drawer after drawer. Thankfully he didn't say anything more. When I didn't find the address book, I began looking in the cubbies above the desk.

Silas repeated my name one more time. I ignored him again, remembering after all these years how much I'd loved him—and how much he'd frustrated me too. Here I was, five minutes after my return, feeling both toward him again. And he, more than anyone, should understand my grief. His father died when we were fourteen. I was there for him every step of the way, and so was my Dat.

I did my best to ignore Silas, and he remained silent. In the last cubby, I found the book tucked in the back. I flipped through the pages. There were hundreds of names. I looked first under *A* for Amos. Then Bachmann. Nothing. I flipped through, skimming over the entries. There were names and addresses of people throughout the United States—New York, Wisconsin, Montana, California—and in other countries too—Canada, Mexico, Ecuador, Haiti. Even Vietnam. All of the handwriting was his. Confusion filled me. I understood the first four countries. He'd been on humanitarian trips to those places, before I was born.

Then, three years ago, after the horrendous earthquake in Haiti, he'd spent two months there. But he'd never been to Vietnam.

"Jessie . . ."

"Don't call me that," I snapped, meeting Silas's eyes. I sighed and tried for a kinder tone. "You can leave whenever you want." I continued to look through the pages, hurt that he belonged at my childhood home when I obviously didn't.

Finally, on the next to the last page, I found two numbers without names. One was my cell phone, and I guessed the other was Amos's. I pulled out my cell and dialed the number as Silas said, "I don't think that's a good idea, without talking—"

I put my hand up, silently begging him to stop, remembering how rigid he was with his rule following.

The phone clicked. "Hello."

"Amos?" I said.

"Who is this?"

"Jessica." I slipped the address book into my purse, noting the disapproving frown Silas had on his face.

Amos didn't answer.

"Your *Shveshtah*." Now I was involuntarily speaking Pennsylvania Dutch.

"My sister?" I could hear him suck in his breath. "What's happened?"

"It's Dat. He's—" My voice cracked.

Silas stepped to my side. I turned toward him, catching a glimpse of Marie and Gail staring in the window. I took a step closer toward the desk. Silas moved with me. His closeness was nearly more than I could bear. Dat's death, mixed with my memory of Silas's last kiss, caused my chest to feel as if it might explode.

"Where are you?" Amos asked.

31

I managed to answer, "Home. I left a few years ago—but I came back, just now. For the funeral."

"I'm coming," he said immediately. "I'll be there tomorrow—or as soon as I can."

I started to ask where Amos lived—a question I'd asked Dat many times, but he'd never answered—but my *Broodah* hung up before I got the question out. I stared at the phone in my hand for a long moment.

"What did he say?" Silas asked.

"That he's coming." As I spoke I was aware someone was standing on the other side of the partially opened door. I suspected it was Mamm.

Silas let out a low whistle just as the door swung open all the way.

Arden and his wife Vi stood in the doorway. "Was that Amos?" Arden asked.

I nodded. There was no reason to try to deceive anyone.

Arden frowned. He'd gained weight over the last three years, his hair had become thinner, and his beard had grown much longer. Some Amish men trimmed theirs. Obviously, Arden didn't.

Vi wagged her finger at me. "Stirring up even more trouble?"

"No," I said, nonchalantly tucking the address book deeper into my purse. "Dat would want Amos to know."

"Dat was too easy on both of you." Arden jerked his head toward the kitchen. "Come out," he said. "You need to be on your way."

I stared at Arden. Obviously he'd forgotten how stubborn I could be. I'd leave Dat's study—but I wouldn't leave my father's house.

32

I followed him out to the table. Mamm had disappeared and so had Silas's mother. Leisel was gone too.

Arden sat at the head, at Dat's place, and Vi pulled out the chair to his left. He motioned for me to sit at his right, which I did. Then he asked Silas to join us, but he shook his head and stood against the far wall, next to the fireplace. Arden seemed miffed but didn't say anything more to Silas.

My brother cleared his throat. "That was a bad idea to call Amos," he said. "You shouldn't be here either. You have no idea how hard your and Amos's betrayal was on Dat."

"He didn't act like it was that hard," I answered.

"What are you talking about?"

"When he came to see me."

Arden's voice rose to a screech. "He didn't go see you."

"He did," I said. "Several times."

Vi leaned toward me, her Kapp ties dangling away from her neck. "Why would you lie to us?"

I ignored her. "And he must have been in contact with Amos too." I caught myself from saying anything more. I didn't want Arden to know I had Dat's address book. And I wouldn't tell him Amos would be here the next day either.

"You need to leave," Arden told me again.

Didn't he know his pronouncements only made me more determined to stay? How dare he try to deprive me of time to mourn my father. Vi leaned back in her chair and crossed her arms. Mamm stepped into view in the kitchen from the pantry. Had she been listening the entire time? She pursed her lips together.

I stood and walked toward her. "Do you want me to go?" I fought back my tears.

The back door banged open and Aenti Suz stepped to my

mother's side, followed by Silas's Mamm. It appeared as if Edith had fetched my aunt.

"What's going on?" Aenti Suz asked, standing toe-to-toe with my Mamm.

"Jessica was just leaving," Mamm said.

"Oh, no she's not." Aenti Suz started toward me, her signature boots clicking across the hardwood floor. "I've been praying you would come. And here you are."

Arden was on his feet. "She really is leaving."

Silas stepped to my side, an empathetic look on his face. I met his gaze for a quick moment.

"No, she's not," Aenti Suz said again, wrapping me in her arms but looking at Arden. "You were there when Gus asked Leisel to call her," she said to my brother. "How could you go against your Dat's wishes?"

– 3 –

Aenti Suz had always had a way of stumping Arden, and he didn't appreciate it, not at all. Nor did he appreciate that his lying had just been exposed, I was sure. My aunt just shrugged as Arden and Vi stormed out the back door of the house.

I glanced at Silas, who now stood with his arms crossed. His expression gave nothing away.

"Your dresses are still in your closet," Aenti Suz said. "Tucked away in a garment bag, including the black one. Go put it on— that will make things go a little more smoothly—and then come out and have a cup of tea with me."

Mamm frowned but didn't say anything.

"All right," I answered Aenti Suz, relieved to have someone give me clear directions.

She hugged me again and then sashayed through the kitchen. She'd always worn her dresses a little long, probably to hide her stylish boots. She'd had jet-black hair, but now it was a beautiful silver. She walked with the same grace and confidence I remembered from throughout my childhood.

Aenti Suz had never married, which was one of the biggest

mysteries of my life. Plenty of widowers tried to court her, but she never seemed to want to marry. I think Mamm would have been happy with Aenti Suz not living in the *Dawdi Haus* behind our home, but my aunt had lived there since caring for her parents when they were ill, and then she stayed on at Dat's request. Dat had built the house for his parents, during his first marriage to Arden and Amos's mother, a woman named Missy. She died when the boys were ten, and Dat married Mamm soon after.

Without glancing back at Silas, I headed toward the staircase, aware of the neighbors in the living room staring at me. If Mamm or Arden had suggested I put on one of my Plain dresses, I wouldn't have done it. But Aenti Suz was the least manipulative person I knew, and I trusted her judgment more than anyone else's, besides my father's. A new sob threatened to undo me, so I hurried up the stairs, squelching it a little more with each step. Mamm frowned on displays of emotion.

When I reached the landing, the front door opened and closed. I didn't dare go back down to see who it was, but then Marie's voice traveled up the stairs. I felt like a calf trapped in a chute. Maybe they wouldn't come upstairs.

I hurried into my old room.

Leisel sat in the comfortable chair by the window, a book in her hand. It was so like her to escape to a quiet place when things were tense. She closed the book as I greeted her and slipped it between her thigh and the armrest.

I put my purse on my old bed. Our room was in a newer wing of the house and actually had a closet. The older rooms simply had a row of pegs along one wall for garments.

"What are you looking for?" she asked.

"My old dresses."

"Why?"

"I'm going to put one on." Maybe I could get changed and out to Aenti Suz's before I had to interact with Marie, Gail, or Mamm again. I found the garment bag in the very back of the closet, unzipped it, and first pulled out my blue dress—the one I'd planned to wear when I married Silas. The black apron I'd made three years ago hung over the hanger too, along with a Kapp. I returned it and pulled out my black dress instead. A Kapp and apron were also attached to it.

I gave the dress a sniff. It smelled fine—fresh even, like soap with a hint of lavender. All of them did.

I turned toward Leisel and held up the dress. Her face reddened. "Aenti Suz added them to the wash a couple of days ago, hoping you'd be coming home sometime soon."

I exhaled. When I inspected the garment bag, sure enough, a sachet hung on a string on the inside. Aenti Suz grew lavender outside her front door and used it to make soap and sachets. My aunt's care touched me.

Leisel had returned to her book. I couldn't read the title, but it didn't appear to be a novel. It was large with a hardcover. I quickly changed into the dress, pulled the apron over my head and tied it, and then transferred my cell phone from my purse to my apron pocket. I found bobby pins in a dish on the dresser, quickly secured a bun at the nape of my neck, and then put on the Kapp.

Next, I hung up my skirt and blouse in the closet, but left my sweater on the bed. The old house was drafty, much colder than I was used to. I opened the top drawer of my old bureau and found a pair of clean stockings. Sitting on the bed, I pulled the first stocking onto my foot just as Marie stepped into the room. Gail was nowhere in sight.

"You can't stay in here." Marie had been furious with me by

the time I left, but she seemed even angrier now. "You'll need to stay in Amos's old room."

"But he's coming," I answered. "Where will he stay?"

Marie harrumphed. "I don't know, but you can't stay in here." She sounded like Mamm.

"I know," I said. "I expected as much. But I won't stay in Amos's room." I put on my other stocking and without looking up asked, "Where do you want me to sleep?"

"How about the Best Western down the road?"

"Stop it." Leisel closed the book on her index finger.

I asked, "How about the extra bedroom down at the end of the hall?"

Marie crossed her arms. "We're using that as a sewing room."

"Is there still a bed in it?"

She nodded. "But it's been ages since the sheets were changed."

"I'll do it," I said.

"I already did," Leisel said, casting her eyes back on her book.

I smiled at Leisel, even though she didn't glance up, and then found an old pair of my shoes in the closet. I hoped to help with chores later, and I wasn't about to wear my dress shoes. Not that they would be deemed appropriate anyway.

No one said anything as I put on the shapeless shoes.

When I'd finished, I said, "I'm going to go have a cup of tea with Aenti Suz. I will be staying on the farm until after the service. Then I'll return to Harrisburg. Marie, if that bothers you, perhaps you could go stay with Gail at her sister's place."

Marie shook her head. "Gail lives here now. Permanently."

"All right then," I said, "let's do our best to get along. I'll soon be gone for good."

Marie put her hands on her hips. "You can't come home and boss me around."

"I'm not," I answered, heading toward the door.

Leisel's voice was loud and firm. "Things are stressful enough as it is. And you know Dat wanted her to come home, so please stop."

"He was delusional," Marie said. "And what Dat wanted doesn't really matter, does it? We should care about Mamm now and put her needs first. Not those of our prodigal sister."

I didn't want to hear any more. Once I reached the bottom of the staircase, I headed toward the front door, not wanting anyone to see me. I had a couple of days to mourn my father—and figure out what Arden planned to do with the farm. Hopefully Aenti Suz would have an idea.

I stepped out onto the front porch to find Gail and Silas huddled in the corner. With all the surprises popping up around every corner, I was beginning to feel like I was back in the haunted house Tom had taken me to last October. He'd been amused by how horrified I'd been, but honestly that had been one of my worst shocks yet.

Until, perhaps, today. Gail stared at me, her eyes rimmed with red. I thought for a moment about telling her everything was fine—Silas would never take me back after what I'd done, if that's what she was worried about—but then I decided it was best to say nothing at all.

Silas simply nodded toward me.

I didn't respond to either of them as I hurried by. I couldn't help but swipe my hand across my backside as I hustled down the stairs. I wasn't used to wearing dresses much anymore and had a sudden fear that it was tucked up in the back. But all seemed fine.

I patted my cell phone in the pocket of my apron. Yes, it was there. I'd call Tom as soon as I had a chance.

I walked next to the fence line as I made my way to the backyard. In the distance, I could make out the pond.

I thought of my older sister, Rebecca. She'd drowned, and it seemed Mamm always blamed Amos, along with me in some odd way, even though I'd been a newborn. Dat put a fence around the pond after that, but even so he taught Marie, Leisel, and me to swim. Dat bought us shorts and T-shirts for our lessons. Mamm claimed he was teaching us to be immodest, but I paid little attention to her comments. What impressed me the most was that Dat was such a good swimmer. After our lessons, he would swim back and forth across the pond over and over and over while we watched. It seemed as natural to him as walking. Finally Mamm would yell for him to get out of the water and bring us back to the house.

It seemed the loss of Rebecca marked Mamm. One time I overheard her tell Dat, as they sat in their rocking chairs on the porch, "You have no idea what it does to a mother to lose her firstborn." Another time, when she was distraught, I heard her tell him she should have been satisfied with one baby. There were five years between Rebecca and me. Did she think God punished her for wanting more? It didn't make any sense to me. Accidents happened, tragically. Even if Mamm had been home, she might not have prevented it.

Rebecca was the sister Marie, Leisel, and I never knew, but still she impacted us every day of our lives. I thought of her when I misbehaved, when I was ungrateful. I was living—something she wasn't allowed. I owed it to everyone to be as perfect as possible. I knew it was *impossible* though. I was the least perfect of the sisters, something Mamm made clear. One time, when I hadn't shared my pudding with Marie, even though she'd already finished hers, Mamm hissed, "Why can't you be more like your sister?"

I knew exactly whom she was talking about. *Rebecca.* Everyone said what a sweet girl she was, an absolute angel. Several times I'd heard people say something along the lines of her being "too good for this earth" and "that God wanted her in heaven."

Even though I felt as if I could never live up to Rebecca, ironically she made the three of us living sisters more grateful for each other. She made us closer. She bonded us together in a way nothing else could. Through our childhood, our years as scholars, and the beginning of our *Youngie* years, we were the best of friends, partly due to the remembrance of our deceased sister.

Until we weren't.

As I turned the back corner of the house, I could see Edith and Aenti Suz across the lawn taking the last of the clothes off the line. Death or not, the household still had to be run. When Aenti Suz saw me she waved and then picked up a basket. Beyond her was the old smokehouse that hadn't been used since Dat was a boy, the old springhouse, and then Mamm's large garden plot. Usually by this time of the year, Dat would have plowed it, lovingly. But it wasn't plowed. The sight sent another jolt of grief through me.

I continued on to my aunt's front door and reached it just as she met me. Once we were inside, I reached for the basket. "I'll fold them," I said.

She handed over the clean laundry. "I'll start the kettle and then help."

The basket was filled with towels and sheets. Perhaps they'd been used to care for Dat on his last day. I buried my nose in the towel on top of the pile, hoping I could catch a scent of

Dat, but it smelled of bleach mixed with fresh air and a hint of woodsmoke. I placed the laundry on Aenti Suz's little table and started with the towels, quickly folding them in thirds as Mamm had taught all of us to do.

Aenti Suz's house was just a bedroom, bathroom, living room, and kitchen. Dat had built it for his parents, with lots of natural light. Windows looked out onto both the backyard of the big house and the field.

The enclosed back porch of the big house was visible too. Original logs, painted white, from the cabin built by Walter Bachmann made up the lower, outer wall of the porch. The top part was glass during the winter and screens during the summer. I'd heard the story that the entire space of the porch was the cabin the first American Bachmann family lived in during their first winter in Pennsylvania, where they'd sought refuge after they'd fled religious persecution in Switzerland in 1752.

There had been one girl and three boys who lived to adulthood. We were descendants of one of those boys. That was as much as I knew about the family. But perhaps now that I'd left the Amish, I had no more right to those stories than to my old bed.

After Aenti Suz started the kettle to boil, she joined me and together we started on the sheets. "I'm so relieved Leisel called you," Aenti said. "I would have if I had your number."

I nodded. I believed her.

"It's what your father wanted, what he requested. But I think Leisel would have figured out a way to reach you regardless."

"I hope so," I answered. Clearly Mamm, Marie, and Arden wouldn't have.

We finished folding the sheets just as the kettle began to whistle. Aenti Suz stepped back into her tiny kitchen, as I stacked everything back in the basket.

Aenti Suz directed me to her couch as she put a tray with the teapot and cups on the side table. There was also a platter of homemade bread, apple slices, and cheese slices. I hadn't had lunch and realized how hungry I was.

As I took a piece of bread, I asked Aenti Suz to give me more details about Dat's illness, saying Leisel had simply said he'd had lung cancer.

"Jah," she said. "It went very quickly. He agreed to one round of chemotherapy but the trips into town and the effects of the drugs took their toll. After his first scans showed no progress, he said he was done with all of that."

"Was he in a lot of pain, at the end?" I asked.

I could tell by the look in Aenti's eyes that he was. "He never complained," she answered. "And Leisel cared for him so well. That girl has a gift. She got it from Gus."

I nodded. Dat did have a gift of healing, and I saw the same in my sister, since she was a young girl. She cared for kittens, chicks, puppies, fledglings, and even baby mice as a child. By the time I was thirteen, I was working with Dat in the fields. By the time she was thirteen, she was assisting Dat with his herbs and supplements. Marie was happy to help Mamm run the house, freeing Leisel and me up, mostly, for what we truly loved to do, although we certainly helped with the inside chores too.

"He told me one day when I was sitting with him, toward the end, that he'd visited you several times. I guessed you were in Harrisburg."

I nodded, taking the last bite of the piece of bread.

"I'm so glad he went to see you." Aenti Suz smiled, but it

was soon replaced with a sad expression. "And then I was in the room when he told Leisel to call you."

I smiled a little. "So he died in his room?"

Aenti shook her head. "No, in his study. In a hospital bed. Once he couldn't climb the stairs anymore, that was the best place for him."

"Oh," I answered, realizing just how much his body had failed him at the end. "Did he ever tell Mamm he visited me?"

"I don't know," Aenti Suz answered as she poured the tea.

He certainly hadn't told Arden. Speaking of my brother, I asked Aenti Suz if she knew what he planned to do with the land now that Dat was gone.

She frowned a little and shook her head. "I'd be the last person he'd confide in as far as that goes."

I nodded, knowing she was right, and retrieved my purse from the table, taking the address book out of it. "I called Amos," I said. "He's coming."

Aenti put her hand to her throat but didn't say anything.

I held up the little book. "I found his number in here."

"Oh?"

"There all sorts of people listed in this book. People I've never heard of."

"Patients?" Aenti handed me a mug of tea as I sat down.

"Some, probably," I answered. "But also people from around the world. South America. Haiti. Those places make sense. But there are even names of people from Vietnam."

"Really?" Aenti took a sip of her tea and then continued to hold the mug close to her mouth.

She'd never been good at being deceitful. Perhaps my confused expression encouraged her to say more. "Your father was a very complex man."

I knew that.

"And reserved."

I nodded. I knew that too—even with his children. Maybe especially with us children. He loved us. He was interested in us. But he was never authoritarian, like many Amish parents. He was authoritative, allowing us to make our own decisions. He didn't demand we overly share about our own lives—and apparently he hadn't overly shared about his own either.

Bishop Jacobs, on the other hand, was authoritarian. I'd learned about different leadership styles in a human development class I'd taken.

Aenti Suz put her mug back on the table. "I take it your Dat never told you he spent a year in Vietnam working in a Mennonite clinic."

I shook my head, baffled.

"He probably felt as if it would be bragging to mention it."

"Of course I knew about his trip to Haiti, and a trip to South America, before I was born. Right?"

She nodded.

"He worked in Vietnam for a whole year? Had he not joined the church?"

"That's right," Aenti said. "In fact, he considered becoming Mennonite for several years."

"But he changed his mind by the time he got home?"

"Jah. He joined the church and then married Missy after he returned. Our parents gave him the farm, and Arden and Amos were born a year later."

"Did the twins know about his time in Vietnam?"

"Probably," Aenti Suz answered. "He wasn't able to write most of his friends in Vietnam, after the war, until the country opened up again in the nineties. When that happened, I think your Mamm didn't want him talking about it, even though he was getting letters on a fairly regular basis. "

"Why?"

"Perhaps she thought it prideful."

That was understandable. She most likely believed his stories would be a bad influence on us girls, too, that they might somehow lead us astray.

"Where in the world would he get the idea to go to Vietnam?" I asked.

Aenti Suz picked up her mug again. "There's actually a long history of that sort of thing in the Bachmann family during wartime," she said.

"What?" I'd never heard any stories about relatives going off to serve during war. We were pacifists. We believed in non-resistance.

"Your great-grandfather worked as a medic in World War II."

"Was he forced to?"

"Jah," she answered. "And your Dat would have been drafted if he didn't go to Vietnam—or he could have joined the church to get a deferment."

My eyes watered at the thought of Dat being drafted. What all had been kept from me?

"Another great-great-aunt, all the way back to the Civil War, worked as a nurse, including at Gettysburg."

I shook my head. "How do you know all of this?"

"Stories have been passed down through the years. My great-aunt told me."

"Was anyone going to tell me?"

Aenti Suz smiled a little. "Jah, first chance I had. Which means today."

I nodded. It wasn't as if Mamm could get mad at her for

telling me about the adventures of my ancestors. Nothing more could inspire me to leave—I already had.

"But the stories go back much further, back to the first Bachmann daughter born in America, way back in 1756, and what her life was like during the Revolutionary War, along with her brother Zachary's."

I let out a low whistle. "You know a story from that far back?"

Aenti Suz nodded. "It was passed down through the generations, as a cautionary tale."

"Cautionary?"

Aenti Suz smiled wryly.

"What are you up to?" I asked, puzzled. "And what was your great-aunt trying to prevent in telling you?"

"That," Aenti Suz said, "is another story. The one *I'm* telling is about Ruby Bachmann. She was the first girl to grow up on this farm. And just like you, her father died and she had to make a decision about going or staying."

"But I already made my decision," I answered.

My aunt cocked her head. "Really?"

I nodded.

"Then what was that look that passed between you and Silas in the house earlier?"

"When?"

Her brown eyes sparkled. "When Arden was trying to force you to leave," she said. "When Silas stepped to your side. You can't fool me. You might have left three years ago—but your heart stayed."

I shook my head. "I've been dating an Englisch man. We've been together for a while now. He'll be here for Dat's service."

With eyebrows tilted upward, Aenti Suz's mouth formed an O, but no words came out.

"I'm serious," I said.

"So am I," she answered.

I may have rolled my eyes. I drained my mug of tea and said, hoping to distract her from any more talk about Silas, "Tell me about Ruby Bachmann."

"Do we have time?" Aenti Suz asked.

"Jah," I answered. It was still a couple of hours before it would be time to start the chores. I planned to corner Arden and ask about his plans for the farm at some point. But right now, there was no better place to pass the time than with Aenti Suz, safe inside her little house.

– 4 –

Ruby Bachmann

OCTOBER 1777

Ruby stood facing Paul Lantz just past the back door of her family's cabin. "Can't you stay and wait for me?" The early October breeze rustled through the leaves of the trees beyond the barn as she reached for his hand. They'd had a seemingly endless run of good weather. Hopefully it would last a few weeks longer. Ruby turned her head up, meeting Paul's blue eyes. "The rebels are on the run."

The British had captured Philadelphia, the seat of the Continental Congress, a few weeks before. For a night, nearby Lancaster had been the new capitol, but then it moved on another twenty-five miles or so to York. Ruby hoped it wouldn't be long until the war was over.

Paul shook his head and his straw hat wobbled a little. "Hans has a good plan. It's our best option."

Hans, Ruby's oldest brother, was leading a migration of Plain

49

folk to Canada, over the border with New York, claiming there was land up north for all of them without the problems in the colonies. There was no reason to risk their lives, he'd said, and all they held dear.

They'd all planned to go together a month ago, but Mamm had been ill and weak. Hans had waited, hoping she'd get better, but now they were running out of time. If they didn't leave soon, they wouldn't have time to build cabins on the new land before the snow began to fall.

Paul's father had died two years before, but his mother was traveling with him. She'd been waiting on the bench of his wagon since they arrived, ready to be on her way. Although Ruby had known her for years, she didn't have a close relationship with the woman. That would have to change once Paul and Ruby married. If only the group wasn't leaving until spring. That would give Mamm time to heal and Paul and Ruby a chance to marry.

Ruby had begged Hans to wait, too, using the same argument she'd just tried on Paul. But he'd told her no, saying again that he'd pledged his allegiance to George II alongside their father when they'd set foot on the docks of Philadelphia back in 1752. Twenty-five years later, his allegiance was just as strong to George III. Paul shared the same loyalty as Hans. They didn't want to risk staying, just in case the Patriots—or "rebel rousers," as Hans called them—won.

Ruby tightened her grip on Paul's hand. "Don't you think the British will win? And life will go on the way it was before?" She loved the Lancaster County countryside and her family farm in particular. It was the only home she'd ever known.

Paul leaned closer. "They'll most likely win, but in the meantime we could be conscripted to fight for the rebels or forced to pay someone else to fight for us. We've gone over this a hundred times."

They had. As the only sister with three brothers, it was expected Ruby would stay behind to care for their ailing mother. Her youngest brother, Zachary, would also stay, while Daniel, who already had a wife and young children, would go with Hans and his family. Zachary had taken over the Bachmann farm when their father died the year before, because both Daniel and Hans already had property of their own, which they'd sold to have money to purchase land in Canada. Hans planned for Ruby, Mamm, and Zachary to join the larger group when they could.

She wasn't sure if Zachary was as loyal to Britain as Hans. In fact, from comments he'd made, she'd suspected that he sympathized with the rebels. She also knew he'd been courting a girl named Lettie Yoder who lived in another Amish settlement, closer to the town of Lancaster. Zachary ventured over every couple of weeks, and one time Lettie had come to a harvest party at the Bachmann farm. Time would tell what Zachary's choice would be—although she doubted in the end that he'd stand up to Hans's plan. However, she knew for sure what her plan was. It was already set in stone. If she wanted to marry Paul, she'd have to follow him to Canada.

"Get word to me when you're ready to leave," Paul said. "In the meantime, I'll build a cabin and barn. Everything will be ready when you arrive. We'll marry then."

Ruby nodded. It was a plan they'd discussed before. Ruby wouldn't leave her Mamm behind, no matter how much she cared for Paul. In God's time, they'd be together again.

But that didn't mean she wasn't distraught at telling him good-bye. Or leaving Lancaster sometime soon. If only there weren't a war going on. If only Paul weren't eager to follow Hans. When Ruby had asked Paul the day before if he felt led by God to go, he'd smiled slightly and said, "I've aligned myself with your family. That's where my future is. We must band together to survive."

The back door opened, and Zach stepped out onto the porch. "Mamm needs you," he said to Ruby. "She wants to get dressed."

Ruby had been up since hours before dawn, doing the chores, mixing up bread dough, and then fixing breakfast for the crowd that had gathered. She hoped she'd have a few more minutes with Paul before he left.

She hurried through the kitchen and the common room. Zachary and Hans stood with their arms crossed, facing each other. Neither spoke. She guessed they'd been arguing before Mamm's call for help interrupted them. There had been tension between the two for months, ever since Hans had decided to move to Canada and mandated that everyone follow him.

As she reached the back of the house, her brothers' voices rose in volume with each word. "Dat would be disgusted with you," Hans said. "You know what life was like in Switzerland for our parents and grandparents. Britain gave us freedom to worship. We can't turn our backs on that."

Zach answered, "The rebels offer the same, minus the taxes."

Ruby knew taxes had been high for years to pay for the war with the French and the Indians, even though it had ended fourteen years ago. Now Britain needed to pay for a new war. No one she knew liked financially supporting violence, and many of their non-Plain neighbors agreed with Zach about the rebels. However, their Plain congregation agreed with Hans and sided with Britain, although their minister, Nathaniel Fischer, wasn't leaving, at least not yet. Regardless, most of the rest of the congregation was going with Hans.

"Maybe you need to come with me now," Hans said to Zach. "So I can keep an eye on you. Dat would agree. . . ."

"What are they fighting about now?" Mamm asked as Ruby entered the back room.

"Oh, I don't know." Ruby pulled the quilt back from Mamm's chin. "Those two can argue about anything."

Mamm frowned a little. She loved all of her children, and it pained her when the boys argued. Through the years, Mamm had lost four children. Two baby boys during their first years of life. A girl to disease when she was seven. And her oldest boy to a wagon accident when he was eleven. Mamm knew the heartache of loss, from her children to her husband. Just the other day, she'd reminded Ruby to hold those she loved close.

Ruby took her mother's aged hands and pulled her to a sitting position and then patted her wrinkled cheek in a loving gesture. It was easy to hold Mamm close. She was kind and caring to all.

Mamm had experienced some sort of incident two months before, after Dat had passed away, right after Hans made the decision to move. Since then Mamm had difficulty walking and her right side was especially weak. With help she could take small steps, but she needed assistance with almost everything—from getting out of bed to getting dressed, and sometimes even eating. She definitely needed to be stronger before she could travel.

"What time does Hans plan to leave?"

"Within the hour."

"Will you help me dress?"

"Of course." Ruby gathered her mother's petticoat, dress, and Kapp from the pegs on the wall. Hans's and Zach's voices rose and fell as she helped her Mamm, but she couldn't make out any more of what they were saying. There was no way Hans could force Zachary to leave with him, not with such short notice. Besides, who would watch over her and Mamm? Two women couldn't live alone in such uncertain times. And someone had to run the farm.

Fifteen minutes later, Ruby helped Mamm to the table. She guessed Zachary was helping Hans load the rest of his family's belongings, which had been stored in the barn for the last week, into their wagon. Hans's eight children ranged in age from three to nineteen. They were excited for a new beginning in Canada.

As she fed Mamm a bowl of porridge, Ruby kept glancing out the window at the activity in the side yard. Every once in a while she could make out Paul's voice. Mostly, she heard Hans giving orders.

After Mamm took her last bite, she said, "Go on out."

"I'll help you to the front porch first," Ruby responded. "You can sit and watch."

"*Denki*," Mamm said. "I appreciate it." Despite her illness, she hadn't lost her sweet spirit.

They shuffled across the planed floor that Dat had nailed down a decade ago. Ruby had been eight and remembered it well. It was the first big expansion of their home, and it had turned the cabin into a house, one of the largest in the area. Of course, Ruby would never say it out loud—it would be seen as prideful—but she secretly hoped she and Paul would be blessed with a home as fine as Mamm and Dat had.

When they reached the porch, she helped Mamm to sit in her rocker, and then returned for a quilt to wrap around her, even though the morning was already warm. When she returned, Paul stood on the porch beside Mamm, telling her good-bye, along with Hans and Daniel and their families.

Ruby's heart swelled as she tucked the quilt around her mother's legs.

"Go on now," Mamm said to Ruby, her eyes sparkling. "You and Paul need to say your good-byes in quiet."

Ruby followed him around the side of the house to where his wagon was hitched with his Mamm sitting on the bench like a queen in her carriage. He stopped. Ruby longed for a bit of privacy but didn't say anything. Tears filled her eyes.

He gazed down at her. "There's no need for sadness," he said. "We'll be together soon enough."

A tear escaped, and then another. She'd told herself she wouldn't cry. He was right. She would be with him soon. In the meantime she needed to serve her Mamm well, caring for her the best she could, helping her to grow strong enough to travel.

He kissed the top of her Kapp, a rare display of affection for him, as Hans yelled, "Time to go!"

"Good-bye," Paul said, releasing her quickly. He seemed anxious to go, which left her with an emptiness inside. She yearned for a longer hug, for a real kiss. For loving words. But that wasn't Paul's way. Still, she knew he would be a good husband, father, and provider. And a strong leader in their community in Canada.

He stepped toward his wagon and climbed up to the bench, next to his mother.

Ruby's heart lurched as the seven families from their congregation rolled forward. Hans turned onto the road. No one in his family or Daniel's glanced back at Mamm on the porch or the old place, but Paul did turn once and gave Ruby a final nod. Her heart swelled as she waved, reaching to the sky, but then he repositioned himself on the bench to face forward, and her hand remained suspended in the air for a long moment, then fell to her side.

Commotion across the fence distracted her from watching Paul turn onto the road, followed by a shout from a distance. She couldn't tell at first what was said, but then a man yelled, "Out of my garden!"

Old Man Wallis lived next door. He was Scottish and had been sympathetic toward the Paxton boys, who murdered twenty-one Indians from Conestoga Town back in 1763. Ruby had been seven then, but she remembered Dat and Mamm's horror over the incident. The Indians were peaceful and owned a deed from William Penn. Old Man Wallis supported the killings, believing the lie that the Conestoga aided other tribes in raiding and burning the homes of settlers. Mennonites had tried to help save the Indians, and the Amish were horrified by what had happened. Being neighborly to Old Man Wallis had been a challenge ever since.

"Git!" It didn't sound like Old Man Wallis. The voice was much younger.

Ruby glanced around for Zachary, guessing the ruckus had to do with the calf. When she didn't see her brother, she hurried to the fence, shading her eyes.

The half-grown beast was in what was left of the neighbor's garden, tromping through the corn and squash. Ruby yelled for Zach, but when he didn't reply, she climbed over the rail fence, lifting her skirt and apron, and started through the dewy pasture. The expansive oak *Bohm* on the Wallis's property was a silhouette against the low morning sun.

Again a man yelled, and the calf began to bawl. Ruby came around the tree. A tall, thin man with reddish hair and fiery brown eyes held a crutch high in the air, trying to get the calf to move. Instead it stood wide-legged and bawling.

Ruby began to run, wishing she'd grabbed a rope. "I'll get him," she called out in English. Even though they spoke a Swiss-German dialect at home, Dat had insisted all of his children learn English.

The man turned toward her. He was much younger than Old Man Wallis, probably in his mid-twenties or so, and wore woolen trousers and a vest over a fancy shirt. "Who are you?" he barked.

She wanted to snarl back at the man, but she heeded her manners. "Ruby Bachmann," she answered. "My family owns the farm next door."

He grunted and then limped toward the calf, raising the crutch again when he stopped, yelling as he did.

Ruby reached the garden and yelled at the calf, too, flapping her apron as well. The calf cut to the left, stepping on a pumpkin. Ruby leaped closer, dropped her apron, and reached for his head. She grabbed it with both arms and held on, but the calf jerked, snorting as he did. She slipped and, still hanging on to him, slid in the mud at the edge of the garden. She caught herself before she fell, but the mud caked her boots and the hem of her skirt. Old Man Wallis had a spring on the other side of the garden, which fed a pond out in the field. Obviously the spring needed to be tended—most likely the stone brim around it had been damaged. Soon enough the rains would come and all the farms would be muddy, but with such fine weather there was no reason for a muddy garden now.

The man slung a rope off his shoulder.

She tried her best to keep hold of the squirming animal.

The man stepped closer and managed to slip the rope over the calf's head. He held on to it as Ruby let go, but the animal lurched and pulled the man down. The calf jerked the rope out of his hand, headed in the opposite direction of the Bachmanns' property.

Ruby lunged for the rope, and this time she landed in the mud. However, she managed to grab hold of the rope and yank on it as the twisted hemp burned both of her hands. The calf bawled in protest but then stopped and stared at her, as if waiting for his next opportunity to bolt.

The man managed to stand and then crutched his way to her side and extended his free hand to her as he sank his crutch in the mud to brace himself. She was so annoyed with him that she hesitated to take it, but she'd have a hard time extracting herself from the mud any other way. Her dress and apron were nearly covered, as were her hands and arms.

Reluctantly, she took his hand, trying not to pull too hard and upset his balance, and managed to stand. She wiped her muddy hands, one at a time, on her apron. Keeping her eyes downcast, she muttered, "Thank you."

He nodded curtly. "Now keep that beast away from here."

Annoyed, she answered, "I'll return the rope."

"No need to. Leave it on the fence," he said. "I'll retrieve it later."

"Speaking of the fence . . ." Ruby replied. This time she met his eyes. "My brother will repair it."

"I expected as much." The man's gaze fell toward the Bachmanns' farm. "That was quite a caravan that took off this morning. I'm surprised you have any brothers left."

Her face warmed, even in the cool air. "One stayed, along with my Mamm."

"And where are the rest headed?"

Tears threatened her eyes. "Canada."

"Oh." The word fell flat. "Loyalists then."

She nodded. "They made a pledge to the king."

He exhaled. "Yes, didn't we all? Some of us were just wee ones, but still . . ."

Ruby didn't answer, wondering how he'd injured his leg. "Who are you?" she blurted out.

"Duncan Wallis." He nodded toward the neighbor's house. "I'm James Wallis's nephew."

"Oh," she said, wondering what his politics might be. She guessed the old man was a Patriot. Perhaps Duncan was too. Maybe he injured his leg fighting for the rebels.

"It seems you had a hard good-bye this morning," he said, changing the topic back to his previous observation.

She guessed he'd been spying on her and Paul. The man was as rude as his uncle.

Ruby yanked on the calf and trudged around the garden, toward the lane, pulling the beast along, without saying good-bye. She felt the man's eyes on her as she marched along.

As she neared her family's farmhouse, the thunder of hooves coming from the opposite direction as Hans, Paul, and the others had traveled startled her. The calf bawled and then lurched. She held on tight, wincing at her burning hands, as a band of a dozen or so Patriots, wearing mismatched uniforms, came into view.

She rushed toward the property past the porch as she held up a finger to her lips in response to her mother's concern, and then around the cabin with the calf. Zachary stood at the woodpile, an axe in his hand. "Patriots," she said. "Hide!"

He swung the axe into the stump and then stood straight, shaking his head. "No," he said, "They're with the 1st Regiment. I'll go speak with them."

"Zachary, that's ridiculous. I'll go tell them all of my brothers have left."

"That would be a lie," he said. "Put the calf away. And then see to Mamm." He smiled at her. "After you wash up." He marched determinedly away from her as the thunder of the hooves came to a halt in front of the Bachmann farmhouse.

–5–

Jessica

It took a moment for me to realize the knocking noise came from the front door of Aenti Suz's Dawdi Haus and not from 1777.

"Excuse me," Aenti Suz said, putting her empty mug on the doily on the end table.

She opened the door. A boy held a straw hat in his hands. He squinted a little into the living room. I stood. Was it Milton? Arden's oldest son? My nephew had been eleven when I left—which meant he was fourteen now. Done with school. Doing a man's work. Most likely taking over for Dat. Milton loved the land. At least he had three years ago.

He stood taller than Aenti Suz, and he had that almost-a-man look with his broad shoulders, deep voice, and the acne sprinkled across his face.

"I heard Jessica's home," Milton said to Aenti Suz.

"She is." My aunt swept her arm wide. "Come on in. Would you like a cup of tea?"

"No," Milton answered. "I've got to figure out how to get the tractor working." He squinted again. I was sitting under the window and perhaps the light was making it hard for him to see. "Is that you?" he asked.

I stood. "Jah, Milton, it's me." I wanted to give him a hug but feared it would be too forward.

He moved his hat from one hand to the other and then back. Poor boy. He was nervous. My heart hurt, wondering what Arden and Vi had been telling their children about me the last few years. I'd heard all the things they'd said about Amos. It was easy to imagine what they said about me.

"I can't get the tractor going. I think it's the carburetor."

"Oh?" It had been three years since I'd worked on a tractor. "Where's your Dat?"

"He went into town, to the funeral place. With my Mamm." He paused and then added, "They said I shouldn't work today, but we've fallen so far behind. I don't think they'll be back anytime soon."

"Can Silas help?" I asked.

He shook his head. "Dat said not to bother him about it—a few weeks ago."

But because Arden hadn't thought to tell Milton not to bother me, he felt he could. Pleased, I said, "I'd be happy to take a look." I turned to Aenti Suz. "Denki for the tea and the story."

"Come back for more when you get a chance." Her eyes sparkled. "I love to tell it. It's been a while since the last time. . . ."

I cocked my head. "How long?"

She placed the fingertips of both hands to her temples and whispered, "Before Amos left." She dropped her voice even more. "I would have told it to you three years ago if I'd had any idea. . . ."

"I'll be back," I said, not wanting Milton to overhear his

great-aunt. Perhaps she was getting a little sloppy in her old age. If Milton repeated anything she said to his parents, they'd have a field day with it. In fact, I could imagine Arden adding it to reasons to move Aenti Suz off the property.

Aenti Suz offered me her warm work coat to wear, and I gladly accepted it.

"Wear it while you're here," she said. "I don't plan to help with the milking or plowing or working on the tractor in the next few days." Her eyes sparkled again.

I smiled, grabbed the coat, and waved at Aenti Suz, and then followed Milton out the door, wishing I could wear a pair of jeans and a sweatshirt instead of a dress and Kapp to work on the old tractor. To think, for years, I didn't have an inkling that farming in a dress was odd to everyone in America who wasn't Amish or Old Order Mennonite.

Learning to drive a car hadn't been that hard for me after driving the tractor since I was thirteen. I loved Dat's tractor and had since my toddler days. In fact, the vehicle was what had initially hooked me on farming. In time, I found the engine just as fascinating as the steel wheels, dented red body, and torn black seat.

The tractor was adapted to only go in the fields. The steel wheels meant no one could take it far on asphalt roads, and the taped seat meant the driver couldn't get too comfortable no matter what. The upside of the steel wheels was that we never had to repair a flat.

The red paint was uncommonly bright, but Dat had never bothered to change it after he bought the vehicle. The tractor was a Ford 3000, 1975 model, three-cylinder engine, forty-seven horsepower. Dat bought it thirty years ago from a local Englisch farmer.

The engine was gasoline and fairly simple to work on. Back in

Harrisburg, in my research for the Department of Agriculture, I used to troll online forums and read comments about tractors just like this one. Many considered it antique, which made me laugh. I had no idea what the tractor was actually worth, but rebuilt engines were available for around four hundred dollars. Dat had rebuilt ours about ten years ago. Hopefully it would keep going strong for another decade or so. If not, Arden could replace it for a reasonable cost.

Milton and I stepped out into the wind and a few spitting raindrops.

"It's in the far field," Milton said.

Of course. I hurried to keep up with him, breathing in the earthy scent of spring emanating from the ground as my steps pressed against the grass. "How've you been?" I asked.

"*Gut*," he answered.

I thought about asking him how he knew I was home, but that might force him to be disloyal in some way to his father. Arden was adroit at gossiping—a skill Milton didn't seem to share. At least not when he was younger, and hopefully he hadn't developed it since I left. It didn't appear he had.

When we reached the tractor, Milton opened up the hood. "I don't know that much about it," Milton said. "After you left, Dawdi or Silas always worked on it."

"How long has it not been working?"

Milton's face reddened. "A month. I kept trying to get my Dat to help me with it, but he was busy."

"What have you been using then?" I asked, wondering exactly what Arden had been up to.

"The mules," Milton said. "But that takes so long."

I stepped up to the engine and peered inside. "Is the choke open?"

"Jah," Milton said.

"When were the spark plugs changed last?"

Milton shrugged.

"Go ahead and start it," I said.

He jumped up into the seat and gave it a go. It took a couple of tries, but once the engine took, it quickly slowed and sputtered to a stop. Most likely too much gasoline was going through. I checked the fuel level, but it wasn't set too high.

I checked the air filter. It was filthy. "Is there a new one in the barn?"

He shook his head.

"I'll go buy one," I said. "Want to come with me?"

He shook his head again. Of course not. Vi and Arden wouldn't allow that, even though Milton was at least a few years from joining the church and technically it wouldn't be against the *Ordnung* for him to ride with me in my car.

"I'll take this one with me," I said. "And go grab my purse."

Milton followed me to the house.

"Were you sad to be done with school?" I asked, trying to make conversation.

He nodded.

I remembered how sad I was. I'd loved school, and I knew Milton did too. I longed to tell him about getting my GED but held my tongue. We walked the rest of the way in silence. When we reached the house, I took the back stairs two at a time, thinking of Ruby Bachmann as I did. Surely the steps had been replaced many times over the years but to think the same logs still held up the back of the house amazed me. And perhaps the planked wood floor I walked over, that was nearly gray from all the years of use, was original too. There was a fireplace that we seldom used anymore along the far outer wall of the enclosed porch. It was made of river rock, and although I'd never thought of it before, I was certain now that it was original too. I shivered as I realized that Ruby probably cooked breakfast over that fire on the morning Paul and her older brothers left for Canada.

I stepped into the kitchen, which was empty. But Mamm and several others, including Leisel, Marie, and Gail, sat in the living room. I couldn't help but think of Ruby again and her love and care for her sweet mother all those years ago. My heart hurt again. I longed to be able to show love to my own mother. Even though she'd never been very affectionate when I was a child, being estranged from her broke my heart, over and over.

No one said anything to me as I swung around to the staircase and hurried up to the second floor. I quickly grabbed my purse and hurried back down the stairs. When I reached the bottom, I held up the air filter and announced, "I'm going to go buy a new one of these. For the tractor."

Mamm simply nodded, but Leisel said, "Thank you for helping with that. I know Milton needs it working again."

It was such an easy fix, I couldn't believe Arden hadn't seen to it. "I'll be back soon," I said.

As I came down the front steps, Milton paced around my car, bending down every few steps to examine a tire.

As I neared him, I asked, "What's up?"

Still squatting, he looked up at me. "Just looking."

"Want to look at the engine?"

"Sure," he said.

I opened the passenger door and popped the hood. Before I stepped around, he had it up and secured.

"Is it an automatic?" he asked.

"No. Standard." I enjoyed driving a clutch.

Milton took off his hat, pushed his bangs off his forehead,

put the hat back on, and then leaned over the engine. "You keep it nice and clean."

I did. I changed my own oil and did my own tune-ups too. If Bishop Jacobs had thought I was too involved in the running of the farm and the upkeep of our equipment, he'd be appalled at what I did in my Englisch life. Not to mention dating Tom.

The sound of a buggy approaching distracted me. Expecting another neighbor, I stepped out from under the hood—to find Arden and Vi staring at me from their buggy. Obviously their trip to the funeral home had taken less time than expected.

"Milton," Arden commanded. "Get back to your work."

He sighed and then gave me a furtive look before he strode away.

"I'm going to go get a filter for the tractor," I said, once again holding up the old one.

"It's not necessary," Arden said. "I'll see to it later."

"No," I answered. "It's no trouble." I slammed the hood of my car and then strode to the driver's door. Perhaps my brother said something more to me. If he did, it was lost in the wind. Vi's steely stare nearly pierced me as I climbed in, buckled my seat belt, and then turned on the engine. I waited a moment for them to proceed to the barn. When they didn't, I backed my car up and maneuvered around them, anxious to have a few moments alone in the car.

I found it difficult to mourn Dat amongst the drama of my family.

When I returned home, neither Arden nor Milton was in the field. I headed to the tractor, installed the filter, and then started the engine. It turned over. It was rough but didn't stall. A tune-up was most likely in order.

I shifted into first and headed toward the big shed by the barn, where the tractor was usually stored. I hoped being exposed to the elements for the last month hadn't caused too much harm. Dat never would have treated a piece of equipment so poorly.

I put the stick in neutral, set the brake, and left the tractor idling as I opened up both doors of the shed. Dat's service would be held in the wide open space, but I'd park the tractor in it until it was time to clean the shed for the service. The afternoon light wafted through the high windows and over the wood-planked floor. The structure was ancient, although I doubted it dated all the way back to Ruby's time.

I jumped back on the tractor, released the brake, and drove it inside. It lurched a little and then sputtered to a stop before I turned the engine off. It definitely needed more work. In the old days, Silas and I would have worked on it together.

The old familiar ache settled in my chest as I jumped down from the tractor. He'd been my best friend. For most of our school days we competed against each other, for the best grades and in whatever game or sport we played during recess. I mostly chose the games. Looking back, I was pretty bossy, but at the time it all felt so natural. I was used to my sisters following my lead and expected everyone else to also.

I stood in the middle of the shed, looking out the open doors to the field. Silas and I were very different. We were almost always team captains, on opposing sides, when it came to sports. I chose my teammates for their athletic skills mostly. He chose his randomly, at least it seemed that way to me. His first choice might be the youngest or the smallest or someone who was having a bad day.

Not surprisingly, his team mostly lost to mine.

I thought he was ridiculous until his father died when we were fourteen, toward the very end of our last year as scholars. I cried and cried for Silas, in what was my first encounter with true empathy. We both had older fathers, in their late fifties. And I knew I'd be devastated if Dat died.

I started being kind to Silas after that. For the last weeks of school, I chose the younger students for my team and left the better athletes for him. I stopped being as bossy. We truly became friends.

And then a few weeks later Dat hired Silas to work on our farm, against Arden's wishes. I still remember the fight they had. Well, the argument Arden tried to have. Dat wouldn't respond.

Silas and I grew closer as we worked together, even though we continued to compete. We'd see who could complete their chores first. Milk the most cows. Cut the most hay. The fall after Silas first came to work on the farm, we were each plowing opposite ends of a field, racing teams of mules to see who could pass the middle mark first, when Silas abruptly stopped and jogged toward the woods. I couldn't figure out what was happening, except that I had noticed Milton slinking off that way. But I kept on plowing, determined to win. Fifteen minutes later Silas returned, with Milton, who was six at the time. He'd been crying because Arden had been yelling at him for not latching the chicken coop properly. Soon Milton stood in front of Silas, holding the reins while Silas guided him.

Of course I won the plowing competition that day, but not really. Silas most definitely had the better heart, something even I could see. But the experience did give me a marker of when I first knew I was falling in love with him—before he'd even started shaving.

We plowed and planted and pruned together. We fixed the tractor. Picked apples. Branded calves. Harvested the corn. Bailed hay. Fertilized the fields. Vaccinated the cows and calves. I rushed through my housework, much to Mamm's disdain, to get outside and farm with him. Life with Silas had been so easy and fun and fulfilling, until Bishop Jacobs, along with Marie and Arden, began to interfere.

Tears stung my eyes as I closed the doors to the shed and decided to see what I could do to help with the chores. It was time to start the milking. I needed to do whatever I could to stop thinking about Silas. And I needed to speak with Arden about the farm.

A few minutes later, I squinted as I pushed the barn door open. Straw covered the floor along with a few piles of manure from the morning milking. Dat never would have allowed that either. I stopped. No, I couldn't come in criticizing Arden. He was in mourning, like all of us. Perhaps it wasn't him at all. Most likely neighbors had helped with the chores. Perhaps they hadn't cleaned up. I grabbed the shovel and began scooping, a little surprised that whoever was doing the evening milking hadn't started.

It wasn't until I had the place swept, too, that Silas stepped through the barn doors. "Oh," he said when he saw me. "Is Arden around?"

I shook my head. "Aren't neighbors helping?"

"There was some sort of miscommunication. Arden will probably be here soon. I'll get started."

"I'll help," I said.

"No," he said, "I don't think that's a good idea."

"Silas . . ."

"Arden doesn't want you around his kids." Silas appeared uncomfortable again as his gaze fell behind me.

Milton approached, along with his brothers Luke and Leroy, who were ten and eleven. I'd been over the moon when all of my nephews and nieces were born and had played with them and later babysat whenever I could. Back then, Vi and Arden liked me and were eager for me to help with their children. Luke and Leroy both gave me a half smile. At least they remembered me. They'd grown too, although they hadn't changed as much as Milton.

"Where's your Dat?" Silas asked Milton.

"In the big house, talking things through with Mammi."

"We'll be fine," Silas said to me. "You should help your sisters or something."

I bristled, but Silas seemed oblivious to what he'd just said. That had been the main problem before—that I did too much outside and didn't help in the house enough.

The boys headed farther into the barn. Silas looked as if he'd perhaps registered what he'd just said and wanted to say something more, but then Arden started toward us. When he grew closer, he said, "The viewing will be tomorrow night and then the service will be Wednesday morning at nine a.m." The burial would be in the cemetery a half-mile away from our house, on land the Bachmann family had donated years and years ago to be used by all in our community. He didn't need to tell us that.

I nodded in response and said, "I wanted to speak with you."

"About?"

"The farm."

His eyes narrowed as if he were angry with me, but then he burst out laughing. "Nothing has changed in the last three years, Jessica. The farm was never any of your business."

"I just have a few questions," I said.

He shook his head. "That I'll not entertain."

"Please listen."

He started walking past me. "Never," he hissed.

I stood frozen for a long minute. I didn't turn to watch him go, to see Silas staring at me, as I expected he was. Instead, I slipped away, patting my phone in my apron pocket, through the thickness of the coat. I obviously wasn't welcome to speak with Arden about anything at all. I wouldn't challenge that, at least not for the time being.

I strolled, slowly, around the pond. There was an underground spring closer to our house, where our water came from. Good clean water that had sustained the Bachmann family for generations.

The pond sustained the livestock all these years, along with the land. Water was life. The green budded boughs of the willow tree at the far end of the pond swayed in the breeze, along with the bare cattails. The murky water smelled of mud and fish and plants. A flock of ducks congregated under the willow, while two ventured out into the water. I stepped away from the reeds and soggy ground and continued through the field, concentrating on each inch of land my feet stepped on. The spicy scent of spring, the new growing grass, and the hint of woodsmoke in the air comforted me. But still, coming home felt like that first day Dat tried to teach me to swim—as if I might flail my way under the water. But being home without Dat here, without his arms around me, was worse than feeling as if I might drown.

I made my way to the woods and then picked my way along the slippery trail. The day grew colder and darker under the boughs of the evergreen trees. I could hear the traffic from the highway—tires rolling over the asphalt, horns honking, the occasional squeal of brakes. The trees muffled the noise but couldn't hide it entirely. Arden felt the property was useless, but I disagreed. It was a buffer between the farm and the world. The trees helped cleanse the air, provide shade for the animals, and nourish the soil. It also provided firewood through the winter. If Arden sold the property to a developer, an apartment complex would look over the property instead of us enjoying our own mini forest.

I was sure that after he sold one parcel off, he'd be more likely to sell another. And then another. Until nothing was left.

I took a deep breath, sucking in the clean pine scent and the smell of the fertile soil beneath my feet. I blew it out slowly. I loved the woods. I leaned against a tree, aware of the puzzle of the bark through my coat, and tilted my head upward. The breeze blew high in the boughs, swaying them back and forth. A needle fell against my cheek, and I turned my face back down, scanning the ground. Ferns of all sizes covered the ground. Green shoots curled out from the stem. How many times had Silas and I played hide-and-go-seek with Leisel and Marie through these trees? And Milton, and even Luke and Leroy. A few times Dat had played with us. I remembered him chasing Silas through the woods. I remembered him scooping my youngest nephews up, one under each arm. I remembered the pure joy on both Leroy's and Luke's faces. Jah, my Dat had a gift with people, no matter their ages.

I fought the urge to sing "How Great Thou Art." I couldn't bear to even think of it. As a child, I thought the line *"Consider all the* worlds *Thy hands have made"* was *Consider all the* woods. . . . I only confessed my mistake to Silas when we were fifteen and we'd started to court, as covertly as we could because Mamm insisted we wait until we were sixteen. He sang the line as *Consider all the woods* forever after. I couldn't help but smile at the thought of his voice, his smile, his soul . . . his hazel eyes twinkling down at me as he sang.

I don't know how long I stayed in the woods, but it grew so dark that I finally headed back toward the oak Bohm, thinking about the Wallis property next door. Today an Englisch family owned the farm, but I knew they weren't descendants of the Wallis family. They'd bought the property from a Mennonite family ten years before.

For a moment the sun seemed as if it were stuck in the oak tree, casting a golden hue over the green buds. But then it shot a moment of pink and orange across the horizon before disappearing.

"Jessie!"

I turned slowly toward Silas.

"Do you have a minute?"

I nodded, hurrying away from the tree. The last thing I wanted was to stand in *our* spot with Silas.

"We didn't really have a chance to talk earlier, not much at least."

The last thing I wanted was to talk with Silas. The day had been hard enough as it was.

"How do you like Harrisburg?" he asked.

It seemed so far away. Had it only been this morning that I'd left? "It's great," I answered, the image of my peaceful apartment coming to mind.

He tilted his head toward the house. "You might have guessed that Gail and I are courting."

"Jah."

"Since last November. That's when I started taking Gail home from singings."

I swallowed hard. "Look, we don't need to have this conversation. You and I—we were a long time ago. I'm happy for you and Gail. Honestly." I took a step toward the fence and stumbled a little. He reached for me, grabbing my hand.

A sob formed in my throat, and I swallowed hard again. I would not be vulnerable in front of Silas. Not for anything. I resolved to remain on guard. Against him. Against Arden. Against the world—at least the Amish one.

I pulled away from him and retrieved my phone. "I need to make a call."

"It's almost time for supper."

"I'll be right in," I said, dreading where I'd have to sit.

Silas didn't budge.

"Go on," I said. "I'll only be a minute."

As Silas retreated, I hit speed dial for Tom. As I held it to my ear, Silas reached the barn.

Tom picked up on the third ring, and I immediately burst into tears.

"What's the matter?" he asked, his voice low and soothing.

I took a deep breath, not ready to try to explain all of the emotions I was feeling. "I'm sad," I answered. That was true. "I wanted to let you know when the service will be." I gave him the time.

"Where?" he asked.

"On our farm." I rattled off the address. "Do you still think you'll come?"

"Of course," he answered. "I'll arrive early, by eight thirty."

"Perfect." That would give me time to explain everything to him.

A rustling caught my attention, and I turned around. Arden was striding toward me. "I've got to go," I said. "I'll call tomorrow." I said good-bye as quickly as I could.

Arden had his hand out, and I tucked my phone back under my coat, into my pocket.

"Give it to me," my brother said.

I shook my head.

"I'm in charge now, and I don't allow cell phones on my farm."

"I'll be here less than two days." I kept my voice as calm as I could. "I promise I won't use it where your children can see me."

He pointed toward the barn. Milton stood there, watching us.

"I'm sorry," I said. "I'll do better next time."

"There won't be a next time."

"Of course not," I said, striding past him. I kept marching toward the house.

I glanced over my shoulder. Arden followed several paces behind. Milton followed his father, but his eyes were on me.

– 6 –

I washed up at the sink on the back porch and then hung Aenti Suz's coat on the only empty peg on the wall. Next I kicked off my shoes and entered the kitchen in my stocking feet. The smell of roast beef, part of the meal a neighbor had dropped by, made my stomach growl.

Mamm didn't look up from where she pulled out a container of mashed potatoes, but Aenti Suz gave me a smile as she placed biscuits in a basket. Leisel, who filled a pitcher with water, smiled at me. Marie and Gail stood with their backs to me at the island. Neither glanced my way.

My mouth watered. I hadn't had a good home-cooked meal since . . . I left home. I scanned the dining room table. It was fully set, which meant Arden's family was probably joining us, along with Silas. I turned toward the far wall. The shunning table was exactly where I expected it to be. Still, shame grew inside of me.

I stood at the end of the table. For a moment I thought about running up the stairs, grabbing my things, and fleeing out the front door. But then my stomach rumbled again. Jah, I was hungry. But it was more than that. I'd chosen to come home. I knew what was in store. I wouldn't run now.

By the time Mamm, Aenti Suz, and the girls gathered around the table, Arden, Vi, and their five children filed in. Milton gave me a nod. The youngest, Pammy, rushed at me and threw her arms around my waist. She was seven, and frankly I was surprised she remembered me.

I hugged her back as Arden cleared his throat and then said, "Pam, remember what we talked about. Take your seat."

The oldest girl in the family, Brenda, shook her head at her little sister as if in disgust. Brenda was only nine. Hardly an authority figure yet, but apparently peer pressure was working well in their family. Milton avoided eye contact with me and quickly pulled out a chair between Luke and Leroy.

Arden sat down in Dat's place, and Vi and Mamm sat on either side of him. I'd been wrong about Silas. He wasn't joining the family for dinner.

I shuffled toward my table and slinked down in the chair, surprised at how humiliated I felt even though I certainly expected the drill.

Arden led the silent prayer. I bowed my head along with everyone else, but no prayer came. That had been a problem ever since I'd left—I'd thought the freedom of being away from Bishop Jacobs, Marie, and Arden would free my spirit. But the opposite had happened. I struggled to pray, to feel connected to God.

My face grew warm and I forced myself to pray. I needed it now more than ever. I asked God to help me to be kind. To not be harsh. To love my family.

As Arden said "Amen," the back door slammed.

"You're late." A smile spread across Gail's face as she looked into the kitchen.

Silas stopped at the side of the table. "One of the cows is

ready to calve," he said, not moving. "I'll go check on her again after supper."

Everyone began passing food and chatting. Jah, their voices were subdued, but it was still a racket. Luke and Leroy were arguing about something until Milton gave them a withering look that reminded me a little too much of Arden. Then Pam knocked over her glass of milk.

Silas hurried into the kitchen as Vi said, "Honestly, can't we have one meal without an accident?"

Leisel grabbed her napkin and threw it over the spilled milk as Silas returned with a dish towel and handed it to Vi.

I expected Silas to sit beside Gail, but instead he picked up his plate, silverware, glass, and napkin and walked toward me. Gail gasped. I froze as everyone turned.

"Ignore them," Silas whispered as he took the chair closest to the wall, the one facing the big table.

I complied, trying to stare straight ahead, but I couldn't help but sneak a look at Silas. His eyes seemed tired but as kind as ever. I whispered, "You can't sit with me. It's against the Ordnung."

"Not for me."

"What are you talking about?"

"I haven't joined the church."

A shiver raced up my spine. "No, you did. The Sunday after I left."

"I didn't," he answered.

My stomach tightened. "Why not?"

"I wasn't ready," he answered. "I went through a . . . spiritually dry time."

I shivered. That pained me. "But you're ready now?"

"Jah," he answered. "I started taking the class again two Sundays ago."

"I see." Most likely so he could marry Gail.

I glanced toward the big table. Gail had her head bowed as if she were praying—or crying. Marie glared at me. Mamm pushed back her chair and then came toward me, quickly. She snatched up my plate. I thought perhaps they'd pass the food our way, since Silas had sat down with me, but that didn't appear to be the plan.

"Come fill your plate," she said to Silas, over her shoulder as she returned to the table. I knew her dishing up for me was part of the shunning.

He followed her. Rebellious yet compliant. That had always been the paradox of Silas. He could be such a rule follower, but then he also always stuck up for the underdog, too, which in this case was me.

Mamm returned before Silas and placed the plate in front of me. I managed a quick thank you before she retreated. This was difficult for her. No Amish mother wanted her child to leave. I'd hurt her deeply.

I breathed in the savory scent of the roast beef and the gravy spread across the meat and mashed potatoes. Cooked carrots, green beans, applesauce, and buttermilk biscuits.

Marie continued to glare at me, which didn't prevent me from enjoying the food. I savored every bite.

Silas shot me a smile. I ducked my head, not wanting to smile back. After I first moved into my apartment, I used to flick the lights on and off for the pure joy of it. I loved the way the entire room lit up. I strung lights around the inside of my apartment too and purchased extra lamps. I loved the light.

That was how Silas's smile felt to me. Like a room full of brilliant lights.

I kept my head down as if I were concentrating on my eating. I'd need to do my best to avoid Silas, especially his smiles.

And I needed to do my best to simply accept my shunning, whether Silas continued to sit beside me or not. There was no reason to challenge or protest it. I wouldn't have to suffer through it for long.

I wondered if Ruby's family shunned anyone. Perhaps not. Perhaps no one ever left. Although it sounded as if Zachary was a bit of a rebel. Like me, he wasn't willing to do his older brother's bidding.

"Clearly Thomas Wolfe was right." I stood in the middle of my childhood bedroom. "You can't go home again."

Unfortunately my sisters and Gail were all in the room with me. I should have kept my mouth shut.

Marie bounced off her bed and landed on her feet a few inches from me. We were eye to eye. Jah, she'd grown even prettier in the years I'd been gone. "You're the one who left," she said. "This is your fault—not ours."

"I get it," I answered. "Completely." I'd never written a letter to someone who'd left the faith, but I truly understood the motivation. If Silas had left instead of me, I would have done everything possible to plead my case for him to return. Same with Marie and Leisel too.

"You can't come back for a day and expect things to be as they were." Marie planted her hands on her hips as if she were five. "You're not in charge anymore."

"I was never in charge," I muttered. If I had been, I never would have left. I started toward my bag to retrieve my pajamas.

Marie couldn't seem to stop. "You're the one who chose the ways of the world."

I spun back around. "Is that why you think I left?"

She nodded.

"What ways, exactly, do you think I chose?"

"A car. Probably a TV and a computer too." She sneered as she shifted her gaze to my pocket. "Definitely a cell phone."

"You think I left my family because of *stuff*? Who told you that?"

She shrugged.

"I know Dat didn't."

"No, he didn't say anything about you. It was as if you were dead to him."

I crossed my arms. I didn't believe that, not at all. "Then why did he come visit me?"

Marie shook her head in disgust. "Don't lie." It was the same response as Vi's. Where did they think Dat had gone on those days he totally disappeared?

"I'm not lying." I turned back toward my bag. The last thing I wanted was to fight with Marie. I pulled my perfectly modest pajamas from my bag—but I still knew Marie wouldn't approve.

I took off my Kapp, shook out my hair, and untied my apron. Next I wiggled out of my dress and hung it on a hanger and put it away in the closet. It was only then that I remembered I had on bright red Victoria's Secret undergarments. I should have undressed in the tiny room down the hall.

"First Timothy 2:9," Marie quoted. I knew what was coming. "'In like manner also, that women adorn themselves in modest apparel—'"

I spun around, grasping for some sort of smart remark, but the look of surprise on Leisel's face stopped me. When my gaze met hers, she broke out in laughter. I couldn't help but join her. I stood there with my pajamas against my chest with

Marie and Gail shooting nails with their eyes. But at least my sister hadn't quoted any more of the verse.

I couldn't stop laughing.

"Come on, Gail," Marie said. "Let's come back later. After Miss Englischer has calmed down." They both headed toward the door.

Leisel abruptly quit laughing and spun around. "You have no right to treat Jessica in such a way. She's our sister."

"She's no sister to me," Marie retorted as she reached the door. She yanked it open and then slammed it after she and Gail both passed through. The sound echoed down the hall and into the room.

I slipped the pajama top over my head and then whispered "Sorry" to my little sister.

"It's not your fault," Leisel said. "Marie keeps getting more and more . . . uptight?"

I nodded, verifying the word she'd chosen as I pulled on my pajama bottoms.

"Dat referred to her behavior as legalistic one time."

"Really?" That surprised me.

"She hangs on every word that Bishop Jacobs says and reads her Bible all the time, but not in a way that worships God. More in a way to catch people and tell them they're wrong."

I groaned.

"Jah, I was reading a medical book about Dat's illness a week ago, and she quoted 'Proverbs 19:15.'"

I gave her a questioning look. I couldn't remember that one.

Leisel took her nightgown out from underneath her pillow as she quoted, "'Slothfulness casteth into a deep sleep; and an idle soul shall suffer hunger.'"

"You're kidding."

"No." She stepped toward the closet to hang up her dress. "She was mad that I wasn't helping with the cooking and cleaning more."

"Wow, I don't remember her being that bad before."

"Jah, she's steadily gotten worse over the last few years. And when Dat was diagnosed with cancer, she said it was because of sin in the family. He was paying for the sins of others." Leisel pulled her dress over her head.

My stomach sank. "Whose sin?" I asked as I grabbed my toothbrush and toothpaste from my bag.

"Guess."

"Mine, I imagine."

"Jah." Leisel pulled off her beige slip, revealing a pair of old-lady beige underwear and a beige bra. Mamm purchased our underthings. I shuddered, grateful she no longer purchased mine. "And she blames Amos too."

"But he's been gone so long." Poor guy. He had no idea what he'd be walking into tomorrow.

"She's convinced the two of you have shamed our family and caused some sort of—" My sister stopped.

"Some sort of what?"

Leisel shook her head. "Not curse . . ."

"Consequence?" I asked.

She nodded.

I rolled my eyes before I could stop myself. "And she thinks that was why Dat got cancer?"

"Jah. She said it was your fault Dat died. If you two hadn't left like you did, God wouldn't have needed to . . ." This time Leisel's voice trailed off.

"Strike Dat? Torture him with cancer? Kill him?"

Leisel looked so innocent in her white nightgown with her

blond hair halfway out of her bun. Tears welled in her eyes. "Convict the two of you of your sin."

"That's so harsh." Before she could respond, I headed down the hall to brush my teeth, not wanting to raise my blood pressure further by discussing Marie. I could hear voices below as I walked. Serious voices. Marie, most likely, tattling to Mamm about what a horrible person I'd become. Or had always been. The latter was probably more likely Marie's view.

I stepped into the bathroom, shut the door, and turned on the water, completely drowning out their voices as I began to brush my teeth. I'd been the best of friends with my sisters. Sure, there was normal competition between us, but not anything too drastic. Then, about six months before I left home, Marie became self-righteous about pretty much everything. She started keeping track of how much time I spent working in the fields. She thought it wrong that I helped pull calves, that I fixed the tractor, that I stood up to Arden when I disagreed with him.

She agreed with everything Bishop Jacobs did and said, saying he was exactly what our district needed. "We were getting too liberal," she explained, more than once. She began measuring the distance from her ankle to the hem of her dress, the length of her Kapp ties, and even the brim of Dat's hats. She avoided riding in cars unless it was absolutely necessary. Then she started measuring Leisel's and my dresses too.

She pointed out, more than once, that the previous way of thinking in our district had affected me more than anyone else. "Be careful, Jessica," she used to tell me. "You need to rein yourself back in before it's too late. We're called to be submissive. We need these rules—and roles—to preserve our way of life. You're much too bossy. You expect the men to take orders from you instead of the other way around."

I ignored her. Dat had always encouraged my interest in farming and my initiative to try new things. Before, when Arden tried to dampen my spirits, Dat had intervened in a kind way.

Marie ended up going to Bishop Jacobs to "talk" about me. The bishop then went to Arden, who confirmed everything Marie had said, most likely adding more trespasses to the list. Soon every one in the district was feeling sorry for Silas, except for Silas and me and Dat.

When Bishop Jacobs finally spoke with my father, instead of just with my sister and brother, Dat told him he didn't think there was a problem. "She's acting within her gifting" was the rumor of what Dat had said. Even though I asked Dat what his exact words were, he never told me, claiming the conversation was private.

Soon after, Arden approached Dat about selling off the woods to a developer who wanted to put an apartment building in on the highway. Dat was opposed to it, but wasn't as firm with Arden as I thought he should be. Then I overheard Arden bring up the possibility of fracking with Dat.

I was livid. Again, Dat said he wasn't interested in the idea, but he didn't shut Arden down the way he needed to. True, we used some oil and gas products as Amish for our generators, propane appliances, and tractors, and also when we hired drivers to take us places. But we didn't believe in blindly consuming resources. We didn't wear jewelry and therefore didn't play a part in the geopolitical warring over gold and diamonds, something that I'd Googled recently. We tried to heat our houses with wood as much as we could, rather than gas or coal, although I knew woodsmoke was a pollutant—but it was also renewable. We managed our woods as best we could, replanting seedlings for every tree we cut down.

Much of what I knew about natural resources, I learned from all the research I did after I left the Amish—but it taught me to value, even more, the Plain approach to the consumption of those resources. Even without having all of the background information, I'd been raised to be a good steward of the land.

And I had firm opinions about how our land should be treated. I couldn't reconcile how fracking or developing a section of a two-hundred-plus-year-old farm was good stewardship of what God had entrusted us with.

Even though we'd been raised the same, it was obvious Arden didn't want to farm and was doing everything he could to make money off our land in other ways.

I'd given him a piece of my mind, and he told me it wasn't any of my business. I told me it was. "No, it's not," he said. "You have no stake whatsoever in this property. It will never be yours."

Soon after that, the bishop requested a meeting with me. Arden was there too—but not Dat. At the time, he was in Haiti for a two-month period, helping to house, feed, and care for victims of the 2010 earthquake.

During that time, both the bishop and Arden wanted to discipline me. I'd gone against the Ordnung. I'd stepped out of my role as an Amish woman. I'd been prideful. I'd tried to manipulate my brother.

I'd asked for them to wait until Dat was home. The bishop agreed, saying he'd set up a meeting for as soon as Dat returned. I talked with Silas over and over about what was going on. Clearly, it all made him uncomfortable. Jah, he felt they were being unfair to me. On the other hand, it was the bishop and my older brother. They deserved my respect.

As it drew nearer to Dat's return, I thought about how a

meeting with the bishop, my brother, and father would play out. I would be pitted against Arden and the bishop with Dat in the middle. My father hated conflict, especially between his children.

And Arden was right. I had no future on our farm. I was a woman—I could never be a Bavvah.

I'd had no idea what Silas and I would do, what would make it possible for us to farm together. We saved every cent we made, but we wouldn't be able to buy property of our own. The land he lived on was only ten acres, not enough to make a living from. And he and his Mamm didn't even own it—a distant relative allowed them to live on it.

I shivered as I spit into the sink, rinsed my mouth, and then turned off the water, hoping my gums wouldn't be sore from my overzealous brushing as I pondered the past.

Marie had started a snowball effect, for sure. But as it sped down the hill, picking up pebbles, rocks, and then boulders, I was the only casualty when it hit the bottom. And Silas wasn't there to catch me. It was his one fault—being too passive. Bowing to authority too quickly. Being influenced by my brother and Bishop Jacobs. Silas didn't actually side with Arden, but he never unequivocally defended me either. Jah, he was supportive. Jah, he thought I should have a say in how the land was managed, but he wouldn't say it to Marie, Arden, or the bishop.

My heart raced at the memory. It was definitely my choice to leave. That was true. But really, what option did I have?

When Dat returned, absolutely physically and emotionally exhausted, the bishop scheduled a meeting. I balked, fearing it was a bad idea. Dat was the quietest I'd ever seen him. He'd helped dig through the rubble of Port-au-Prince. He'd comforted widows, widowers, and orphans. He'd cared for the injured and the ill.

I didn't want to cause him more pain, nor did I want to stand up to Arden and the bishop on my own. Because even if I did, what would I gain? I would always be viewed as suspicious by both of them. There was nothing I could say that would change their opinion of me.

So I decided to leave, sure Silas would follow. But he was taken aback by my plan and begged me to reconsider. "Everything will work out," he said.

I knew he was wrong and begged him to come with me. Then I screamed at him, commanding him to come. Not surprising, neither method was effective. He finally said, "We need to give it time if we can't come to a mutual decision. In the meantime, we should leave it alone."

It wasn't the first time he said we should leave something "alone."

Instead of doing what he asked, I left on my own, giving Silas one final chance before I did. He declined, tears in his eyes, his voice raw with emotion as we said our farewells.

When I told Marie good-bye, she cried, which shocked me. Jah, she was petrified about my soul, but then she asked, "How can you leave me?" That shocked me even more. I thought she'd be happy to have me go.

When I told Leisel I was leaving, she simply shook her head at me. "Why?" she asked.

"Because it's what I need to do."

She hugged me tightly and whispered, "Godspeed."

I called a driver, whom I knew had a connection with an ex-Amish woman in Harrisburg who could help me. I stayed with her for a few weeks, and she helped me get the job in the coffee shop, work I was thankful for even though I hated being cooped up inside. Slowly I grew used to it though. Once I contacted Dat and let him know where I was, I believed Silas would come join me. It didn't happen. When Dat visited me for the first time, I was sure Silas was waiting on the sidewalk, that any minute he'd burst through the door of the coffee shop and surprise me. It didn't happen.

I soon gave up hope that Silas would leave and ended up asking Dat not to tell him where I was. I didn't want to be forever wishing he'd show up.

Did I regret leaving? Jah, nearly every day. At the time, it felt as if I'd made a rational decision, but looking back I'd been impulsive. I should have waited and talked with Dat. And I should have worked things out, one way or the other, with Silas.

Did I regret not being under my brother's thumb? Under the bishop's whims? Under Marie's constant criticism? No, never.

Thankfully, Dat had told me later that he'd insisted Arden give up the fracking idea. I couldn't help but think I'd at least been an influence for good on that account, that I'd raised questions that perhaps my father might have overlooked.

I washed my face, dried it, and then grabbed my toothbrush and toothpaste and headed back down the hall, feeling drained from reliving all those memories. I'd avoided them as much as I could once I started dating Tom.

When I reached the bedroom, Leisel was gone. I collected all of my things so I wouldn't have to bother Marie again and headed down the hall. When I reached it, Leisel was in the double bed, her face toward the wall. A lamp was lit on the small table. I crawled in, missing my own pillow, my own bed, my own apartment, but I was thankful for my baby sister's presence.

And I couldn't help but breathe in the scent of the fresh sheets. It was the smell of home. "Good night," I said.

She didn't answer and for a moment I wondered if she'd already fallen asleep, but then she asked, "Do you go to church in Harrisburg?"

"Yes." I didn't tell her I went each week with Tom. "It's a little church, not far from my house."

"What kind?"

"Nondenominational."

"Is it anything like our church?"

"We sing 'How Great Thou Art' and 'Amazing Grace.'" We used to sing those at Youngie singings and sometimes in church. "Except with music. There's both a piano and an organ." I hesitated a moment and then added, "Of course all of the scripture and sermons are in English. And the congregation is smaller. Only seventy-five or so." Our Amish district had over one hundred fifty people in it. Many of those were children though, far more than at my little church in Harrisburg. I was one of the youngest people in the congregation, which still felt so odd to me.

"What else is different?"

"A woman preaches sometimes."

Leisel popped up in the bed. "What?"

"Jah," I said. "She preaches at another church in town, but she fills in if our pastor is gone."

"Wow." Leisel put her head back on her pillow. "Don't tell Marie."

I laughed. "Believe me, I won't."

"Do you know other women who do men's jobs?"

"Like?"

"Doctors."

"Being a doctor isn't necessarily a man's job."

"You know what I mean."

I shook my head. "More women go to medical school nowadays than men."

"Really?"

"Yes. And more men are going to nursing school than ever before. Women are lawyers. Engineers. Pilots. Men are teachers and daycare workers. Women, like me, can work at the Department of Agriculture."

"Tell me about your job."

First I told her about the job in the coffee shop below my apartment. Then I told her about the receptionist job I got with the State Department of Revenue and how I worked hard to get my GED. "Then I got my job as an administrative assistant in the communications office at the Department of Agriculture." I added that I mostly did filing and updating documents and that sort of thing.

She asked me more about my GED and I told her about my classes, my voice finally trailing off. "Why do you want to know?" I asked, growing suspicious.

"Just curious."

"Leisel," I said, panic rising in my chest. "What are you up to?"

"Nothing." She yawned. "Good night."

"Talk to me," I said.

She rolled over. "I have nothing to say, honestly."

I exhaled slowly. If Leisel left the Amish, Mamm, Arden, and Marie would never forgive me. Everyone adored Leisel. They'd all blame me.

I blew out the lamp. As much as I enjoyed spending time with Leisel, I knew I needed to return to Harrisburg as soon as possible. It was stressful for my family to have me around, and I no longer belonged in Lancaster County. I'd leave as soon after the funeral as I possibly could. My being home would only lead to more heartache for all, me included. But probably not for Silas.

Dat had told me, the last time he came to visit, that Silas had grown into a fine man with real leadership qualities. "I'd be proud to have him as my deacon," Dat had said. "Or bishop. He has a kind and gentle way about him, of course, but he's not afraid to stick up for what is right too."

"Are we talking about the same Silas?" I'd asked.

Dat nodded. "He was only nineteen when you left, Jessica. Show him some grace."

I appreciated Dat sticking up for Silas—I just wished Silas had stuck up for me.

The next morning I ate breakfast at Aenti Suz's, devouring a bowl of oatmeal as I stood at her kitchen counter.

"Come sit with me," she said.

I shook my head. "I don't want anyone rushing in and busting you."

"Who would do that?"

"My Mamm. Marie. Arden. Take your pick." Just as I finished, there was a knock on the door.

I stood up straight, expecting the door to fly open. "See?"

"No one's rushing in," Aenti Suz said. She walked to the door, her head held high.

She opened it to reveal a thin man standing in the doorway. I gasped. Arden and Amos were identical twins, but they no longer appeared as if they were. Amos was at least fifty pounds lighter than Arden. He also wore jeans, a work coat, and a cowboy hat and boots and looked as if he'd stepped out of an old Clint Eastwood movie.

But when he took off his hat, even though his face was thin, the resemblance to Arden was still evident. The heavy blue eyes, the round nose, the thin lips.

"Aenti Suz," he said.

"Amos!" She threw her arms around him.

I stayed back for a long moment but then started toward him. He let go of our aunt, and said, "Jessica?"

I nodded.

"Same dark hair," he said. "And brown eyes." Marie and I had Mamm's eyes, but Leisel's were blue like Dat's and the twins'. Amos gave me a half hug. "I thought you said you'd left."

"I did." I lifted my apron. "I'm dressed this way to appease . . ." My voice trailed off. Mamm. Marie. Arden. The usual suspects.

He smiled a little. "Well, I won't be appeasing anyone."

"Of course not," Aenti Suz said. "We're just so glad you're here. But you must be exhausted."

He shrugged. "I slept some on the plane."

"Then how did you get here from the airport?" Aenti Suz asked.

"I rented a car in Philadelphia." He ran his hand through his hair. It had more gray than Arden's did, and he had far more wrinkles on his face. "I forgot how beautiful the landscape is here," he said. "It's a different sort of beauty than in Colorado."

So that was where he'd been living.

Aenti Suz offered Amos breakfast, but he said he'd grabbed a bite at the airport.

"You're staying with me," she said. "In the spare bedroom. If you'd like, you can nap now."

He shrugged again. "I'll wait. I'd like to take a look around the farm and see Marie and Leisel."

I wondered if he had any desire to see Arden. Or Mamm. Neither of them ever spoke kindly of Amos. I'd been six when he left—he'd been gone sixteen years. Although Marie was five, she always claimed she didn't remember him. Leisel was only three, and of course she didn't remember him at all.

Aenti Suz asked, "How about a cup of coffee?"

He agreed to that, and we all sat around the table. This time I didn't caution Aenti Suz about sitting with us. I doubted anyone, except maybe Leisel, would venture into the Dawdi Haus to intentionally see Amos. Hopefully Marie, Mamm, and Arden wouldn't be rude to him.

We soon found out. Leisel and a neighbor were hanging laundry on the line when we ventured out, so I introduced Amos to her. She gave him a hug, her blue eyes dancing. "Oh, I've wondered about you my whole life," she said.

He blushed and glanced down at his cowboy boots.

"You're much what I imagined," she said.

That made him chuckle. "Well," he said, "you're nothing like what I imagined. I've been thinking of you as a little girl all of these years."

Leisel frowned in response. "I can't imagine how much has changed since you left." She pinned a sheet on the line as she spoke. "And I'm so sorry you weren't able to see Dat before he passed. I planned to call once Dat gave me your number, but then he faded much quicker than we thought he would. He spoke of you often."

Amos looked at his boots again and toed the lawn.

"I'm sorry," Leisel said.

"No, it's fine." He raised his head and met her eyes. "What did he say?"

"He talked about you working as a ranch hand. He kept the photos you sent beside his bed and looked at them over and over."

That surprised me—first that Dat had told Leisel far more about Amos than he had me. That stung, honestly. Second, I was surprised that Mamm would allow Dat to keep the photos Amos sent.

Leisel continued. "He was proud of the life you made. He wished he'd gone to visit you."

Amos's eyes grew teary. "I would have liked that."

I was truly blessed that Dat had been able to visit me. I couldn't imagine how much harder all of this would be if I hadn't seen him since I left, which was Amos's reality.

"Leisel took care of Dat," I told him. "Once he was diagnosed with cancer."

Amos put his hat back on, probably to shade his eyes from the morning sun. "That sounds as if it would have been a big job."

Leisel grabbed another sheet and more pins. "I was happy to do it," she said. "I've always enjoyed caring for others. It was a privilege to do so for Dat."

A commotion across the fence distracted us. Milton chased a cow while Arden sauntered along after them, his face turned away from us.

Amos asked, his voice low, "Is that him?"

I nodded. "And his oldest son, Milton."

Amos exhaled. Arden and Vi married soon after Amos left and had Milton less than a year later.

"I suppose I should get this over with." Amos started toward the fence. I followed, wishing Aenti Suz had come with us, but she'd stayed behind to clean up after breakfast.

Milton chased the cow toward the barn, but Arden stopped as we approached.

"Brother," Amos called out.

Arden put his hands on his wide hips.

Amos had reached the fence line, but Arden stayed put. Finally he said, "Amos, is that you?"

"Yes," Amos called out, his voice calm and crisp.

Arden shifted his cold gaze to me even though he spoke to Amos. "No one told me you were coming."

Clearly he felt that had been my responsibility, but why would I? I sighed. It wasn't like last night at supper I was going to shout across the room, *"Oh, by the way. I called Amos and he'll be arriving in the morning."*

"Sorry," I muttered.

Amos waved his hand in my direction, as if dismissing my words. "How have you been?" he asked his twin.

Arden crossed his arms. "What are you doing here?"

"I've come to mourn my father. And to see my siblings. My Aenti. My stepmom."

"No one wants you here."

Before I could state Arden was wrong, Leisel started toward the fence line, waving a wet sheet as she called out, "That isn't true. I want him here. So does Aenti. So does Jessica." Her voice was calm, but strong.

"Jessica doesn't count," Arden said.

Leisel reached Amos's side. She put her free arm around him as she spoke to Arden, still waving the sheet. "Dat would be so ashamed of you."

"Ashamed of me?" Arden rocked back on his heels and began to laugh. The breeze caught his long beard and blew it to the side. Abruptly he stopped, pivoted ninety degrees, and started off toward the barn, after Milton.

"Ignore him." Leisel's eyes flashed.

"Only if you will," Amos replied. He patted her back. "Thank you for coming to my defense."

"Jah." Leisel clenched the sheet. "I'm so tired of the self-righteousness demonstrated by two of our siblings. How did such a loving father have children who are so judgmental?"

She didn't wait for either Amos or me to answer. Instead she marched back to the clothesline, waving the sheet again. It might have looked like a flag of surrender, but it was anything but.

Amos smiled at me. "Looks like I missed out on a lot."

"Your brother's wrath?" I asked.

"Jah," he said. "But also what strong women my sisters became."

I sighed. "Wait until you meet Marie."

"Oh?"

I nodded. "She's squarely on Team Arden. So is Mamm. And of course, Vi is too."

Amos winced but didn't say any more.

Throughout the rest of the day, none of them let me down when it came to my assessment of them. All were rude to Amos, in one way or another. By the end of the afternoon, he and I were both hiding in Aenti Suz's Dawdi Haus. I didn't dare to offer to help with the chores or even assist the neighbors who swept out the shed and set up the benches for Dat's memorial service the next day. I saw the neighbors come and go through the front window of Aenti Suz's little house. One time Arden marched by, his head held high in determination, or more likely arrogance. Another time Silas hurried by, glancing toward the house as he did. I couldn't help but wonder if he was looking for me.

Later, over Aenti's chicken potpie and homemade bread, I announced, "I'm going home after the funeral tomorrow. As soon as we get back from the cemetery."

"I don't blame you," Amos said. "My return flight isn't until Saturday. Right now, it feels as if it might be a long week."

I put down my spoon. "Sorry it's this way."

He shrugged. "I expected it, kind of. I mean, I hoped it would be better. That everyone would welcome me with open arms. Or at least not be rude." He picked up his water glass. "At least I have you. I'm thankful for that."

"I'm thankful for you too." I picked up my water glass too and gestured a toast.

He laughed and clinked my glass as Aenti Suz watched over her reading glasses. "Don't forget that God is at work," she said. "He wants nothing more than to heal this family."

I believed that too—but I doubted that everyone wanted to be healed. A buzz in my pocket took me to Aenti Suz's porch. I stood with my back to the big house in case Arden was spying on me. The text was from Tom, of course. *Looking forward to seeing you. I'll be there by 8. You're in my thoughts and prayers.* He signed off with an emoticon blowing a kiss. My heart warmed. I didn't need my family. Or Silas. My life belonged in Harrisburg. The sooner I returned, the better.

I still needed to learn the rest of Ruby's story, but tonight all of us had Dat's viewing, which would be held in the front room of the farmhouse.

—7—

The next morning at eight I stood on the front porch wrapped in my Englisch coat, waiting for Tom. The morning had dawned icy and cold with a thick cover of fog. The viewing the night before had progressed without incident, but breakfast had been tense, to say the least. Amos and I sat together at the table in the corner while our family ate with neighbors and friends. I suggested that we stay at Aenti Suz's until it was time for the service, but Amos said he wanted to see the inside of the farmhouse and he figured he might as well do it in the morning, before there were even more people around.

I hoped the fog wouldn't slow Tom down. I felt as if I couldn't wait another minute as I mulled over the last two days. The most frustrating part of all of it was that the drama took away from me mourning Dat. Instead of thinking about his life and honoring him, I was putting all of my energy into avoiding Marie and Arden and Mamm.

I felt the worst about Mamm. Didn't a girl need her mother? But it was as if I never had one, or at least one I could count on. I'd always relied more on Dat.

There were times when I wondered why Mamm and Dat

ever married. He was a widower with ten-year-old twin sons, whose first wife had died from blood clots in her lungs. Mamm was twenty-six and never married. She worked at a bakery in Paradise. He stopped in one day on his way to his favorite bookstore. He went back to the bakery the next week and then the next. Soon they were courting.

Aenti Suz said Mamm fell head over heels in love with Dat from the beginning and adored Arden and Amos. I sighed, squinting into the fog. How far we all had fallen.

Buggy after buggy headed up the lane. A few of the drivers waved but most stared straight ahead and then veered toward the barn. Youngie were waiting to unhitch the horses and put them in the pasture closest to the barn. Finally headlights appeared. Then a silver sedan. I breathed a sigh of relief. It had to be Tom. I started down the steps, waving. But by the time the car turned toward where my car and Amos's rental were parked I could tell it wasn't Tom. The driver was a lot older. He parked and climbed out, revealing a rumpled suit. The man had short gray hair and a round face. My hand fell to my side. The driver waved at me though, and I smiled in return although I'd never seen him before.

A minute later, another silver sedan came toward me. This time it was Tom, and I lost sight of the other Englischer. Apparently he'd made his way toward the shed. It appeared he was familiar with the farm.

Tom slowed his car and lowered the window.

"Hi there," he said to me.

"Hi there yourself," I answered.

"What's with the costume?"

I glanced down, then up again, and smiled. "I'm just trying to fit in—although it's not working."

He grinned and then asked, "Am I late?"

I shook my head. "I was just anxious is all." I stepped closer to the car. "I'm so glad you're here."

He smiled, his eyes shining.

"Park over there," I said. "Then we can walk around before we head over to the shed."

"The shed?"

I nodded. "That's where the service is." I stifled a laugh. No Englischer would ever hold a funeral service in a shed.

The other members of my family, besides Amos, had gathered in Dat's study and then planned to walk into the shed together. I had no desire to do so. I'd sit in the back. I figured Tom could sit with Amos.

First I led Tom around the outside of the farmhouse, pointing out the back porch. "Those logs are original," I explained. "From 1752. Then over the years, more and more rooms were added."

"Do I get to see the inside?" Tom asked.

"Jah—"

"Pardon?"

"Yes," I answered. "But not until after the burial. We'll come back here for the meal." I pointed toward the gate to the pasture. "And then we'll leave. I'll follow you home."

He stopped. "Home?"

I nodded. "Jah," I said. "Harrisburg is home now. My time here has made that absolutely clear."

He smiled. He'd heard me talk about how homesick I was, how much I missed my community. Coming home had shown me how little I had in common with the people who were once my entire life.

I led the way through the gate. "There's the pond," I said, pointing to the far end of the pasture.

"And the oak," Tom said, increasing his pace toward the tree. I'd told him everything I could think of about the farm, describing the pasture, the fields, the dairy herd, the barn, the tractor, the corn and soybean crops, the garden, the pond. The oak tree.

"It's beautiful," he said as he stopped below it. Tiny buds of green covered the branches above our heads. "How old is it?"

"Well over two hundred and fifty years." My understanding was that the tree was established by the time the original house was built. That meant it existed long before Ruby Bachmann lived on the farm. I scanned over to the next property. There was no sign of an oak tree there, as mentioned by Aenti Suz in her account. Or perhaps it had been cut down long ago, while this one survived.

Perhaps Ruby and Paul Lantz had stood under this one, like Tom and I were now. Like Silas and I used to. A wave of sadness swept through me.

Tom put his hand against the trunk. "Just think of everything that's transpired around this tree in all these years."

A shiver ran down my spine, and I diverted my attention toward the shed. A group gathered by the front door. Men in their black jackets, women in their black capes and bonnets, and children dressed like replicas of their parents. And the Englisch man I'd seen earlier. He was speaking with a few of the Amish men. Slowly they filed in.

"Should we go over?" Tom asked.

I shook my head. "Not yet." I stepped closer to Tom, as if being nearer could warm me, and zipped my coat all the way to the top. Then I clapped my gloved hands together. I wished I'd brought a scarf.

"I could put my arm around you," Tom said.

I smiled as I shook my head. "Not a good idea."

"Oh? Who would say something about it?"

"My brother Arden. My Mamm. My sister Marie. The bishop. They all think I'm fast and loose as it is."

Tom shook his head. He certainly knew better.

"Jah, you might think I'm a Goody-Two-Shoes in Harrisburg, but here I'm seen as a wild woman."

Tom wrinkled his nose but didn't say anything.

I turned my attention to the back porch as Arden led the way down the steps. Vi, their children, Mamm, Marie, and then Leisel followed him. Once they reached the shed, I said to Tom, "Let's go." My family would all sit in the front together. I was sure they'd allow Tom and me to sit with them, and Amos, but that wasn't what we wanted. Not today. Partly because none of them had actually asked us.

Leisel looked this way and that as she walked, most likely looking for Amos and me. Her sweet disposition hadn't changed at all.

Tom and I snuck in the back, and I motioned for him to sit on the men's side, on the back bench next to Amos but closest to the aisle. I sat in the exact same spot on the women's side. Tom gave me a questioning look. I stared straight ahead, realizing I hadn't explained things thoroughly to him.

I knew I'd told him how long the sermons could last, all in Pennsylvania Dutch with the scripture readings in High German. Poor Tom. It would prove to be the longest morning of his life, I was sure. Amos leaned over to him and whispered something, perhaps an explanation. I was grateful for that. Before Amos sat back up straight, I noticed the gentleman with the gray hair and rumpled suit sitting past him. He looked as if his back hurt, poor guy.

My eyes filled with tears at Bishop Jacobs spoke. "Augustus

Bachmann was a deacon in this district, a loving husband, and a devoted father. He was a man who loved the Lord, his family, and the Plain folk of this district. He also loved farming, tending both animals and people, and telling a good story."

That stopped me. I didn't remember Dat telling stories. He was so afraid of gossiping that he hardly told any stories at all, not even about the past. But maybe he told stories to other people, just not to his children.

A sob started to well up inside me. My father was dead. He'd never come to Harrisburg to visit me again. I couldn't ask him—ever—about the farm or about his life. I couldn't ask him about his time in Vietnam—one story of many, probably, that he'd chosen not to tell me. Or exactly why he fell in love with Mamm. Or why Arden was so awful to Amos.

I'd lost my father, a lifetime of stories, and the only true connection I had to my past.

If only I could sit by Tom now instead of all alone. I'd never felt so isolated, not even when I first left. Once the sermon started, the back door opened. Perhaps someone helping in the house had decided to sit in on part of the sermon. A second later, Aenti Suz slipped by me on the bench. As she sat, she reached for my hand and squeezed it. Relieved, I relaxed a little. I wasn't alone, not entirely. She should have been up front with the family, but she'd chosen to be with me.

After the service ended and Dat's casket was loaded into the wagon, we all made our way to the cemetery. Amos and I rode with Tom in his car at the very back of the procession. By the time we reached the cemetery, most of the mourners had already gathered around the grave. As we stepped through the gate of the white picket fence, people turned and stared. I kept my head down and stopped on the edge of the crowd instead of joining my family in the front. Aenti Suz sat beside Mamm, while the rest stood around them.

Gail had positioned herself directly behind my sisters, with Silas at her side. His Mamm was just a few feet away from him. I wondered if Gail realized what a jewel Edith Kemp was.

I didn't see the man with the gray hair and rumpled suit anywhere.

All of the newer gravestones were exactly alike, and the old ones were small and unpretentious, unlike those in some of the Englisch cemeteries I'd seen where wealthy families purchased ostentatious memorials for their deceased relatives. The last thing an Amish family was allowed to do was draw attention to itself.

My gaze fell to the oldest section. Was Ruby buried there? If so, her marker had probably deteriorated with time.

Bishop Jacobs read a scripture from Revelation: "Blessed are the dead which die in the Lord from henceforth: Yea, saith the Spirit, that they may rest from their labours; and their works do follow them." He spoke again about how Dat had served others. It was true. He had, in a humble and unassuming way. He never bossed others around. He never tried to manipulate people. He never even tried to control people, including his children.

As the bishop led us in a silent prayer, I thought of when Dat called me back after I'd left a message on his machine in the barn that I'd left home. He simply asked me questions about what I planned to do. He never tried to shame me. That came later from Mamm, Marie, Arden, and Vi in their letters that condemned me. Both Arden and Vi wrote that unless I confessed and rejoined the church, they never wanted me to visit the farm or be around their children.

Bishop Jacobs said, "Amen" and then motioned for the pall-bearers to lower the casket. Tears stung my eyes. After it was in the ground, one of the pallbearers picked up the shovel leaning against the tree and began scooping dirt atop the casket. Then another pallbearer took a turn. Then Arden stepped forward and took the shovel. He flung several scoops of dirt onto the casket and then stepped backward, the shovel still in his hands.

Then he stumbled. My heart swelled in sympathy for my brother, thinking he was overcome with grief. But he dropped the shovel and stumbled again and took a couple of big steps away from the others. Then he began to fall. I stepped forward as if perhaps I could catch him from fifteen feet away. Milton hurried to his father's side and reached for his arm, but Arden kept falling.

I gasped and started forward. I sensed Tom following me as I wove through the crowd. By the time I got to Arden, Milton was kneeling beside him with Vi standing a few feet away. I bent down, my hand falling to Arden's neck. I couldn't find a pulse. And no breath was coming from his nose or mouth.

I made eye contact with Tom. "Call 9-1-1." We'd had a CPR training at work just a few months before.

I wedged Arden's lips apart and swiped his mouth. It was clear. As I placed my hands on his chest, Leisel fell to her knees beside me and said, "You do the compressions, I'll breathe."

We started, counting out compressions and then two breaths. Dat knew CPR, and I guessed that he'd taught Leisel. I could hear Tom ask someone exactly where we were and then recite the information. A minute later, he kneeled beside me, asking if I wanted him to take a turn.

I did. I knew Tom could get more compressions in per min-ute than I could and his big hands covered more of Arden's chest. The three of us worked together and continued even as we heard the sirens approaching. The circle around us spread thin when the paramedics arrived. As they reached us, one took over the chest compressions and Tom and I stood and stepped back, bumping into Milton. I put my arm around him. Vi and the other children stood behind Leisel, who was now standing too. All appeared as stoic as could be. Mamm had sat back down on her chair, but Aenti Suz stood, one arm on the back of my mother's chair, trying to see through the crowd as best she could.

The paramedics took out a defibrillator and shocked Arden. He jumped with the first jolt of electricity. Another zap and one of the paramedics said, "We've got a heartbeat."

The paramedics had arrived quickly. Hopefully enough oxygen had gotten to his brain as Leisel breathed for him. I began to shake, and Tom put his arm around me. I didn't care what anyone thought now. Except maybe I did because my eyes sought out Silas. He still stood beside Gail, but he was staring at me.

As the paramedics loaded Arden into the back of the ambulance, I urged Vi to go with him.

"May I?" she said.

"Yes," I answered. "We'll meet you at the hospital." I glanced at Tom, hoping he'd be willing to drive. He nodded.

I turned to Mamm and asked if she'd ride with us.

"I can't ride with you," she said.

I grimaced. "Tom's driving."

"All right, in that case, jah. Maybe I can be of some comfort to Vi."

Marie quickly rounded up Vi and Arden's children, and with

the help of Gail and Silas and Aenti Suz, herded them toward the buggies.

"May I go with you?" Leisel asked me.

"Of course," I answered. But then it dawned on me that we should take another car because Vi would need a ride home. I suggested we swing by the house so Amos could get his car. But then that meant I needed to ride with Amos because Mamm couldn't, due to his being shunned, and she wouldn't want Leisel to either.

Ten minutes later, Amos led the little caravan away from the buggies heading back to our house. A meal would be served to all of those who attended the service.

As Amos turned on the highway, headed toward Lancaster, he commented on all of the changes in the last sixteen years.

"Did you ever consider coming back?" I asked.

"To visit?" he asked. "Or to stay?"

"Both," I answered.

"Yeah," he said. "All the time at first. I thought I'd made the biggest mistake of my life."

"Why did you leave?" I'd asked both Mamm and Dat over the years but neither gave me a satisfactory answer.

"Well, now . . ." Amos had both hands on the wheel. "Didn't anyone tell you?"

"Not really," I answered. "After you left, Dat said that you were traveling, and he wasn't sure when you would come back. After a couple of years he said perhaps you weren't."

"It's true that I thought maybe I would return. At first I simply felt I needed some time away."

"Why?"

When he didn't answer for a long time, I feared perhaps I'd offended him.

Finally he sighed and said, "Arden and I weren't getting along. That was mostly the problem."

That didn't surprise me. "Did you try to work it out?"

"Yeah," he said. "For six years I tried to—but nothing changed."

Six years. From the time I was born. Or more likely from the time Rebecca had died.

We'd reached the hospital, so I didn't ask any more questions. Amos turned into the parking garage, and Tom followed us. A minute later we were parked and on our way to the emergency department. Once we checked in at the front desk, we settled in the waiting room.

Time slowed to a crawl. I asked at the desk several times but was told they couldn't reveal any information. Finally Amos asked, and a doctor, followed by Vi, came out to speak with us.

The doctor explained that Arden had had a heart attack and was now stable. He was conscious and answering questions, so it seemed the oxygen deprivation hadn't done any permanent damage. "We'll do more tests," the doctor said. "But most likely he'll have surgery in the next few days."

Leisel asked, "Will he be transferred to a critical care unit?"

"Yes," the doctor answered. "I've ordered that. Once all of his tests are back, I'll schedule the surgery."

I glanced at Vi, wondering if she had any questions. When it seemed she didn't, I asked, "Should one of us stay with him?"

"Not necessarily," the doctor answered. "He's tired. He needs to rest. And he said, specifically, that there were a couple of family members he didn't want to see." The doctor glanced at Vi, who looked pointedly at Amos and me.

I concentrated on keeping my face expressionless.

Tom asked, through clenched teeth, "Does he know Jessica saved—"

I put my hand on his arm, appreciating his trying to defend me but not wanting to stir up trouble. "It doesn't matter." I turned toward Vi. "Do you want to stay? Tom could give you a ride later."

She pursed her lips.

I added, "Or we could call for a driver."

She shook her head. "Arden does need to rest. I should go home and speak with the children."

"I'll stay," Leisel said. "If that's all right with you, Vi."

Our sister-in-law seemed relieved by the idea. I pulled Leisel aside as I dug in my purse for some cash so she could get something to eat in the cafeteria. "Call my cell phone when you want a ride home," I said. "I'll come get you. It will be dark. No one will notice." Hopefully no one from our own family would report her to the bishop. Then again, she hadn't joined the church yet so, technically, it wasn't against the Ordnung.

"Denki." She slipped the money into the pocket of her apron and then gave me a hug. Tears filled my eyes, and I quickly blinked them away.

By the time we returned to the house, Aenti Suz and a kitchen full of women were cleaning up after the meal. However, they quickly heated up the soup and pulled out the sliced ham, cheeses, and bread that had been served, along with several of the remaining pies.

I could tell Tom was impressed with the house. He excused himself to use the bathroom, and when he returned he whispered, "There are granite countertops in there."

"I know," I whispered back. Perhaps he thought I'd grown up in a shack. "Dat got a good deal."

His eyes grew large at the sight of the kitchen. Mamm and

Dat had remodeled it the year before I left. The countertops were quartz, not granite, but the malachite perfectly matched the tiled floor that ran throughout the house. And both the new propane-operated refrigerator and stove had been installed at that same time.

I could hear voices in the backyard.

Vi turned toward me. "Would you come out with me to tell the children? In case I don't have the details right?"

Surprised, I nodded as Tom and I both followed her through the back porch and out to the yard. Gail, Marie, and Silas played a game of volleyball with the children. When they saw their mother, the children froze.

I waited a moment for Vi to say something, but when she didn't, I called out, "Your father's okay." I feared they thought he'd passed. "He's in the hospital. Leisel is staying with him."

Vi seemed to find her voice. "I came home to tell you what happened. He had a heart attack."

She turned toward me with a look of panic on her face.

"The doctors are doing tests," I said. "To see what the damage is to his heart. He's in a special unit at the hospital where they can take extra good care of him. He'll probably have surgery soon—they'll let us know tomorrow."

"Did he have an attack because Dawdi died?" Luke asked.

I shook my head. "Something was already wrong with his heart. If it didn't happen now, it would have happened soon." Thank goodness it happened today and not while he was alone in the field. Or in the middle of the night when Vi would have had to run to the barn to call for help. I shivered at the thought.

Silas ruffled Luke's hair and said, "How about some pie?" He glanced up at Vi. "They wanted to wait until they had word about their Dat."

My heart constricted. No matter how harsh Arden was with me, he was a father and a husband. He was loved and cherished.

"Jah," I said. "Let's all go inside. It's chilly out here."

The children lifted their coats and capes from the grass and started toward the door, following their Mamm. I hung back and introduced Tom to Silas, Gail, and Marie. Even Marie was cordial.

Once we were back in the house, I nodded to the table in the corner and whispered to Tom, "You can sit at the big table or here with Amos and me."

He wrinkled his nose and muttered, "This shunning is hard to take."

I shook my head and whispered, "Don't worry about it."

"I'll sit with you, of course." He scowled as he sat down.

As we ate, Tom asked Amos about Colorado. Soon we were having an animated conversation about farming practices. Amos used his hands as he gestured how wide open the ranches were out there. "I worked on one that was twenty thousand acres," he said. "It takes a lot of land to graze a steer out there. We had three thousand on that one."

Tom whistled. "I've always wanted to visit Colorado. I've never been west of Chicago."

And I'd never been west of Harrisburg.

As we chatted away, I realized that those sitting at the big table were quiet. Mamm, with Aenti Suz's help, was headed toward the staircase. Vi stood and said, "Children, we should head home."

Luke groaned. "Why do we have to go so soon?"

"We should get going is all," Vi said. "I'm tired."

Tom gave me a questioning look. I stood too. "I'm going to show Tom the rest of the farm. Don't mind us."

"I'm going with them," Amos said.

We all picked up our dishes and headed toward the kitchen. Milton gave me a questioning look as we passed by, but everyone else kept their heads down, including Silas.

After we left our plates in the kitchen, we hurried onto the back porch, and down to the lawn again. "You saw the shed," I explained. "Usually there's an old tractor in it and tools. That sort of thing. Now I'll show you the barn. We can walk through, but it's just about time for milking. Maybe we can help."

Our barn was a typical large Amish dairy barn, whitewashed both inside and out. "I'm guessing there's not much dairy farming in Colorado," Tom said to Amos.

He laughed. "Not around where I live. We strictly raise beef."

Silas and Milton came into the barn to start the milking, along with a neighbor. "Mind if we help?" I asked.

Silas glanced at Milton, who shrugged. Finally Silas gestured toward the milking machines. "Why not?"

I put on a vinyl apron over my coat and Tom did the same. Amos didn't bother. Instead he took off his coat and rolled up the sleeves of his shirt. He went to the door and called the first group of cows, who began parading in one by one with a little nudging from Silas and Milton. We had eighty all together, which meant two milkings. The neighbor and Amos began securing them in their stalls. Tom joined in, while I began giving each of the cows her feed. All in all, they ate over a hundred pounds a day. We mixed hay and silage, plus grain and a concentrate that contained carbohydrates, proteins, fats, minerals, and vitamins.

Milton and Silas began sanitizing the cows' teats and then drying them, which kept everything cleaner and also sped up the milk letting down. They quickly attached the milking tubes that connected to the vacuum pull from the machine.

Once the cows were all in their stalls, I showed Tom what to do and every once in a while Amos too. A lot had changed in the barn in the last sixteen years.

Silas took charge of the milk vat. He stepped into the office at least once—maybe to record numbers or retrieve some sort of supply. I wasn't sure.

It only took around five minutes for the machine to milk a cow, but it took much longer to get everything set up and then to finish the process. We spoke some as we worked, but it wasn't like the old days when Silas and I used to joke around as we did the milking.

As Tom and Amos herded the last of the cows back out to the pasture, I stepped toward the office, my eyes landing on the phone. I touched my apron pocket. Surely Leisel would call my cell phone and not the barn phone. I knew she had my number, at least at one time. I should have asked her if she remembered it. I decided to check the answering machine just in case.

The red light was blinking. I hit the button and the recording said, "You have five messages." Two were from yesterday, both neighbors who offered to help with the chores. The third one was from a Mr. Carlson from this morning. He simply said he would see the family at the service. I guessed it was the gray-haired man in the rumpled suit.

The next message was blank. Someone had hung up after the beep.

The last message was from Leisel. "This is for Jessica," she said. "Could you call me back with your cell number? I've forgotten it. Oh, and Arden had the tests the doctor talked about soon after you left. We don't have the results yet." She rattled off the number I could reach her at. I took my cell phone from my pocket, punched in the number, and then as it rang my eyes fell to the papers on top of the desk.

The top one looked like some sort of a contract. I picked it up just as Leisel answered my call. "Got a piece of paper and a pen?" I asked.

"Uh-huh," she said.

I gave her my number. "Do you want me to come get you soon?"

"No," she answered. "I'll spend the night."

"Are you sure?"

"Jah," she said. "It's good for Arden to have someone with him."

"All right," I said. "Call me in the morning."

She assured me she would. We said our good-byes, and as I disconnected the call, I turned the document around. It was from an oil company. Our address was printed at the top. My heart sank. What was Arden up to? I looked for a date. Had he requested the plans be drawn up three years ago? Or was this something new?

"Jessica?" Milton stood at the office door. "What do you need?"

I looked up slowly. For a moment I could see a hint of Arden's harshness in his face. I nodded toward the phone on the desk. "Leisel left a message." I started toward the doorway, feeling the old familiar shame. But this time from my fourteen-year-old nephew. I'd come back and look at the papers later.

As I came out of the office, Tom stepped to my side. "Are you ready to go home?"

I shook my head. "I'm going to stay another night." I'd see if Aenti Suz would tell me the rest of Ruby's story, and I'd help with the milking in the morning. "I'll stop by the hospital to-morrow," I said. "And see what the doctors say about Arden. Then I'll come home."

Tom seemed to understand. I walked him to his car and

thanked him for coming. "I don't know what I would have done without you," I said sincerely. "I'll text when I'm back in town tomorrow. Life will soon be back to normal."

He nodded and put his arm on my shoulder. "I'm looking forward to that." Then he quickly released me and climbed into his car. I knew he had a meeting at church at 7:30 p.m. that he'd hate to miss.

Silas and I had always spent every second we could together, but Tom was so busy with meetings and basketball games and projects that we had to squeeze time in together. We weren't starry-eyed teenagers like Silas and I had been. This was normal life, or at least that's what I told myself.

I watched as Tom's car disappeared up the lane, and then I headed to Aenti Suz's. Thankfully she was there. And so was Amos.

"How about some supper?" she asked. "I gathered up enough leftovers so you and Amos can eat here tonight."

I thanked her and said I'd eat later—I wasn't hungry yet. "I was hoping for the rest of Ruby's story," I said. "I'm going back to Harrisburg tomorrow."

"So soon?"

I nodded.

"Well," she said. "Where did I leave off?"

"The Patriots had just arrived. Ruby wanted Zachary to hide, while she said all of her brothers had gone to Canada."

"That's right," Aenti Suz said. "But Zachary said he'd speak to them." She sighed. "Here Ruby had stayed behind, thinking she'd have Zachary to protect their mother and her. But all that changed in the course of a day."

– 8 –

Ruby

Ruby followed Zachary to the front yard, still tugging on the calf, still covered in mud, dismayed that her brother would be so foolish.

He turned toward her and hissed. "Go secure the calf. Do you want them to take him?"

She stopped. He was right. They needed to protect everything they could. She'd heard of the rebels raiding barns, cribs, smokehouses, and cellars. They'd sent so much food with the travelers that she'd have to scramble to preserve enough food for Mamm and Zachary and herself as it was. She'd need to start with the baskets of apples waiting for her in the shed. There was a hog to butcher as soon as the cold weather arrived, and they'd butcher the calf by spring.

Zachary's face had grown serious. "Go on."

"All right," she said. "But why aren't you hiding?" The rebels had been forcing men to attend military musters and join

118

companies of soldiers. Zachary had to avoid such a thing at all costs. "You're in more danger than the calf."

He shrugged, and she shuddered. Zachary hadn't been himself lately, not at all. She dragged the calf back to the barn and secured it in a stall, leaving the rope. She'd return it to the fence later.

Then she washed in the trough as best she could and hurried back to where she could see Zachary. Not only was he not hiding, he wasn't staying in the yard either. He kicked up the dust as he headed to the road. She quickly counted twelve Patriots, dressed in mismatched blue uniforms and ratty tricorn hats. A motley crew to be sure—so unlike the crisply dressed British soldiers with their red uniforms and black hats. The Patriots mocked them by calling them Lobsters.

Ruby was surprised, for a moment, with how tall Zachary appeared. Had he grown in the last year without her noticing? Or was he simply holding himself upright with his shoulders squared?

"We heard there was a crowd of Loyalists around here," one of the older soldiers shouted. "We're here to find out if that's true."

"I'm the only man here," Zachary said.

Oh, why hadn't he hidden and let her talk with the soldiers?

"Where are the rest?" the man asked.

"They left for Canada."

The man smirked and a couple of the other soldiers laughed.

"Point proven," the man said. "What about you? Why didn't you leave?"

"My mother's ill." Zachary nodded toward Mamm, who still sat on the front porch. "My sister and I stayed behind to care for her."

"Is that right?" the leader asked, eyeing Ruby. She hurried to Zachary's side.

But he nudged her and said, "Go sit with Mamm."

Ruby turned toward the porch, walking slowly, hoping to hear more of the conversation.

The man jumped down from his horse. "Why haven't you signed up to fight with us?"

"I'm nonresistant," Zachary said. "It's against my faith to fight."

"Have you paid the war tax?"

"No," Zachary answered.

"You need to pay the tax or hire someone to fight for you." The man paused, and then said loudly, "Or join us and fight like a man."

"Even though I'm the only one to run the farm?"

The man smirked. "Let your sister do it."

"Let me think on it," Zachary said. "Come back tomorrow, and I'll give you my answer."

The man didn't seem happy. "We can force you to go with us now."

"I know," Zachary said. "But another day won't make any difference in the long run. I'd appreciate it if you'd give me a chance to figure it out. To either come up with the money or put my affairs in order so my mother and sister will be cared for."

The man glanced toward Ruby again. She was only halfway to the porch, shuffling backward. As his gaze fell on her, she turned around and started walking forward again. She couldn't hear any more of the conversation as she reached the porch and stopped beside her mother.

"What's going on?" Mamm asked.

"Patriots," Ruby answered. "They're asking Zachary some questions."

Mamm exhaled but kept quiet.

Zachary nodded toward the house again and then called out, "Ruby. How about if you get a basket of apples for our guests?" For a moment he sounded so much like Dat that she almost wept. Their father had been hospitable and kind, even to people he disagreed with. Instead of crying, Ruby marched as calmly as she could to the shed, all the way to the back, and picked up one of the baskets of apples. Dat had planted several apple trees on the far side of the house before Ruby was born. Each year the trees produced more and more, which they made into applesauce, dried apples, apple butter, and cider for the family. Ruby had sent full baskets with Hans and Daniel. But she'd kept several baskets for until Mamm, Zachary, and she left for Canada.

When she returned, the soldiers had all pushed into the yard. She held the basket in front of them, one by one, and they grabbed as many as they could, filling their pockets, until all of them were gone.

"Thank you, miss," the oldest one said, tipping his matted felt hat.

"You're welcome," Ruby said and retreated back to the porch.

Finally the soldiers left, taking off in the direction they'd come from, and Zachary started toward the cabin. Ruby met him in the yard.

She knew Hans had taken most of the money their father had managed to save through the years and would combine it with what he and Daniel had from the sale of their properties to buy land. Paul had money of his own from the sale of the farm he'd inherited from his father. "What are you going to do?" she asked Zachary. "There's no money to pay a tax or hire someone to fight for you."

Her brother shrugged. "Give me some time to think it through. We'll talk later."

Ruby nodded. There was no reason to worry Mamm about it.

"Let's get you back inside," Ruby said to her mother. "I need to get changed and then stoke the fire in the oven and get the bread started." She'd sent all the loaves she'd made that morning with the travelers, along with the baskets of apples, hams, corn, potatoes, and squash from the garden.

Jah, she was thankful the Patriots hadn't raided the little food Ruby had left to feed Zachary and mother through the winter, if needed. It was a good thing Zachary offered the apples.

They only had a few sacks of flour left and a little sugar. The inn on the edge of Lancaster, where the Bachmanns sometimes traded, didn't have much in the way of supplies, and the prices seemed to climb higher by the week.

Zachary would need to spend some time hunting to fill the smokehouse. She sighed. They'd have to come up with the money, somehow, to pay for someone else to fight for him or pay the special war tax, even though Hans was against both. Otherwise their land would be confiscated. Where would they live while Mamm recovered?

Once Ruby had Mamm settled at the table, she changed out of her muddy clothes and then tended the fire out back in the oven. After she shaped the remaining dough into loaves, she set them on the worktable near the fireplace. While they rose, she began cutting apples to dry. Hopefully the days of sunshine would last. The warm autumn weather was a blessing.

Mamm began to hum "Das Loblied" and Ruby sang along with her. She'd learned everything she knew about life and housekeeping and cooking from her mother, while Dat had instructed her in the faith and taught her to read and write, too, along with mathematics and English. Together her parents had given her a well-rounded education.

Ruby had a happy childhood with her brothers. Secure and mostly worry-free, until the war started. Now, as she'd grown into a woman, everything had changed. The problems between the Tories and the Patriots had strained the community. Most believed the taxation was too high, but they wanted to settle the problem with the British, not rebel against them. Before the war, the community experienced freedom in both civil and religious matters. Once the war started, however, the Patriots began taking away freedoms. Some of the Loyalists had their land taken away. Even those who simply refused to pledge allegiance to the Patriots or the Loyalists were harassed, often by both sides.

Now there was the war tax to pay.

Before Dat had died, he urged his sons to dedicate themselves to serving all men and preserving lives. "Don't ever take up arms or support either side—there is no freedom in assisting in the destruction of life," he'd insisted. "Instead pray to God for us and them."

That was why Hans had decided to move to Canada. He'd decided that praying was no longer the only viable solution. He had to take action to save himself and his brothers from fighting or having to support the war.

If only Mamm hadn't fallen ill. They'd all be on their way to Canada, instead of Zachary being forced with making a decision that, no matter what, would disappoint Dat—and Hans too.

Ruby worked hard all day, cutting apples, baking bread, and then preparing a supper of ham slices and corn cakes. Afterward, she got Mamm down for the night.

When she returned to the kitchen, Zachary sat at the big oak table with a lit lamp in front of him.

Ruby sank into one of the chairs her Dat had made so many years ago. "Do we have enough money?"

"For?" he asked.

"The war tax." Surely Hans had left *some* money.

"We don't need it," her brother replied.

She shook her head. "What do you mean?"

He stared at his hands, resting on the table. "I'm going to fight."

"No!" Ruby cried. "You can't."

He raised his head and met her eyes. "I've made up my mind."

The realization hit her. "You didn't just decide today. . . . Did you have this planned all along? Is that why you decided to stay?"

"No, I hoped not to have to fight. But I didn't want to go to Canada either. This is home. I didn't agree with Hans about leaving."

"But why would you fight now?"

"I don't have the money to pay the tax."

"Surely Hans left some. . . ."

Zachary shook his head. "No. He said he might, but he must have changed his mind."

Ruby shook her head, but she wasn't surprised Hans had put his family's needs before the rest of them.

She stood and walked to the desk, opening drawer after drawer. The money had been stored there before, but there was nothing to be found now except for a few coins that had been left to buy flour and sugar. She turned back to Zachary.

He shrugged. "Obviously he took it all."

Ruby crossed her arms. "We can go ahead and sell the farm and board in town until Mamm is strong enough. Old Man Wallis—"

"Ruby, no."

"We're going to sell it soon enough anyway."

Zachary looked as if he might cry.

"What? Isn't that what we need to do? Sell out and go to Canada?"

"No," he said. "That's never what I wanted. You weren't listening to me."

Ruby struggled to speak. Finally she managed to ask, "What do you want?"

"To stay here, on our land. I'd rather fight than leave."

"Zachary, what are you saying?"

He stood. "When the Patriots come back, I'm going with them."

"What about Mamm and me?"

"I spoke with the neighbor."

"Old Man Wallis?"

"No, his nephew. He's from Philadelphia. Duncan Wallis is his name."

"The one who walks with a crutch?"

Zachary nodded. "He said he'd keep an eye on both of you and the farm too."

"No." Ruby stepped toward her brother. "That won't do, not at all."

"He seems nice enough."

"He's not. He was quite rude this morning." Her face grew warm. She'd forgotten to return the rope. "And he's in no shape to help with anything. He couldn't even get the calf out of his garden."

"He was injured at the Battle of Trenton, fighting for the Continental Army. He wants to help."

"Zachary, he's an Englischman. You can't possibly think this is a good idea."

"What do you propose I do? Have the Patriots confiscate our land? Then what will become of us? We won't have any money to get to Canada. We'll be destitute here."

"Go ask Old Man Wallis if he'll buy our property. We can leave tomorrow."

"And what about Mamm? You know how weak she is."

Ruby grabbed the lamp from the table and started for the door. "I'll go ask Old Man Wallis."

"Rube."

Zachary had never betrayed her like this. Out of all of her family, he was the one she trusted most. How would she ever get to Paul if Zachary went off and fought in the war? Then again, what was she thinking to force Mamm to travel when she was still weak? She couldn't do that.

But it would be better to sell now before it was confiscated. Perhaps they could board with one of the families who hadn't left for Canada. She hurried out the cabin door, pulling her shawl tight, and marched toward the neighbors', breathing in the cool autumn air.

A light burned in their window, and she hurried up to the door. She began knocking before she lost her nerve.

The man—Duncan—came to the door with his crutch in one hand and a musket in the other. "Who's there?" he barked.

"Your neighbor." Ruby held up the lamp. "We met this morning."

"What do you want?"

"I need to ask Old—your uncle—something."

"He's asleep." Duncan said. "What do want to ask him?"

She inhaled sharply. "If he would like to buy our farm. He's been interested for years, and we're finally ready to sell."

Duncan frowned and then shook his head. "His health isn't good."

"What about you?" Ruby asked. "Would you like to buy it?"

Duncan pointed to his bad leg. "You think I'd make it as a farmer? I'll sell this place as soon as he dies and head back to Philadelphia. God willing, the British will be forced out soon." He smirked a little. "Perhaps your family would be interested in buying this place."

Ruby shook her head. She'd been foolish to come over. But she had one more question. "Why did you tell my brother you'd keep an eye on my Mamm and me if you don't plan to stick around?"

He shrugged. "I was being neighborly and wanted to help out a fellow Patriot. Besides, I probably won't be going anywhere before next spring—hopefully your brother will be back by then." He held up the musket. "And I might be lame but I can still shoot a gun. Scream if you need me." He started to close the door, but Ruby stuck her foot out and stopped him.

"Are you always so rude?"

He sneered. "I answered the door, didn't I?"

"Listen," Ruby said. "I won't need your help while my brother is gone. You stay on your side of the fence, and I'll stay on mine." She jerked her foot out and the door slammed shut, followed by a crash on the other side.

She gasped and then pushed the door open again. Duncan was sprawled on the floor reaching for his crutch, one hand on his bad leg.

"Get out of here," he bellowed.

"I'm so sorry." She stepped over him and grabbed his crutch with her free hand. "Here," she said, holding her lamp so he could see. "Let me help."

"You've done enough," he said as he snatched the crutch from her.

"Let me pull you up."

He held the crutch against his chest. "I don't need your help."

She was afraid he did, but by the look on his face he wasn't going to accept it. "I'm sorry," she said again, ashamed of what she'd done.

"Go!" he ordered. "And shut the door."

She slipped back out the door and pulled it closed behind her. But she didn't head home. Instead she listened. She could hear the crutch against the wood floor, a shuffling noise, and a push against the door. Then the click of the crutch against the floor again and a shuffle-step pattern. She breathed a sigh of relief that Duncan was up and able to walk. What had possessed her to yank her foot out of the doorway like that, causing him to fall?

Ashamed, she hurried home, asking God to forgive her for being uncaring. She couldn't rely on Duncan Wallis, not after what she'd done. Come what may, it seemed she'd have to figure out a way to care for Mamm and run the farm on her own.

– 9 –

Ruby hardly slept that night, remembering the thud of Duncan falling against the wood floor and then the look of despair on his face. When she did fall asleep, she dreamt of Patriot soldiers and war and of Paul riding off in his wagon, leaving her behind. Finally she rose, hours before dawn, and dressed in the dark.

When she reached the kitchen, Zachary sat at the table with the lamp lit and two books in front of him. She didn't need to look to know what they were. The family Bible and *Martyrs Mirrors*. Dat and Mamm had brought both from Switzerland. The Bible was closed and pushed to the middle of the table. The second was open, and Zachary was staring at it as if in a trance.

"Convicted?" Ruby asked.

Without glancing up, he asked, "Of what?"

"Going off to fight. Aligning yourself with soldiers."

He closed the book and pushed it to the middle of the table also. "No," he answered. "I'm going off to save our land—for now, at least."

"Think what you want if it will make you feel better." Ruby turned toward the fireplace. "In the meantime, go fetch me

129

some water and then do your chores. At least give me one last morning with only my own work to do."

She stirred the fire first, bringing it back to life, and then built it up. She stood, warming her hands against the flames until Zachary returned with the water from the springhouse. Then she put the kettle on to boil and began making porridge for their breakfast. Zachary came in with the milk, and she told him they would go ahead and eat. There was no reason to wake Mamm yet. Ruby knew a good sleep made for a better day for their mother.

She sat at the table across from her brother. After he led them in a silent prayer, they ate without speaking. Once they were done, Zachary retrieved the Bible again and read from Matthew 5, including, "But I say unto you, Love your enemies, bless them that curse you, do good to them that hate you, and pray for them which despitefully use you, and persecute you." Ruby wondered how he could read such scripture on the day he planned to go off to war without obeying it, but she kept her mouth closed. She knew Zachary's conscience was at work. Perhaps he'd change his mind yet. At this point, she figured it would be better if their land was confiscated than for him to go off and fight. What if he had to kill someone? How could he live with that on his conscience his entire life? Or what if he were killed? She felt as if she might be sick.

If only Hans had waited a day to leave. He should have been the one dealing with the rebels.

Zachary closed the Bible, thanked Ruby for breakfast, and then stood. "I'm going to go chop as much wood as I can before I leave."

Ruby thanked him. Before she could say any more, the sound of Mamm's voice pulled her to the back room. After she dressed and fed Mamm, Ruby separated the milk, fed the chickens, then killed, feathered, and cut up an old one and put it in a pot to boil for Zachary's farewell meal. Then she sliced turnips, potatoes, and carrots and added them to the pot. She could hear the ring of the axe over and over and over as she worked.

Her hope rose as time passed by. Maybe the rebels wouldn't come back. Maybe they'd moved on to the other side of the county. Maybe they'd forgotten all about the Bachmann place.

At noon, Zachary came in for his dinner. They ate silently again. Finally, in her slurred speech, Mamm asked about the soldiers. "Tell me what's happening. You two are hiding something from me."

Zachary gave Ruby a hopeless look.

"We don't know, not exactly," Ruby finally said. "We'll have to see if the Patriots return or not."

Mamm didn't ask any more questions, but Ruby doubted she was content with the answer.

In the midafternoon, while Mamm rested, Ruby went out to the garden to harvest the rest of the squash and onions. As she loaded her baskets with produce, thundering hooves once again descended on the farm. She stood for a moment, waiting to see what would happen, but then Zachary stepped from the barn in his coat with a leather bag over his shoulder.

She dropped an acorn squash and then jumped back so it wouldn't land on her foot. Zachary marched straight ahead.

"You need to tell Mamm good-bye," Ruby shouted.

"Tell her for me. Say I won't be gone long. I don't want to wake her."

"Zachary . . ."

He turned toward her, looking for a moment like a little boy. "I can't, Rube. I just can't. Don't make this any harder."

"Harder? I'm the one who will have to explain things to her. Don't be a coward."

He hesitated but then nodded his head. Ruby led the way to the porch. Zachary waved to the oldest of the men, the one who had done all the talking the day before, and then dropped his bag on the porch. Then he followed Ruby into the house, to the back room. Mamm slept soundly, her white hair fanned out around her head.

"Mamm." Ruby gently shook her shoulder. "Can you wake up? Zachary is leaving and wants to tell you good-bye."

Her eyes fluttered open and then closed again.

"Mamm," Ruby said again.

She opened them again and this time they didn't flutter. Ruby repeated that Zachary wanted to tell her good-bye.

"Where are you going, son?"

"I'm not sure." His voice was so low Ruby wondered if Mamm could even hear him. "But I'm leaving with the Patriots. I'll come home as soon as I can."

He bent down and hugged her. She clung to him for a long moment and then released him. "Don't forget your faith," she said.

He nodded, seemingly too choked up to speak. Again, he seemed like a child. Whatever his reasons, the task ahead of him wasn't easy either.

"Don't forget your home."

"Never," he managed to answer.

Neither said good-bye as he quickly left the room.

"I'll be right back," Ruby said to Mamm and then rushed after Zachary. "What instructions do you have for me, as far as the farm?"

He stopped at the front door. "Harvest the corn in a couple

of weeks. Butcher the hog next month, once the temperatures fall." She knew that. "Keep the spring clean. Plant the garden like you always do. Plant the corn in late March. If there's any trouble, like I already said, ask Duncan Wallis for help."

When Ruby didn't respond, he bent down and hugged her. "I'm sorry, Rube. This isn't fair, I know. I'll pray for you and Mamm every day."

"What about Lettie?" she asked.

"I'll send her a message—she'll understand," he said. "I already asked her to wait for me, no matter what might happen. . . ."

Ruby couldn't imagine Zachary going off to war would set very well with the girl's Dat, but she didn't say so out loud.

He pulled a letter from his bag. "I've written to Hans about my predicament, about my decision. I've asked him to return to see to you and Mamm and sell the farm if he can."

"But I thought you wanted to keep the farm."

"Jah, I'd like to, more than anything. But the safety of you and Mamm is my biggest concern." He slipped the letter back into his bag. "I'll send it to Hans as soon as I can."

Ruby thanked him and then said, "Take care of yourself."

He nodded and then rushed out the door. She followed him, but stopped on the porch. The soldiers had a string of horses they hadn't had the day before. They were probably confiscated from Loyalists. The Bachmanns only had a pair of workhorses left—Gunnar and Gustaf. Hans had taken the other ones. He'd left the two workhorses so Zachary could plow in the spring, if needed.

The man who'd done the talking the day before directed Zachary to the first horse. He quickly untied it and slipped on to its bare back. He glanced at Ruby once but didn't wave.

Tears filled her eyes, but then the sound of Mamm calling her drew her back into the house.

After Mamm and Ruby both dried their tears, she helped her mother to the porch to enjoy the last sunshine of the day. Dark clouds had started to gather on the horizon. Leaves from the trees along the roadway swirled in the air, and the smoke from the dying fire in the fireplace floated down toward them from the chimney when the breeze shifted. Ruby peeled apples while they enjoyed the sun.

About the time Ruby was ready to help Mamm back inside, someone called out a hello. She stood and shaded her eyes from the lowering sun.

"It's me," the voice said. "From next door."

"Oh." Why in the world would Duncan come over? But then she remembered the rope. She hadn't put it on the fence like she said she would. "Oh, your rope!" she called out. "It's in the barn. I'll go get it."

"I'd forgotten about it," he answered. "It can wait."

"No. I'll get it now." She turned toward Mamm. "This is Duncan Wallis, Mr. Wallis's nephew."

Mamm extended her hand and in her broken English asked, "How is your uncle?"

Ruby excused herself as Duncan answered. She slipped away to the barn, grabbed the rope, and then returned to the porch. Duncan was sitting in the chair beside Mamm. They were somehow, with Mamm's poor English, talking about Old Man Wallis.

Duncan said, "It's been several weeks since he fell ill."

Ruby felt bad neither she nor her brothers had checked on the man. He'd leased out his property to another farmer, so there had been no indication by the state of the farm that he wasn't doing well.

"When did you arrive?" Ruby asked Duncan, wondering just how long Old Man Wallis had been on his own.

"Just a week ago. We had a letter from my uncle that the farmer leasing his land had gone off to fight, so my parents sent me."

"Have you been here before?" Ruby asked.

The man shook his head. "This is my first time to Lancaster County." Duncan stood, told Mamm it was nice to meet her, and then told both of them good-bye. Ruby handed him the rope and thanked him again for loaning it to her.

"I see your brother got the fence fixed."

Ruby hadn't noticed. She wondered if Zachary had slept at all the night before. She glanced toward the woodpile, guessing she had enough to get through the next couple of months at least.

"I saw him leave," Duncan said. "With the Patriots."

Ruby nodded and then took a deep breath. "Are you all right? After last night? I don't know what got into me—I wasn't thinking, not at all, when I pulled my foot away like that."

His eyes darkened a little. "I'm fine." He held up the rope and said, "I'll be on my way."

Ruby watched him step and then shuffle, step and then shuffle away, leaning against his crutch with each movement, sure he was limping more than he had the day before. She returned to the porch and finished peeling the last couple of apples and then helped Mamm inside as the rain clouds darkened on the horizon.

She did the evening milking, fed the cows, calf, and workhorses, and herded the chickens into their coop. Then she heated their leftover dinner for supper.

Never in Ruby's life had there been only two people around the old oak table.

She thought of Paul and wondered how far they'd traveled in two days, alarmed they'd only been gone that long. It felt as if it had been weeks already.

That night, after she got Mamm settled in her bed, Ruby took out her mending and sat by the flickering fire. As she repaired a tear along the hem of her most-worn dress, she said the Lord's Prayer silently and then prayed for the travelers, for the new soldier, for Mamm, and for herself. Just as she finished, the rain started. It sounded like a downpour. Ruby shivered, thinking about the muddy mess the farm would soon turn into. She didn't know how she would possibly keep up with all of the chores. Feeding the animals. Mucking out the stalls. Keeping the calf in his pen. Harvesting the corn. *Lord*, she prayed. *Give me the strength to do all I need to. And to serve Mamm as you would.*

She sat quietly for a moment, watching the flames flicker and sputter. Her thoughts fell to the events of the day, and she felt compelled to pray for one more. *Lord, please bless Duncan Wallis and heal him, body and soul. As only you can do.*

It rained for the next week. On the sixth night of rain, a loud knocking woke Ruby from a deep sleep. She hurried to the door, making out voices on the other side. She checked to make sure the latch was down and then crept to the window. Three Patriot soldiers stood on the porch. One knocked again. She waited, crouched by the window, contemplating if she should sneak out the back door and solicit Duncan's help. Finally the soldiers left on their own.

Perhaps she'd need more help than she'd anticipated. And

not just with safety. The corn needed to be harvested soon. She'd hoped their minister, Johann Fischer, might assist her, but she hadn't heard from him since Hans and Paul and the rest departed.

The more it rained, the deeper and deeper the mud grew and the more restless the calf became. On the first somewhat dry morning, it escaped the pen as Ruby tried to muck it out and headed toward the Wallis place. By the time Ruby reached it, the calf had broken through the fence again. Ruby's tears fell like the rain. She still needed to get Mamm up and fed. And then get the bread started.

Ruby stepped over the snapped boards and onto the neighbors' property. The calf had headed straight for Old Man Wallis's field of corn. Ruby hurried after the calf just as Duncan came out, leaning against his crutch and waving a scythe. Ruby couldn't fathom what he was doing with it.

"Sorry," she called out, trying to get ahead of the calf. "Once I get him back home, I'll fix the fence."

Duncan waved the scythe in his hand and stepped wide, leaning on his crutch. The calf cut to the left just as Ruby stepped forward to block the way. She untied her apron and pulled it out from under her cape and began waving it, turning the calf back toward home. Duncan limped along on the other side with the scythe spread wide, trying to persuade the calf not to head toward the Wallis cabin. The calf turned toward him, but he yelled and the calf staggered back, heading toward the fence. Once Ruby and Duncan herded the calf through, Ruby got him back in the pen and then secured the gate.

She called out to Duncan, who stayed by the fence. "I'll make the repairs this afternoon."

"I'll see what I can do now," he said.

"What were you doing in the cornfield?" she asked.

He held up the scythe.

"It's too wet," she called out. "Wait a day or two." She stepped closer to the fence. She hesitated, fearing perhaps she was being to forward, but she decided to ask anyway. "In fact, perhaps we could help each other."

"That wouldn't be very fair now, would it?"

Her face grew warm. He hadn't seen her work—he had no idea what she could do. "What do you mean?"

He pointed the scythe toward his bad leg. "I doubt I can keep up with you."

"Oh goodness," she said. "I saw you swinging that thing. But you need to wait until the stalks dry out. A few days of sunshine and we should be able to complete the task together." If he could do the cutting, she could bundle up the stalks. They both needed the feed for their livestock.

Duncan bowed a little. "Thank you for the instruction."

Ruby wasn't sure if he was being sarcastic or not. Perhaps her face showed her confusion because he said, "I meant that sincerely. I'm not a farmer. Far from it."

He'd said that before.

"My father is a businessman. I'm used to people and trading." He gestured with the scythe toward the calf and then back to his field of corn. "Not cattle and crops."

"Well," Ruby said. "I don't have much experience farming either except watching my father and brothers my entire life. But I think, together, we can figure it out." She would need someone's help if she and Mamm were to survive, and at this point Duncan was available while the remaining men in her community didn't seem to be. It wouldn't hurt to accept his help, and help him in return.

She called out, "Have you repaired the brim around your spring?"

"Pardon?"

"Your spring was flooding. The stonework needs to be re-done."

He shook his head. "No."

"I'll do it for you," she said, stepping over the downed boards of the fence. It didn't take her long to reset the stones, stopping the overflow that flooded the garden. The springs on both farms were invaluable to the properties. Good, clean water was price-less. Dat had often talked about how if they followed Christ, living water would flow from them. Working on the spring reminded Ruby of that.

The good weather held, and two days later Ruby and Duncan worked together, first in the Wallis cornfield and then in the Bachmanns'. The work was slow and tedious, and they didn't talk much. Ruby took breaks throughout the day to check on Mamm. Old Man Wallis seemed to be doing better. He trudged out to the field a couple of times to oversee the work, and once he ventured over to the Bachmanns' front porch and said hello to Mamm.

"He seems to have rallied," Duncan said, watching his uncle totter across the field.

"Will you be staying, then?" Ruby asked. "Or going back home?"

"I'll be staying," he answered. "At least through the winter." He didn't seem happy about it, and Ruby couldn't help but wonder if there were other reasons for him to be in Lancaster County, besides helping his uncle.

Still, relief washed over Ruby. The man had been rude, but perhaps that wasn't his usual way. The truth was, Duncan could do more than he realized, and she appreciated having him next door.

The day after they finished the work in the cornfields, Ruby baked two apple pies and took one over to Duncan and Old Man Wallis. She could hear the axe ringing out as she approached. Duncan had braced the foot of his bad leg against one stump, and then used another stump to split the wood. He didn't see Ruby for a few minutes. When he finally did, she waved and then held up the pie.

"I'll put it on the porch," she said.

"You can put it on the table, inside the house," he answered, and then started swinging the axe again. Perhaps if he took a break, it would be hard to get resituated again. She let herself into the house, calling out a hello. No one answered. Perhaps Old Man Wallis was resting.

She hadn't noticed a thing about the inside of the cabin the night she'd caused Duncan to fall. Now she did. There wasn't much furniture. Just a table and two chairs and a bed in the corner where Ruby realized Old Man Wallis slept. Ruby tiptoed to the table and set the pie in the middle. She wondered what food the two men had for the winter. Old Man Wallis had planted his garden in the spring but it hadn't been well tended—and then her calf had damaged it. She'd have to see what she and Mamm could spare. She left the cabin as quietly as she'd entered. The truth was, Mamm was eating less and less. Ruby had been so sure that her mother would recover, but day by day she was trying to be as realistic as possible. Mamm's speech hadn't grown better or worse, and yet she seemed to be talking less and less. And the use of her arm hadn't grown any better.

Several times, through October and early November, Ruby delivered food to Duncan and Old Man Wallis. A bag of potatoes. Then some turnips. A crock of dried apples. When it came time to butcher the hog, Ruby asked Duncan to help, saying she'd give him a ham and shoulder after they were smoked for his troubles. On a clear, frosty mid-November morning, Ruby and Duncan got to work. Thankfully, Duncan was fine shooting the hog. It wasn't that he relished it, but for a city boy he was a perfect marksman. Ruby guessed his military training probably played a role.

They waited until the animal stopped convulsing and then carried it to the hook and pulley hanging from the pole her father had installed many years ago. Somehow, Duncan managed to carry the head with one arm while crutching along with the other, and then he was able to help Ruby string the animal up and then lower it into the cauldron of hot water below. Next, Duncan helped Ruby scrape the hair off the animal, cut up the meat, and then salt the pork and pack it in barrels, which were stored in the smokehouse. In a couple of months, Ruby would hang the meat and then start the fire.

The work was long and hard, and by the end of the day Ruby was exhausted. She couldn't imagine how Duncan's leg must have ached, but he never complained.

She noticed that a few times he managed to take a few steps without his crutch. She hoped that meant it was still getting better. She didn't ask though. His leg definitely seemed to be a touchy topic.

In the middle of December, Duncan ventured to the inn in Lancaster. Ruby asked him to stop by the minister's farm on his way and tell him that Mamm wasn't doing well. She also gave Duncan the small amount of change she had and asked him to buy sugar for her from the inn, if he could. She hoped to at least do a little Christmas baking. When he returned, he said the minister's wife had been ill and therefore he was unable to visit Ruby and her mother.

And he handed her the money. "They haven't had any sugar for weeks," Duncan said. "But I have something else for you."

He held up a piece of paper. It was a letter from Paul.

Ruby thanked him and slipped it into her apron pocket. It was the first word she'd had from him, or from anyone who had headed north, and she wanted to read it in private. She hadn't heard a word from or about Zachary. She supposed that in his case no news was good news.

After Duncan left, Ruby sat beside the fire and read the short letter. It was dated the middle of November, four weeks ago.

We've settled on the land Hans secured for us. Three cabins are nearly completed. We'll build more, including one for you and me and my Mamm, in the spring.

Her heart warmed at the thought of sharing a home with Paul.

The first snow has fallen. The hunting is good. We'll not be short of meat. If you're not already on your way, encourage Zachary to bring you and your Mamm and the rest of the livestock soon, before the snow makes it impossible. Hans said he can return in the spring to secure a buyer for the property.

That was all. Obviously Hans hadn't received Zachary's letter. Obviously Paul was overly optimistic. Even if Zachary hadn't left, there was no way they could make a trip with the remaining cows, calf, and the workhorses. And Mamm. She was growing weaker every day.

Ruby folded the letter and slipped it back into her pocket,

wishing Paul had written something more personal about missing her. But he probably didn't have extra time, ink, or paper to write such things. She wrote Paul back, explaining that Zachary had written to Hans, but obviously the letter hadn't arrived. She explained that Zachary had joined the Patriots. And that Mamm was growing weaker. She asked him to return as soon as he could and bring Hans with him. She had no power to sell the land on her own.

The next day, she asked Duncan to take the letter to the inn for her and post it. Even though the day was wet and cold, he rode his mare into town. The day seemed to drag on forever. She couldn't get Mamm to leave her bed, and all she ate were a few bites of porridge. After the evening milking, when it was dark, Duncan finally returned. When he knocked on the cabin door, Ruby bid him in by the fire.

Rain dripped from his hat and oilskin coat. "The temperature is dropping," he said. "We'll either get ice or snow by morning." He shivered.

"Take off your coat," she said. "I'll get you a blanket and make you a cup of tea."

He obliged. Ruby took his coat and then pushed a chair closer to the fire for him. He reached into his bag before he sat. "You had two letters today."

Her heart raced. Perhaps Zachary's letter had arrived in Canada after all, and Paul had written to say he would soon be arriving.

She hung Duncan's coat on a peg and then returned for the letters. One was Paul's handwriting, but the other she didn't recognize. She opened Paul's first.

Zachary's letter to Hans arrived the day after Paul sent his letter.

Hans asked me to write to you. He's been ill and is just now recovering. He has no strength to travel and needs me to stay to complete the cabins, plus my Mamm has fallen ill, too, and I can't leave her now. At this point, Hans says you should stay on the farm until spring. If Zachary hasn't returned by then, Hans will return to Lancaster County and sell the farm.

Goodness. She folded the letter and placed it on the table, suddenly aware that Duncan watched her.

She quickly unfolded the second letter.

It was written in charcoal and smudged and hard to read.

I'm writing for your brother, Zachary Bachmann. He was injured last week. We're now at Valley Forge. He wanted you to know that he won't be home anytime soon.

Ruby gasped.

"What is it?" Duncan asked.

"Where is Valley Forge?"

"This side of Philadelphia," Duncan answered. "Why?"

"Zachary's been injured. That's where he is recuperating."

"I heard Washington's army retreated there," Duncan said, "after crossing the Delaware." He frowned.

"What is it?"

"I don't know if this is accurate, but I heard today at the inn that they're building structures for shelter for hundreds of soldiers and that they're ill-equipped—as far as both supplies and food."

"Of course it's accurate." Ruby stood. "I'll go get him," she said. "Why should he be cold and hungry at Valley Forge when he could be fed and warm here?"

"Ruby," Duncan said. "It's nearly sixty miles. How will you get there?"

"The workhorses and wagon. I'll get started in the morning."

"What about your mother?"

Ruby hesitated. Mamm wasn't doing well, not at all. "Can you care for her?" It was a lot to ask of Duncan, she knew. Perhaps with his uncle's help they could do it. "Perhaps Zachary is badly wounded. What if I don't go and he dies?" She felt ill. What if both Mamm and Zachary left her?

Duncan grabbed his crutch and stood. "It's not safe for you to go. I'll do it for you."

– 10 –

Jessica

When I woke up the next morning just after four, I thought of Duncan's words: "I'll do it for you." He was a true friend to Ruby. That was the sort of friend Silas had been to me, before our last fight. Before I left. He'd shown his friendship again, though, the other night when he sat with me during supper.

Tom was that sort of friend too. What would I have done without him the day before? He'd been there for me, absolutely.

I thought of Paul and his terse letters. So he was a man of few words. But that didn't mean he didn't care for Ruby. They were definitely committed to each other. Ruby hadn't wanted to leave Lancaster, but she was willing to go to Canada for Paul. I climbed out of bed and dressed quickly in the cold, dark bedroom.

I couldn't help but wonder which of the Bachmann brothers ended up with the land. Did Hans come back with his family? Or maybe Daniel? Hopefully Zachary survived his wounds.

I slipped out of the bedroom and down the landing, deciding I'd skip making coffee and head straight to the barn. I put on Aenti Suz's work coat on the back porch and slipped my feet into a pair of rubber boots, guessing they were Leisel's. Then I headed out to the barn in the still-dark morning. Surprisingly the lights were on already. I glanced at Aenti Suz's house. I hadn't expected Amos to arrive before me.

At first I didn't see anyone. Then I heard whistling. My heart began to race as Silas stepped through the far door with the first of the cows. He smiled a little and waved.

I waved back. He kept his distance from me, but even so, we worked well together, each doing different tasks without conferring about what we were doing, just like old times.

It was nearly five before Amos showed up. "Sorry," he muttered. "I haven't adjusted to the time change yet."

"No worries," I answered. It was three a.m. in Colorado.

"Aenti Suz and I stayed up late after you left. She filled me in on the first half of the story she's been telling you." He took off his cowboy hat, then grabbed one of the vinyl aprons and put it on over his jacket. "I was thinking about all the Bachmann brothers leaving in that story. Did you feel like Ruby did when I left? Abandoned?"

I shrugged, trying to think how to explain how I had felt. We had Dat, so it wasn't as if our safety was threatened. But in a way I did feel abandoned. Amos had engaged with me in a way Arden never did. He taught me how to do different chores. How to ride a horse. He listened to me read. I missed him horribly when he left and wondered what I'd done to make him leave. It was foolish, I knew now. But, in the way that children often do, I took responsibility for him leaving.

I attempted to answer his question. "Mostly I felt *ferhoodled*

147

by what others were saying about you. Not Dat. When he talked about you it was only good things. Same with Aenti Suz."

"But your Mamm? What she said wasn't so nice?"

My face grew warm. "I shouldn't have brought it up."

"No. It's fine. I've known all along what she said about me. She said it before I left too."

Specifically, Mamm had said Amos was lazy, selfish, and untrustworthy. Being late for the milking occasionally was actually the worst thing I could think of that I ever knew he'd done, though. Arden was late for the milking all the time. The different ways Mamm treated my two brothers had always confused me.

Silas came in with more cows and interrupted us. Amos greeted him and then got busy with the milking machines. At one point, when Silas was outside, I ducked into the barn office. The fracking plans were no longer on the desk. I poked around a little, looking in the drawers and on the shelves along the wall, but couldn't find them.

When we'd finished, on the way back to the house, I fell back from the other two and checked my phone for a message from Leisel. There wasn't one. But I did have a text. From Tom.

How is Arden this morning? How are you? With Arden not around, I wasn't as concerned about using my phone. I stopped so I could text Tom back. *Not sure about Arden yet. Hopefully I'll hear from Leisel soon. Guessing no news is good news. How are you?*

He texted back. *Good. See you tonight?*

Yes, I texted back. *I'll let you know once I'm home.*

My heart swelled at the thought of being back in Harrisburg. I started walking at a brisk pace. Hopefully I could get Aenti Suz to tell me the rest of Ruby's story. I might not be back to Lancaster for years. Maybe never. Another wave of grief swept over me. Grief for Dat. Grief for the land. Grief for the relationship I once had with Silas.

I'd stop by Dat's gravesite, too, on the way to the hospital. I didn't have a chance to say my farewell, not in a proper way, not with Arden nearly dying. I shivered at the thought of it. As much as Arden tormented me, I couldn't fathom him passing away so young. Vi needed him and his children needed him. And Mamm and Marie did too.

By the time I reached the back porch, Silas and Amos were already in the house. I paused for a moment, wanting to retreat to Aenti Suz's. I didn't mind working with Silas, but being around him in the house was difficult. I hoped he wouldn't try to have a conversation again. I wrinkled my nose. He wouldn't, not in front of Gail. He hated conflict. I shivered a little. He was like Dat in that way.

I slipped out of the boots and hung up the coat. When I opened the back door, loud voices greeted me. I stepped inside the kitchen but then stopped.

Leisel and Vi were arguing.

"You need to go up there. He keeps asking for you."

"I don't know what to do," Vi said.

"They opened up his arteries with a stent yesterday, but it wasn't as successful as they hoped," Leisel said. "They may need to do surgery. I'll go back up later and spend the night again, but I think it's strange that your husband is in the hospital and you're here."

Vi said, "The children—"

"Are fine," Leisel answered. "Marie and Gail can watch them." Her voice dropped a little. "This is serious. He's still in ICU. The doctors will need to speak with you."

"It will take a while for a driver to get here," Vi said.

"You weren't listening. My driver is waiting. But you need to leave now. He's on a tight schedule."

Mamm spoke up, saying, "I'll go with you, Vi."

"Denki," Vi answered.

I stepped into the kitchen and said, "Vi, I'll come up later before I leave for Harrisburg."

She gave me a withering look in response but didn't add any words. She had dark circles under her eyes and appeared overwhelmed.

Silas stood next to Gail at the island. He gave me a kind look but didn't say anything either.

"That would be good, for you to go up," Leisel said to me. "I'll take a nap and then get a ride with you."

"Leisel," Mamm said. "You can't—"

"Of course I can," she answered as she pivoted in the direction of the staircase. "Good night." My easygoing sister stormed off without another word.

Everyone was silent for a long moment until I asked, "What happened?"

"She's frustrated," Marie answered. "With Arden it seems . . ."

And Vi. That had been obvious.

"How is Arden doing?"

Marie crossed her arms. When no one else said anything, Silas said, "It sounds as if he's been uncooperative."

I exhaled slowly. Amos smiled.

A horn honked outside.

"We'd better go," Mamm said. "The driver can stop by your house so you can get your purse and things. And we can grab a bite to eat at the hospital."

Vi didn't seem happy about it, but she followed Mamm to the front door. Over her shoulder, she said to Marie, "The kids need to keep busy today. Chores. Homework. They'll return to school tomorrow."

"Of course," Marie said. "We'll see to everything."

After the front door closed, Marie and Gail started getting breakfast on the table. I noticed the little table in the corner was set for two.

"I'm going to fill up my plate and go eat at Aenti Suz's." I glanced at Amos. "Want to join me?"

He smiled.

Marie put her hands on her hips again. "That's not how this works."

"Of course it is," I said.

She stepped between me and the main table, where the food was.

"Look," I said. "I'm leaving today. You won't have to deal with me again. Ever. Don't bother to be all self-righteous. It's not going to do any of us, let alone you, any good in the long run." I barged past her, aware that my outburst hadn't left me feeling satisfied. I felt worse than ever. I missed Marie and the relationship we used to have.

As I grabbed a plate from the big table, she said, in a begging voice, "Silas?"

He shrugged. "Don't ask for my help. I'm staying out of it." He sat down at his usual place on the far side of the table.

Amos and I quickly dished up a couple of sausages, scoops of scrambled eggs, and pieces of toast. Hopefully Aenti Suz would have coffee at her place. On our way out the back door, we heard Marie yell, "You'd better bring our plates back."

Our. That single word threatened to undo me. I was no longer part of *our.* No longer welcome at *our* big oak table. No longer wanted in *our* home. No longer part of the three sisters.

No longer one of *our* Dat's daughters. Jah, there was so much that I'd lost.

Tears stung my eyes. Perhaps the rest of Aenti Suz's story would distract me, but as we neared the Dawdi Haus she stepped out of it, wearing her cape and bonnet.

"Where are you going?" I practically wailed.

"Over to Edith's house for work party. We're making soap and candles for Edith to sell at the market, along with her floral arrangements." That was how Edith and Silas survived—on his labor and whatever Edith could make and sell.

"When will you be back?"

She shrugged. "Before sunset anyway."

"But I'm leaving," I said, "by this afternoon." I'd leave sooner with Aenti Suz gone except that I just told Leisel I'd take her back up to the hospital. It wouldn't do to wake her up in an hour to go. I tried not to whine. "I wanted to hear the rest of Ruby's story."

As I steadied my plate, Aenti Suz gave me a half hug. "You'll have to come back."

I grimaced as she released me. "I'm pretty sure I won't be welcome. This could be my last visit."

"You'll always be welcome at my place."

I couldn't help but wonder how long she'd have her place but didn't say so. I doubted Arden would want her to stay on the property.

She gave Amos a half hug too. "At least I'll have another couple of days with you," she said.

He nodded.

I opened the door and headed into her cozy kitchen. Amos and I sat at the table and ate in silence. Finally he asked, "When are you leaving?"

"Early afternoon," I answered. "I should give Leisel a chance to sleep."

"Want to go for a walk around the place?" he asked. "One last time?"

"Yes," I answered. "I'd like that very much."

After we washed our plates and left them in Aenti's drying rack, we headed out the door. My goal was to spend the next five hours distracted by the beauty of *our* land. Yes, I'd pretend it belonged to me, too, one last time.

We walked the entire fence line, along the pasture, through the woods, along the field that would need to be planted soon. I would love to be a part of that—but I wouldn't be. Most likely Silas and Milton would do it.

We skirted along Arden and Vi's yard. Just like Mamm's, their garden hadn't been plowed yet either. I looked for the children, hoping to tell them good-bye, but Marie and Gail must have had all of them in the house. "Dat had told me, at one time, that I would have this property," Amos said.

"Really?"

"Jah, way back when."

"Arden didn't get it right away," I said. "He and Vi lived on her folks' property at first. I remember him asking Dat for this parcel over and over, though."

"The last time Dat asked me if I was coming home, if I wanted the property, I figured Arden was asking for it," Amos said. "I told Dat to give it to him—that I was never returning."

"Why did you leave?" I asked, as we approached the pond. I felt bolder than I had last time we chatted. "Did something happen? Because no one ever really talked about the why of it all."

Amos stopped and stared at the pond. "I don't want to criticize your Mamm. It was a lot for her to marry Dat, to be the stepmother to two boys like us. When Rebecca was born, she was easier to get along with even though it was five years until you came along."

I held my breath, hoping he'd say more.

Finally he did. "I was watching Rebecca that day while Arden was supposed to be dragging the field, but he wasn't getting the work done, so I told him I'd do it, which meant it was his job to watch Rebecca. She'd been playing on the swing set.

"As I pulled the tractor over by the shed, he started yelling Rebecca's name and then running toward the pond. We reached it at the same time. Rebecca's Kapp was floating in the water. We both rushed in, and I pulled her out. She screamed right away. We were both so relieved.

"Dat had just come home from the hospital to pick up some things for your Mamm when he heard the yelling. He ran to the pond, too, and then carried Rebecca back to the house. All seemed well. Arden did manage to mention that I'd been watching Rebecca. I started to set the story straight but decided not to. She was fine. There was no reason to start a fight. Dat grabbed what he needed and said you and your Mamm would come home the next morning. Then the driver took him back to the hospital.

"I put Rebecca to bed that night. She had a little bit of a cough, and I thought perhaps she'd gotten a chill." Amos paused.

I swallowed hard. Part of me wanted him to stop. This was about my older sister. About her *last* night on earth, which occurred my *first* night on earth.

My brother stared into the greenish water of the pond and

then said, "The next morning she was cold. I sent Arden to call for an ambulance even though I knew she'd passed. I didn't know what else to do. After he called the ambulance he called Dat at the hospital. Your Mamm answered and Arden told her Rebecca was very ill. He repeated the story that I'd been watching her the day before when she fell into the pond.

"The paramedics said she'd been dead for hours. They called it a secondary drowning, said she'd gotten water into her lungs. Dat simply said, 'The Lord giveth and the Lord taketh away.' I tried to tell him that I hadn't been watching Rebecca when she got to the pond, but he said it didn't matter who'd been watching her. I said it mattered if one of us was lying.

"Your Mamm directed her anger at me. And soon someone else began to also."

"Who?" I asked.

"Vi. We'd been sweet on each other, but Arden told her Rebecca's death was my fault, and after a while she wouldn't have anything to do with me. I was pretty sure, after I left, she and Arden would start courting."

"But you stayed for six years after things got bad, before you left. What made you finally go?"

"At first I thought it would all blow over. Maybe Arden would take responsibility and free me. Then when Marie and then Leisel were born so soon after you, I thought your Mamm would let go of her anger. I hoped Dat might see all the damage that had been done and try to fix it, but for all of his good qualities, he seemed in denial about the rift caused by Arden's deception."

I nodded. Dat had so many positive qualities, but he was often overly optimistic when it came to his children. "You're right about Vi and Arden. I do remember they started to court soon after you left." And then married right away.

The wind had picked up and blew ripples across the pond. Perhaps something blew into Amos's eyes or perhaps it was his emotions, but he rubbed at both of his eyes.

"It was only a few months later that Dat called and said Arden and Vi were married. That was the first time he asked me to come home, farm with him, and claim the piece of property he'd set aside for me."

"What property had Dat set aside for Arden?"

"The section that borders the woods."

"Really?" That had always been one of my favorite parcels of land on the farm. "Why didn't he want it?"

Amos shrugged. "Because he always wanted what I had. My land. My girl. My story about the day Rebecca fell into the pond."

I could see that about Arden. He always seemed discontent with his own life, always wanting something different, including making a living from exploiting the land instead of farming it.

"Wait. Dat asked you to come home and farm with him?" Amos nodded.

"What about Arden? Dat didn't want him to farm?"

"At the time, Arden wanted to set up some sort of business."

"Like?"

Amos shrugged. "I'm not sure."

The Amish men I knew who had businesses made things like cabinets and furniture or buggies. Arden didn't like to make things. Or some business owners repaired small machines, like lawn mowers. Arden didn't like to repair things either.

"What was Arden like when you two were younger?" I asked. "Did he ever like farming?"

Amos shook his head. "He liked school. Numbers. Math. He should have been an accountant. He never liked the land."

I could see that. He was happiest working in the office in the barn, not doing the milking or dragging the fields or planting or harvesting or doing any of the many chores that needed to be done to keep the farm running—and profitable.

Amos turned away from the pond and I followed him to the oak tree. Dat had chosen Amos to farm with him. He was the one from our generation who was meant to protect the land.

If only we could keep it safe until Milton was ready to take it over.

We stopped and listened to the wind whistle through the branches of the tree. I was tempted to stay and have a good cry about Dat but decided that would have to wait until I reached the cemetery.

As we started walking again, my brother said, "Don't be too hard on your Mamm."

Shocked, I realized my mouth had fallen open. Finally I found a word to say. "Really?"

He nodded. "She's gone through a lot. Rebecca dying. Years of mourning. Now Dat passing. She's never been strong, not the way you are."

"But she ruined your life."

He shook his head. "She didn't ruin my life. She believed Arden is all."

I couldn't help the pitch of my voice. "Is all?"

He nodded. "I forgave her long ago. Arden too." He stopped. "I'm sorry if it didn't sound that way just now, when I was telling the story of what happened."

I shook my head. I hadn't questioned whether he'd forgiven them or not. I was just surprised at his sympathy toward Mamm. Honestly, it was a lesson for me—probably one that I needed.

As we reached the yard of the big house, Silas came out the

back door. A second later Gail rushed out, yelling, "You have to keep your job! What will the Bachmanns do without you?"

"They'll figure it out," Silas said. "I'm tired of being in the middle."

Marie came running out next, followed by Leisel. "Silas!" Marie called out.

Leisel yelled, "He's right. Let him go." Milton followed her out.

Silas brushed past Amos and me, headed for the barn.

"What's going on?" I asked him.

"I quit," he said, over his shoulder. "Your family is going to have to find someone else to do the milking and vaccinate the calves and do the plowing and planting and listening and mediating. . . ." He was halfway to the barn, his voice trailing off in the wind.

Gail and Marie rushed by us too.

"Stop!" I called out.

The girls didn't obey.

I sighed as Leisel and Milton approached. They did stop.

"What happened?" I asked as we all watched Silas flee into the barn.

"Marie and Gail were bad-mouthing you, and he got sick of it. He said he didn't want anything to do with their gossip and that he was going to find another job. They both freaked."

I cocked my head at Leisel's word choice. *Freaked.* But then disregarded it. "Can Arden hire someone else?"

Leisel shook her head. "Mamm or Vi will have to do it. We can't burden Arden with this now. I didn't want to alarm Vi this morning, but he really isn't doing well." Leisel's eyes grew even more serious and she lowered her voice as Milton trekked after the others. "Can you two stay another couple of weeks or so?" she asked me. "Until Arden is doing better?"

I couldn't help but laugh. "No one wants me to stay."

"I do," she answered.

"Well, you're the only one."

"Please?" Leisel said.

I shrugged, not knowing what to do. "I'll take you back up to the hospital and see if Mamm and Vi have any ideas. Then I'll decide." I turned toward Amos. "Want to come along?"

He glanced back toward the pond. "No. I think I'll go take a nap in the Dawdi Haus." He started to walk away but then turned back around. "Good luck."

I decided to stay in my dress, guessing I might be coming back to the farm for a few days. But I packed my bag just in case.

– 11 –

Leisel didn't speak as we left the farm. When I turned my car onto the highway, I asked why she thought Silas quit. "Maybe he feels the way you felt when you left—fed up." She didn't say any more. Instead she closed her eyes and put her head back against the headrest. I concentrated on driving.

When we reached the outskirts of Lancaster, she said, "You were talking the other day about how you got your GED. I need to tell you that I got mine too."

I glanced toward her, swerving as I did. "What?"

"Watch the road!" she shouted.

I'd veered onto the shoulder and quickly corrected. "When? How?"

"Last year. Dat allowed it. I have no idea what he told Mamm—maybe that I was getting some kind of special training. I'd hoped to go on and become a certified nursing assistant, but then Dat got sick."

"You don't need a GED for that," I pointed out.

"Right."

I expected her to say more, but she didn't. "Leisel, what are you planning?"

160

She shrugged. "I'm not exactly sure yet. I just know . . ."

"What?"

"That there's something more for me."

"Than?"

"Staying here. Getting married. Having children. Gossiping with Marie and Gail. Watching Mamm grow more and more negative."

"What do you want to do?"

She sighed. "The truth is, there's only so much I can do. Right?"

"Wrong," I answered. "You already have your GED. You managed that—there's probably no limit to what you can do, but it would mean a lot of hard choices."

"That's it," she said. "I want something more. But I don't want to lose what I have."

I nodded. She and I both knew it was an either-or situation. Both couldn't happen simultaneously. "I'm sorry," I said.

"Whatever for?"

"That you're facing this."

She scooted down in her seat a little. "Jah, well, you paved the way. If I do decide to leave, it will probably be easier for me than it was for you."

I didn't respond, but I doubted it. She wouldn't have Dat as a buffer, and Mamm would be more heartbroken to lose Leisel than she was to lose me. Leisel was her baby. Her last born. And her easiest, at least compared with me. The only thing in her favor was that she hadn't joined the church, so she wouldn't be shunned the same way I was.

Arden was still in the ICU, and Mamm and Vi were sitting in the waiting room. "How is he?" Leisel asked.

"All right," Vi said.

Mamm gave Vi a confused look and then said, "He needs to have surgery, more than the initial procedure. Open-heart surgery."

"Oh dear," Leisel said.

"When?" I asked.

"Tomorrow."

Leisel sat beside Mamm. "How long will his recovery be?"

"Two or three more days in the hospital, then he'll need to rest at home and do rehab. It will be weeks before he can return to work." Vi glanced at Mamm, who shrugged. Vi continued, "Arden says we need to sell the woods."

I bristled. "Why?"

"Hospital expenses."

I shook my head. "Won't the mutual aid fund cover it?"

Mamm and Vi both sighed in unison, and then Mamm said, "They already covered your Dat's medical costs."

"That doesn't matter. Lots of families have multiple medical costs at one time." When neither of them responded, I said, "Don't you understand? Once that land is sold, that's it. The farm will never be the same. We'll never get it back—after over two hundred and fifty years, it will all be gone."

"Listen," Mamm said, in a shrill voice. "Land isn't everything. Once you're older, you'll understand."

"No," I said. "I won't understand. Instead of selling it, we should be working at managing what we have. Caring for it."

"We?" Mamm stood. "Jessica, this has nothing to do with you."

My face grew warm but before I could speak, Leisel said, "We need to talk with the two of you about something else. Silas quit today."

Mamm turned toward me. "What did you say to him?"

162

"Nothing."

She frowned. "Then why would he quit?"

"He seems to be fed up with all of us," Leisel said. "The gossip. The backbiting. The hypocrisy."

Mamm pursed her lips.

"All the negativity toward Jessica, especially."

Mamm's eyes flashed a hint of anger.

"That means there's only Milton to do the work. Jessica could stay for a few more days and help, though. . . ." Leisel's voice trailed off.

Vi clutched her purse to her chest as she shook her head. "Leroy and Luke can do more. So can you and Marie."

Leisel rolled her eyes. "Jah, we can do the milking, but we're not going to be much help with the plowing. Or the planting. Arden never allowed it—we don't even know what to do."

Arden had much more control over my sisters than he ever had over me.

"We'll have to hire someone else then," Mamm said.

"Jah, we can try," Leisel answered. "But I can't think of anyone who's looking for a job right now."

"I have vacation time," I said. "I can help Milton."

Mamm and Vi's eyes met and both grimaced. "No," Mamm said. "That won't be necessary. . . . You know what Bishop Jacobs said."

My face grew even warmer and I stepped back. "All right. I'll go ahead and be on my way then."

My mother gave me a nod, and Vi waved her hand a little. I started toward the elevator.

"Wait!" Leisel hurried after me. "Don't leave yet."

"There's no reason to stay." I brushed away my tears, surprised at how rejected I felt. What did I expect? That I would become the heroine and save the day? Save the farm? Somehow save myself?

I gave Leisel a hug and whispered, "You have my number. Keep in touch."

She nodded, and I stepped on the elevator.

I thought about texting Tom to tell him I was on my way but decided to wait until I was back in my apartment. As I pulled out of the parking garage, my heart warmed. I'd soon be in my cozy apartment, away from the angst of my family. Perhaps I could finally mourn my father.

Dat. I hadn't gone by the cemetery. Going now meant backtracking, but it would be worth it.

When I arrived at the cemetery, the rain had just started. I wished I'd changed into my Englisch clothes. Sure, I fit in here. But by the time I reached Harrisburg I'd feel like a chicken off the farm. I parked on the edge of the cemetery—thankful no one was there—and started toward Dat's grave by the far fence. As I walked, the rain fell harder, and I pulled the hood of my coat over my Kapp.

Of course there was no marker at Dat's grave yet, and when it was installed it would be as plain as all the others. It was one of the things I truly appreciated about the Amish. Modesty wasn't just about dress—it applied to all areas of life. No one was to be showy. No one was to appear better than anyone else. We were all equal in God's eyes. Well, mostly equal. Men, it seemed, were worth more. I chided myself. That wasn't true, not at all. Dat had never made me feel that way, and I'd seen Dat serve Mamm, over and over. I'd seen him serve us all. And the Amish truly cherished each member of the community and saw each person's value and worth, within prescribed roles.

But I wasn't normal. Couldn't Mamm understand that? I know Dat never minded that I was different. If only he'd stood up to Bishop Jacobs. But then what? Would he have been forced out? Would he have to have chosen to become Mennonite? Would that have been so bad?

The mound over Dat's coffin had settled some. I bowed my head and forced myself to say a prayer, thanking God for giving me a loving and caring father. True, he didn't always know how to handle conflict between his children, but he tried, mostly by giving us the opportunity to work it out ourselves. He loved all of us. And he never bad-mouthed one of us to the other. Jah, I was very grateful for a father's care and love. It had molded me into who I was.

Just as I turned to go, my phone buzzed in my apron pocket. I lifted my coat and fished it out. It was the hospital number. Panic seized me. Hopefully Arden hadn't grown worse. I answered quickly. It was Leisel.

"Hallo," she said. "I'm with Arden. Vi and Mamm are still in the waiting room."

"Is everything okay?"

"Jah," Leisel said. "Well, the same anyway. Listen, Arden wants to speak with you."

"What?" He was in the ICU for goodness' sake. And I stressed him out. What could he possibly have to say to me?

"Jah . . ." I sensed worry in Leisel's voice.

"What about?" I asked.

Leisel didn't answer my question. Instead she said, "I'll put him on."

In a weak voice, Arden said, without saying hello or any other greeting, "Stay and help with the farm. At least until I get home."

"I was told not to," I answered.

"I'll talk with Vi and your Mamm. They don't understand. You'll probably still need to get neighbors to help, but I can't expect other people to fix the tractor or work with our ornery mules or know what to do as well as you. If you can stay until I'm home, that would help."

"All right," I said, without giving it a moment of thought. "As long as you make your wishes known."

"I will." He handed the phone back to Leisel without saying good-bye.

"I guess I'll see you back at the house," I said to my sister.

"*Gut*," she answered, her voice the lightest I'd heard in days. "I'll come back tonight and then head back here early in the morning before surgery."

"Are you sure you're up to all of that?"

"Of course," Leisel answered. "I wouldn't miss a chance to speak with the doctors. And that way I can let Mamm and Vi know how Arden is doing." I surmised they didn't plan to be at the hospital during the surgery. I knew Dat would have been.

After the call ended, I stood staring down at the mound of soil again. "What do you have for me?" I said out loud to God. "What good can possibly come from all of this?"

I slipped my phone back into my apron pocket and headed toward my car. Only time would tell. At least I'd get to spend more time with Amos, and chances were I'd get the rest of Aenti Suz's story.

A driver brought Mamm home and then took Milton up to the hospital just before Amos and I started on the afternoon milking. Soon after I reached the barn, Silas arrived.

"I thought you quit," I said.

"I did," he answered. "But I'll just help tonight. Gail told me Milton went with Vi."

Had Gail gone by his house? I frowned at the hint of jealousy in my thoughts. *Hint?* Who was I trying to kid? I needed to stop.

The truth was, Silas and Tom were very similar. Except that Tom was a better version. More honest. More responsible. More ambitious. More likely to stick up for me.

When we finished the milking, Amos said he was going to drive into town and get some supper. "Maybe I'll stop by the hospital," he said, a twinkle in his eye.

He started toward his car, and I walked toward the house, expecting Silas to head toward his buggy.

"Jessica," he said.

I turned around.

"May I talk with you for a moment?"

That was the last thing I wanted.

"Please," he said. "Where no one will hear us?"

I tried to speak, but a lump had lodged tight in my throat. Finally I said, "Let's head toward the field." The last rays of the sun faded over the woods. It was the moment before dusk fell over the farm, when the sun hung low. Sometimes pink or lavender filled the sky. Even if the sky was gray, it was a magical moment. I shivered, thinking of Ruby experiencing the same thing all those years ago.

Silas and I wouldn't have much light.

He stepped to my side, and I led the way. Neither of us said anything. When I reached the closed gate, I stopped and said, "What's up?"

"Let's keep going." He opened the gate. This time I followed him. He didn't stop until we reached the oak tree just as a splash of orange spread across the horizon. Then the sun completely disappeared and dusk fell.

"I wanted to explain why I quit," he said, his voice as muted as the sky. "And then why I came back to help today."

"You don't need to," I said. "I'm sure your reasons for both are valid."

He shook his head.

My heart raced. Whatever was still between us seemed as elusive as it had that night I left. The only thing I was sure of was that I needed to get back to Harrisburg and to Tom. Standing under the oak tree with Silas made me feel as if I were nineteen again and madly in love—with him.

"After you left, it was as if your family couldn't bear it. I think there was the feeling that if they kept me around, perhaps you would return. Then when it was obvious you weren't going to, the next best thing for them was to match me up with Gail."

My face grew warm. "Whom are you talking about? Dat?"

He shook his head. "No, your Mamm. And Marie."

"Once Gail moved in and essentially took your place, everyone was thrilled when we started courting." He paused a moment and then said, "You know how much I love this farm, this land. It's not as if I ever expected to own any of it, but I would have been happy to work here for the rest of my life. . . ."

"Except?" I prodded.

"Except I always feel as if I'm in the middle of everyone's business—even when I try not to be. All these years I wouldn't stand for anyone talking negatively about you, and they mostly respected my wish when I was around, but once you came home they couldn't seem to help themselves."

When I didn't answer, he said, "I'm sorry. I thought you knew."

"I do know they vilify me. I mean, I get it, I left. But it still surprises me that Marie and Mamm show so much animosity toward me."

"I think Amos leaving felt like a fluke to your Mamm, and then to Marie too, once she was older. But you leaving made them feel marked, is if it were a sin on the family name. Your Dat didn't believe that, though. Not at all. He never acted that way."

Again, I didn't answer.

Silas leaned toward me. "He'd tell me when he'd go to see you—not where you were living but just that he'd seen you."

"Really?"

Silas nodded. "He told me that you were dating Tom too."

"Oh?" That surprised me.

"Your Dat thought he was a fine fellow. In fact, he told me once that I shouldn't wait for you, that I shouldn't expect you to return."

I cocked my head. "And yet you haven't joined the church. And you haven't married Gail yet."

He nodded. "But I plan to."

"Join the church? Marry Gail?"

He nodded. "Both."

"Why has it taken you so long?"

He shrugged. "It was hard for me to get over you."

Was. "Leaving was the hardest thing I've ever done." My voice wavered involuntarily. I couldn't manage to say, also, that leaving him was even harder than leaving the land, than leaving my family.

He didn't respond to my confession. Instead, he changed the subject and said, "I quit because all of you Bachmanns need to work things out. There's how Amos was treated. And then you. And the way your Mamm and Marie gang up against you. None of it is right. Your Dat didn't want to meddle in the lives of his children, so all he could do was let you and Amos know he loved you and hope the rest of them would figure it out. He hoped all of you would reconcile at some point."

Tears filled my eyes. Dat was the least-controlling person I knew. It sounded as if he'd confided in Silas.

"I would have worked with your Dat forever," Silas said. "He took me under his wing and cared for me like a father after my Dat died." He shook his head slightly. "But I can't, in good conscience, keep working here with him gone. Your Dat wouldn't allow Marie to treat you the way she does, and he wouldn't allow Arden to . . ." Silas stopped and shook his head.

"To?"

He shrugged.

"To what?"

Silas sighed. "I keep going back and forth whether I should tell you this."

I inhaled sharply. He had no intention of addressing the topic of us. He was concerned about Arden . . . maybe about the land. "Does this have to do with something Arden wanted to do?"

"Present tense," Silas answered.

"Wants?" I crossed my arms. "Does this have to do with some documents I saw on the desk in the barn? About fracking?"

"I'm guessing he's pursuing that again." Silas met my eyes. "Every farm needs an advocate—someone who loves the land more than money. First this farm lost you. Now it's lost your Dat."

"Maybe Milton will step up and be the next advocate."

Silas nodded. "Maybe. But perhaps by then there will be an

apartment complex over there." He pointed toward the woods. "Jah," he said. "He talked about that again, too, once your Dat became ill." Then he pointed down toward the ground. "And a fracking operation here."

"Here? Where the old oak is?"

Silas nodded.

"No," I whispered, imagining the rocks and natural gas deep in the ground. "How could Arden even consider such a thing?" I pressed my hand against the tree. "Why is he so certain he can't make a profit off farming?"

"Maybe because he doesn't like working the land. He wants to take shortcuts. Volunteer to take on other duties in the district, like managing the mutual fund and things like that, instead of spending his time farming."

"Do you think the land can be profitable?"

"Sure, with some extra work." As darkness settled, the wind picked up and rustled through the branches.

"I wish I could do something to help," I said. I couldn't see Silas's eyes.

"Pray," he said. "And remember, there's a spiritual connection to the land. God gave it to your family. He desires that it be cared for and protected. Ask for wisdom and for direction about what to do."

I nodded in agreement as tears stung my eyes again. Silas understood. He'd always understood. How many times, before I left, had he reminded me to pray? How many times, because of his calm spirit, had I actually followed his suggestion? Even toward the end, he encouraged me to pray. And I did, until I couldn't stand it any longer. Until I decided to leave. Until I screamed at him, to no avail.

I couldn't overreact now, not if I wanted a solution.

Maybe there was something I could do. Maybe working the file on the Stoltz fracking case could give me an idea on how to deal with Arden. I could go back to Harrisburg—Tom! I hadn't texted him.

"Oh dear," I said, pulling my phone from the pocket of my apron. "I need to text Tom that I'm staying here longer. I completely forgot. . . ."

"And I need to get home," Silas said.

We started back toward the gate.

"You're not coming in for dinner?"

He shook his head.

"Because of all the Bachmann drama?"

He hesitated a moment and then said, "And because of my Mamm. I've been neglecting her for the last several months."

I didn't respond. *His Mamm.* I'd asked him to leave with me without a thought to Edith. Nausea swept through me for a moment. Had I thought she'd come with us? Had I actually thought she'd be okay by herself if she didn't?

When we reached the gate, Silas headed toward the barn for his horse. I started to text Tom as I walked toward the house. But then I decided to call him.

"Hey," he answered. "Are you home?"

Home was not where he expected. "I ended up staying," I said. "Silas quit and there was no one else to help."

His voice fell flat. "Jessica, are you sure?"

"Jah." I winced at how easy it was for me to slip into my old way of speaking. "They need me."

"Even when they treat you so poorly?"

"I'm doing it in my Dat's memory," I said, "and because of the land. That's all."

He sighed.

"Sorry," I said. Clearly he was disappointed in me. "I'll need another few days off work—except, I was thinking about driving up tomorrow and getting the Stoltz file. I'll send Deanna a text to let her know. The Stoltz farm is close to here. I thought I could go by and ask some questions."

"All right." His voice was back to normal.

"Want to have lunch?"

"Sure," he said.

We spoke for a few more minutes about Arden and the farm. "Why did Silas quit?" Tom asked.

"It's a long story," I said. "He feels caught in the middle of all of my family's drama."

Tom chuckled a little. "Silas is a good man."

I smiled. Both Tom and Silas were good men. And if they didn't live in such separate worlds, they'd probably be friends.

After we said our good-byes, I slipped my phone back into my pocket. Instead of going into the house, though, I backtracked to the Dawdi Haus. Aenti Suz came to the door wearing her bathrobe and slippers.

"I have beef and barley soup on the stove and freshly baked bread," she said.

"Perfect," I answered.

A few minutes later, as I ate, she said, "I heard Silas quit." I nodded.

She frowned. "That poor boy. He's been moping around here ever since you left."

"What do you mean?" She couldn't pull that trick again. She'd already tried once. "He's been courting Gail."

"True," she said. "But why hasn't he joined the church? Why hasn't he married her?"

"He's going to," I answered.

173

She shook her head. "He's been leaving room for you to come back."

"I don't think so," I said. "Besides, I don't want to talk about Silas. I'd rather you told me the rest of Ruby's story."

She yawned and quickly covered her mouth. "Maybe not the rest, but more," she answered. "Where were we?"

"Ruby had just received the letter that Zachary was badly wounded, and Duncan offered to go to Valley Forge for her."

"That's right," Aenti Suz said. "Because she couldn't leave her Mamm."

I nodded, ready to forget my own problems. Listening to Ruby's story was like a good book—except it was set on my childhood farm and I shared DNA with the protagonist.

–12–

Ruby

Ruby didn't feel right about Duncan traveling that far by himself. He'd have to take the wagon to be able to bring Zachary back. If a wheel or axle broke, it would be nearly impossible for him to fix it. And Ruby wasn't sure if he'd know how to care for Zachary either.

But she couldn't leave Mamm. She considered trying to hire a local girl, but she feared Mamm might be dying and felt it too much to ask of another person. There was the matter of the chores too. There weren't any older boys and young men left—they'd all been conscripted as soldiers or had fled.

The next morning, Mamm opened her eyes but didn't seem to focus on Ruby, although she managed to say, "Trust the Lord, dear one. Pray that His will be done."

She didn't speak, nor did she eat after that. Ruby asked Duncan to wait a couple of days before he left. She couldn't bear the thought of being alone if Mamm died.

Ruby sat beside Mamm's bed as much as she could, moistening

her mother's mouth with a damp cloth and reading to her from Dat's Bible. She prayed silently for Mamm and Zachary, too, throughout the day.

That evening Mamm's breathing grew raspy. Ruby sat up with her, leaving the lamp burning, feeling destitute at the thought of her mother passing. At some point, toward morning, she dozed, and when she woke, she realized her Mamm was gone. She sat until the sun rose and then staggered over to the Wallis farm, overcome with sorrow, and asked Duncan to go fetch the minister. There was no reason, with most of the congregation gone, to wait to bury Mamm. The ground was only going to grow colder and would be harder to dig.

While Duncan was gone, Old Man Wallis did the milking and Ruby washed Mamm one last time. When Duncan returned, saying the minister would arrive soon, he and his uncle made a pine box from boards they found in the barn. By the time the minister arrived, Duncan, Old Man Wallis, and Ruby had managed to get Mamm's body into the box.

The minister was ill, but he went with Duncan to the small plot on the edge of the farm where Ruby's Dat and her siblings who had died young had been buried and dug another hole for Mamm. At least the weather was warm enough and the ground still soft. Old Man Duncan said he could feel it in his bones that a cold snap was coming though.

Ruby hitched the workhorses to the wagon, and when Duncan and the minister returned, they all managed to carry the box, with Old Man Wallis's help, out to the wagon and then transport it to the burial plot. The minister said a few words and led them in a silent prayer. Then the four of them lowered the box into the ground. Duncan worked at shoveling the dirt on top and then Ruby took a turn, saying she wanted to have a part in it, but honestly she was afraid it was all too much for Duncan. She didn't want him to reinjure himself. The minister ended up completing the job, but then fell into a coughing spell.

When they all arrived back at the cabin, Ruby fed the men ham and sweet potatoes and biscuits. She told the minister about the letters she'd received, the two from Paul and the one from Zachary.

Duncan explained that he would go find Zachary at Valley Forge. Ruby didn't say anything because she was sure the minister wouldn't approve, but since Mamm had died she could go with Duncan. That was what she planned to do—if Old Man Wallis could keep up with the chores on both farms. It would be a lot for him, she knew, but the essential tasks were to feed and water the animals. She thought he could manage that.

Before the minister left, he pulled Ruby aside. "I'm grateful for the help of your neighbors, but I don't think it's safe for you to stay here alone. Come stay with my wife and me."

Ruby politely declined, saying that Zachary would be back soon and she'd need to nurse him back to health. The minister seemed troubled but didn't say anything more and soon left. She was grateful he didn't meddle in the affairs of others, even though, because of his position, he had the right to. For the first time in her life, she was making decisions on her own instead of relying on her parents or brothers to make them for her.

Before Duncan left for home with his uncle, he said he would leave in the morning for Valley Forge.

"Could we talk things through? Before you go in the morning?" Ruby asked.

He nodded, a questioning look on his face, but didn't say anything more.

After he left, Ruby realized it was Christmas Day. She sank

down in front of the fire and let the tears roll down her face. For her mother. For Zachary. For Paul. Never in her life had she been alone. Finally, she rose, washed her face, and thought through her plan.

The next morning, before she milked the cows and fed the calf, workhorses, and chickens, she packed food for the trip, a basket of food for Old Man Wallis, and a bag of cabbage, turnips, and onions plus a ham and a slab of bacon from the year before to contribute to the feeding of the soldiers at Valley Forge. The food wouldn't go far, and she certainly didn't agree with what the soldiers were fighting for, but the thought of people going hungry pained her. Then she collected bedding from the cabin and stacked it by the door.

Old Man Wallis was right. A morning frost had blanketed the farm and a heavy fog hung low. After she finished her chores, she hitched Gunnar and Gustaf to the wagon and loaded the supplies in it, expecting Duncan any minute. When he didn't appear, she grabbed the basket and marched across the frosty field to the fence, climbed it, and then continued on to the Wallis home.

Duncan opened the door, dressed in his oil coat and hat, a cane in his hand instead of his crutch. "I was just coming down," he said. "I'm sorry I'm late."

"He fell again," Old Man Wallis said, "and couldn't get up—"

"I'm fine." Duncan shot his uncle an annoyed look and then turned toward to Ruby. "It wasn't bad, really."

Ruby stood tall and squared her shoulders. She wore an old coat Zachary had outgrown years ago. "I'm going with you to Valley Forge." She looked past him. "If Mr. Wallis can see to my chores too."

"I can," he answered.

But Duncan said, "It's too dangerous for a woman to go."

She knew if she said it was too dangerous for him to go alone that he'd be offended. So instead she said, "I don't want to get in your way on the trip there, but I think I should be along for the trip home. We have no idea how bad Zachary's injuries are. It would be difficult for you to care for him and drive the team. It might delay you a day or two."

He seemed to be considering it but then said, "An army camp is no place for you."

"We won't be there long."

"She should go with you," Old Man Wallis said. "Two is better than one when it comes to a journey. And the weather may turn. It wouldn't be good for you to be out there alone in the cold."

Duncan hesitated again, but then said, "All right."

She placed the basket of food on the table and told Old Man Wallis it was for him.

"Thank you," he said. "I'll see to things on both farms."

Ruby thanked him, regretting how she'd misjudged him through the years. Or perhaps he'd changed. Perhaps they all had.

Once she and Duncan were on the road, with several wool blankets tucked around their legs, Ruby began having second thoughts about traveling alone with a man who wasn't part of her family, let alone her congregation. Perhaps she should have spoken to the minister first. Perhaps she should have asked him to go with Duncan to fetch Zachary. Except that wouldn't have worked. Minister Fischer was still ill and his wife was pregnant. He couldn't be tasked with such a trip and caring for Zachary too.

Ruby's gaze fell to the right and she shivered. The frost hadn't thawed and still hung from the bare tree branches along the creek. She'd come to a manageable working relationship with Duncan through the last couple of months, but being alone with him in the wagon made her feel as if he were a complete stranger again. She sighed. That wasn't true. She didn't feel the animosity that had been between them at the beginning. Working with him had made him seem familiar in a way that she hadn't even felt with Paul—probably because they hadn't worked together. He'd farmed while she'd cooked and cleaned and tended the garden. But with Duncan, she'd had to work with him to survive. She couldn't imagine what her life would have been like since Paul and the rest left if Duncan hadn't moved in with his uncle.

The road was full of ruts because of the rains that had made a pathway of mud, which then froze. Soon they passed through a wood, then by an inn, and then onto the road to Philadelphia. Ruby had been to the city years before, when she was nine. Her father had business to attend to for supplies to expand the house, and she and Zachary had gone along.

In places, stones lined the surface of the road, but in others it was rutted too. Overall, the road was in better shape than she remembered.

Duncan said he knew of an inn past the halfway point where they would stay that night. Again a feeling of unease came over Ruby. She doubted Mamm would approve, and she knew Paul wouldn't. She'd been impulsive to say she'd come along.

However, she knew Duncan was a gentleman, despite their first encounter. Mamm saw his tender side too. But Paul would never believe an Englischman could be so kind.

Still, she truly believed this was what would be best for Zachary. *God*, she prayed, leaning back against the bench, *I hope I wasn't foolish to come. Please watch over*—she nearly said *me*, but then changed it to *us. Please watch over us. Please lead us to Zachary. Please care for him and comfort him until we can arrive. Please keep Duncan safe and from further injury.*

The horses trotted along. Duncan remained silent and soon Ruby dozed. When she awoke, the day had warmed above freezing. Toward midafternoon, clouds gathered on the eastern horizon, growing larger and darker as they traveled. Dusk had fallen as they neared the inn.

Duncan sighed, most likely relieved to reach a safe place before nightfall. A stable boy helped him unhitch the horses, and together they all worked to unharness and brush them down. Ruby wondered about leaving the food in the wagon and didn't want to ask about it in front of the stable boy, but then Duncan said he would sleep in the wagon and keep an eye on everything.

After a bowl of stew and a slice of bread, eaten at the end of the table crowded with rowdy men, Ruby and Duncan stood by the fire a little longer. Some of the men left, probably ones who lived nearby, but the others appeared to be staying at the inn that night. Ruby turned toward the fireplace to warm her hands.

Duncan stepped closer to her and whispered, "Will you be all right?"

"Jah," she answered. "I believe I'll be fine." The truth was, at this point, she'd rather sleep outside near Duncan, but that wouldn't be acceptable either.

"All right," he said, "I'm going to go check on the horses and then bed down. Let's leave at first light." Then, in an even softer voice, he said, "Barricade your door with a chair. If anyone tries to get in, yell out the window, and I'll see to you as quickly as I can."

Ruby nodded her head and started toward the stairs. But then she heard Duncan greet someone. A woman, close to Ruby's age, had just come through the door. She was well dressed and carried herself with confidence. Duncan was hugging the woman, an expression of joy on his face. Obviously he knew her.

A wool jacket covered the woman's bodice and waist, her fashionable skirt, open in front above the hem, revealed a lacy petticoat. She wore slippers on her dainty feet and silk stockings. The woman wore her hair in ringlets piled high on her head, partially covered by a fancy hat.

Ruby touched her simple Kapp. Her plain wool coat mostly covered her plain dress and apron. Jah, she was *so* plain. And the woman was *so* beautiful.

"Isabelle," Duncan said as he released the woman. "What in the world are you doing here?" Ruby was surprised at the pang of jealousy she felt and tried to ignore it.

"Mother and Father decided I needed to leave Philadelphia and sent me by coach. I'm headed to Lancaster County. To stay with you."

"Oh dear," he said. "I've had a bit of a diversion. We'll need to figure this out." He glanced up, a smile on his face. "Ruby," he called out. "Come meet my sister."

Ruby almost gasped. In all this time she'd known Duncan, he'd never mentioned a sister. But then she'd never asked him about siblings. Her face warmed.

Ruby stepped forward. By the way his sister was dressed, Duncan's family was wealthier than he'd let on.

Duncan introduced Isabelle and then said, "This is Ruby. My neighbor back in Lancaster."

After greeting Ruby, Isabelle turned toward her brother. "Goodness, you seem to have settled into farm life."

He nodded. "It sounds as if you'll be soon doing the same."

"Never," Isabelle replied with a laugh.

The innkeeper greeted Isabelle and said that he'd show them both the room upstairs for women.

"I'll wait and sit with you," Duncan said to his sister.

As they reached the landing, Isabelle said, "So you're Uncle Wallis's neighbor?"

"Jah," Ruby answered, continuing on to the room.

"Why are you traveling with Duncan?"

"He's helping me find my brother at Valley Forge."

"Oh my," Isabelle said. "But why are you dressed *so* simply? Are you a servant?"

"No." Ruby stopped as the innkeeper opened the door, nodded at the women, and then hurried back toward the stairs.

Ruby and Isabelle stepped into the room and continued their conversation. "I'm Anabaptist, but we refer to ourselves as Plain," Ruby said. "The Apostle Peter taught that believers should not focus on outward appearance but on their hearts, having a meek and quiet spirit."

The woman looked Ruby up and down and then said, "How well do you know Duncan?"

"Not well, really. We've worked together these last few months to maintain both of our farms." She quickly explained her predicament, adding that she was betrothed to a fellow Anabaptist named Paul.

That seemed to give Isabelle a measure of relief. Perhaps she feared Ruby had her sights on Duncan. "How in the world does he help much, though? With his injury."

"He actually does quite well," Ruby answered.

"Goodness, my parents didn't want me to stay in Philadelphia any longer, but I doubt if they guessed sending me to Lancaster would make me a farmer." She lowered her voice. "They were afraid if I stayed I'd fall for a 'Lobster' but don't tell Duncan that." Her eyes twinkled, and she laughed. "They were right."

Ruby smiled, guessing the woman wouldn't believe she was a Loyalist—or had been. She couldn't be now, not with Zachary fighting for the Patriots.

Not wanting to continue the conversation, she stepped farther into the room that was dimly lit from the light of the lamps on the landing. Isabelle followed.

"Goodness," she said, "it's not much." There was a narrow bed, basically a cot, and a couple of pallets on the floor.

Ruby said, "You can have the bed."

"Oh, no," Isabelle said. "You were here first. I'll sleep on the floor."

Ruby didn't respond. She couldn't imagine sleeping on the bed and letting Duncan's sister sleep on a pallet. Ruby started to step inside, planning to go to bed while Isabelle got something to eat and caught up with Duncan.

"Come back down with me," Isabelle said. "The more the merrier."

Ruby inhaled. She'd hardly fit in, listening to Duncan and Isabelle talk about their fine life.

"Please?"

"All right," Ruby replied. How wonderful for Duncan to get to see his sister, and how nice that Ruby would have a roommate for the night. The least she could do was sit with the two. And the truth was, she found Isabelle fascinating. She seemed so comfortable with herself, and so carefree—despite the war going on around her.

The three sat closest to the fire. Duncan asked Isabelle about their parents, who were doing fine. Shamefully, Ruby hadn't put much thought into his life. She knew his father was a business-man, but that was all.

Isabelle talked about Philadelphia, about how things had been before General Howe marched in with his troops. "We knew they were coming," Isabelle said. "So all of the supplies and weaponry were moved out, even the Liberty Bell. That made the British furious." She dropped her voice. "They've just started to move supplies in. Of course, we hid our food. Father had a false wall built in the cellar."

"Was it hard to leave the city?" Ruby asked.

"Yes, partly. But I'll survive. So far, the day has been fascinat-ing. We got a late start out of the city because—" She nodded her head toward the group of men at the far end of the table who came in with her. "They're all businessmen, headed to York to work out deals with the Patriots. Back in Philadelphia, they do deals with the British."

Ruby's mouth dropped open.

"Shhh," Duncan said.

Isabelle nodded. "That's the way of the world."

Ruby folded her hands together on the tabletop. That sort of duplicity and deceit were exactly why her people stayed apart from the world.

Isabelle took another bite of stew and then looked up at her brother, who sat directly across the table from her. "What do you hear from Jane?"

Ruby watched as a pained expression passed over Duncan's face.

Isabelle kept talking, as if she hadn't noticed her brother's response. "I haven't spoken with her in months, not since right after you left. I hoped she's written to you."

Duncan shrugged as if he didn't care about this Jane, but

Ruby was sure that he did. Or at least had. "We need to talk about you," Duncan said to Isabelle. "If you continue on the stage to Lancaster, I doubt Uncle Wallis will be able to collect you, even if you send a message. You'll have to hire a driver. Why don't you come to Valley Forge with us?"

Isabelle wrinkled her nose. "Do you have a carriage?"

"No," Duncan answered. "A wagon."

Isabelle pushed back her plate and folded her hands. "I'll go on to Lancaster and hire a driver to take me to the farm."

"Sister . . ."

"I've heard horrible things about Valley Forge," Isabelle said. "Bert told me all about it." She raised her eyebrows as she gazed at her brother.

"Oh?" Duncan said.

Isabelle nodded.

Duncan turned to Ruby. "I served with Bert—otherwise known as Captain McLeod. But now he's with the 1st Regiment that Zachary is with."

"Yes," Isabelle said. "He was at Valley Forge, but he left for York about a month ago. I'm assuming he made it. He was grateful not to have to stay at Valley Forge. I definitely don't want to go there from what Captain McLeod said, and, in fact, I was thinking of continuing on the coach to York." She raised her head and looked Duncan in the eyes again. "I'd like to see Bert again."

Duncan shook his head.

Isabelle smiled. "I'll tell him hello from you. I told him you were in Lancaster, but I'm surmising he didn't stop on his way to York."

"You knew he wouldn't," Duncan said.

"Well," Isabelle said. "You know he has to get over his guilt sometime. He didn't mean for you to get shot."

"Please." Duncan grabbed his cane. "Let's concentrate on matters at hand—not the past. What's done is done." He swung both of his legs over the bench and then leaned on the cane and stood. "Good night, Ruby."

She could barely see his face in the flickering light of the fire.

He turned toward Isabelle. "Good night, sister."

Isabelle smiled. "I'll see you in the morning."

After Duncan had reached the door, Isabelle directed her gaze on Ruby. "So how is he really doing? He didn't want to talk about Jane. He didn't want to talk about Bert. What does he like to talk about?"

Ruby shrugged. He hadn't mentioned Jane or Bert, but apparently both had contributed to his wounding, internally and externally. "We talk about the animals and preserving food. Butchering the hog. That sort of thing."

Isabelle wrinkled her nose.

"He's awfully kind," Ruby said. "To help me like this, by going to find my brother."

Isabelle drained her mug. "That's the way he was when we were small. Kind. But he hasn't been much of late."

"He traveled to Lancaster County to help your uncle."

"Oh, that wasn't his idea," Isabelle said. "That was Father's doing." She stood. "Goodness, our parents certainly manage to push us out of town, don't they?"

Isabelle grabbed one of the candles from the table, and the two women walked upstairs. Ruby insisted Isabelle take the bed, and finally the woman agreed to the offer. Then Ruby pushed a chair under the latch to the door.

"Good thinking," Isabelle said.

"Duncan and I are leaving at first light," Ruby said.

"The stage is too," Isabelle answered.

"Are you sure you won't come with us?"

Isabelle smiled. "If he was with anyone else, I fear I should. For propriety's sake. But considering you're betrothed, and—what do you call it?"

"Anabaptist."

"Yes. Well, I doubt I have to worry about the two of you at all." Isabelle grinned. "Not the way everyone keeps worrying about me."

Ruby could only guess at how worried Isabelle's parents must be about such a headstrong girl. Then again, if her family knew what Ruby was up to, they'd see her as headstrong too. Still, she couldn't help but be concerned about Isabelle.

"Wouldn't it be best for you to travel with your brother?"

Isabelle shrugged and for a moment resembled Duncan. "He'll join me soon enough."

Ruby stepped to the window, and Isabelle slid under the quilts on the bed. "What are you looking at?"

"My family's wagon," Ruby said. "Duncan is sleeping in it."

"Goodness," Isabelle said, "he really has turned into a farmer."

Ruby supposed Duncan was more of a farmer, at the moment, than anything. He certainly wasn't a soldier anymore. Nor a merchant. He'd done well managing his uncle's farm the last few months. He'd surprised both of them.

Once Ruby settled on the pallet, she tossed and turned, her thoughts drifting to Paul. She wished he were journeying with her. She'd feel cherished and loved instead of so Plain. He was used to the way she looked.

Soon, she would be with Paul in Canada, and Duncan would return to Philadelphia and his family. To Jane, whoever she was. He'd help his father oversee their businesses.

Of course, first they needed to find Zachary and get him

home. Then Ruby needed to nurse him back to health so he could take her to Canada. Step by step, she'd reclaim her life.

Isabelle's breathing slowed, and it was obvious she'd fallen asleep. Ruby could hear the laughter of the men below. Finally, their voices quieted and she drifted off to sleep too.

– 13 –

Ruby dreamt during the night that her Mamm stood out back at the home place, behind the original cabin, gazing at the neighbor's property. At the oak tree. Two people stood under it, a man and a woman. Ruby woke with a start. The room was dark, but she sensed it was near morning and rose quickly. As she stepped to the door, a slight knock startled her. She moved the chair and opened it to find a maid holding a pitcher of water. Ruby took it from her, washed at the basin, and then quietly said Isabelle's name.

The woman stirred, opened her eyes, and groaned. "It's not morning yet, is it?"

"Jah," Ruby answered. "I'm going to go on down to the fire." The room was icy cold, and she wanted to make sure Duncan wasn't waiting for her.

He was.

"How long have you been up?" she asked.

"I just came in." He stepped closer to the fire and leaned against his cane.

"Did you stay warm enough?" she asked.

"I have no complaints," he answered.

The same maid came out with two bowls of corn mush. They sat and had just begun to eat as Isabelle joined them.

"When will you get back to Uncle Wallis's farm?" Isabelle asked.

Duncan wrinkled his brow. "Day after tomorrow, God willing."

Isabelle seemed to weigh his answer. "I think I'll go on to York then."

Duncan shook his head. "That's not a good idea. Hire a driver in Lancaster and ask him to take you to the Wallis farm on Oak Road. Don't go see Bert—perhaps the two of us can go later."

A pout settled on Isabelle's face.

Duncan shook his head. "Trust me, sister. Please."

Isabelle nodded, but by the smile on her face, Ruby wouldn't be surprised if the girl actually wasn't in agreement.

Ruby couldn't imagine what it would be like to have Isabelle living next door. Would she help with the chores? Cook? Expect to be entertained? She'd find all of it much, much simpler than what she was used to. Ruby had never met anyone like Isabelle. She wouldn't mind having her close by, though. It would be nice to have another woman as a neighbor.

Ruby finished her bowl of mush, remaining silent as the other two talked. As soon as Duncan finished his breakfast, he pushed his bowl to the middle of the table and asked Ruby if she was ready to go.

"Jah," she answered, hoping by the end of the day they would have found Zachary. It was hard to be away from home. The Englisch ways were not her ways. As much as she appreciated Duncan's help, the two of them were as different as could be. And it was even worse with Isabelle.

Isabelle stood and walked around the table, giving Duncan a hug. "I'll see you soon." Then she turned her attention to Ruby.

"It's been a pleasure to meet you. I look forward to seeing you again." She grinned and then added, "Neighbor."

Ruby curtsied and said, "Likewise."

As she followed Duncan toward the door, she pulled her plain brown cape tighter around her shoulders, bracing for the cold.

Ruby commented about Isabelle and how remarkable it was they'd ended up at the same inn.

"Not really," Duncan said. "I'm not surprised Father forced her to leave Philadelphia."

"But what a coincidence," Ruby said, "that we ended up at the same inn on the same day."

"Yes," Duncan said. "That's true."

"Isabelle seems to be a kind person."

Duncan gave Ruby a sideways glance. "Isabelle is many things. Intelligent. Creative. Conniving . . ."

"Well, she was kind to me."

"Then perhaps you brought out the best in her," Duncan said. "I doubt it was of her doing."

They rode silently after that. The dark clouds from the day before had grown heavier. Snow would soon fly at the lower elevations. They didn't speak as they traveled until they stopped to water and feed the horses. After a small meal for themselves, they continued on.

It was midafternoon when Duncan waved at a wagon driver headed the other direction, gesturing for him to stop. "Are we close to Valley Forge?" he asked.

"Take a right at the next road," the man called out. "I just came from there. Delivered a load of cabbage."

"Thank you." Duncan tipped his hat and urged the horses to continue on.

Ruby said another prayer that they would soon find Zachary. Before long they were on a rutted road that, thankfully, was frozen. If they'd come a few days ago, they'd most likely be mired down in mud. The road headed away from the river and up toward the ridge. Smoke drifted down toward them. The sound of axes rang out in the distance. Most likely trees were being felled to build more cabins. Hopefully Zachary was under some sort of shelter.

When the road curved around for the last time, the camp came into view. Tents and hundreds of cabins lined the ridge with cooking fires scattered among them. Several women, bundled in capes and coats, tended food over the fires, and some appeared to be doing laundry, which surprised Ruby.

"Do the women serve among the men?" Ruby asked.

"They're camp followers," Duncan explained. "The soldiers couldn't survive without them. They cook, wash, and mend. Bandage wounds. Everything that makes life bearable. Last time I went to the inn, I heard that General Washington's wife is here too. Martha. She's sewing, nursing the sick, and doing everything she can."

"Goodness," Ruby said. "I wouldn't expect a fine lady like that to serve in such a way."

Duncan smiled wryly. "Fine ladies can be a surprise," he said, stealing a glance at Ruby. She had no idea what he was implying, but her face grew warm under his gaze.

Hundreds of horses were penned in a makeshift corral. Bedraggled soldiers wearing mud-covered uniforms worked on building more cabins.

Duncan asked a soldier about Zachary's regiment. The soldier pointed to the north, and Duncan drove the wagon along a wide trail. Snow began to fall as they continued on. Duncan asked again, and another soldier pointed to a group of wagons a few yards away. Duncan set the brake, climbed down, and then came around to Ruby and helped her, leaning on his cane as he did.

They walked, side by side, to the cabins. "We're looking for Zachary Bachmann," Duncan said to a soldier sitting on a stump, sharpening a knife.

The soldier nodded his head toward a cabin. "Look there."

Duncan led the way. Ruby's heart raced as she prayed for strength. Duncan pushed against the door. "Zachary Bachmann! Are you in here?"

A moan greeted them. Ruby followed Duncan into the cabin, squinting in the dim light. Another moan followed and then a deep, wracking cough.

She stepped inside. A fire in the middle of the cabin burned in a circle of stones, sending smoke up through a hole in the roof. But the interior was freezing—as cold as it was outside—besides being filled with smoke. "Zachary," Ruby said. "Is that you?"

"Have you come?" He was curled in a ball on a layer of hay that covered the bare ground. "I've prayed and prayed you would."

"Jah, it's me," Ruby said, "and Duncan Wallis. We've come to take you home."

"Not so fast." A gruff voice from the doorway startled Ruby. "He's not so bad. Others are worse. All he needs is another week of rest or so. Then he'll be fit as a fiddle."

Ruby turned toward the man, ready to tell him not one soldier she'd seen yet appeared as fit as a fiddle.

But Duncan grabbed her hand and said to the man. "Sir, perhaps you and I could speak in private while this sister tends to her brother?"

"Perhaps I don't have the time." The man's uniform was in better repair than any she'd seen so far.

Duncan pulled something from the pocket of his coat and held it out. Even in the dim light she could tell it was a flask. Scotch, she guessed. She'd never seen Duncan drink, despite his pain, or even smelled it on his breath. Perhaps he brought it along for such an occasion.

"Perhaps a drink together?" Duncan offered. "And we have food in the wagon too. For you and the other soldiers in Zachary's squad."

Ruby did her best to care for Zachary as she told him Mamm had passed. She couldn't tell in the dim light if tears filled his eyes, but his voice caught as he thanked her for caring for their mother and seeing to her burial. Ruby nodded in acknowledgment, swallowed hard, and then concentrated on his wounds. He had a gash across the back of his head that was bandaged with a rag. His left arm was riddled with open wounds, and his forearm was broken and held against him in a ratty sling. But the worst was his cough and how thin he was. When he'd left in early October, he was a strong and healthy young man. Now he was as weak as a baby.

"Has a camp physician seen you?" Ruby asked.

"No," he replied. "There aren't many."

"Do others have the cough?" she asked.

"Jah," he said. "Many do."

"Have you been eating?" she asked.

"I had a bit of soup yesterday."

She went outside the cabin to ask Duncan if he could locate some water, but he wasn't in sight. She asked a soldier walking by where she could find some. He pointed to a barrel a few cabins over. Unfortunately there was only a bit of brackish water in the bottom. She leaned in and scooped up what she could.

First she gave Zachary a drink and then tore a strip from her petticoat to use to wash his wounds. Then she tore more strips and bandaged them. After she finished, Duncan returned without the other man.

"We're free to go," he said.

"It was that easy?" Ruby asked.

Duncan nodded.

"For now." Zachary struggled to sit. "They'll expect me back as soon as I'm well though, isn't that correct?"

"Something like that," Duncan muttered.

Ruby frowned but then redirected her thoughts. It did no good to borrow trouble. Besides, by spring they'd be in Canada.

"We should get going." Duncan stepped closer to Zachary and leaned on his cane. "Can you walk? Unfortunately I can't carry you."

"I think so," Zachary said.

Ruby helped him up off the ground and then wrapped her arm around his waist. Duncan added as much support as he could on the other side. Together they shuffled out of the cabin. Zachary leaned against the wagon as Ruby made a bed in the back for him. Then she and Duncan helped Zachary as much as they could into the wagon. After she made him as comfortable as possible, she sat down beside him.

Duncan climbed on the bench and pulled the horses around, heading back to the road. Later, when they stopped to water the horses, Duncan said he thought it best if they camped for the night. "You two can sleep in the wagon bed and I'll sleep under it." He pulled off the road into a stand of trees. A creek ran nearby.

Duncan started a fire while Ruby stepped down to the creek and filled the bucket with icy water. After giving Zachary a drink, she watered the horses. Duncan said he'd unhitch and then feed them while she saw to their supper.

She had cold ham and more cheese for them to eat, and she fried corn cakes in the cast-iron skillet she'd brought along. She also heated water over the fire and used the little bit of tea she had left.

As Duncan sat on a rock by the fire, eating his supper, Ruby climbed into the wagon and helped Zachary eat. When he finished, she tucked the blankets around him and told him to sleep. By the time she joined Duncan, he'd finished eating and was stirring the fire.

As Ruby finished her tea, Duncan said, "Hopefully we can make it all the way home tomorrow."

"We'll have to see how Zachary does," Ruby answered. She knew all the jostling and bumping around was hard on her brother. She lowered her voice. "Who was the man you spoke with?"

"A sergeant."

"Did he say how Zachary was injured?"

"No," Duncan said. "But he did say that they had heavy losses at White Marsh. That was the last battle before they headed to Valley Forge."

"What do you think happened to Zachary?"

"He was clearly fired upon."

"What about his broken arm?"

"Perhaps he fell on it. Or a cannonball could have landed nearby and sent him flying."

Ruby nodded toward Duncan's leg. "How were you injured?"

He stared into the fire, and for a moment Ruby thought he

hadn't heard her. But then he winced, and she felt bad for asking him. Perhaps the memory was too difficult.

"I'm sorry," she said.

"No," he answered. "I don't mind you asking." He glanced up, and in the shadows from the fire she could see the hint of a smile on his face. Then it grew serious again.

"It was Christmastime, last year. The Battle of Trenton, the first one. We followed our commander-in-chief across the Delaware in icy conditions, and then we fought the Hessians."

Ruby had no idea who that was, and her expression must have given her ignorance away.

"German soldiers," Duncan said. "A contract militia hired by the British."

Ruby's stomach sank. It made no sense to her for one country to hire soldiers from another. She'd never understand the ways of men.

"Toward the end, as they retreated, it was obvious we'd won, something we sorely needed for morale. The platoon next to me, led by their captain, began celebrating too soon, and the Hessians got one more cannon shot off. It landed near me, sending shrapnel ripping through my leg. I feared I'd lose it at first."

"I'm sorry," Ruby said.

He shook his head. "Like I said, it could have been much worse." He shrugged. "I was fortunate. Many died. More were horribly wounded. Maimed. Severely crippled." He slapped his leg. "I was wounded just badly enough not to have to fight again."

"Jah," Ruby said. "Thanks be to God."

He shook his head. "I'd rather be able to help my fellow soldiers."

"Like Captain McLeod?"

Duncan shook his head a little. "He's not the man Isabelle thinks. In fact, he was a bit of a fool that day. If he'd kept fighting, I probably wouldn't have been injured."

"Oh?"

Duncan shook his head. "I shouldn't have said that. Forgive me."

It seemed Captain McLeod was the officer who led his men in the premature celebration. For a moment they were both silent, but then Ruby gathered her courage again and said, "Tell me about Jane."

"There's not much to tell," Duncan answered. "We grew up together. Probably similar to you and Paul. I thought she cared for me, but when I came back home wounded, it appeared she'd changed her mind."

"And she's a friend of Isabelle's?"

"Yes," Duncan said. "Best of friends." The fire had died down and Duncan pushed himself up with his cane, put another piece of wood on the fire, and then sat back down on the rock. "There are times I envy how simple your life seems." He met her eyes. "You seem so resolute. So sure of your path in life."

Her heart lurched. It was true that her family's expectations of her were clear. But there were moments when she felt less than sure about everything. She wouldn't admit that to Duncan, though. "Jah," she said. "That's true."

When he didn't respond, she said, "But surely there are lessons you have learned from your hardships during this last year."

His gaze met hers, and for a moment she feared she'd insulted him. But then he smiled a little and said, "Yes."

The flames of the fire flickered and the smoke shifted, obscuring his face some.

"Such as?" she asked.

He sighed. "I've learned how important it is to be honest with oneself. To know one's own heart."

She nodded, although she wasn't sure she knew hers all that well.

"And," he said, "I've learned that the hard things in life are the ones that mold us. Sometimes for the better. Sometimes for the worse. It's up to us. If we're willing, I believe God truly does use those hardships to make us better, to allow us to serve Him more."

An ache settled in Ruby's chest. Never once had Paul spoken about God's work in his life, not directly.

Duncan continued to stare at her. "Thank you for asking. It was good for me to give that subject some thought, to vocalize what I believe." He smiled, and an expression of calm settled on his face.

Ruby didn't feel as calm as Duncan appeared. Instead, she felt unsettled to have him share so easily with her, even though she'd asked the question. In that moment she felt a spiritual connection with him that she'd never experienced with Paul.

It was too much. She had no idea how to respond, so instead of trying, she stood quickly and gathered up their dishes and the skillet. She quickly cleaned them as Duncan continued to watch her. When she was done, she wished Duncan a good night and headed toward the wagon, her heart racing as she left him alone at the fire.

Just before dawn the snow began to fall again. Ruby woke to the wet flakes on her face and the shuffle of Duncan's cane and footsteps. She rose quickly, pulling her cape tight against the wet cold. Duncan worked at getting the fire started again.

"I'll water and feed the horses," Ruby said. After she finished, she hitched the horses to the wagon as she watched the few swirls of smoke from Duncan's fire. The snow was coming down too hard for it to take.

"Let's get going," Ruby said. "We can eat cheese and bread on the way."

At first the wagon rolled along just fine, but as the morning progressed and more snow fell, the going grew more difficult. A couple of times the wagon slid. Thankfully, Duncan was a good driver and kept the horses calm and moving forward. They passed the inn where they'd stayed two nights before.

By midafternoon the horses were struggling through the snow. Duncan stopped under a willow tree to let them rest. Zachary woke, and Ruby told him they'd only be delayed for a moment.

He assured her he was all right and pulled the blankets over his face. She tucked them tight around his body and then grabbed the buckets and told Duncan she'd get the water. She knew it would be impossible for him to go down a slippery bank.

Duncan came around to help her out of the back, but he slid on the wet snow and then steadied himself against the side of the wagon.

"I'm fine," Ruby said, hurrying over the back and then moving carefully.

Duncan held on to the edge, a disturbed expression on his face. Ruby quickly looked away.

The snow was deep going down the bank, and ice was forming on the edges of the creek. She broke it with the buckets, filled them as best she could, and then struggled back up the bank, spilling some of the water.

Once the horses were cared for, Ruby told Duncan to get

back on the bench. "I'll lead them for a bit," she said. "Perhaps that will help." They only had a couple of hours of daylight left. The last thing she wanted was for Zachary to spend the night out in the cold again.

She took long strides, plowing through the snow, pulling on the horses' harnesses as she did. The horses followed her lead. She glanced back at Duncan, and he smiled at her. She was thankful for the boots Dat had purchased for her before he died. Her feet finally grew warm, as did her face. After ten minutes or so, Duncan slowed the horses and told her to get back into the wagon. Instead of returning to the bed, she climbed up onto the bench. Duncan lifted the blanket and she slid underneath it. Again she felt self-conscious riding beside him, even with Zachary in the back.

Finally, she asked, "Do you think we'll make it home tonight?"

"I hope so," Duncan answered, then nodded toward the back. "How is Zachary doing?"

"About the same." Ruby didn't think he was any worse or any better. She pulled her cape tighter around her throat.

"Take all the blanket," Duncan said.

"No. I'm fine," Ruby said, "but thank you."

They left the main road and headed north toward their farms as dusk fell. Duncan asked if Ruby thought they should set up camp for the night and then go on in the morning.

"No," she said, "it will most likely only get worse."

Once darkness fell, Duncan stopped, and they managed to light the lantern. Immediately it cast a shadowy light across the snowy landscape. Ruby said a silent prayer of gratitude, realizing how tense she'd felt all day, afraid they wouldn't get home. Now they were almost there. She rubbed her hands together, and then asked Duncan if he wanted her to take the reins for a while.

"I'm doing fine," he said.

"How's your leg?"

"Surprisingly well," he answered.

She doubted he was telling the truth. They passed the minister's farm. A single light burned in the downstairs window. What would he think once he realized what she'd done?

The horses slowed even more, despite the fact that they were nearly home. They had to be exhausted. The road climbed a hill, and once they crested it, the horses picked up speed on the way down, but then an owl hooted as the road curved and Gunnar spooked.

"Easy boy," Duncan called out, pulling back on the reins. And then he called out, "Whoa!"

Instead of stopping, the horses lurched forward, but in the opposite direction. Zachary stirred in the back as the wagon began to slide.

"Hold on," Duncan said.

Ruby did, looking back at Zachary and grabbing the edge of the bench as the wagon slid toward the ditch.

Zachary was sitting up now, his eyes wide open. "Whoa!" he shouted, his voice surprisingly strong. "Gunnar! Gustaf! Whoa!"

First Gunnar stopped and then with another lurch, Gustaf followed suit. Ruby exhaled. The wagon kept sliding, though.

"Jump down," Duncan said to Ruby, his voice still calm.

She slid to the edge of the bench and then leapt, landing in the soft snow on the road, just as the wagon, back first, slid into the ditch. The horses, wild-eyed and stamping their hooves, stayed on the road. Ruby rushed toward them and grabbed Gunnar's harness.

"Careful." Duncan had managed to stay on the bench. Zachary raised his head again and sat up straight, wrapped a blanket around himself, and climbed to the road side of the wagon. It tipped forward with his weight, bringing the rear wheels out of the ditch, suspended in the air.

"Pull the horses," Zachary said, his voice not quite as calm as Duncan's.

Ruby complied as Duncan snapped the reins. Gustaf sidestepped but then followed Gunnar's lead. Slowly the wagon inched forward and the back wheels landed on the ground. Ruby didn't stop until the wagon was in the middle of the road. Without saying anything, Zachary climbed back under the pile of blankets.

"I'll keep leading them," Ruby said.

Duncan nodded, a pained look on his face.

Ruby continued on, talking softly to the horses as she walked and silently thanking God. The moon rose higher, over the bank of clouds, and a few stars began to shine. They'd averted a tragedy. If the wagon had slid a little farther, both Zachary and Duncan could have been injured, along with the horses.

An hour later, they passed the Wallis farm, where lamps burned in each of the two windows, and then turned toward the Bachmann barn.

"We'll get Zachary inside," Duncan said, "and then unhitch the horses."

As they helped Zachary through the door, Ruby's heart throbbed as the loss of Mamm hit her again. The house was dark and cold, as if it no longer had a soul.

They helped Zachary into a chair.

"I'll build a fire," Ruby said, "and then meet you in the barn."

Duncan shuffled back out the front door, and then she heard the horses' neigh and the wagon roll forward.

By the time she reached the barn, Duncan had the horses in their stalls. Ruby hauled water from the spring to the trough while Duncan brushed them and then fed them. Next she checked on the calf in the back of the barn, where Old Man Wallis must have managed to move him when the snow started.

When Duncan finished, Ruby thanked him. "You made getting Zachary possible," she said. "I can't express my gratitude to you. You've been more than a good neighbor—you've been a dear friend."

Duncan nodded but didn't say anything.

They walked together to the barn door, and then he started toward the Wallis home, while Ruby trudged back through the snow to the back door, missing her Mamm again. But she had Zachary.

He was still wrapped in the blanket, sitting by the fire.

"How are you feeling?" she asked.

"Better, now that I'm home."

As she examined his arm in the dim light, he said, "I see you were able to accept Duncan's help after all."

"Jah," she said. "I couldn't have gotten through the last months without him. He helped me harvest the corn, butcher the hog, do the chores. . . ." She swiped at a stray tear. "He helped bury Mamm." She raised her head. "And I never would have been able to retrieve you by myself."

"My initial impression of him was right then?"

Ruby nodded. "It seems so."

Zachary met her eyes. "You seem taken with him."

Ruby shook her head. "Indebted, jah, but that is all."

Zachary smiled a little. "I don't remember you looking at Paul the way you do at Duncan."

Ruby took a step backward. "You're teasing me."

He shook his head.

She put her hand to her throat. "Don't say such a thing, Zachary. It isn't true."

He shrugged. "Perhaps you aren't being honest with yourself."

"I'm to marry Paul, as soon as we can get to Canada."

Zachary sighed. "Don't marry someone you don't love, sister."

She cared for Paul. And she'd made a commitment to him. She loved him—or at least she had. She couldn't be so frivolous as to throw away all that she had with Paul for her fleeting feelings toward Duncan, for an Englischman. Too much was at stake for that.

Zachary continued to stare at her.

Lots of people, she was sure, married someone they didn't love. She shrugged. "It doesn't matter whether I love Paul or not. We can still have a good marriage."

Zachary shook his head and his eyes grew sad, but he didn't say any more.

Finally, against her better judgment, she asked, "What are you thinking?"

"About when I joined the army. About how certain I was I could fight, but when I was faced with it I realized it went against everything I believed in. I stood facing the enemy, who wasn't the enemy at all, but another man, probably younger than me, in a red coat. Far away from home. Scared. And fighting for what? A king he'd never meet?"

Ruby shook her head. "What does that have to do with me marrying Paul?"

"I went against my conscience," Zachary said. "And I regretted it every day. Especially when I pulled the trigger and shot that young man." His eyes filled with tears.

Ruby stepped toward her brother and placed her hand on

his shoulder. She felt his sorrow and sympathized, but her marrying Paul was a very different matter. She'd heard of women who married men they didn't love, but they came to love their husbands—or at least to respect them. Perhaps she'd never truly loved Paul, but she'd had feelings for him. She was sure those would return, once she was far away from Duncan.

"I have one more thing to say," Zachary said. "You may think you'll be fine marrying Paul, and perhaps you would have been if you'd never met Duncan. But you can't go back, Ruby. You can't pretend none of this happened."

She turned away from her brother and toward the fire, her eyes burning as she did her best not to think about what he'd just said. He had no idea what he was talking about.

As she put another piece of wood on the fire, a knock on the front door startled her. The only person it could possibly be was Duncan. She walked slowly, not wanting to seem too eager, even though her heart raced.

When she opened it, a soldier dressed in a well-kept blue uniform stood before her. But behind him were Duncan and Isabelle.

"Come in," she said, alarmed.

Duncan must have sensed her fear because he said, "This is Captain McLeod. Isabelle mentioned him at the inn."

"Pleased to meet you." Ruby curtsied a little and then stepped aside so all three could enter the cabin. "Come to the fire," she said.

She started to introduce Zachary to Captain McLeod but by the look on her brother's face it seemed he was already familiar with the man. He struggled to stand and said, "Captain McLeod."

"Glad to see you're on the mend," the man said. "You'll be returning to the 1st Regiment, Company H with me in the morning."

"But we've just arrived! And . . . and he's ill," Ruby exclaimed.

The man stepped forward and put his hand against Zachary's forehead. "No fever. No doubt the cough I heard about is fabricated."

"His arm is broken," Ruby said.

Zachary let go of the blanket, showing his arm in the sling.

"I've seen worse," the man said. "He can still work with the horses. And drive a wagon."

Duncan cleared his throat. "I'll take his place."

"No," Ruby said. "Not with your leg the way it is."

"I can work with horses and drive a wagon," Duncan said. "I've proven it over the last few days. Maybe not as well as Zachary, but I can get by."

"I can't let you do that," Zachary said. "I don't want you to take my place."

"Yes," Isabelle said, stepping to Duncan's side. "Don't be ludicrous. You'd break my heart—and Mother and Father's too."

"That's just it," Duncan said. "If something happened to me, you and Mother and Father would have each other. All Ruby has is Zachary."

That wasn't entirely true. She had Hans and Daniel too. And Paul. Her heart fell. But neither felt like family. Not the way Zachary did. Not the way Duncan—

She stopped. She couldn't choose between her brother and her—her what? Neighbor? Friend? Her heart began to ache, and she turned toward Captain McLeod.

He put his hand on his hip. "Frankly, I don't care who accompanies me. But one of you must. I've been put in charge of rounding up our scattered troops. How fortunate that I'll be able to collect one so soon."

–14–

Jessica

Early the next morning, as I mulled over Ruby's story, a driver picked up Leisel and took her to the hospital so she'd be there before Arden's surgery. It was scheduled for 6:30 a.m. As Milton, Amos, and I did the milking, I prayed for Arden and for the surgeon. And for Vi, who didn't plan to go up until later in the day. None of us spoke much. I checked the office again for the fracking plans but once again couldn't find them. After we finished with the milking, Milton asked if I'd work on the tractor so he could start plowing on Monday. He could get more done with it than the mules. I told him I would the next day.

By midmorning, I changed into my Englisch clothes and started for Harrisburg. I couldn't imagine what my office mates would think if I came in wearing a cape dress. As I drove, I thought of Ruby leading the horses home with Zachary in the back of the wagon and Duncan on the bench. Aenti Suz had insisted on stopping the story last night even though I'd begged her to continue.

I couldn't help but compare Duncan to Tom. Both had gone out of their comfort zones to help an Amish girl. Well, I was an ex-Amish girl—but I couldn't help but be grateful to Tom. He'd been nothing but good to me. Patient as I learned the Englisch ways, both at work and in our relationship. He'd been so generous with his time, coming to Lancaster for the funeral. And he'd saved the day helping with the CPR on Arden and keeping him alive until the paramedics arrived.

Another week and I'd be back in Harrisburg for good, moving forward with my life. In fact, I felt a freedom I hadn't before. And it wasn't due to Dat's death. Seeing my Mamm and Marie again convinced me more than anything that I didn't want to live the Amish life anymore. Sure, seeing Silas brought up my old feelings for him. But that was all in the past.

Hopefully some good would come with my time at home. I knew spending time with Leisel had benefitted me, and I already felt closure as far as Silas. God could bring good from anything, even my time with Mamm and Marie. I truly believed that. I said a prayer for each of my family members. Then I realized I was praying for Silas, too, and my face grew warm. I hadn't meant to do that.

I stopped praying for Silas and consciously switched to praying for Tom. But soon my mind wandered off to Ruby and Duncan again, and Paul. I knew what was at stake for her. I was dying to find out what she decided.

Surely Paul would come after her soon—unlike Silas had done for me. But Duncan was so willing to sacrifice for her. Then again, if he ended up at Valley Forge, perhaps he didn't survive.

An odd gasp erupted out of my mouth. A sob. Then another. I gripped the steering wheel harder. I thought I'd cried myself dry over Dat but more tears started to fall. I pulled off on a side road and cried some more, not entirely sure what I was even crying about. The last week had been so emotional.

Finally, the crying done, I flipped down my visor and looked in the mirror. I hadn't put on any mascara at the house. I decided I might as well or I'd look as if I hadn't slept in a week, so I dug in my purse for my makeup. I never wore a lot—just a little foundation, eye shadow, and mascara. A little color on my lips. I had to admit, I hadn't missed wearing makeup while on the farm. In Harrisburg, I didn't leave my apartment without it.

Twenty minutes later, I pulled into the parking lot at work and parked next to Tom's car. After I climbed out of my car, I glanced down at my low-heeled black pumps, afraid they might be speckled with mud. They weren't. My black skirt wasn't wrinkled either. I slung my bag over my shoulder and headed for the building, feeling confident. Jah, I truly was an Englisch girl. No doubt about it.

Tom wasn't at his cubicle, so I continued on down the hall to my desk. The Stoltz file was just where I left it—in my top drawer. I slipped it into my bag, checked in with Deanna to let her know what I was doing, and then waited for Tom by his cubicle.

A few minutes later, he bounded up to me, his coffee cup in his hand. "You're here."

"I said I would be."

He put the cup down. "Did you get the file?"

I nodded.

"Ready for lunch?"

I nodded again.

"How about the sandwich shop on Fourth Street?" he asked.

"Perfect," I answered.

"I'll drive," he said.

He always drove. "I'll drive too," I said. "I should leave from there, instead of coming back."

"Of course," he answered.

Lunch was fine. The sandwich shop only had ten tables and was one of those places where you pay when you order at the counter. I got the chef salad because it was easy to eat, and I didn't have to worry about spilling soup or having the middle come out of my sandwich.

Being with Tom was comfortable. There was no drama. No backbiting. No mean looks shot my way. Tom said work was going fine. He nodded toward my bag where the file was peeking out. "Thank you for going to meet the Stoltz family."

"I'm happy to do it," I answered. "It's a nice diversion."

"Let me know if you think the story is worth pursuing. If so, I'll do the interview."

I nodded.

"Hey," Tom said. "I really enjoyed meeting your family. All of them." He smiled, a little wryly. "They're not nearly as bad as you make them out to be."

My mouth dropped open, but then I realized he was joking. The truth was, I hadn't been negative about my family to Tom. As much as they frustrated me, my loyalty was greater than that. "Well, let's just say you brought out the best in them."

He grinned. "A heart attack? Don't flatter me."

"Well, that was simply unfortunate." I pushed my empty salad bowl to the middle of the table.

Tom finished his water and then said, "I'd better get back to work."

I stood and bused my bowl, cutlery, and glass. Then I slipped into my coat and grabbed my bag. As we walked out of the sandwich shop, I said, "I'll see you next week."

"Ditto," he answered. "I hope the rest of the time with your family goes well."

"I hope the rest of your day . . ." My voice trailed off. He was already at the corner.

He waved and called out, "Bye!"

I stood still for a moment and then shuffled along to my car, feeling dejected. But why? Did I secretly hope Tom would beg me not to go back to Lancaster? As if a week was that big of a deal? Maybe I needed some extra comfort. Maybe he felt as if I didn't. But how could he know? I hadn't said what I needed.

When I reached my car, I opened the file and then entered the Stoltz address into the navigation app on my phone. That was one thing I could, hopefully, do for Tom—get an Amish farmer to talk.

In no time, I left Harrisburg far behind and was back in the farmland that I loved. The Stoltz farm was east of my family farm, off Highway 30. As I drove, my thoughts fell to Ruby again. And once I turned on Highway 30, I realized it was the route she would have taken to Valley Forge. Of course I knew it wasn't the exact route. I guessed a lot had changed in the last two hundred and forty years. But it was the same general vicinity.

I turned off the highway, onto Garden Lane, and then a short time later arrived at the Stoltz farm. It consisted of the typical large white house, several outbuildings—a barn, a shed, and a chicken coop—a large pasture, fields, and a strip of willow trees along a creek. I guessed it was the average seventy acres or so that most Amish farms were in Lancaster County.

After parking, I grabbed my bag and climbed out of my car. As I approached the house, a man walked out of the shed, a red rag in his hand. I called out, "*Guder Daag,*" and headed toward him. He appeared to be in his late sixties, maybe early seventies, and walked with a significant limp.

In English, I explained whom I worked for and why I'd stopped by.

"*Ich non fashtay,*" he said in Pennsylvania Dutch, telling me he didn't understand.

"*Mei Englisch?*" I asked.

He smiled wryly. "I don't have anything to say to you," he replied, still speaking in Pennsylvania Dutch. His tone was polite, but his words were clear. He seemed both timid and gruff all at the same time.

I responded in Pennsylvania Dutch, saying his story could help others.

He looked at me, a hint of smile in his eyes. "You speak Plain even though you're dressed Englisch. Who are you?"

"Jessica Bachmann. My family owns a farm near Leacock."

"One of Augustus Bachmann's daughters?"

I nodded. "Jah, the oldest." Of the living, anyway, but not of the faithful.

"I heard about you," he said. He took off his hat and added, "I was sorry to hear about your Dat passing."

I accepted his condolences. After a moment of silence, I told him that my interest in his experience was both professional and personal. "It seems my brother may have or is entertaining the idea of fracking on our property."

He raised his eyebrows. "Your property?"

"Well, our family farm."

"But obviously you've left."

"That's true," I replied. "But I'm still concerned about the land."

By the skeptical look on his face, I guessed he didn't believe I had a right to be.

"Could I ask you a few questions?"

He nodded toward the shed. "I'm working on my tractor. We can talk in there."

I followed him inside. The place was as tidy as I would expect, and the faint scent of gasoline hung in the air. The tractor was ancient, even older than ours.

"I'm just changing the oil," he said, and proceeded to awkwardly sit down on the mechanic creeper and then slide under the vehicle.

I started asking my questions. Bit by bit his story unfolded. A pickup truck hit his wagon, throwing him out into a ditch, twenty years ago. The accident broke his back, and it took years for him to recover his mobility. He and his wife were childless, so he leased out his land because he couldn't farm it and didn't have any offspring to help.

"But one doesn't make as much leasing out land as farming it," he said. "It became hard to make ends meet."

When he was approached by a fracking operation, he sent them away. But they kept coming back. Finally, he listened to their proposal and decided it was the financial boost he and his wife needed. They'd been praying for an answer to their money problems.

He rolled back out from under the tractor, dragging a gallon jug full of oil. "This doesn't matter, not in the long run, but I found a year after I signed the contract that they paid me seventy percent less than my Englisch neighbor."

"Oh dear," I said.

"Jah. I spoke with a lawyer who said I could sue for fraud, but you well know we don't sue."

215

Obviously so did the fracking company.

He stood and placed the oil on the shelf under his tools. With his back to me, he said, "The actual drilling wasn't a problem, but what it did to our well was." He turned around slowly.

"What happened?"

"First the water grew cloudy. Then there was a funny odor." I told him the story I'd read, about the farmer who lit his tap water on fire.

He smiled. "I tried that—but that wasn't the case with our water. It seemed chemicals from the fracking process had leeched into our well. Mildred started boiling it, but it seems maybe not soon enough. Or perhaps boiling didn't make a difference."

"Why?" I asked. "What happened?"

"She was diagnosed with breast cancer last year." He shrugged. "We can't prove it's from the well water. She's sixty-seven. Perhaps it was age-related and inevitable. . . ." His voice trailed off.

"Is she going through treatment?"

"She did," he answered. "But the cancer is aggressive, not like some. . . ." Again his voice trailed off.

"I'm sorry." I blinked back tears. It sounded as if Mildred was all he had. "Sharing your story could help others. Amish and Englisch alike."

He started to speak and then stopped. Finally he said, "I'd like to think about it. I'll speak to Mildred and then make a decision."

"Of course," I said. I gave him a card with my cell phone number on it. "Could I stop by in a few days?"

"Jah," he answered. "We're home most all the time."

"What about your land now?" I asked. "Are you leasing it out?"

"Some of it. I'm farming some too. Like I said, we don't have any children. . . ." His voice trailed off as his hand fell to the small of his back. "I'm still crippled up some but better than I used to be."

"Oh? What made the difference?"

"Your Dat," he answered. "He gave me some supplements that eased the pain, taught me some exercises, and recommended a good chiropractor. All of that helped."

Tears stung my eyes again. "I'm so glad," I said. "Thank you for telling me."

As he walked me out of the shed, a slight woman, a scarf tied under her chin, stepped out onto the porch. "John," she called out.

My heart swelled.

"Coming," he called back.

"Could I meet Mildred?" I asked.

"Jah," John answered. "But she tires easily."

"Of course," I answered. "I'd just like to say hello."

I followed John up the steps and shook Mildred's bony hand after he introduced me. She smiled sweetly. When John told her I was Gus Bachmann's daughter, she squeezed my hand again and told me how sorry she was to hear about his passing. "Tell your mother hello," she said. "She's such a sweet woman. I know God will use this trial to draw her closer to Him." Instead of looking at me as she spoke, she glanced at her husband.

He pursed his lips but didn't say anything.

Mildred patted my hand, let go of it, and then pulled her shawl tighter. "It's so cold today."

"You should get inside," I said, "and I need to get going."

"Please come in," she said. "I'll make some tea."

"I'd love to," I said, "but I need to be on my way." I quickly explained about Arden's heart attack. "I'm going to stop by the hospital."

"Oh goodness," she said. "So many trials."

I nodded. "But God is with us."

"Jah," she answered. "He will see you through."

I thanked John for his time and said I'd see him next week. He nodded and then followed Mildred into the house.

As I drove away, I thought of our property, of our well. And I thought of my Mamm. What if Arden went ahead with the fracking and she got breast cancer? Or Vi? Or Marie or Leisel? I shuddered.

At least Arden would get a fair price. There was nothing timid about him. He'd find out what others were paid and expect as much or more. I headed west toward the hospital instead of north toward our farm. I hadn't planned to go see Arden until the words came out of my mouth. But it was a good idea. He'd be out of surgery and hopefully out of recovery and back in the ICU. If he couldn't speak with me, I could at least talk with Leisel.

As I knocked on the door to Arden's room in the ICU, my palms grew sweaty. Perhaps it wasn't a good idea. Perhaps he wouldn't be happy to see me. Perhaps he'd ask me to leave.

Leisel's sweet voice called out, "Come in."

I pushed the door open and stepped into the room. Arden was in the bed with his eyes closed. Leisel stood at the window. I greeted her and then in a whisper asked how the surgery went.

"*Gut*," Leisel said. "The surgeon said it was successful."

Someone had trimmed Arden's beard—most likely to keep it out of the way during surgery. "Did Vi come with you?" he asked, without opening his eyes or saying hello. His voice was weak.

"No," I answered.

He opened his eyes and then asked, "Why are you dressed that way?"

"I drove up to Harrisburg to retrieve a work file—and then made a visit."

His eyebrows shot up. "What kind of visit?"

"It's nothing," I said.

"I doubt that," he responded. "You've always got something going on."

"A work-related visit." Already, I regretted coming. "It's not a big deal."

He raised the bed a little. "Whom did you see?"

"Arden," I said. "You just had open-heart surgery. You should be telling me how long your incision is, not grilling me."

"Jessica, answer me. Whom did you see?"

"John and Mildred Stoltz."

"Off Highway 30?"

I nodded.

"About the fracking on their land?"

I nodded again.

"You're meddling," he said.

"No," I answered. "It's a work assignment."

He grunted, as if in disgust. "Don't believe what he said. There's no evidence."

"How do you know what he said?"

"It's all over the county. That he blames his wife's cancer on the fracking."

I shook my head. "No, he blames it on the contaminated well water caused by the fracking."

Arden rolled his eyes. "He doesn't have any proof."

"The water was tested. It shows 2-Butoxyethanol and chloride, among other chemicals—"

"—and natural gasses and hydrocarbons too," he inter-rupted. "His well was probably poorly built, and he's too prideful to admit it."

My jaw dropped. Once I recovered and was able to speak again, my voice was at a higher pitch. "It seems his well was fine for years. Most likely, the chemicals were introduced into the well water by the fracking."

Arden shook his head. "I've done a lot of research into this. It doesn't matter whether they were or not—there's no proof the chemicals caused the cancer. Most likely, it's genetic."

I crossed my arms.

"You don't see us blaming Dat's cancer on anything. Or my heart attack. The Lord allows trials and disease. We weren't made to live forever."

I pursed my lips together. "Cases seem to indicate there could be a correlation between fracking, contaminated wells, and cancer. Clean water is the basis of sustainable life. Why take any chances?"

Arden steepled his fingers on the pillow across his chest. "If it was the well water, wouldn't John have come down with some sort of cancer too? Why just his wife?"

"Because cancer isn't equitable," I answered. "All sorts of factors can come into play. Perhaps the contaminants are more likely to cause breast cancer than other cancers."

"There's no proof," he said again.

"I can show you case studies. And it's not just breast cancer. There are cases of enlarged ovaries. And spleen damage, in both women and men."

His face turned red. "I'm not interested in pseudo-science." He was the most contentious man I knew.

Leisel stepped to his side. "Don't get worked up about this."

"I'm not," he snapped.

"Jah," I said. "I'm sorry." I shot Leisel a concerned look. She shrugged.

A tense silence settled in the room.

Arden turned toward Leisel. "Did Vi call back?"

"Not yet," she answered.

He frowned again. "How about Amos? Has she been spending time with him?"

"Goodness, Arden," Leisel said. "What a thing to ask. I haven't seen her say more than hello to him."

My face warmed at the memory of what Amos told me, about him and Vi being sweet on each other way back when. Arden was still jealous. And worried.

"What do you know?" Arden asked me.

"The same as Leisel," I answered, assuming he was asking what I knew of the present. "I've not seen Amos and Vi having any kind of conversation." I stepped forward. "It can't be good for you to fret." He must have been in horrible pain.

"Jah, enough of this," Leisel said. "No one wants you to worry. Vi's probably on her way here now."

She met my eyes. "Could you pick up rolled oats on your way home? Mamm mentioned last night that she wanted to make a berry crisp for supper. I told her I'd stop, but I may stay until late. Amos said he'd get me, but we'll see. . . ."

"Sure," I muttered but didn't move.

"You should go now," she said. "The sooner Mamm has all of her ingredients the better."

"All right," I answered, getting Leisel's hint that I needed to leave. It had been foolish of me to stop by.

"I don't want Amos coming to visit," Arden said, his voice barely a whisper.

"I'll make sure to tell him that," I responded, unable to check the snarky tone in my voice.

"Bye," Leisel said.

"Bye," I responded, my voice finally contrite. Ashamed, I left the room.

After I'd stopped by the store and filled up a bag with three-minute oats from the bulk bin, I headed on home. As I pulled up, I spied Amos talking with someone along the fence, to the side of the Dawdi Haus.

I parked and then walked to the house, swinging the bag of oats in my hand. But instead of going up to the front door, I walked to the side of the house and peeked around the corner. It was Vi standing with Amos. I hurried into the house. No one was around. I dropped the oats on the kitchen counter and then went upstairs to change into my dress.

When I returned downstairs, I noticed the door to Dat's study was open. I pushed on it a little. Mamm stood at the window, spying on Vi and Amos, I guessed.

"Hello," I said.

She turned. "Oh, you're back."

I nodded. "I brought oats."

"Oats?"

"For the crisp you wanted to make. Leisel asked me to pick some up."

Mamm shook her head. "I have plenty of oats. Besides, I didn't plan to make a crisp."

My face grew warm for the second time in an hour. Obviously, Leisel had thought quickly on her feet to come up with an excuse for me to leave.

A blur of blue went by the window. Vi, walking by herself. Mamm turned again.

"Everything all right?" I asked.

She nodded and held up a rag. "I was just dusting in here."

I told her that I'd stopped by the Stoltz place and that John and Mildred had said hello.

"Oh, that's nice," she said. "How is Mildred doing?"

"She's thin."

Mamm nodded. "I think she's probably your Dat's age. Cancer is such a horrible disease."

I nodded and stepped toward her, putting my arms around her before I realized what I was doing. For a moment I was afraid she wouldn't hug me back. But she did. Tightly. And then she began to cry on my shoulder. I thought of Ruby and her Mamm. Mine wasn't nearly as sweet, but for the moment she needed me—for the first time in all my life, it seemed, since the day I was born.

−15−

After the evening chores were completed, Vi and her children ate at their house, and Aenti Suz said she wasn't feeling well and planned to go straight to bed, which left only Marie and Gail at the big table with Mamm during supper. Amos and I sat at our own private table, as we'd come to call it.

There was no berry crisp for dessert, and Mamm remained quiet all through the meal.

Afterward, she went straight to her room while I helped Marie and Gail clean up. We worked mostly in silence and it seemed to take forever, especially considering how few people actually ate the meal, but the leftover stew had cemented on the bottom of the Dutch oven, and the sticky bun pan from breakfast had been put back in the oven and forgotten, and then Marie insisted that we needed to sweep the living room and kitchen and wipe down the cupboards.

While I swept, Marie and Gail worked on the cupboards, chatting as they did. I half listened as I started in the living room. Their conversation soon turned to Silas. "He's sensitive is all," Gail said. "You know that."

Marie responded, "Well, it wasn't as if what we said wasn't true."

"But we shouldn't have said it," Gail said. "Silas was right."

Marie shook her head. "There's no reason to shy away from the truth. Silas shouldn't have responded the way he did."

Gail didn't say anything more.

I began sweeping around the table.

Marie shifted to the cupboards by the refrigerator. "I know you don't agree."

"No, I don't. It's who Silas is. He's kind and gentle. He doesn't like to hear anyone spoken ill of." Gail glanced toward me. I ducked my head.

She lowered her voice. "I know it wasn't easy for him to speak up like that. It took me a while to realize it, but I'm proud of what he did."

"Quitting? Letting all of us down? You're proud of that?"

Gail hesitated again but then said, "Well, I think he tends to be too soft-spoken at times. Or did. It's good to know he can stand up for what he believes in."

Marie exhaled sharply. "But that's exactly what he shouldn't do. He's putting his own pride before what's best for our family, for our community." Marie glanced over her shoulder.

I was now sweeping the floor on the kitchen side of the table.

"Shhh," she said to Gail.

I smiled but with my head down. Silas had stood up for me, and Gail found it endearing. It made me soften toward Gail. Maybe she wasn't as much of a follower of Marie as I'd first feared. And perhaps Dat was right. Silas was only nineteen when I left. Perhaps he had grown into being his own man after all.

Marie's voice softened. "Don't worry. He'll come around— and all of this won't have any effect on the two of you."

Gail's voice was nearly a whisper. "It already has."

Perhaps Marie didn't hear, or if she did, she didn't respond. Instead, she started humming "Amazing Grace" and then after a few minutes started singing it. She had the prettiest voice out of us girls. ". . . how sweet the sound," she sang. "That saved a wretch like me."

Gail joined in and I did too, quietly under my breath. ". . . but now am found. Was blind but now I see."

If only I could *see* again. But I was more blinded by my hurts than ever. What would it take for me to be released from them? A complete new life in Harrisburg? Marrying Tom? Our own family? Never returning to Lancaster again?

I stopped singing and mulled over *"And grace my fears relieved"* as I finished up the sweeping. I'd been hurt by my family, but somehow those injustices had turned into fears. Fear that I didn't fit in. Fear that no one cared about my opinion. Fear that they'd abandoned me.

Grace was undeserved assistance from God. I hadn't believed His divine care could right the injustice I felt, that it could heal my hurt and ultimately relieve my fears. Instead, I'd fled as fast as I could.

Marie and Gail were halfway through singing "The Old Rugged Cross" by the time I finished the sweeping. As I headed out the door to the back porch, the words "In the old rugged Cross, stain'd with blood so divine, A wondrous beauty I see . . ." followed me. I'd stopped seeing that wondrous beauty when I'd left. Maybe it was because I wasn't working on the farm, out in nature, anymore. Maybe it was the fear I felt. Maybe it was being away from my family and community. And Silas. For whatever reason, I didn't appreciate the miracle of redemption, the beauty of the Cross the way I had as a child and young adult.

A verse we'd memorized in school, that I'd learned faster than Silas, came to mind. *"Fear thou not; for I am with thee: be not dismayed; for I am thy God: I will strengthen thee; yea, I will help thee. . . ."* I'd memorized it, but had I really learned it?

Feeling restless, I hoped Amos hadn't left to get Leisel yet, hoping I could ride along. He had a flight out of Philadelphia the next evening, and I'd hoped to spend more time with him, but his car was gone.

I wandered back to the barn, looking for a place of comfort. One of the workhorses neighed and then a cat meowed. I headed up the ladder to the hayloft, using my phone's flashlight app. Then I headed to the far end and scooped up a barn kitten that had somehow found her way up to the loft. She was young enough that she hadn't grown wild yet.

I settled on a bale and stroked the kitten's soft gray fur. She started purring. As a girl, I used to retreat to the hayloft to have time alone. I thought back to the medley of songs going through my head, and then landed on the lyrics to "Amazing Grace" again, to the line *"And grace my fears relieved."* Silas used to help relieve my fears because he was the one who had shown me grace, over and over. How many times had Mamm shamed me about her believing I'd rushed through my housework or some other perceived wrong, only to have Silas comfort me and speak grace into my life?

And it wasn't just through his words. It was through his example of living a grace-conscious life too. I knew he prayed when he plowed. I knew, when he pulled a calf, that he thought the birth of a newborn was the most amazing miracle in the world. And I knew, when he walked through the woods, that he always sang "How Great Thou Art." All of those things had inspired me to pray, acknowledge the miraculous, and sing praises too.

But the truth was, I'd hardly sung at all the last three years. Jah, I'd mouthed the words in church with Tom, but I hadn't sung. My soul hadn't sung, not like in the song.

I hummed the tune to "How Great Thou Art," the words floating through my mind. *"Then sings my soul, My Savior, God, to Thee. How great Thou art; How great Thou art."*

I shivered at the words, and at admitting that my spiritual life had been dry as a lonely desert ever since I'd left. I'd only been going through the motions.

I shivered again. Perhaps it was just because of the cold. The shutters of the window were open, giving me a view of the house and the driveway. A light still shone in the kitchen window. I imagined Marie and Gail sitting at the table playing a game of Scrabble. I wondered if Silas would have joined them before.

A car started up the drive. I imagined it being Tom. That he just couldn't stay away. That he was so interested in the Stoltz case he couldn't wait until next week. Or that he'd come to do whatever he could to help me, hoping I would return to Lancaster sooner. I cringed. When did I start thinking of myself as needing to be rescued?

The car parked, and just before the lights turned off I could make out Leisel climbing out of the driver's door. I leaned forward, not trusting what I'd just seen, but then everything went dark. Her voice and Amos's carried, but I couldn't make out what they said. Both car doors slammed and then, I assumed, they walked to the house, but I couldn't actually see them.

I'd forgotten how inky black the nights were on the farm when the sky was clouded over. I'd grown used to city streetlights. As my eyes adjusted, I made out a few faint stars where the clouds had thinned. The kitten yawned and snuggled closer. I cradled her in my arms, tucking her against my chest.

A few minutes later, someone opened and then closed the back door of the house. Then a beam shone brighter than a flashlight. I guessed it was Amos and he was using his cell phone app. The beam made its way toward the barn and then disappeared. A couple of minutes later, Amos called my name.

"Up here," I answered.

When he reached me, he said, "Marie thought you'd be here. She said this is where you used to come when you were young."

"Jah," I answered. "She knows me well."

He sat down beside me.

"So you had Leisel driving?"

He chuckled. "She begged me, honest."

I didn't doubt that. "How did it go?"

"Well." He paused a moment and then added, "She wouldn't fess up to it, but I'm guessing she's driven before."

"Really?"

"That girl's got some secrets," Amos said. "But she's like Fort Knox. She's not giving anything away."

A shot of anxiety tore through me. I agreed that it seemed Leisel was up to something. She'd passed her GED. She knew how to drive. Somehow she'd managed to do what I couldn't until I had left the Amish.

I changed the subject and asked how Arden was doing. "Leisel says he's grumpy." Then he sighed. "Probably because of the pain and probably because Vi didn't go up today."

"I saw you talking with her. Did Vi tell you why she didn't go?"

"No." He leaned forward and put his hands on his knees.

"We talked a little, but she didn't say anything about Arden. Mostly she asked about my life in Colorado."

"What did you tell her?" I asked, genuinely curious. In all of our talking, Amos hadn't said much about himself.

"That I married two years after I left Lancaster."

"You didn't tell me you're married."

"Was."

"Oh no," I said, assuming he was now a widower.

"We divorced ten years ago."

"I'm sorry," I said.

He shrugged. "It was mostly my fault. For as good a role model as Dat was when it came to being a husband, I couldn't seem to get it right."

"What happened?"

"Honestly?"

I nodded.

"It was like I was Arden or something. I was too harsh. Too critical. Much too legalistic." He leaned back and took his cowboy hat off. "Cindy—that's her name—grew up in a mainstream church. I didn't think she took her faith seriously enough. I didn't think she feared God the way she should. She was okay with having a glass of wine, with going to a movie, with women preaching."

"Didn't you figure your differences out before you got married?"

He laughed. "We'd only known each other a short time. I think both of us made a lot of assumptions about the other."

"What did you have in common?"

"Horses. Ranching. I worked for her father—still do. We both love riding and hunting and fishing. She's a strong woman, inside and out."

He stopped for a moment and then said, "She was too strong

to put up with my legalism. I was focused on all the wrong things, and it only got worse once she had our baby."

"Baby?" I nearly choked on the word. "You didn't say anything about a baby."

"She's not a baby anymore. She's thirteen."

"Did Dat know?"

"Jah, but I asked him not to tell anyone else. I was afraid it would make it harder for all of you not to have contact with me."

He was right. My heart ached in sorrow. I had another niece. I'd been nine when she was born. She was almost Milton's age.

I took a ragged breath and asked, "What is your daughter like?"

"She's tall and has dark hair, like you and Marie. And she's smart. Straight As in school so far. She wants to go to college and become a veterinarian. I'm grateful she still likes spending time on the ranch so I get to see her at least on weekends. Her mom moved to town after we divorced."

"But you still work for your ex-in-laws?"

"Jah," he answered. "They're good people. Good grandparents too. I'm grateful for that, especially since I was so far from Dat. From all of you." He paused for a moment and then said, "I don't regret leaving—if I didn't I wouldn't have my daughter. But, and I know this doesn't really make sense, if I had it to do over again, I wouldn't have left. I never recovered a part of myself. Surely Arden and I would have worked things out, somehow. And I would have gained a lot knowing Dat as an adult, working with him, living close to him. And I missed out being a brother to you three girls. I left over grief for one sister—and in doing so threw away my relationship with my other three." He smiled sadly. "But I do have my daughter, and I'm very grateful for that."

The ache in my heart grew deeper. I whispered. "What's her name?"

"She goes by Becca," he answered quietly. "But Rebecca is her name. Rebecca Bachmann."

I woke up over and over that night, thinking about the second Rebecca Bachmann. *Becca*. Oh, how I longed to meet her! And to get to know this girl named after my sister. Finally I turned away from Leisel and let the tears roll down my cheeks. I mourned the sister I never knew, my father who was taken too soon, and the niece I'd never met. The losses felt like holes inside of me, as if my heart had morphed into a porous rock. I drew my knees up to my chest and cried myself back to sleep.

The next morning, as we were doing the milking, Amos asked me to promise not to tell any of the others about Becca. Or that he was divorced. "I'd rather they not know how complicated my life is."

"They? Or Vi?"

He gave me a withering look. "I didn't think you'd use what I told you against me."

"Mamm saw the two of you talking yesterday too."

His weathered face grew red.

"What were you talking about?"

"You were blunt when you were little too," he said.

"Well?"

"We were just catching up. Like I already told you, I mostly talked about my work in Colorado." He shrugged. "We told each other what we've been up to over the past seventeen years."

As far as Vi, it seemed pretty obvious. She'd been having kids with Arden. "But you didn't tell her about your divorce or Becca?"

"That's right," he said. "I didn't see any reason to."

I shook my head in wonder. I wouldn't tell anyone about his life in Colorado because he'd asked me not to, but I didn't understand his reasoning. Just like I didn't understand Dat's willingness to accommodate Amos's request. If Arden had known he was an uncle, would he have been more likely to repair his relationship with Amos?

I exhaled. Probably not. Nevertheless, I said a prayer for reconciliation between brothers. And then I felt a pang in my heart. How about reconciliation between Marie and me? Was I willing to pray for that?

Amos said he wanted to change the subject.

"Oh?"

"Jah," he said. "Do you plan to marry Tom?"

My face grew warm. "The subject has come up," I said, "vaguely."

"What about Silas?"

"What about him?" I focused on the udder of the cow before me.

"You don't realize it now," Amos said, "but there's more to your first love than you realize. There's something pure and true about it. It's so much simpler than later loves."

"But I have no plan to return." I finished with the cow and stood.

"What about Silas?" Amos asked. "Would he leave?"

"No." My voice caught in my throat. "We already went through all of that. He'll never leave. I'll never return. That's all there is to it." I thought of Edith as I marched around the cow to the next one, of how obtuse I'd been before. Silas was a good son, loyal and true.

Amos didn't ask me any more questions. Leaving had been such a simple decision for me three years ago, or so I'd thought. Now it felt much more complicated.

After we'd finished, as I hung my apron up on the hook, I asked Amos what time he planned to leave.

"After breakfast," he answered. "I've decided to do a little sight-seeing in Philadelphia before I turn in my car."

Amos and I ended up eating in the Dawdi Haus with Aenti Suz. Leisel came in and joined us, asking Amos if he would give her a ride up to the hospital before he left. It was in the opposite direction of Philadelphia, but he didn't point that out. He simply said he would.

An hour later, Aenti Suz and I hugged Amos good-bye on her front porch and then walked him to his car. Leisel came out onto the porch of the big house and then turned and walked back inside, leaving the door open.

She called out, "Mamm! Marie!"

I winced. My sweet sister was going to force a group good-bye.

Mamm and Marie appeared and then, surprisingly, so did Vi. She wore her coat and carried her purse.

When Mamm reached Amos, she patted his arm and said, "I'm not sorry you came."

I cringed, but it was as close to a positive reaction toward Amos that I'd ever heard from Mamm.

Marie nodded. "It was good to see you again after all of these years."

Amos smiled at both of them and then reached out and hugged Mamm first. She stiffened. Marie didn't do much better when it was her turn. "I'll come out again in a few years," he said.

"Oh . . . all right," Mamm answered. It seemed she thought she was done with him.

He turned to Vi. "It was good to see you too. And meet your children."

Vi nodded. "I talked with Arden last night." I imagined Vi in the barn office, on the phone. "He and I are both hoping I can get a ride to the hospital, since you're taking Leisel." It must have been quite the talk.

"Sure, I can take you," Amos said.

"And perhaps you would come in and see Arden."

Amos shook his head. "I've had specific instructions, from the boss himself, not to."

"He'll be all right about it with me there," Vi answered and then climbed into the backseat of the rental before Amos could respond. She looked up at me and said, "I've already arranged for a driver this afternoon to get back home."

I nodded. I didn't expect her to ride with me, but for a minute, I considered going along. If I hadn't told Milton I'd help him, I might have.

Amos hugged me last and said, "Come out to Colorado and visit me."

I hugged him back and said, "I'd love to." And, of course, meet Becca, but I didn't say that out loud.

I told Leisel I'd pick her up that evening.

"Good," she said. "I think Arden will come home on Monday, but I doubt he'll ride with you, so we'll arrange for a driver."

I nodded. I wouldn't have expected Arden to ride with me. But I was shocked that Vi—and Arden—were okay with her riding with Amos. I was even more shocked Marie hadn't said anything.

Mamm and Marie headed toward the house before Amos started the car, but I stayed and waved as he headed down the driveway. Before he turned the corner, Amos honked a final farewell.

My throat constricted and gratitude filled my heart. I had a brother who loved and cared for me. I mourned the years we'd lost, but I was thankful to have a relationship with him again.

As I started toward the tractor shed, Milton drove the team of mules into the field. My nephew was growing into a responsible man. He seemed to value the land. Hopefully it would stay intact long enough for him to own it.

I finished working on the tractor in the afternoon. After he'd finished plowing for the day, Milton had used the gas tiller to do both the gardens and was cleaning up when Vi arrived home. She went directly to her house. Milton and I did the milking together, and then I left for the hospital to get Leisel instead of going into the house for supper.

Arden had been transferred out of ICU onto a different floor, but he was asleep and I didn't speak with him. Leisel put her finger to her lips when she saw me, grabbed her cape and bag, and then slipped out of the door.

"He's tired," she said. "He stayed awake the whole time Vi was here."

Thankfully Leisel didn't ask to drive and I didn't give away her secret by asking if she wanted to. I was sure I didn't have the nerves of steel that Amos did.

She didn't say much on the way home. It wasn't that I didn't give her an opportunity since I asked question after question. About Vi. About Arden. About if Amos said anything to Vi on the way to the hospital.

"Jessica," she finally said. "What are you implying?"

"I'm just curious is all," I said.

"It seems a little gossipy, all of these questions."

"Sorry," I said. "I didn't mean it that way."

Leisel put her head back against the seat and closed her eyes, her dainty hands resting in her lap. My mouth remained silent the rest of the way home—although my mind certainly did not.

When we reached the farm, I expected to see Amos's car and had to remind myself that he'd left. Another sense of loss and grief swept through me.

Sunday morning Milton and I finished the chores and then I had breakfast with Aenti Suz again.

After we'd finished, she said, "We'd better clean up and be on our way to church."

Jah, it was Sunday morning. I'd considered going back to Harrisburg for the day instead of spending an uncomfortable morning being stared at by people from my past. Dat's service had been bad enough, but at least then I could be the grieving girl. Now I was simply the prodigal daughter.

It wouldn't do for me to drive my car. "May I ride with you?" I asked Aenti Suz.

"Of course," she replied.

We left before Mamm and the girls. When we arrived, I stood by Aenti Suz and a couple of the widows in the congregation. When Mamm and the others arrived, Leisel took me under her wing.

All of the congregants filed in with their age groups. Leisel ended up following Marie and Gail into a row of young women. I perched on the end of the bench, hoping to remain inconspicuous. But of course I couldn't.

Mamm filed in with Aenti Suz behind her. A lump formed in my throat. It was my mother's first service as a widow. True, all these years she'd never sat with Dat, but she'd always come and left with him.

After Aenti Suz was Edith. She smiled at me as she passed by. I anticipated Silas sitting on the men's side with the other men who were in their early twenties, but he never appeared.

I sang the hymns along with the rest of congregation, surprised that none of the words to the songs in German were lost to me. It felt as if I'd only missed a few services, not three years' worth.

A deacon I didn't recognize read the scripture from 2 Thessalonians. "Therefore, brethren, stand fast, and hold the traditions which ye have been taught, whether by word, or our epistle." Then Bishop Jacobs walked to the front to preach. I'd hoped someone else would be doing the honors. I straightened my aching back. I wasn't used to sitting on a hard bench for three hours, even after sitting through Dat's service. The padded chairs from the church I attended with Tom seemed opulent compared to what I sat on now.

Bishop Jacobs's voice boomed, startling me. "For the law was given by Moses, but grace and truth came by Jesus Christ." He stared at all of us for a long moment and then said, "That's what John wrote in his Gospel after he'd seen the glorified Christ. He knew Christ had fulfilled the law."

Puzzled, I sat up even straighter. The Amish certainly had their own laws—well, rules anyway. The unwritten Ordnung, a word for order, covered everything from the length of dresses to the width of hat brims to the tires on our tractors. I wondered exactly what his point was.

Bishop Jacobs's voice grew louder as he said, "John had

experienced the grace and truth of Christ over and over." He continued to talk about John's life with Jesus and what he saw and learned. I listened as intently as I could, considering that a sharp pain had settled between my shoulder blades. I wondered if all of my time in front of my computer at work, compared to my all-day workouts on the farm in my former life, had made me grow weak. Perhaps sitting on benches for three hours at a time created a super strong core that I'd lost in the last few years.

My mind began to wander until Bishop Jacobs's voice boomed again. "We can't have grace without truth, and we can't have truth without grace. Some might say we have our own laws, but those aren't to gain favor with God." I hoped Marie was listening.

"Those are to allow us to live in community with each other. To keep us modest—all of us. To keep us from coveting what our neighbor has. To keep us caring for each other."

I bristled. Had he thought me wanting to farm immodest? Or that someone might covet my role? Or that it would keep me from caring for others?

"But our main focus has to be on grace and truth, not rules."

I wanted to shake my head. That certainly hadn't been my experience three years ago.

"We can best point others to truth when we have a relationship with them," he said. "We can best extend grace to others when we've admitted our own need for grace—and accepted it."

He smiled wryly. "There was one man in particular in our community who extended grace to me over and over, especially when I first started as bishop, when I needed it most." He paused for a moment as if to collect his thoughts or perhaps his emotions. "That man was Gus Bachmann. I won't go into details, but even when he was hurt by my actions, he extended me grace."

The bishop continued. "Right now, his family is going through a hard time. They are grieving him while caring for Arden, who's in the hospital. Gus's son Amos came for the service, but has returned to Colorado. Jessica . . ."

I bristled, alarmed that he'd mentioned me by name.

". . . is here, too, helping out."

I kept my eyes on the floor.

"And as you can imagine, Bethel, Marie, and Leisel . . ." Someone sniffled down the bench. Marie, I assumed.

The bishop continued, ". . . along with Vi and the children are grieving for Gus as they care for Arden. My prayer is that just as Gus extended grace and truth to me, I can do the same for his family."

Odd that we hadn't seen him since the service. I sighed. Perhaps Bishop Jacobs had been up to see Arden. And he'd probably been over to see Vi too. Maybe he'd stopped by to see Mamm when I'd been gone.

The bishop then listed other concerns in the community. A broken leg. A cancer diagnosis. I cringed and thought of Mildred Stoltz, even though she wasn't in our district. He mentioned a stillborn baby. My stomach dropped. Life was full of heartache. I'd grown up knowing that. But somewhere along the way, I began to think that my heartache was special. My change in thinking went against the teachings of the church. Is that what led to my leaving? Or had my leaving led to my change in thinking?

The deacon returned and read another scripture and then closed the service. As we filed out, I noticed Silas outside coming into the shed through a side door, probably to help move the benches.

After Aenti Suz and I had a bowl of soup and bread with

peanut butter spread, she asked me if I was ready to go. Of course I was.

Edith overheard us and asked if she could get a ride home. "Silas will be staying to clean up," she said, "and I'd rather not wait that long."

Of course Aenti Suz agreed to give Edith a ride. The truth was, it hurt for me to be around Edith. For years I believed she'd be my mother-in-law, and honestly, I got along with her better than I did my own mother. It was hard for me to be around her, but not as difficult as it was to be around Silas.

She sat up front with Aenti Suz while I sat in the back. The day had grown warmer and the constant wind from the week before had finally calmed down to a breeze. Daffodils waved as we drove by. Green shoots peeked through newly planted gardens. A pair of lambs frolicked along a fence line.

The day Silas's Dat died, the two of them had been working for a farmer, cutting the first crop of hay. The tongue to the baler broke and the workhorses dragged his Dat. Silas ran to the phone shed and called 9-1-1. Silas stayed at the road to show the EMTs where the gate was, so they could drive the ambulance into the field. But when they all reached his father it was too late. He'd died from internal bleeding.

Silas blamed himself. He should have gone back to his Dat instead of waiting for the ambulance. Everyone told Silas it wasn't his fault. It was his Dat's time to go. There wasn't anything to be done. My Dat explained, in detail, that there wasn't a thing he could have done to stop the internal bleeding. Still, it weighed heavily on Silas.

I wondered if Gail and Silas would move to Ohio where her family had relocated. Maybe Edith would go with them. There wasn't much to keep them in Pennsylvania. I remembered Arden telling me, several times, that if I wanted to live on a farm I should marry someone besides Silas.

Edith invited us into her house. "How about a cup of tea?" she asked.

Without consulting me, Aenti Suz accepted her offer.

The Kemp home was much smaller than most Amish houses. It had two bedrooms but wasn't much bigger than Suzanne's Dawdi Haus.

Aenti Suz went into the little kitchen with Edith, but I settled on the couch. Of course the room was spick-and-span. The sunlight coming through the picture window made the linoleum shine. There was no clutter and only a few books on a single bookshelf. A Bible. *Martyrs Mirror*. An *Ausbund*, our ancient Anabaptist hymnal.

By Englisch standards, it might seem sterile. But it wasn't. Just extremely tidy.

When the women returned with the tea, I was surprised that Edith asked me about my life in Harrisburg. No one besides Leisel had. I told her about my job and apartment. Then she asked about the Englischman who'd been with me at Dat's service, who had helped save Arden's life.

I told her I worked with him.

"Oh?"

I cringed a little, knowing she could see right through me. "And we've dated some."

"I'm happy for you," she said. "I really am." She smiled, but it didn't seem to be exactly sincere. I couldn't imagine her not being happy about Silas courting Gail, but then I realized I hadn't actually seen her interact with Gail at all. Not at our house. Not during Dat's service or burial. And not during the church service or meal either.

"Denki," I managed to say.

During a second cup of tea, a buggy turned into the driveway. I doubted Silas was home already, but no one came to the door.

Edith remembered the arrangement of dried flowers she'd forgotten to give Aenti Suz. "Jessica," she said, "would you go out to my shed and get it? It's the only one on my workbench."

I guessed she could just grab it when we left and wondered if she had an ulterior motive, but I went anyway. There was no sign of Silas as I hurried to the shed. A basket held the arrangement—larkspur, statice, avena, dried wheat, and millet grass. I picked it up carefully from the bench, not wanting to damage it in any way.

As I headed back to the house, I heard whistling. *Silas.* I kept my head down and charged ahead, not looking up until I saw a shadow out of the corner of my eye coming around the side of the house.

Silas and I collided, crushing the dried bouquet between us. As he stepped away, I tried to hold on to the arrangement, but it slipped through my hands to the ground. Then I stumbled over it and started to fall. Silas grabbed my arm and steadied me. His warm hand felt soft against my skin.

"Sorry," he said.

"I didn't see you," I muttered, kneeling down to gather up his mother's work that we'd just destroyed.

He bent down, too, and plucked up the wheat that had broken off. He raised his head just as I did mine, and we collided again. His hat went flying, and his long bangs fell across his forehead.

"Sorry," he said again, starting to stand. I stayed put. He reached for my hand and helped me up.

"I'll pick up the pieces," I said, wanting to avoid another

243

collision. Once I had all the flowers collected, I held them up, not sure what do. I felt horrible about Edith's arrangement.

"Put it back on Mamm's bench," Silas said, retrieving his hat and placing it back on his head. "She'll put it back together."

I headed to Edith's little shed, expecting Silas to go into the house, but instead he followed me.

"How are things going at home?" he asked.

"All right. Milton and I are managing. Arden may come home tomorrow, but of course it will be quite a while until he can help." I met Silas's gaze. "How are you doing?"

"Good. I'm looking for another farmhand job."

A light bulb went off in my head. "I know of someone looking for help. John Stoltz, way over on Garden Lane. I met him on Friday."

Silas cocked his head as if asking why.

"He leased out his land, for fracking. Then his well got contaminated."

Silas's expression darkened. "Oh."

"Anyway, he's partially disabled, and his wife has cancer. He leased out his fields before, but he figures he can make more if he hires someone to farm for him."

"I'll go by tomorrow," Silas said. I expected him to leave the shed, but he stayed by the doorway, smiling just a little.

I fidgeted, itching to get to the door but not wanting to be obvious about it. It was hard being in the same county with him, let alone in the same tiny shed.

"I should get going," I said. "I need to tell your Mamm I destroyed her work, and I think Aenti Suz is ready to get home for her Sunday afternoon nap."

He nodded. "When are you returning to Harrisburg?"

"Soon. We'll need to find someone to help Milton. . . ."

Silas grimaced. "I feel bad about that. . . ."

"You could go back to working for Arden once I leave, right? Or I could go back to Harrisburg tomorrow and you can start up again." I wished I could thank him for sticking up for me, but it would be foolish to bring it up. "I'm the problem, right?"

He shook his head. "No, you're not the problem at all. What Arden wants to do with the land is the problem. And . . ." His voice trailed off.

"Any drama caused by me will soon be over."

He shook his head. "But the hearts behind the drama won't have changed," Silas said. "The way one sister treated another. The way another person treated an outsider."

I shrugged. "They were only following the directions of the leader of this community."

"Who, by the tone of today's sermon, is hopefully changing." Silas lowered his voice. "Remember Elijah? His youngest son?"

I nodded. He was Marie's age.

"He went off to Florida, to Pinecraft, to work last year, before joining the church. It sounds as if he's been partying some, that sort of thing. Anyway, all of the other kids in the family towed the line. They're getting their first taste of dealing with a rebel."

I shrugged again. However—and for whatever reasons— Bishop Jacobs might be changing hardly had any impact on me, not now.

"Go back to the farm," I said to Silas. "Pretend I never came back."

He leaned against the doorframe of the shed, crossing his arms as he did.

I took a deep breath. "I'm not saying this to gossip, but I think it would be good for you to know. Gail defended you"—I smiled—"defending me. She was quite impressed with you. I can tell she cares for you deeply."

Under the brim of his hat, his eyes met mine. But he didn't respond.

I began to feel uneasy by his gaze, which caused me to continue rambling. "So tell Arden you'll take the job back. If you'd like, I can get word to him today."

He shook his head. "No, I'm going to go talk to this John Stoltz. It would be good for me to work with someone else. It meant a lot to me to work with your Dat, but Arden is an entirely different person." His gaze intensified. "You should probably know where he keeps his important papers."

"What?"

"Just in case. On the bottom shelf of the cupboard behind—"

The back screen door banged shut and then Aenti Suz called out, "Jessica!"

Silas stepped out of the shed. "We're over here," he said.

I followed him out, not sure why he'd want me to know where Arden kept his important papers. Unless Silas had seen the fracking plans on the desk too. . . . If he was trying to help me with that, it was a kind gesture. But it didn't matter. No one believed I had a right to an opinion concerning the farm, especially not Arden.

Edith followed Aenti Suz out of the house, and I quickly explained that I'd dropped the arrangement and apologized for it. But then Silas said it was his fault, that he'd clumsily bumped into me.

Edith smiled and assured us she'd put it back together. "Don't give it another thought," she said.

After Aenti Suz and I told Edith and Silas good-bye, we climbed into the buggy and headed up the drive. The day had grown even warmer—so different than the day we'd buried Dat. The daffodils along the fence line swayed in the breeze like a hundred little suns.

"Silas seems a little lost again," Aenti Suz said as she pulled onto the highway.

I didn't respond.

"Edith was worried about him when you left. He mourned as if someone had died."

A lump began to form in my throat. I'd felt the same way. But he'd gotten over it. We both had.

Aenti Suz didn't say any more for quite a while. I stared out the window, watching the fields go by. Even in the few days I'd been in Lancaster the grass had grown greener.

"I'm sorry," Aenti Suz finally said.

"For what?"

"I know how much you and Silas cared about each other."

I nodded but didn't turn my head toward her. I'd tried to convince myself we hadn't really loved each other, that we were too young, that we didn't know what we wanted back then. But none of it was true. We had loved each other.

"I don't know if you've ever heard about this or not, but I was in love way back when."

I shook my head. No one had ever mentioned it.

"With a Mennonite man."

"Really?" I turned toward her. "What happened?"

"He was killed."

I gasped. "How?" I imagined a buggy or farming accident.

"He was with your Dat in Vietnam. They went to work as orderlies in a hospital."

Wanting more information about this part of my Dat's life, but sad about Aenti Suz's loss, I leaned forward and asked, "What happened while they were there?"

"The hospital was attacked by the Viet Cong. Jake was injured badly. Your Dat tried to save him but couldn't."

I sat back, too dumbfounded to know what to say.

"Your Dat came home soon after that. It wasn't as if I'd vowed not to wed anyone else, but I never found anyone else I wanted to marry. I never found anyone else I wanted to live with, day in and day out."

"You were going to leave the church?"

She nodded. "He was conservative Mennonite. So there's that."

I didn't intend for the pitch of my voice to increase with each word, but it did. "But you were going to leave?"

"Jah," she answered.

"Like I've left?" I was a note away from being shrill.

She shook her head. "I was going to leave to marry one specific man. You left for other reasons, right?"

I nodded.

"My great-aunt told me the story of Ruby Bachmann as a cautionary tale, hoping to persuade me not to marry Jake." Aenti Suz looked me straight in the eye. "But that's not why I'm telling you."

"What are you saying?" I'd expected a predictable story, especially if it had been wielded as a cautionary tale.

Aenti Suz gave me a pathetic look. "I'm not going to give the ending away."

"Then tell me the rest of the story," I said.

"I will," she answered. "Well, some, anyway. When we get back to my place."

"I thought you wanted to take a nap."

She smiled. "I'll have plenty of time to do that after I tell you a bit more."

I nodded in agreement, and then focused my eyes back onto the landscape. When we reached the farm, I squinted over to the neighbors' property in the distance, sad that the oak tree Ruby had chased the calf around had been cut down. "So did Duncan take Zachary's place? Did he do that for Ruby?"

"I said once we get back to my place," Aenti Suz said, "and make a pot of tea."

We rode along in silence the short distance to the farm. I guessed Aenti Suz was thinking about Jake. And I was thinking about Silas. I leaned back against the seat, forcing myself to think of Ruby instead.

–16–

Ruby

Ruby stepped around the table and faced Captain McLeod. By the light of the fire his square jaw appeared set.

"You know Duncan can't go," she said. "And we don't have the money to pay the tax."

"Then I'll seize your land. I'd be satisfied to have this parcel for myself. I've come to appreciate the Lancaster countryside."

Even in the dim light, Ruby could tell Duncan's face was growing red. "Don't be ridiculous, Bert," he said. "You'll not seize the land of these people. That's unconscionable."

Captain McLeod shrugged. "No, it's quite reasonable. This is war, and they're not doing their duty."

Duncan groaned, as if in disgust. "Like I've already said, I'll go."

"You can't," Ruby answered. Panic nearly overcame her. Duncan had survived his time in the Continental Army once—what if he didn't a second time? It would be her fault.

Captain McLeod ignored Ruby and focused on Duncan. "Very well. We'll leave for Valley Forge tomorrow."

"Wait until spring," Ruby said.

"No, I'm going now. Who knows when I'll be back this way. I can take your land—or either Zachary or Duncan with me in the morning."

"There aren't enough supplies there." Ruby could feel her voice grow louder with each word. "Soldiers are starving. Why add yourself and Duncan to the chaos?" She couldn't bear the thought of Duncan being sent there, not after they'd just rescued Zachary from it.

"I'll go too," Isabelle said to Captain McLeod. She turned to Duncan. "We can go home first and ask for Father's help."

Ruby didn't want Isabelle to ask their father for help. Not for her and Zachary. She wanted to be able to take care of things herself—or for her family to at least see to their own problem. But she didn't have the resources to save Zachary on her own. Panic gripped her again, this time tighter. *Casting all your care upon him.* How many times had Mamm recited that through the years? Ruby had barely listened because she'd never had much to feel anxious about—until now. Thank goodness the scripture had stayed with her, regardless.

She said a silent prayer and then asked out loud, "May I speak with you, Duncan? In private?"

She led the way to the back door and registered he was following as his cane clicked against the floor. She stepped outside onto the back stoop. The snow had stopped and the moon now rose in the sky, casting a measure of brightness across the wintery world.

Duncan stopped beside her, leaning against his cane.

"I appreciate you wanting to help us, but I can't let you do this," she said. "I'd rather lose our farm than have you go to Valley Forge."

"Rubbish," he said. "Nothing is going to happen to me. And hopefully Bert is only bluffing anyway."

Ruby swallowed hard.

His eyes grew tender. "We work well together, remember? We'll figure this out."

We'll. Her heart lurched. But it could never be. And, regardless, he hadn't meant it that way.

"Please don't go" was all she could manage to say.

"I'll come back as soon as I can, I promise. Then we'll figure out a way to get you on your way to Canada. I'll even drive you there myself, if needed."

She appreciated his kindness, but at the same time her heart sank at the thought of telling him a final good-bye. And of him being willing to deliver her to Paul. "No, I'll send for Hans," she said. "Or if he's too ill, I'll ask Paul to come down and help us sort it all out." That was how it should be. After all, Paul was the man who would soon be her husband.

A flicker of pain passed over Duncan's face, and he shifted his weight more to his good leg. "It will take time for a letter to reach them and then more time for one of them to make arrangements to travel. I'm not saying don't write to them, but don't expect immediate help. Let's see what I can figure out when I get back. Hopefully, that will be soon."

"Shouldn't Captain McLeod wait until Zachary is better before making you go?"

"By Bert's standards, Zachary is well enough."

Ruby grimaced. "What about the weather?"

"It's warming," Duncan said. "The snow should melt soon."

She shook her head. Their trip home had been so treacherous.

"We'll make better time on horseback," he said. "Something will work out."

"What about a horse? Ours won't do you any good."

"Bert has two—Isabelle rode one of them." He inhaled sharply. "Will you watch after my uncle?"

"Of course," Ruby said. "So Isabelle will go with you?"

He shook his head. "Father sent her away for a reason. I don't want her going back." He paused for a moment. "Actually, could she stay here with you?"

"She's not used to such a simple home as this."

He smiled. "Our house isn't that fancy. She'll be fine."

Ruby couldn't decline him the favor, not after all he'd done for her, but the thought of Isabelle living with her seemed a little daunting.

"I'd have her stay with Uncle, but she hardly knows him, and he's so crotchety—I'm afraid she'd expire from boredom."

"Well, I'm hardly entertaining," Ruby replied, shaking her head just a little.

Duncan smiled again. "That may be, but you're hardly boring either." He paused for a moment. In the moonlight, his eyes sparkled and Ruby's heart lurched again. Perhaps it was best he was going away. She hardly knew what she was feeling.

He opened the door and motioned, with his cane, for her to lead the way.

The next morning dawned much warmer. By the time Ruby served breakfast to Zachary, the icicles hanging from the eaves of the back part of the house had begun to melt, and the snow on the road was turning to slush.

After she'd cleaned up the dishes, there was a knock on the

door. She hurried to open it, drying her hands on her apron. Duncan and Isabelle stood on the porch, with Captain McLeod perched on the bottom step.

"Come in," she said.

Duncan shook his head. "I just walked Isabelle over. Bert and I need to be on our way."

Ruby had prayed for a change of Captain McLeod's heart, but it didn't seem God had answered it the way she'd hoped. "Be careful," she said. "And thank you—" Her voice choked. "For everything."

Duncan nodded and returned the thanks for her care of Isabelle and his uncle. "He seems tired today. Would you check on him, to make sure he's eating and resting? And help him with the chores?"

"Jah." Ruby would cook for the old man herself. There was no reason for him to do any cooking.

After they said good-bye, Isabelle followed the men toward the road, waving as she walked along, the hem of her dress soaked by the melting snow. Isabelle seemed awfully sweet on Captain McLeod. She'd never seen a girl look so longingly after a man. Ruby thought he was a horrible choice, especially when Isabelle had such a kindhearted brother who had set a good example. Didn't Isabelle care about what the man had just done?

Isabelle returned with a frown on her face, but it quickly dissolved into a smile. The girl had an adventurous attitude, although her bold affections could likely get her into real trouble. At least there were no possible suitors anywhere nearby with everyone having gone off to war—or Canada.

The days marched on without any word from Duncan. Ruby started the fire in the smokehouse and hung the meat with Isabelle's help. Soon the savory scent of the smoke permeated the farm, bringing a sense of comfort to Ruby. Zachary grew stronger and managed to help some with the chores. He couldn't chop wood, but he could help feed the animals.

Ruby sat down and wrote a letter to Hans, asking him to come and help sell the farm. It wasn't something she could do on her own, and she feared Zachary didn't have the motivation to do it now. She understood Zachary's hesitancy. She felt the same way. But she knew it was the right thing to do.

She walked the three miles to the minister's house, doing her best to make her way through the muddy woods. He was at the woodpile, and a few of his younger children were marching toward the house, their arms filled with kindling.

She asked after his wife.

"She's improving," he said.

"And the baby?"

"The Lord giveth and the Lord taketh away. . . ." His voice trailed off.

"I'm sorry," Ruby said.

He shrugged, but his eyes grew misty. He quickly blinked the tears away. She asked how he was feeling, and he said he was still weak but seemed to have recovered.

She apprised him of Zachary and his condition, without giving away too many details, and then asked if he knew of anyone who was heading north soon.

He put his finger to his lip and said quietly, "Our oldest son," he said. "The Patriots are after him, so he intends to sneak away sometime soon."

Ruby handed him the letter. "Could he give this to Hans?"

The minister nodded.

"Do you plan to go?" she asked.

"We'll wait until spring. The weather is too uncertain with

my wife . . . You and Zachary can travel with us then." He seemed eager to leave, to perhaps put the sadness of the winter behind them. "We'd be a help to each other."

She nodded in agreement. Hopefully Hans would make the trip down by then and lead the way.

On the walk back, snow began to fall. She turned her face to the sky, up to the big, fluffy flakes. For a moment she felt a sense of delight, but then a wave of sadness washed through her. Four months ago she could picture a new settlement in Canada, even though she was reluctant to leave Lancaster, but now it felt beyond her imagination. She could barely recall the excitement she'd once felt at a new beginning. Now all she wanted was what was familiar—and for the last four months that had been the farm. Tending it alone, with only Duncan's help, had made her love it all the more.

Ruby tried to get Isabelle to help with the cooking, cleaning, and washing, but she was worse than useless. More often than not she made a mess that Ruby had to sort through. Still, the girl found it all amusing and she never lost her sense of humor, even when she failed miserably.

Finally, one morning when Ruby had instructed Isabelle to make bread, the girl admitted that her family had servants to do all of the work, which Ruby had long ago suspected. She was sure Duncan had misrepresented his family's wealth.

No matter.

"Do you want to learn to make bread?" Ruby asked as she added flour to the much-too-sticky dough.

Isabelle pursed her lips together.

Ruby laughed. "The skill might keep you from starving someday."

"All right." Isabelle wrinkled her nose. "Give me a lesson."

Ruby did. And also lessons on milking a cow, churning butter, scrubbing a floor, and washing clothes. And fixing dinner. Old Man Wallis came over for every meal, and although cooking for only four was much easier than what Ruby had done for much of her girlhood, it was still an effort.

So was doing the chores. The weather turned cold again, more snow fell, and the ice had to be chipped in the watering trough several times a day. Zachary took over that chore, using the axe with his left hand to do the job. Besides feeding the animals, he began mucking out the stalls as best he could and spreading hay too. Slowly, he was able to do more and more. She realized he'd gained enough strength back that he was probably stronger than most of the soldiers at Valley Forge. But he wouldn't have been if Captain McLeod had taken him. She shivered at the thought of what Duncan's condition might be.

"What else needs to be done?" Zachary asked toward the end of a day in early February after he'd carried buckets of water from the springhouse to fill the trough.

"Would you go check in with Mr. Wallis and see what he needs help with? And then accompany him over for supper."

Zachary complied, and Ruby headed back to the house to teach Isabelle how to thicken the stew.

As they worked, Ruby asked Isabelle more about her uncle.

"He's my father's oldest brother," she said. "He and his wife never had any children." The wife had died years ago, when Ruby was a girl. "He's said all along that his land would go to Duncan when he died."

"Oh?" They all knew, with Duncan's injury, that it would be hard for him to farm, to make a living at it.

"But he will also inherit the house in Philadelphia, and I

know Father expects Duncan to join him in his business." She shrugged. "But everything's upside down now. Both Father and Duncan took big risks to align with the Patriots. Father's import business is all but nonexistent now, considering the Tories in town are furious with him." She sighed. "Of course, not all of the British are awful." She grinned again. "I've met one or two I'm quite fond of."

Ruby could imagine.

Isabelle grew serious again. "Now that Duncan's permanently injured, working with Father seems to be the best plan for him."

Ruby couldn't disagree. She'd go on to Canada. Duncan would end up in Philadelphia. There was no reason to pine after something she couldn't have. And didn't even want. She was Plain. He wasn't. She was of the Anabaptist faith. He was Presbyterian.

She'd been behaving like a foolish girl, like Isabelle.

As they continued to work, Isabelle began talking about Captain McLeod. "He and Duncan went to school together. He can be a bit of a brute, but I like a man who takes charge," Isabelle said as Ruby instructed her to stir water into the flour. "Don't you?"

"Take charge, maybe, but never one that's a brute." Ruby lowered the pot on the fire and then motioned for Isabelle to add the flour and water mixture to the stew to thicken it. "Goodness, wouldn't you rather spend time with a kind man? One who didn't force your brother to go back to war?"

Isabelle shrugged. "Captain McLeod is just doing his job. Duncan knows that."

Ruby didn't understand how a good friend could act in such a way, but there were many things she didn't understand about the Englisch. Another was why Isabelle had never been taught to cook or clean, even if the family did have servants.

A week later, when Old Man Wallis came down for dinner, he brought a letter for Ruby that another neighbor had brought from the inn in Lancaster. For a moment she thought it might be from Hans or Paul, and her heart sank. Would they be coming soon?

But as she opened it, she didn't recognize the handwriting. She scanned it to the bottom—*Duncan.*

He was at Valley Forge, and the conditions were more deplorable than before. An epidemic of measles was going through the camp, food was in even shorter supply than when they'd rescued Zachary, and even the horses he was caring for were starving and should probably be eaten before all the meat on them disappeared.

Ruby shuddered.

Bert hadn't allowed him to go on to Philly, and he wanted Isabelle to go back home. *Would you go with her?* he wrote.

Take the stagecoach. Don't let Isabelle out of your sight and make sure she returns with you. Show this letter to Uncle Wallis. He'll give you the money I left behind in case of an emergency.

I've written my father, for the third time, telling him what I need from him too. I fear none of my letters are getting through, though. If this letter reaches you, make sure to take it with you and then explain everything to him.

He signed the letter, *Your friend, Duncan.*

Ruby slipped the letter into the pocket of her apron, unsure of what to do. She couldn't imagine riding a stagecoach with

Isabelle and going to Duncan's family home. But Duncan had risked everything for Zachary—and now he needed her help.

She had to go.

Isabelle was thrilled to be returning to Philadelphia. Ruby feared she looked like Isabelle's maid, sitting next to the elegantly dressed young woman, and fought anxiety the first few hours of the trip. She hadn't had a chance to cook ahead for Zachary and Old Man Wallis. Hopefully they'd be able to feed themselves and keep up with the chores.

Ruby and Isabelle stayed at the same inn again, and then reached Philadelphia by noon. Once they arrived at the station closest to the Wallis home, Isabelle sent a note to her father to send the coach.

When it arrived, Mr. Wallis was inside. "I've been expecting you," he said out the open door, and then turned to Ruby and introduced himself. "Duncan said he hoped you'd accompany Isabelle."

"Goodness," Ruby said. "You've heard from him then?"

The man nodded. Obviously one of Duncan's letters had gotten through.

Ruby examined the man more closely. Silver hair showed under his hat and along his temples. He had a kind face, much like Duncan's—when he wasn't trying to catch a wayward calf.

A man, perhaps a servant, helped the women up into the coach, and they settled on the bench across from Mr. Wallis. The coach seemed fancy to Ruby, but as other coaches on the street passed by, she realized it was simple in comparison to some. The servant turned out to be the coach driver, and soon they were on their way.

As they rode along, Mr. Wallis asked Ruby to tell him the story of what happened. When she finished, she took Duncan's letter from her pocket and extended it to the man.

He waved his hand and said, "As you probably guessed, I finally received a letter myself. I don't need to read yours."

Ruby nodded and then said, "It's really my doing that Duncan ended up at Valley Forge. I never expected that Zachary would be forced to return so soon, or that Duncan would volunteer to take his place."

"Yes, that surprised me too." Mr. Wallis smiled. "After he nearly died, I didn't think anything would drag him back to war, but I should have anticipated his care for a fellow soldier might."

Ruby's heart swelled. Duncan had done it out of pity for Zachary and also for her, she knew that. But she wasn't sure why he felt as if it were his responsibility.

"But I haven't been able to get an answer out of him." The man smiled.

"What?" Ruby gasped. "You've seen him?"

"He's back at the house. I sent for him, and he arrived this morning."

"Oh my," Ruby said. There had been no reason for her and Isabelle to travel after all. She wanted to ask if Duncan would return to Lancaster County, but she couldn't bear to voice the words. Chances were he wouldn't. And perhaps Isabelle wouldn't either.

Isabelle and her father began to chat. "Has Duncan seen Jane?" Isabelle asked.

Mr. Wallis sighed. "Not yet, although I hope he will. Perhaps you could send her a message? I feel so certain he'd stay in Philadelphia if they could patch things up."

Isabelle didn't say anything, which was a surprising turn of events for the girl who never seemed to hold back from speaking her mind. Ruby's heart raced. It was obvious that Duncan's family liked this Jane.

Isabelle changed the topic to Old Man Wallis. "You're nothing like your brother," she said. "He's so crotchety and outspoken. Ruby's the only person he likes. Well, maybe Duncan, a little anyway. But certainly not me. I can't understand how the two of you can even be related."

"Well," Mr. Wallis said, "we're nearly twenty years apart in age, and he's gone through much harder times than I have, I'm afraid. He's done well for himself considering his wife died so long ago and he never had children to help him see the world with fresher eyes."

Mr. Wallis reached across the coach and squeezed Isabelle's hand. "I hope you showed him some grace, for my sake."

She smiled sweetly. "I simply followed Ruby's lead and treated him quite well, thank you very much."

"I'm grateful for that," Mr. Wallis said and then smiled at Ruby.

Embarrassed, she ducked her head.

Isabelle's smile disappeared and she said, "I bet Duncan's relieved to be at the house."

"Actually, the British overtook our home last week," Mr. Wallis said. "We're currently living in the servants' quarters."

"Oh dear," Isabelle said.

"Yes, it's not an easy situation. But I'd rather stay close by so that I can keep an eye on things." He sighed. "I'm afraid we've only been able to retain our coachman. The British demanded Cook and the others work for them."

"I see," Isabelle said, sitting up straighter. "You'll be happy to know that I can make bread and churn butter, thanks to Ruby."

Mr. Wallis smiled as if he didn't believe her.

"And scrub a floor and wash clothes." She pulled one glove off and held her red hand up to her father. "Here's proof."

"Goodness, daughter," he said with a smile. "You'll make your poor Scottish grandparents proud after all."

Isabelle smiled mischievously and pulled her glove back on. "Any sight or sound from Lieutenant Anderson?"

Mr. Wallis's face reddened. "No," he snapped. "And don't ask after him again."

Isabelle's eyebrows shot up as if asking a question, but she didn't say anything. Ruby suppressed a gasp. The girl was un-conscionable. Ruby had never met anyone like her. First Captain McLeod and now a Lieutenant Anderson? One a Patriot and one a Redcoat? Two men on opposite sides of the war. Ruby couldn't imagine such a thing. Her face grew warm. Did she not care for two very different men, herself? She exhaled slowly and tried to relax against the bench as Isabelle changed the topic back to Lancaster and how lovely the countryside was.

A minute later, the carriage turned up a driveway. The house ahead was large and stately with columns on each side of the front door. Several British soldiers gathered on the porch. Isa-belle pressed her nose to the carriage window until her father gently pulled her away without saying a word.

The carriage continued on as the driveway curved behind the house to the left and on to a much-smaller building not far from the stables. The coachman helped the women down, and then Mr. Wallis led the way toward the house. The door was open. Mr. Wallis and Ruby must have both smelled smoke at the same time, because they both started running toward the house.

"Mary! Duncan!" he called out.

Ruby followed him over the threshold.

"We're in the kitchen," Duncan called out. "And everything's fine. It's just the bread that burnt."

He stepped to the doorway with two blackened loaves half wrapped in a rag. "I was just going to throw these out the door into a puddle." He laughed, his gaze meeting Ruby's. "But you caught me in the act."

He was thinner than he had been when he left Lancaster, but his disposition seemed good. "You've met my father," he said and then glanced over his shoulder. "This is my mother, Mary."

A petite woman, smaller than Isabelle, appeared. Duncan had her fiery eyes, but his father's height. It was obvious he also had his mother's laugh.

She threw up her hands. "I haven't made bread in fifteen years—it used to be so easy." She stepped forward, wiped her hand on her flour-covered apron, and extended her hand. "Dear Ruby," she said. "I'm so pleased to meet you. Welcome to our home." With that, she burst into laughter again too. "Oh dear," she managed to say. "I'm usually better mannered."

Mr. Wallis stepped toward his wife and put one arm around her shoulder. "The Lord giveth and the Lord taketh away."

Ruby thought of the minister quoting the same passage.

Mary Wallis responded with, "Blessed be the name of the Lord." She leaned her head against her husband's shoulder, smashing her loose bun. "And we are blessed. Both of our children are alive, and both are with us today."

Isabelle stepped forward and hugged her mother too.

Ruby took a step backward. She wasn't used to families showing each other affection that way.

"Well," Mary said. "I'd better get started on a new batch of bread."

"I'll help," Ruby said.

"So will I," Isabelle chimed in.

"Goodness." Mary led the way into the house while Duncan and Mr. Wallis stayed outside. "Some things do change! You girls go clean up, and then you can help. Isabelle, everything is ready for you in the maids' bedroom."

"Mother," Isabelle said. "I have no idea where that is."

"Down the hall, third door on the right. You can't miss it. Then come help me. And, just so you know, I've invited Jane for dinner tonight."

Isabelle spun around abruptly. "Did you tell Duncan?"

"Not yet," Mary sung out.

"He won't be happy," Isabelle said under her breath. Ruby followed her down the hall, both looking forward to meeting this Jane and also dreading it. She couldn't help but be curious, but she knew she'd feel even plainer than she already did.

Everything about the Wallises seemed to shout money and influence. The house might have been the servants' quarters, but it was much nicer than her family's home. She didn't revel in the family's bad fortune, but she felt some measure of relief at not having to stay in their big house. Just being with the family was hard enough. Nothing in her background had prepared her for being in Philadelphia in the company of a wealthy Englisch family.

-17-

Ruby helped with the bread and offered to make the soup for their supper.

"No," Mary said. "You're our guest."

"Then let me assist," Ruby said. "You'll be doing me a kindness to allow me to help after what your family has done for mine."

No one said a word about the future and not much about the past either as they worked together. Ruby longed to find out how Duncan got away from Valley Forge, but she didn't have the courage to ask, not in front of his parents. Perhaps whatever his father did to secure his release wasn't her business. Still, she knew something had transpired that had freed Duncan. She wondered if Zachary's debt was paid or if they could expect Captain McLeod to return to Lancaster County.

Just as she determined the soup was done, a knock fell on the door. "Who would that be?" Duncan asked.

"Oh, I asked a certain someone to join us," his mother replied.

Duncan stood and leaned against his cane. "You didn't."

"I did," his mother said sweetly.

Isabelle headed to the door and opened it. A young woman, wearing a wool cape over a stylish dress, stood in the doorway. Isabelle hugged her, invited her in, and then introduced Jane to Ruby.

The woman took off the hood of her cape, revealing auburn hair styled in curls piled on her head. She looked as if she were going to a party—not to a supper of soup and bread. She swung the cape off her shoulders, showing a green velvet dress. Ruby slid her hands down her plain apron. As the woman stepped forward, her silk stockings showed under the hem of her gown.

"Duncan," she said. "It's so good to see you."

"Jane," he responded, taking her hand and kissing it. Ruby slipped into the kitchen, not wanting to witness any more of their greeting.

Ten minutes later, after they all were seated at the small table in the kitchen, Mr. Wallis led them in prayer. It was a heartfelt petition of the Lord, said out loud. He thanked God for his family, for the safety of the children and Ruby, and for Jane's presence. Then he asked for direction for the near future. Ruby couldn't help but think he was referring to Duncan.

Mr. Wallis added, "Lord, help us to love the soldiers who have taken over our home. They are your children too. Help us to show them kindness—" he paused a moment—"but not too much kindness." Obviously the qualification was directed at Isabelle. Then he asked God to bless the food to their bodies and to keep them strong in spirit. He closed with a loud "amen" that was echoed by the others in his family and by Jane too.

In Ruby's family, all of the prayers were spoken in silence, and she wasn't used to such a verbal outpouring to the Lord. Tears stung her eyes. These were good people.

She stayed silent as the bread was passed, and Mary filled up the soup bowls and passed those too. Isabelle asked Jane how life had been in Philadelphia.

"Boring without you or Duncan here," Jane replied. "And the shopping has been dreadful."

"Your dress looks new," Isabelle said.

"I purchased it before Christmas. It's the last new thing I've had."

"Oh dear," Isabelle said.

"And, as you can see—" She spread her hand across the table. "It's getting difficult for all to buy decent food."

Duncan cleared his throat.

"Is it not true where you are too?" Jane asked.

Duncan shook his head. "We have plenty where we are, thanks to Ruby's skills."

"But you look so thin," Jane said.

"Well, Valley Forge is an entirely different matter. It takes a lot to feed an army."

Jane was quite pretty, even when she frowned. "That's what the British say."

"'Tis true," Duncan said and then took a bite of soup.

"Perhaps we should share some of our food with the soldiers next door," Mary said. "As a way to love our enemies."

"We have a couple of loaves of bread cooling in the slush," Mr. Wallis responded.

"Oh goodness," Mary replied. "I meant a couple of loaves that Ruby made—not the ones I failed at."

Impressed with Mary's kindness, Ruby said, "I could make more bread tomorrow."

"No." Duncan held his spoon in midair as he turned his gaze toward his mother. "We're returning to Lancaster in the morning. Uncle needs our help, and you sent Isabelle away for a reason." He glanced toward his sister, who simply shrugged. "Plus Ruby needs to get back to her brother and their farm."

"You're leaving so soon?" Jane said to Duncan. "But you've just arrived."

"Couldn't Ruby go back and then you follow in a few days?" Mary asked.

Duncan exhaled and then shook his head. "Of course not, Mother. I'll be returning with her. You and Father can decide, of course, what you want Isabelle to do." He glanced toward the large house as he said it and then directly at his sister.

She shrugged her shoulders and smiled again. Jane continued to frown.

Isabelle's parents shared a look, but Ruby couldn't decipher the meaning behind it. She guessed she'd find out soon enough what they planned for their daughter.

After dinner, Mr. Wallis hauled water into the house from the well in the backyard while Isabelle and Jane sat in the small parlor with Duncan. Ruby insisted on organizing the dishwashing, even though Mary begged her to join the other young people. Finally Ruby said that she'd much rather have a task to do than sit idly.

Mary finally accepted her help and asked her questions about her family as Ruby stoked the fire to heat the water.

"Oh, you poor thing," Mary said after Ruby explained both of her parents had passed away. "At least you have brothers who are looking after you. Do you have any prospects, as far as marriage?"

Ruby told her briefly about Paul. "I'll need to get to Canada. . . ."

"Oh my," Mary said. "Does that mean you're a Loyalist?"

"Not really," Ruby said. "We're nonresistant. We don't believe in fighting."

"But your brother did."

"Jah," Ruby said. "It's all so complicated, isn't it?"

"I'm afraid so." Mary poked her head out of the kitchen and then returned to the dish basins that Ruby had just filled with water. "War seems to change everything. Before Duncan left, I was certain he and Jane would marry. Now he doesn't seem interested in her, not in the least. Somehow she's managed not to experience any hardship through all of this except for how it's affected her shopping and food consumption. I've asked her more than once to assist me when I work at the poorhouse, but she's refused each time. After all Duncan's seen and lost, I think he finds her disposition tedious. War brings out the worst in some people. This evening, I saw for the first time that perhaps she isn't who Duncan needs to navigate life with." Mary sighed. "It was foolish of me to try to meddle."

Ruby smiled at the woman. "You're his mother. You want what's best for him."

"I do," Mary said. "And at this point, I think that's simply to pray that God will guide him."

Ruby warmed even more toward the woman. She saw God's grace in this family, plus the love of Christ for each other and those less fortunate too.

Halfway through the dishwashing, Isabelle came in to join them, saying that Duncan was going to walk Jane home.

"Oh?" Mary said, clearly hoping for more information.

Isabelle shrugged. "It was Duncan's idea." She turned toward Ruby. "Jane lives across the boulevard. So far, the British don't have their eyes on her family's house."

After the women finished, Mary said she was tired and headed down the hall to the second room. It seemed that Duncan hadn't returned. Perhaps his mother was wrong about how he felt about Jane.

Isabelle said she was tired, too, and Ruby followed her to the room they were to share. Five small beds and two bureaus filled the room, barely leaving enough space to walk around the furniture. They soon had their nightclothes on and settled into the cold beds. With time, Ruby began to warm, but she had a hard time falling asleep as she thought about Duncan and his family. Just as she was starting to drift off, Isabelle climbed off her cot and started to dress in the dark.

"What are you doing?" Ruby sat up in bed.

"Oh." Isabelle froze and then said, "I'm just getting some fresh air."

"It's freezing in here—I can't imagine how cold it is outside," Ruby answered. "You need to get back under your covers."

"I just need to go on a little walk, that's all."

"Please don't lie to me, Isabelle," Ruby said. "Get back in bed."

Isabelle shook her head, grabbed her coat, and picked up her boots. "I'll be back in a few minutes."

"Do you run after every man you meet? This Lieutenant Anderson? Captain McLeod?"

"Oh goodness." Isabelle froze at the door. "Please stop. Besides you're running after my brother—and you're to be married to another."

Ignoring her, Ruby got out of bed and followed Isabelle as she left the room, calling out after her, "Don't go."

"Stop fretting over me," Isabelle hissed, her voice low but firm, and then slipped out the door at the end of the hall.

For a moment Ruby wasn't sure what she should do. Yell and wake up the house? Barge into the girl's parents' room?

She snuck down the hall to the room she guessed was

Duncan's and knocked on the door, hoping he was home. No one answered. She opened it and whispered, "Duncan."

Still no answer. Starlight shone through the window.

"Duncan," she said louder.

He startled and then jerked his head up, appearing frightened.

"It's me, Ruby."

He rubbed his eyes and then his head fell back down onto the pillow.

"Isabelle snuck out."

"What?"

Ruby said, "Tell your father."

"No, I'll go after her."

Duncan couldn't go alone. "I'll go with you," she said. "I'll go get dressed. Meet me at the back door."

A few minutes later, Duncan, carrying a lamp, met Ruby, and together they stepped out into the night. Ruby took the lamp, hoping Duncan could concentrate on his balance.

"Is Lieutenant Anderson staying in there?" Ruby asked, pointing toward the big house.

"Yes," Duncan answered. "He kept pursuing Isabelle. That's why Father sent her to Lancaster County. She has no discernment when it comes to men. You saw how she acted with Bert. She was the same with this captain. Mother and Father are beside themselves."

"Perhaps they're in the stables," Ruby said. "Or the woods."

"I doubt it," Duncan said. "It's too cold for the woods, and the stables probably haven't been mucked out. And Isabelle would want to be in our house, if at all possible."

When they neared the porch, Duncan struggled up the steps, his cane clicking on the wood, and to the door. Ruby followed, holding the lamp high.

He pounded on the door. When no one answered, he yelled, "I fear there's a young woman in the house, without permission."

In no time an older man, holding a candle and wearing only his long underwear and a nightcap, opened the door. "What's all the racket about?"

"My sister may be within these premises, accompanied by Lieutenant Anderson."

"Impossible," the man bellowed.

"Take a look," Duncan shot back.

The man turned around without closing the door, and Duncan and Ruby stepped into the house. Candles lined the entryway. A wide staircase straight ahead led up to the second floor. The man shouted for help and then veered off to the right. Three men came running down the stairs.

"We're looking for Lieutenant Anderson and my sister, Isabelle Wallis," Duncan barked.

"That fool," one of the younger men said. Then he shouted, "Andy!" as he veered off to the other side of the hall. A moment later he called out, "They're in here!"

The old man charged across the hall and into the room, followed by Duncan. Ruby stayed in the entryway, staring up the staircase, still dumbfounded by the grandeur of the home, even in her concern for Isabelle.

The old man was shouting now at Lieutenant Anderson. Duncan came through the door, his arm around Isabelle. Her hat was off, her hair was falling out of her bun, and her jacket was open.

"Get her out of here," the old man bellowed.

"I am," Duncan shot back.

"Out of Philadelphia!"

"We're headed west at first light." Duncan started toward the door, pulling Isabelle along. *We're.* The word comforted Ruby. He called out over his shoulder, "Thank you, sir!" as he motioned to Ruby to follow. She did, taking one last look at the inside of the home. Duncan might be returning to Lancaster, but she doubted he would stay. There was far too much in Philadelphia to entice him back.

The next day, Mary swiped at her tears as Isabelle told her good-bye. They weren't able to get on the morning coach and had to wait until noon. Ruby didn't let Isabelle out of her sight.

"You behave yourself," Mary said. Neither Duncan nor Isabelle told their parents what had happened the night before. Ruby could only hope Isabelle had learned her lesson.

Mary turned to Ruby and whispered, "Please take her under your wing. You're a good influence. I'm afraid we've spoiled her, without meaning to."

"I'll watch over her," Ruby said, not adding *for as long as she was still on the farm.* She might be headed to Canada soon. She watched as Isabelle hugged her father. Did the girl have any idea how blessed she was to have both of her parents still living? And a brother to care for her?

They were soon back on the stagecoach. Once it left Philadelphia, Isabelle quietly apologized to Duncan. "That was foolish of me," she said. "I only wanted to tell him good-bye."

Then she turned to Ruby. "Thank you for coming after me. I'm afraid Lieutenant Anderson's thinking wasn't as innocent as mine." Ruby wasn't sure if Isabelle was telling the truth or not, as far as her intentions, but she seemed to genuinely regret what she'd done.

Isabelle's voice grew lighter. "Duncan," she said. "How did your evening end with Jane?"

He wrinkled his brow. "I spent an hour in her parlor with her father glaring at me. Apparently I've failed to live up to the expectations of both her family and mine."

"Oh, I don't know about that," Ruby blurted out, realizing as she did she should have kept quiet.

Duncan gave her a questioning look.

Ruby's face grew warm. "It's just that your mother said last night she needed to trust the Lord with you. . . ." She wouldn't add that Mary had regretted asking Jane to supper.

Duncan's face relaxed a little. Finally he said, "Perhaps there's hope, then."

Ruby couldn't guess what he hoped for. Maybe just to make his own decisions in life. She wondered what that would be like. From the time she was young, it was assumed she and Paul would marry. If she didn't marry Paul, she absolutely needed to marry someone else in her community—and there weren't that many choices. Especially not now. It was also assumed she'd go to Canada because that was what Hans had dictated, and she was his responsibility, since the moment their father died. No wonder he was anxious for her to marry Paul.

She didn't believe Zachary felt the same way, though. She didn't feel as if she were a burden to him. He'd already guessed she didn't love Paul. And he'd guessed she had feelings for Duncan.

She turned her head toward the window and stared out at the landscape passing by, feeling as if she'd been kicked in the stomach by the calf. She couldn't have survived the last few months without Duncan's help, and yet she regretted ever meeting him, ever allowing him to become her friend. Knowing him, caring for him . . . jah, all of it had tangled her life in a way she didn't know how to unwind.

Ruby turned toward Duncan. "Tell me—or at least Zachary—what we owe your father, for however he arranged for the army to let you go."

Duncan shook his head. "I have no idea what he did, and I don't plan to ask."

"Please," Ruby said. "We don't want to be beholden to you."

Duncan rubbed the bridge of his nose and said. "Should I feel I must compensate you for sounding the alarm about Isabelle last night?"

Isabelle grinned. "Or should we compensate you for bringing Duncan back from the deep, deep darkness of his—"

Duncan elbowed his sister and the two began to laugh. Ruby decided to let Zachary speak to Duncan when he had the chance—clearly he wasn't taking her seriously.

Duncan, Isabelle, and Ruby spent the night again in the inn and then arrived the next day in Lancaster. From there, Duncan hired a driver in an open buggy to take them to their farms. He instructed the driver to go to the Bachmann farm first and drop Ruby off. They sat close together on the back bench, Isabelle in the middle, trying to stay warm in the late-February cold. The temperature had dropped as they traveled, and the dark clouds looked as if another snowstorm was on the way.

As the driver turned the horses and buggy toward the Bachmann house, Ruby gulped for air. Their old wagon was there.

Hans had returned.

She felt for sure as if the calf had kicked her.

"Who's here?" Duncan asked.

"My brother," she answered. "Hans."

A cloud passed over Duncan's face. "From Canada?"

She nodded.

"Then you'll be leaving soon?"

"Perhaps . . ."

He reached across Isabelle and grabbed for Ruby's hand. "I need to speak with you before you go. Please. In private."

She wanted nothing more than for him to keep a hold of her hand, to never let it go. Tears stung at her eyes.

"Ruby?" She turned toward the voice coming from by the corral. The speaker wasn't Hans.

It was Paul.

— 18 —

Jessica

A enti Suz smiled at me and then pointed to her window. The afternoon sun hung low in the sky. "I think I'll rest for a while after all," she said. "Even though it's so late."

"What about the story?"

"It will have to wait," she said. "I'll finish it tomorrow, before you leave."

I would have rather she continued, but I respected her need to rest. She'd had a hard week, like all of us. I thanked her for the story so far, and then left her little house, stopping on her porch. I could empathize with Ruby. She cared for two different men, as I did.

Ruby had to make that decision years ago. And I'd made that decision too. I had loved Silas, more than I realized. But that didn't mean he was the man I should marry.

I exhaled, as if blowing my worries away, and then headed back to the house. The late afternoon breeze sent a chill right

278

through me. Before I reached the back door Leisel, Marie, and Gail came out, dressed in their capes and bonnets.

For a moment, I visualized Ruby walking along with them, the hem of her plain dress drawing attention to her hand-knitted socks, her wool cape flowing out around her. But then I was back in the present, watching my sisters and Gail march toward me.

"We're going to the singing," Leisel called out, her voice pleasant. "Want to come with us?"

I shook my head. That wouldn't go over well with Bishop Jacobs. "Is Mamm around?"

Leisel nodded. "She's in the living room, reading."

I told them to have a good time. Marie nodded as she passed by me, Gail smiled, and Leisel gave me a quick hug.

Then I continued on inside. Mamm sat in her rocking chair, the family Bible in her hands. She'd always been tall and lanky, but I noticed how thin she looked. Had she been eating? She continued reading, and I stepped to the bench near the door where I'd left my bag.

Then I returned to the living room and said, "Mamm." She glanced up with a surprised look on her face. "Do you mind if I sit in here with you?"

She pursed her lips together, but then said, "Go ahead."

I sat down on the end of the couch closest to her, remembering how I used to sit on her lap when I was young, usually jockeying for position with Marie and Leisel, too, but because I was the oldest she'd ask me to stand. She would read to us—the Little House books were what I remembered the most. It was so easy to imagine the Ingalls as Amish with their horses and wagons and old-fashioned farming and quaint ways and sayings.

I took Dat's address book from my bag. "I found Amos's phone number in here."

She nodded as she closed the Bible and left it to rest on her lap.

I handed the book back to her and she took it. "I shouldn't have kept it," I said. "I'm sorry."

She pursed her lips again.

"I noticed addresses from Vietnam. Aenti Suz told me last week that Dat lived there for a year. And then began corresponding with people from there about twenty years ago."

Mamm's face clouded.

"I wish he'd told us about it."

She shook her head. "I didn't want him giving you ideas."

"There's so much I don't know about him, though," I said.

"You know the most important parts."

I had to agree with her. At least I hoped I did. He'd poured those parts into me. Dedication to the land. Care for others. Faith in God.

I sighed. I doubted I'd ever get more information about my father's life from my mother. "I plan to go back to Harrisburg tomorrow," I said. "Milton is doing well with the farm, and with Arden coming home, I think it's better that I leave."

She nodded, hugging the book to her chest.

"But Mamm, if you have any influence over Arden, could you discourage him from selling off the woods? And from allowing fracking on our land?" I wouldn't mention the dangers of fracking as far as the well water. I honestly felt the less defensive I made them all feel, the better.

Mamm shook her head. "Arden isn't considering fracking."

"No, he is."

She pursed her lips together. "He told me he wasn't."

I wasn't sure what to say. I'd seen the paperwork. But I didn't want to get in a power struggle with her.

"Well, Milton would like to have land left to farm, to earn a living when he's grown." If I left it that Milton needed a livelihood someday, I figured she might be more receptive.

For the longest time, Mamm didn't respond, but finally she said, "I'll think about what I can say to him."

"Denki," I said and then, "I need to speak with you about something else."

She lifted her eyebrows and pursed her lips again.

I quietly said one word. "Amos."

Her expression collapsed into a frown.

"He's carried a heavy burden all of these years. Perhaps Dat told you."

She nodded. "He told me what Amos claimed."

"But you didn't believe he was telling the truth?"

She shook her head again. "That would mean Arden was lying."

"Jah," I whispered. "It would."

She put the address book on top of the Bible, resting both in her lap. "Jessica, don't do this again."

"Do what?"

"Try to stir up trouble. Bishop Jacobs warned you once."

I exhaled slowly. "Arden does lie," I said. "He lied about Rebecca. He lied about Amos. He won Vi's affection based on his lies. And he *is* pursuing fracking."

Tears filled her eyes. "What makes you hate your brother so much?"

"I don't," I answered, doing my best to keep my voice calm. "But I do love our family and our land. I think it's time we seek the truth."

"It doesn't matter," she said. "You have no proof."

"Not that he lied about Rebecca," I said. "But I do about the fracking."

She wrinkled her nose. "No, he told both your Dat and me, just last month, that he wasn't considering any such thing."

"Come out to the barn with me," I said. "I'll show you." I hoped the plans were in the cupboard, as Silas indicated.

She complied, placing the Bible and the address book on the table and then putting on her cape and bonnet. She followed me out the door and trudged beside me to the barn, completely silent.

I remembered what Amos said about feeling sympathetic toward her, for all she'd gone through. I didn't know what it was like to lose a child, to have two others leave, to lose my husband. I prayed for compassion, to see her hurts and disappointments.

I held the barn door open for her and then led the way to the office. I hurried behind the desk and opened the cupboard, kneeling down. There were a couple of boxes filled with tax records. I pulled out the boxes. Up against the back of the cupboard was a cardboard tube. I took it out, imagining that Milton had stashed it back there after he saw me looking at the plans. I took off the lid and pulled out the paperwork. Bingo.

"Arden left these here," I said, turning around to my mother and then spreading the plans on the desktop.

She bent down and scanned the papers for a few seconds and then looked up at me. "Maybe these don't belong to Arden."

I concentrated on not rolling my eyes. "Who would they belong to? Amos?"

"Don't be sassy," Mamm snapped.

"Don't be in denial," I replied.

She crossed her arms.

"I'm sorry," I said, disappointed that I hadn't been more gentle, even after intending to. "Mamm, these absolutely belong to Arden." I held up the side of the tube with the address.

"Look. This has Arden's name on it. And the postmark was nearly four months ago." I held it up so she could read it.

She did and then struggled around the desk and sat down abruptly in the chair.

"What is it?" I asked.

She opened her mouth and then closed it again. Finally she managed to say, "That was the week after your Dat was diagnosed with cancer."

The next morning Milton and I did the milking with Luke and Leroy's help. I'd decided I'd done all I could to stop Arden—the rest would be up to Mamm. I could go back to Harrisburg knowing I'd done my best.

The children, except for Milton of course, were all returning to school that day, and right before we finished, Vi came out to tell Luke and Leroy it was time to eat breakfast and get ready for school.

"You go along, too, Milton," I said. "I'm going to go run an errand, but I'll come back and help you get started with the plowing."

The boys ran across the field to their home as I started toward the big house, but Vi asked me to wait a moment and then said, "May I speak with you?"

I stopped. I knew Mamm hadn't told her about Arden's lies, but I still felt anxious about all of it. Did she suspect that he'd lied to her?

"I have a driver coming to take me up to the hospital as soon as the children leave for school. Leisel is going with me."

I nodded. That sounded like a good plan. "I'll tell you good-bye now." I doubted seeing me would be good for Arden, and I certainly had no intension of confronting him about his lies. I'd leave that up to Mamm. "I plan to leave by early afternoon."

"I suspected you would leave today." She shoved her hands into the pocket of her coat. "We all appreciate your help this last week, even Arden."

"You're welcome," I said. "It was good . . ." My voiced trailed off. Good to see everyone? Good to be back? Good to be shamed and shunned? I didn't say any of that. "Tell Arden I hope he'll heal quickly."

She smiled, just a little. At one time, she'd been a big sister to me. Now I struggled to see her as a friend and not an enemy.

"Take care," I said, squinting into the rising sun.

"You too." She turned and walked away slowly, as if every step were an effort. But then she turned and cleared her throat. "I'm sorry for the way I treated you when you first arrived. And that letter I sent after you left. Well, it was required of me. . . ."

I nodded. I imagined either Bishop Jacobs or Arden insisted she write it.

She took a few steps toward me and then I walked toward her, meeting her halfway.

She took a deep breath and then exhaled slowly. "It was helpful for me to see Amos, to remember what I was like at your age."

I tilted my head and then smiled at her. "I remember. You were kind and generous. And good to me."

She closed her eyes for a moment and whispered, "Denki. I needed that." She opened her eyes. "I need to be reminded that perhaps I can be that way again."

I reached for her hand, and she let me take it. It wasn't as cold as I expected it would be, considering the frosty morning. "What's going on, Vi?" A shiver ran through me.

284

Her face grew pale. "I don't want to say too much, but somewhere throughout the years I got caught up in Arden's negativity. It started with how critical he was of Amos. Then it jumped around to various people through the years—your Dat's leniency, then you, then Silas."

"He was critical of Silas?"

She nodded. "His recent negative talk has made others in the community suspicious of Silas. He implied Silas was courting Gail to get back at you."

"Oh" was all I could manage to say.

She frowned. "And I never said a thing to him. Never. Not about Amos, whom I knew was a better man than Arden ever admitted. Not about your Dat or you or Silas. At first, I believed Arden was the man I needed to marry, the one who would care for me. And then I figured no husband was perfect and there were simply things I needed to put up with. So instead of asking him to stop criticizing others, I joined him."

I squeezed her hand in support. "Is that why you've been avoiding him?"

She nodded. "Your Dat dying. Having you return. Seeing Amos. Arden's heart attack. All of it hit home for me. I knew I needed to stand up to Arden, but I couldn't do it while he was in the hospital." She sighed. "But I will. In the meantime, will you forgive me?"

"Of course." I squeezed her hand again. Her words had lifted part of the cloak that had been clinging to my soul for the last three years.

"Don't give up on Silas," she said.

I let go of her hand. "Pardon?"

"I regret Arden and I weren't more supportive of the two of you when you started courting."

· "You weren't unsupportive. . . ." Actually, come to think of it, they were. Arden was so critical of me and my "unladylike ways." And even back then he was weirdly critical of Silas, implying he wasn't strong enough to stand up to me and that sort of thing.

When I didn't finish my sentence, Vi said, "I hope you'll give him another chance."

I shook my head. "That was all so long ago. Water under the bridge . . ." Again my voice trailed off.

She smiled a little. Was she thinking of Amos? My much kinder, gentler brother. My brother who was actually a lot like Silas. I shuddered and spoke quickly to interrupt my thoughts. "Thank you," I said, "for talking with me. I hope things will go well for you when you speak with Arden."

She smiled again, this time a little broader, and then turned her head back toward the field.

I knew her children were waiting for her. "Go," I said.

She did. I watched as she walked away. Vi had been passive, beginning when she chose a lie over the man she loved. But she was determined, now, to do what she could to right her course.

I decided not to go into the house for breakfast. I was grateful for my encounter with Vi, but I wasn't ready for more drama with Marie and Gail. I decided to go to the Stoltz farm instead, without changing out of my milking dress. Hopefully John Stoltz had decided to share his story as a cautionary tale to others, my brother included.

As I started up my car, Leisel rushed out onto the porch. I rolled down my window. "Come tell me good-bye," I called out, as I pulled around in front of the house and put the car in Park.

I climbed out and gave her a big hug. "Hopefully I'll have

a chance to give you a second good-bye this afternoon, but if not, come see me sometime," I said.

She hugged me back, then pulled away, and wrinkled her nose. "Can you imagine how that would go over if I just took a trip to Harrisburg?" She shook her head. "Not well."

I hugged her again and then, choked up, climbed back in my car and sped away. I'd expected coming home would be hard, but I hadn't anticipated the pain I'd feel at leaving again.

In less than ten minutes, I pulled in front of the Stoltz house and climbed out of my car. The brisk spring breeze stung my cheeks as I looked around. After detecting no sign of activity in the open shed, I started toward the house.

Mildred Stoltz opened the door for me. She again wore a scarf over her bald head. After greeting her, I told her I wanted to speak with John.

"He's out in the barn with the new fellow."

"Oh?"

"Jah, John hired a farmhand."

My heart raced. I'd only told Silas about the possibility yesterday. "What's the new farmhand's name?" I asked.

"It starts with an *S*," Mildred said. "Simon, maybe?" She shrugged.

"Silas?" I asked.

"Perhaps." She shrugged. "Go on out. John will be happy to see you."

As I entered the barn, I called out a hello. When no one answered, I walked on through it and out to the field. In the distance, John stood with a younger man at the fence line. I headed toward them. Halfway across the field, I could confirm the young man was Silas. He'd certainly acted quickly on my tip, and it was crystal clear he really was done working on our farm.

For a moment, I considered leaving. Seeing Silas hurt. It hurt me over and over and over. Why inflict more discomfort on myself right before I returned to Harrisburg? But if I didn't speak with John in person, I'd have to leave a message on his answering machine. And then he'd need to call me back. That could go on for days. It would be much better if I arrived in the office in the morning with a positive report for Tom.

I called out a hello and waved. Both men turned toward me and then John waved back.

Pasting a smile on my face, I trudged forward, determined to be as cordial as possible.

"Hello, John!" I said as I reached him.

He greeted me and turned toward Silas. "It seems you two already know each other."

"Jah," I answered. "We're old friends."

Silas gave me a nod, his hazel eyes sad. I quickly redirected my attention to John. "May I speak with you?" I asked.

"Certainly," he answered.

Silas said to John, "I'll go finish up in the barn. Denki for the explanation here."

John nodded. "Denki for your input. I appreciate it."

"I stopped by the house and said hello to Mildred."

"*Gut*," John replied. "She's doing well today. We're thankful for that. And at least now, on the bad days, Silas will be here."

Perhaps letting Silas know about the job was the right thing to do. Silas was a fatherless young man, and John and Mildred were a childless couple. I could see how the arrangement might benefit them in many ways.

I asked John if he'd had a chance to think about sharing his story. "Well," he said, "I was going to tell you no, but then I discussed it with Silas and he encouraged me to think about some other aspects."

"Oh?"

"Jah, he said what you did. That I might be helping others, both Amish and Englisch. That it's information everyone should have. He told me that water safety is one of the most important issues—other than spiritual ones—that we have. It's no coincidence that Jesus used water to explain His plan for us, using terms like *wells of salvation*, *living water*, and *water of life*. Clean water is essential to our physical survival—just as Christ is to our spiritual survival."

I nodded in agreement.

"So, jah," he said. "I'll speak with this Tom fellow. I'll tell him our story—that's all. But I won't allow any photos."

"How about photos of your land?" I asked. "But not you or Mildred."

He paused for a moment but then said, "All right. I guess we can allow that."

"Denki." I wanted to hug the man, but I knew he wouldn't have been receptive to that.

He nodded shyly. "Denki for sending Silas out to me. I'm grateful to have a hard worker to help me. I knew his father—he was a good man too."

"I'm so glad it worked out," I said. I told him that Tom would come out by the end of the week to interview him and then said farewell. I headed back, walking around the barn instead of through it, but when I reached my car Silas was waiting for me.

"Jessie," he said. "Could we talk for a moment?"

I nodded, afraid that if I spoke the growing lump in my throat might dislodge.

"When are you going back?"

"This afternoon," I managed to say.

He stepped toward me. "May I ask you something?"

I nodded.

"Do you love Tom?"

I inhaled sharply. I tried to answer, but I couldn't find the word. Instead I nodded my head.

"All right," he said. "I'll leave it alone." I thought about when I'd begged him to leave with me before, and he asked me to stay and work things out. When I wouldn't, he'd said the same thing. *"I'll leave it alone."*

I hated it when he said that. I always had. How many times had I wanted him to push? To pry? To react? And he'd simply left it *alone.*

"I've got to go," I stammered, climbing into my car.

He stepped back as I started the engine, his hat in his hand. Tears clouded my vision as I put the car in Reverse. Once I turned around, I glanced in the rearview mirror. Silas stood still as a statue, watching me go—once again.

By the time I returned to our farm, I'd managed to compose myself. I quickly sent Tom a text, telling him John Stoltz had agreed to be interviewed, and gave him the man's phone number. Then I added that I would be home that evening and would give him all of the details at work the next day. I ended the text with: *I miss you! Can't wait to be back to normal life.*

Then I headed straight to Aenti Suz's Dawdi Haus, hoping she had a sticky bun or cinnamon roll I could eat—but mostly that she would have time to tell me the rest of Ruby's story. I needed to know what happened all those years ago. Aenti Suz had left Ruby sitting in the buggy with Duncan holding on to her hand, as Paul called out to her. Choosing Paul would mean losing Duncan and leaving her farm. Choosing Duncan would mean leaving her family, faith, and land.

We had that one thing in common. Ruby had to leave the Bachmann property no matter what, just as I did. Land for a daughter was something completely different than for the one son from each generation who would inherit the farm.

I knocked quickly and then opened the door to the comforting scent of cinnamon and the sweet smell of icing.

Aenti Suz stood at her oven, smiling at me. "I've been waiting for you," she said. "Are you ready for the last of the story?"

"Jah," I answered, thinking of Ruby facing Paul as Duncan held her hand.

– 19 –

Ruby

Pulling her hand away from Duncan, Ruby stared at Paul for a long moment.

"Zachary said you'd been to Philadelphia." Paul stepped toward the buggy.

Ruby stood, and Duncan quickly did too, stepping down. He started around to help Ruby, but Paul extended his hand. Instead, Duncan helped his sister.

Ruby quickly introduced the two to Paul and then said, "Duncan took Zachary's place to keep him from having to go back into the army."

Paul nodded at Duncan and said, "It's unfortunate Zachary ever got himself mixed up in such a thing, but I appreciate you helping him." Then Paul turned toward Ruby. "Hans wants me to help sell the farm immediately, and then all of us will travel to Canada."

"Oh, surely not so soon," Isabelle said. "Can't it wait? Until summer at least?"

Ruby wanted to laugh. There was so little Isabelle understood. But she couldn't help but find some consolation in how oblivious the girl was. Even though her family had suffered, too, Isabelle remained optimistic. Life continued to be one long adventure for her. Ruby turned toward Isabelle. "We'll have some time yet. A few weeks at least." She couldn't imagine Zachary and Paul would find a buyer right away.

She turned toward Duncan, aware of how stilted her voice sounded as she spoke. "Thank you again for everything you've done for us."

He nodded as a complicated expression passed across his face. Perhaps a bit of anger, but also sorrow. Her stomach dropped.

He turned and grabbed his bag from the buggy and directed Isabelle to do the same. Then he paid the farmer and said, "We'll walk to our place from here."

Isabelle hugged Ruby and said, "I'll be down tomorrow for my next lesson."

Ruby hugged her back. "I'll be expecting you." Then Isabelle caught up to Duncan and walked beside him, chatting away. Bless the girl. Ruby really did find her endearing.

After thanking the farmer, Ruby collected her bag, too, and then turned toward the house. Paul stepped to her side. "I worried about you being gone like that, with strangers."

Ruby started walking. "They're not strangers."

"They're not friends," Paul countered.

Ruby shrugged, trying to appear as if his words didn't matter, but they did. They were her friends, but she wasn't going to admit it to Paul.

"Zachary was vague about how he returned home. Tell me what happened."

They reached the porch. Ruby took the steps quickly, and then opened the front door. "How about some supper?" she asked. "I'm guessing there must be some sort of food available."

"We had ham last night. There's some left."

"*Gut*," she said. "I'll see what else there is."

"Ruby . . ."

She kept moving toward the back of the house.

"What are you hiding?" It was quite a forthright question for Paul.

"Nothing." She kept walking. "Go tell Zachary we'll eat soon." After she placed her bag in the back bedroom, she found the ham and several potatoes in the cupboard, but all of the bread was gone. She'd make more in the morning.

She sliced the ham and the potatoes, and then fried both in the pan over the fire. By the time she was done, Paul returned with Zachary and a pail of milk for her to separate. She dished the food onto plates and then they all sat at the table.

After Paul led them in prayer, he said he wanted to know the entire story of Zachary's rescue. Ruby glanced at her brother, hoping he'd do the explaining. He shrugged and looked down at his plate.

"Zachary wrote that he was ill and wounded." She went on to explain that she'd gone to Valley Forge and brought him home.

"I understand that," Paul said, "but how did you get there?"

"The wagon." Ruby sighed. There was no getting around the truth. "Duncan went with me."

"You traveled unaccompanied with a man you don't know?"

"I do know him," Ruby responded. "We worked together for four months to keep our two farms running. He offered to go alone to get Zachary, but I insisted on going with him."

Paul took another bite and asked, "Why?"

"Because Duncan was injured in the war. He'd been walking with a crutch but had just started using a cane. If there was a problem with the horses or the wagon, he might not have been able to manage alone."

"So he's a soldier then too?"

"Was."

Paul remained silent as he continued eating. Ruby concentrated on her food, but she didn't have much of an appetite as shame seeped through her, and then flowed into her soul. Justifying her actions to Paul felt humiliating. Jah, none of it looked good, but she'd had no other choice.

Finally he said, "So why did you need to leave again?"

She explained about Captain McLeod coming to take Zachary back to Valley Forge. "Like I said, Duncan took his place."

Paul wrinkled his nose. "I remember you said that, I just find it surprising."

Ruby agreed. "So did I—but once he did, we couldn't just leave him there."

"Why not? He's a soldier."

"*Was.* And an injured one at that. Plus the place is rife with disease, and there isn't enough food or other supplies." She explained that it seemed his father made the payment for Duncan to leave, although Duncan didn't seem to know exactly what happened.

"I'll pay the Wallis family back," Zachary said. "I promise I will."

"You can try, but they don't expect you to," Ruby explained, "although I agree with you that you should."

Paul swallowed his last bite. "So they're wealthy then?"

Ruby nodded. "Jah, but not as wealthy as they were. The

British have confiscated their home in Philadelphia and are using it as a headquarters."

A look of satisfaction settled on Paul's face.

Ruby frowned. "They're good people. I don't know what I would have done without Duncan's help. The farm would be in disarray. Mamm's final days would have been much harder. Zachary would probably have died. I owe a debt of gratitude to the entire Wallis family."

"Of course," Paul said. "It's just that none of this seems in keeping with our way of life."

"No, it doesn't, does it?" Ruby stood. "I wrote to you and Hans and told you I needed help. You knew Mamm was ill. You knew Zachary had been conscripted. When neither of you came, I had to do the best I could. I had no choice."

She picked up her plate.

Neither Paul nor Zachary said a word. She put her plate in the bucket and headed out the back door. She had longed for Paul to come get her, but now she no longer did. Not at all. She agreed with Isabelle. Why couldn't he have waited until summer?

She found herself at the fence line, gazing at the oak tree on the Wallis property, missing Duncan. If only she could talk with him now. If only she could freely share how she felt.

That night a light dusting of late-February snow fell, but not enough to keep Zachary and Paul from riding over to the minister's farm the next morning. Ruby stayed to make bread with flour Paul had brought from Canada, and to give the cabin a good cleaning. Late in the morning, a knock fell on the front door. Ruby hurried to open it, finding Isabelle on her stoop.

"Come in," she said, glad to see her friend. But she couldn't ignore the fact she wished Duncan was with her.

"How are you?" she asked Isabelle as she motioned her into the kitchen.

"Just fine," Isabelle said, following Ruby to the kitchen. "But things are pretty grim over at Uncle Wallis's house."

"Why?" Ruby asked as she turned her attention back to her bread making.

Isabelle rolled her eyes. "I'm the one who's supposed to be daft—not you."

Ruby shook her head. "I have no idea what you're talking about."

"It's not what—it's whom."

Ruby bent over her dough and began to knead it, digging her hands into the sticky mess.

Isabelle flung herself onto the stool by the fire. "Duncan's been pining over you ever since—"

"Stop," Ruby gasped, surprising herself and Isabelle both. She stood up straight and pulled her hands from the dough. "I'm sorry," she said.

Isabelle took a deep breath.

Tears stung Ruby's eyes. "Please don't say any more."

"Why?" Isabelle stood and put her arm around Ruby.

"Because . . ." She'd burst into tears if she said another word.

Isabelle pulled her closer. "Because why?"

Ruby knew she couldn't answer that—she needed to take care with what she said. She took a deep breath, exhaled slowly, and then said, "Let me finish kneading this. After it rises, you can shape the loaves."

"You're not going to answer me?"

Ruby ignored her again. "We'll get four out of this batch. You can take two with you."

Isabelle sighed. "Please answer me."

"I can't." Ruby pulled away from her friend. "I'm sorry." She dug her hands back into the dough.

She guessed that Paul believed she'd grown too close to the Englischers, that she'd been influenced by their fancy ways. But that wasn't what had happened at all. She'd been influenced by their care. And Duncan's sacrifice.

Jah, and their love. They were different from her Plain community—oh, so different—but in many ways they were the same too. Helping your neighbors, loving your family, honoring the Lord. All of those things were important to them too.

She finished kneading the dough and then scooped it into the greased bowl, placing it on the table close to the fire. She put Isabelle to work sweeping the entire cabin, while Ruby started the water to boil for the laundry.

An hour later, Isabelle shaped the loaves. Later, Ruby took them out to the oven in the backyard, following her footsteps in the snow from when she'd done the chores earlier. She slipped them inside, over the fire, welcoming the blast of heat against her arms and face. Then she gazed over to the Wallis property.

It was a mistake. Duncan stood under the oak tree, looking her way. He waved and started toward the fence. "Ruby!" he called out.

She waved but turned away from him, hurrying toward the house.

"Wait," he called out.

She kept going.

Isabelle met her at the door. "Go talk to him."

"I can't," Ruby answered, remembering her wish from the

night before. But the truth was, she'd never talk to Duncan again. She couldn't trust herself. She hadn't been wrong to help him and accept his help. She hadn't been wrong to go to Valley Forge with him. Or to Philadelphia with Isabelle. But she had been wrong to let herself have feelings for him.

As she brushed past Isabelle and into the house, she heard the hooves of horses. Paul and Zachary were back.

A moment later, Zachary called out a hello to Duncan, but she couldn't make out any more of a conversation. Later, when her brother and Paul came into the house, it seemed Paul wasn't happy to see Isabelle, but he didn't say anything. However, he did stay in the cabin, perhaps to monitor their conversation. When the bread was done, Ruby wrapped two loaves in a cloth and sent them home with Isabelle.

Paul sighed as Ruby closed the door. "I didn't think she'd ever leave." He stood. "I'll go out and work until it's time for dinner."

"You stayed in here just to keep an eye on me? To see what we were talking about?"

He smiled, but in an odd way. "I have good news. Minister Fischer thinks his Englisch neighbor's son might be interested in the farm. He's going to see if he can come up with the money to meet the price Hans wants. We could be on our way soon." The expression on his face was undeniably smug.

Ruby turned toward the fire, and Paul continued on out the door, seemingly oblivious to her reaction. She grew cold regardless of the warmth of the flames.

That night, after Paul went to bed, Zachary stayed by the fire as Ruby finished mending one of his shirts.

Her brother hadn't said much all day. Tired of his silence, she asked, "How are you feeling?"

"Not as strong as I used to but much better than I was," he said. "I think I'll be back to normal soon." He extended his arm and wiggled it. "Maybe not normal but good enough."

She nodded. He'd be able to do everything he needed to farm, to make a living.

He leaned forward in his chair. "Could we speak frankly? The way we used to before I left?"

She nodded again and then knotted her thread.

"Are you looking forward to moving to Canada?"

"Well," she said, and then broke the thread with her teeth. "I suppose so. There are many things to anticipate favorably. We'll be with family again. With our people. We'll be away from the soldiers and the fighting." She looked up at her brother, his face in the shadows bouncing across the wall from the flickering flames.

He appeared to be sad.

"What is it, Zachary?"

"I like it here," he said. "This is our land. Our place. This war will end. Why should we move to Canada?"

"Because our family is there."

"Mamm and Dat left their families in the Old Country to come to Pennsylvania. They'd understand us staying."

"Us? What foolishness are you saying? I'm going to Canada."

"Why? To marry Paul? You don't even love him."

She lowered her voice even more. "Zachary, how can you say that?"

"It's obvious."

An icy coldness swept through her. "Shhh," she said.

"You don't want Paul to overhear us? To realize what's going on?"

"Nothing is going on. You know I'd never deny our Lord

and church, deny my commitment to our faith." Her face grew warmer and warmer as she spoke, even though the dying fire had left the room cold.

Zachary shook his head.

Ruby stood and folded the shirt, putting it on the table beside her brother. "I'm going to bed. I'll see you in the morning."

Zachary picked up the shirt and clutched it to his chest. "I'll make no apologies for what I said."

"That's fine," Ruby responded. "Just don't say it again." Sure, Zachary could decide to stay, although Hans was expecting the money from the farm. He'd said the sale of the farm would buy Zachary land in Canada, but she guessed Hans felt entitled to some of it too.

Hans would be furious with Zachary, but her youngest brother could ultimately decide for himself. On the other hand, she had no choice but to go, and at this point the sooner she left the better.

Once she was far away from Duncan Wallis, she was sure her feelings of affection for Paul would return. She couldn't deny that she once thought very highly of him. Those feelings would come back once she left Lancaster. They had to.

The weather turned warm again by the next morning, and all the snow melted, leaving more mud than usual. As Ruby fed the chickens, she heard Paul and Zachary in the barn, their voices raised.

"We all had a plan," Paul said. "You can't abandon it now."

"Dat always intended for this farm to be mine. He helped Hans and Daniel buy their own farms, which they sold. Why does Hans feel I must contribute from the sale of this farm to the entire group?"

"You'd mostly be contributing the money toward your own farm up north," Paul said. "Your brother is a good man. He has all of our best interests in mind. A little extra cash will give us all a bit more land."

Ruby stepped closer to the barn, hoping to hear more. Paul sounded as illogical as Hans.

"Think of your sister," Paul said. "She'd be devastated to have you stay. Family should remain together. And besides, how would you survive down here without your brothers? Or your community? Whom would you marry? Whom would you worship with?"

"More are staying than you and Hans led us to believe," Zachary responded. "Closer to Lancaster, an entire group is staying."

"Well, you're not," Paul said.

Her brother didn't respond, but a moment later he came bursting through the open barn door and started marching toward the road.

"Where are you going?" Ruby called out.

"To speak with Duncan."

She didn't say anything more, not even when Paul stepped out of the barn, glancing from Zachary to her and then shaking his head.

Ruby continued on with her work, hoping Isabelle would come over and keep her company. But she didn't.

On Sunday, Zachary rode toward Lancaster and attended church with Lettie Yoder and her family. It was the first time that Ruby knew of that he'd seen the girl since he'd come home from Valley Forge. When he returned, he called Paul in from the barn and asked him to sit at the table with Ruby. Then he told both of them that he'd decided to keep the farm and stay. "And marry Lettie," he said. "We've set a date for next month."

Paul banged his hand on the table. "Hans will be furious," he said, turning toward Ruby. "We're leaving tomorrow. Pack your things."

"Will you marry first?" Zachary asked. "Before you go?"

"We'll marry in Canada," Paul answered.

"What about the propriety of traveling together when you're not married?" Zachary sneered. "Won't you be ashamed of yourself?"

Paul banged his hand on the table again.

Alarmed, Ruby stood and calmly said she was going for a walk.

"That's not a good idea," Paul said.

"I'm going to the graveyard is all," Ruby answered, stepping to the back door and grabbing her cape.

"I'm afraid you've strayed from the Ordnung with me gone," he said. "You'll soon be back to living the right way."

She didn't bother to respond but slipped out the back door. As she walked down the road to the edge of the property, she pulled her cape tight against the cool spring wind. At the end of their farm, she turned into the small plot where her Mamm and Dat were buried. She stood there, feeling lost and lonely. Tomorrow she would leave the only home she'd ever known to go to live near two brothers she wasn't close to and marry a man she didn't love. How would that draw her closer to the Lord Jesus? How would that allow her to serve Him and others more?

Dear Lord, she silently prayed. *What should I do?*

The wind whipped at her bonnet and stung her eyes. Soon real tears formed, and a few slipped down her face. She quickly swiped them away. Wallowing in her sorrow would do no good.

She turned to leave as a horse and rider approached in the distance. For a moment, she thought it might be Paul. Perhaps he'd come to apologize. But why would he ride such a short way?

It wasn't Paul. It was Duncan.

She turned to face him—and the wind. Duncan clutched his cane as he dismounted and started toward her. "Zachary told me you'd walked down here."

Ruby nodded.

"So you're leaving? Tomorrow?"

"Jah," she answered. Zachary had told him.

Duncan stepped closer. "I know you don't want me to say this, but I have to, before you leave."

She shook her head. "Please don't."

He ignored her. "I care for you, Ruby Bachmann." She put her hand up to stop him, but he shook his head and continued. "Truth be told, I love you."

She stepped backward, unable to bear his words.

"My entire life has changed since meeting you. I'm now grateful for my injury—I can truly see the good God is working in my life. He used you to show me that there's so much more than business and connections, than life in Philadelphia, than my family's fortunes. Isabelle was right—you saved me from a dark place. Your gentle faith brought me back to what I believed as a child. I can see God's work in my life, and I long to see what He holds for my future."

He stepped toward her. "I'll stay here in Lancaster and farm Uncle's land. I'll live as simple a life as I possibly can, for you. I don't believe I can join your church, but I do believe we already worship the same God. I won't stop being a Patriot, but I won't pursue war or violence of any kind. I will be the best husband I can to you."

Her eyes filled with tears again. As she brushed them away, Duncan reached for her hand. She pulled it away from him.

He smiled, just a little, and then said, "Tell me that you love Paul. Tell me that you don't love me. Because I don't believe either, not for a second."

She turned toward Old Man Wallis's woods, where she used to play as a child, keeping her face as stoic as possible. She could dart across the field to the trees. He wouldn't be able to follow her.

"Think about what I said. I'll come say good-bye in the morning. It won't be too late to change your mind."

She turned and began marching toward the woods, away from him. He had no idea what it would mean for her to reject her family, to reject her faith, to reject Paul.

Jah, it seemed they did share the essentials of faith, but their families had chosen very different ways of living.

"Ruby!" Duncan yelled. "Come back."

She waved but marched even faster.

"Ruby!" he yelled again. But his voice was distant now.

She crossed her family's farm, and then at the very back of it, climbed the fence. She marched through the Wallis's field, past the oak tree, and then around the pond. By the time she reached the woods, tears flowed down her face.

She slipped into the trees and stumbled her way to the middle of the woods. Then she collapsed on a fallen log and cried her heart out. No one, not even Duncan, would ever know how much it hurt her to reject him. Her heart shattered as she sobbed. Tomorrow morning she'd tell him good-bye and never see him again. For the rest of her life, she imagined, she'd struggle to forget him, to force his memory from her mind.

She couldn't imagine how bleak her marriage to Paul would

be now. Not only did she not love him, but never had he ever spoken about seeking God's guidance or will. All of his talk had been about following the Ordnung, about following the rules.

"Our Father which art in heaven . . ." She silently prayed as the wind blew above her in the high branches of the trees. *"Thy kingdom come, Thy will be done. . . ."* She'd have to trust God to heal her broken heart and guide her future.

The next morning she awoke long before sunrise, completed her packing, and then made porridge for breakfast. She could hear Paul and Zachary arguing again before they reached the house after doing their chores.

"Hans will expect me to bring the plow. He specifically said not to leave it."

"He has his own plow."

"It's not as good as your father's."

"You mean as *mine*," Zachary said. "You're not taking it."

As they came through the door, Paul said, "Ruby, talk some sense into your brother."

She didn't bother to answer. Paul wouldn't hear her anyway.

After the men finished their porridge they went back outside, and Ruby cleaned up—for the very last time in her childhood home. When she finished, she stood by the fire and remembered the evenings when Dat would read aloud to all of them while Mamm mended their clothes. She thought of the meals she helped Mamm cook, of all the laundry they did together. She hoped her parents knew back then how much she appreciated them, even though she'd failed to tell them as often as she should have.

She packed what food she felt fair in taking into the basket on the table. It was a good thing Zachary planned to marry soon—otherwise he would most likely starve.

Then she retrieved her bag from her room, put on her cape and bonnet, grabbed the basket and bag, and left the cabin without looking back. She'd cried enough yesterday. She wouldn't cry again today, especially not in front of Paul.

A few tools sat in the back of the wagon. A rake, a scythe, and an axe. And a crate that held a few chickens, the beginning of her own flock.

"Ready?" Paul asked.

She nodded, placing the basket and then her bag behind the bench. She hugged Zachary good-bye.

"I wish you'd stay," he said.

She nodded. "I know." Then she told him that when the time came, he owed Duncan a ham and shoulder from the smokehouse for helping her butcher the hog.

"Of course," Zachary said. "He won't let me pay his family the debt I owe, but hopefully he'll take that."

"He will," Ruby answered. At least she hoped so.

Paul jumped up on the driver's side while Zachary helped her up onto the bench. As she sat, Isabelle called out her name and then yelled, "You can't leave without saying good-bye!"

Ruby shielded her eyes from the morning sun. Isabelle looked like an angel, wearing her white cloak, coming toward her.

Paul held the reins tight, ready to go.

"Wait," Ruby said, relieved it was just Isabelle and not Duncan. Thankfully, it seemed he'd changed his mind about coming over.

She scrambled down from the bench and ran toward her friend as Paul set the brake and then jumped down too. She wasn't surprised that he followed her.

Ruby and Isabelle hugged. "Will I see you again?" Isabelle asked.

307

"I don't know," Ruby answered. She'd like to think that someday she and Paul would return to visit Zachary, but she doubted it.

"Thank you," Isabelle said, "for being like a sister to me."

Ruby hugged the girl again, and as she did Duncan rounded the corner from the road. She released Isabelle.

"We need to go." Paul took Ruby's elbow.

"Wait," Ruby said as her heart lurched.

Paul pulled on her arm, but she stood firm. On the way home from Valley Forge, beside the fire, Duncan had said that being injured had helped him know his heart, and that the bad things that had happened had helped shape who he was, and how he saw both God and the world.

She couldn't deny the same had happened to her in the last several months. Could she trust God enough to believe she could make a choice different from what her family expected? A choice filled with love and a spiritual connection? Perhaps God had been shaping her into the person He wanted her to be, one who could choose love over safety, and spiritual growth over what was familiar and expected.

When Duncan reached them, he held out his hand to her. Time froze.

Paul spoke again, this time more forcefully. "We need to go."

Ruby's eyes stayed on Duncan's hand. The message was clear, most likely even to Paul. She could leave with Paul for the predictable life she'd expected since she was a girl, although in Canada, not Lancaster County, and put all of this behind her. Or she could take Duncan's hand and forge an unknown life with the man she loved, with a man she truly wanted to spend the rest of her life with.

Jah, Hans would be furious.

And Paul's pride would be hurt, but she wasn't sure that in the long run he'd be that sorry. He'd easily find another girl to marry.

"Ruby." Paul's voice was harsh. And demanding.

She shifted her gaze to Duncan's face. His expression was kind. Gentle. His eyes brimmed with tears.

She reached out and took his hand, stepping away from Paul's side. Duncan pulled her into his arms as she did.

–20–

Jessica

Aenti Suz stood and started toward her kitchen. "How about some tea?"

I fell against the back of her sofa. "How about the end of the story?"

"That is the end of the story. She chose Duncan."

"And left the Amish?"

"Jah," Aenti Suz said. "It's not what you expected?"

"I thought you said it was a cautionary tale."

"It is," Aenti Suz said, her back to me as she filled the teakettle.

"Oh come on," I said. "Generations of Amish aunties have *not* been telling that story as a cautionary tale. That wouldn't discourage any Amish girl from marrying an Englisch man. In fact, it would encourage every one of them to leave."

"Well," Aenti Suz said, turning on the burner. "I may have embellished a little, focusing more on Ruby's feelings than other generations did." She turned around and smiled.

I had no doubt she embellished it—and I was glad she had. That's not what I had a problem with. "Why would you tell it to me of all people? I do plan to marry an Englischman." God willing.

"But that's not the point of the story," Aenti Suz said. "Ruby recognized that God had worked the difficult things in her life to mold her, to make her stronger. Through that, He opened her heart to accept and return Duncan's love, and trust God with her future."

My face began to grow warm. "What are you saying?"

Aenti Suz shrugged. "I simply told a story. The questions you should be asking yourself are What has God been teaching? And where is He leading?" She busied herself with her tea basket. "Let's see. Should we have a pot of peppermint? Or orange spice?"

"I need to go," I said, patting my apron pocket to make sure my phone was still inside.

"So soon?" She bit her lip, maybe to keep herself from saying any more. But then she spoke anyway. "I had one more thing I needed to tell you."

I tilted my head.

She stepped toward me and lowered her voice. "I heard Silas and Gail have stopped courting."

"When?" Tears stung my eyes, even though I guessed it was probably just a rumor.

Aenti Suz shrugged. "I'm not sure exactly. But I heard Silas finally called it off for good."

I wasn't sure how to respond. Was she implying he'd tried to break it off before? I simply hugged Aenti Suz and said, "Thank you for everything."

She hugged me back. I understood Ruby's fear of being

separated from her family. But as it turned out she didn't have to be. She still had Zachary. And I still had Amos, even though he was half a continent away.

All I had to do was grab my bag and try not to think about Silas. I'd change out of my dress, for the last time, once I reached Harrisburg. Milton would need to get someone else to help him finish the plowing. I couldn't bear to stay five minutes longer.

I hurried to the house, ran up the stairs, collected my things, and then sought out Mamm to tell her good-bye. She was in Dat's office, sitting at his desk, going through papers.

"So this is it?" she said.

I nodded.

"You won't stick around and confront Arden with me?"

I shook my head. That was the last thing I wanted to do. I'd already taken that route, more than once. It'd only brought me heartache.

She stood and gave me a hug. When I pulled away, I grabbed a piece of paper from Dat's desk and a pen and then wrote down my address and phone number. "Contact me if you need anything. And you're always welcome to come to Harrisburg. . . ."

"Denki," she said. "I may call or write sometime, but I won't be coming to visit."

I nodded. I really didn't expect she would. Dat felt comfortable traveling all over, but Mamm never had.

"Tell Leisel good-bye," I said. "I told her I'd hoped to be here when she returned, but I should get going." I knew Leisel would call me if she wanted to, but I didn't mention it to Mamm. I didn't want her to worry about Leisel any more than she probably already did.

"All right," Mamm said. "What about Marie and Gail?"

"Where are they?"

"Down at Vi and Arden's doing their wash."

I paused a moment. Marie didn't want to see me, but then I thought of all the years of sisterly friendship we'd shared.

"Please," Mamm said. "Just stop by."

"All right," I answered. I'd do it for my Mamm. Ruby had lost both of her parents, but I still had one of mine, and chances were she'd be alive for a long time yet. True, I wouldn't see much of her, but I didn't want to add to the tension between us. I felt as if we'd experienced some healing. I'd do what I could to keep it that way. Besides, I needed to tell Milton that I couldn't help him with the plowing.

I drove back up the lane, then on to the short stretch on the highway, and then turned down Vi and Arden's lane.

After parking my car, I walked around to the side yard where Milton was planting the garden plot. I waved and he stopped.

"I'm going to head back to Harrisburg," I said. "You'll do fine finishing plowing."

He frowned but didn't respond.

"It was good to see you." I wanted to hug him but knew that wouldn't go over well. "I'm so glad you like farming, that you love the land."

He nodded and a bit of a smile crept across his face.

"You're doing a good job."

He nodded again, grinned, and returned to the planting.

No clothes were on the line yet, so I guessed Marie and Gail were in the basement using the old wringer washer. I headed to the front door, knocked, waited, and then let myself in.

Arden and Vi's house was especially plain. No decorations on the walls, not even a calendar. The weren't any books in the house either, besides a Bible, *Martyrs Mirror*, and *Ausbund*, all on a corner shelf in the living room. The house barely looked lived in.

As I started down the stairs, I heard my name, but in conversation—not as if anyone was calling out to me.

"At least she's leaving today." That was Marie talking.

"It seems as if she's been here forever," Gail said.

"Jah, I never thought I'd feel this way about my own sister."

My throat constricted as I realized I had three choices. I could leave without saying anything, I could get mad, or I could try my best to love my sister, the girl who had been my best friend until three years before.

As I descended the rest of the stairs, their voices continued but I stopped listening. I thought of the day I told Marie I was leaving. She wouldn't stop crying. She was afraid for my soul. And for my life. But over and over she said, "How can you leave me?"

Of course she'd find a new best friend.

I stepped onto the concrete floor and said, "I came to say good-bye."

Both Gail and Marie stood at the washing machine, feeding towels through the wringer, with their backs to me. Slowly, Marie turned around. Red blotches crept up her neck to her face.

"It was good to see both of you," I said. The tears that stung my eyes took me by surprise. "I'm sad to say good-bye."

Marie's surprised expression turned into a frown, but she stepped toward me. She opened her mouth but no words came out. Gail nudged her, but then tears filled her eyes too. She wasn't as heartless as she'd seemed.

"Jessica," she said. "I'm—" She stopped. After a long moment she said, "I'm sad, for what has happened."

"Me too," I answered.

We didn't hug or say any more except for our farewells. It felt like a step in the right direction for me, though, simply because I'd been honest instead of defensive.

As I pulled back onto the highway, a van turned down Arden and Vi's driveway. Someone in the front passenger waved. *Leisel.* A driver was taking Arden home from the hospital. For a moment I contemplated going back, but I didn't. I didn't have the stamina to be confronted by my brother, not even to tell Leisel good-bye again.

Driving through the countryside, I thought of Ruby and Isabelle. Aenti Suz owed me more of an ending. Did Isabelle stay? Did she and Ruby continue to support each other? When did Ruby and Duncan marry? Did they move back to Philadelphia? If they stayed in Lancaster, did Isabelle stay with them?

I tried to sort out what the property lines would have been back in 1777 and what they were now. There wasn't an oak tree in our neighbors' field—obviously the oak tree on the Wallis property hadn't survived. I was grateful ours had, although there was no mention of it in Aenti Suz's account. The activity around me soon brought me back to the present.

The warm spring day brought out a workforce of both Englisch and Amish farmers, who were plowing and planting. I would never grow tired of the Lancaster County landscape with the lush green fields, rich soil, and tree-lined horizons. It had to be one of the most beautiful places on earth.

When I reached Harrisburg, my heart felt hollow, as if the center of it had been scooped out. Already I missed the farm. And there was no denying I missed Silas too.

I got a few funny looks as I climbed out of my car wearing my cape dress. I grabbed my bag and hurried up to my apartment. Even though the day was warm, my apartment was cool. I quickly went through it, turning on the heat and then turning all the lights on, including my string of tiny bulbs. Next I opened up the curtain.

But not even the fresh green buds on the plants down in the courtyard brought me comfort. I felt hopelessly alone. The hollow feeling expanded. I thought of when the low branches on the oak tree rotted and how at first we feared the trunk might be rotting too. Dat said the tree wouldn't live forever. I'd felt hollow then, fearing the tree might die. Thankfully, pruning the dying branch was all that was needed.

Changing into jeans and a sweatshirt didn't ease my angst. Neither did looking into my empty refrigerator. I curled up with my laptop to see what I'd missed on social media, but that only made the hollow feeling grow even more intense. I closed my computer. It was only 2:30. I decided to go into work for the rest of the day.

I quickly changed into slacks and a blouse and then grabbed the Stoltz file on my way out the door.

Tom wasn't at his desk when I walked down the hallway, but a couple of my other co-workers greeted me and offered their condolences. I graciously accepted. I worked with good people.

When I reached my desk, I booted up my computer, opened the file, and then started a report, writing it from the notes I'd jotted down while speaking with John Stoltz. Hopefully he wouldn't change his mind about the interview. An older Amish man who had been deceived would offer credibility—and garner sympathy—that another farmer might not.

Once I finished the report, I attached it to an e-mail to Tom and cc'd Deanna. Then I started catching up on my e-mails. Twenty minutes later Tom started toward me, a smile on his face.

"You're back," he said.

"Jah," I answered, and then shook my head and smiled. "Did you get my report?"

He nodded. "I skimmed it. I'll go through it more thoroughly later. Can you go with me on Friday? I've already made an appointment with Mr. Stoltz."

"Do you want me to?"

"Of course," he said. "I think the interview will go much better with you there."

I suspected it would too, but I didn't want to see Silas again. Especially not with Tom.

After work, I hoped Tom would want to hang out, but he had a meeting at church. The next day at work he was tied up in meetings over lunch and then had his usual Tuesday night basketball game. On Wednesday after work, we grabbed dinner together, but then he had to rush off for his usual men's Bible Study at church. Every night that week I sat alone in my apartment with all the lights on, missing home. Jah, I missed everyone. Even Marie. Even Arden.

I used to see Silas as passive, but now I realized just how passive I was in my relationship with Tom. While he bounced around from meeting to game to meeting, I sat at home pining after him. What had I become?

I made myself a cup of chamomile tea and sunk down into my couch. I couldn't help but wonder how Mamm's conversation with Arden had gone. And how Vi was doing. And how the farming was going for Milton.

When I first left Lancaster, I felt so wounded that I seethed with disappointment toward my family and community. But going home made me realize something. Even though neither my family nor our Amish district was perfect, they still offered me something I'd hadn't found yet in the Englisch world: Community. Service. Traditions. It didn't mean Englischers didn't have all of that—I knew they did. Tom had it in both his family and church. It was just that all of it still felt unreachable to me.

I remembered the day I joined the Amish church, proclaiming my faith in Christ Jesus before my community and family. I believed following His teachings and the traditions of the church was what was best for my spiritual life and for my future. I believed salvation came, alone, through my faith in Christ. I believed the support of my family and community would help me live out that faith and serve others in a way I never could on my own.

And I came to those conclusions mainly through my conversations with Silas. True, he was ready to join the church as soon as I was, but he didn't. Some, including Arden, saw that as a moral failing on his part. But I knew that was just Silas. I knew first that I loved him. I knew first that I was ready to join the church.

Silas was more thoughtful than I was. Perhaps a little slower to arrive at a decision. It wasn't a moral failing; it was simply his personality. We were different, that was all.

But perhaps that was changing. He'd quit working for my family without looking back. And he'd taken the job with Mr. Stoltz. And he planned to join the church, regardless of the fact that he was no longer courting Gail.

Then again, maybe what I saw as passivity when we were younger was actually wisdom.

I sighed. But the shaming by Bishop Jacobs and Marie and Arden toward me destroyed much of my hope, regardless of Silas's thought process. I was stripped of my dignity. Stripped of self. If only I'd been able to trust Christ through my trial, but by then, in my mind, my church represented Christ. I found no comfort in them—so I found no comfort in Him either.

That had left me isolated, more than anything. Perhaps that, along with the unfamiliarity, had left me adrift when it came to the Englisch church and traditions. It wasn't as if I didn't enjoy worshipping in the Englisch church, but I never felt as if I truly belonged.

Tom was my one connection. Was it fair to put so much of my hope in him, when I should be putting it in Christ and expecting a community to support me, not just one person?

I leaned back against my couch and closed my eyes, completely filled with the emptiness that I'd become more aware of since I went back to Lancaster County. The thing was, if I married Tom, he'd continue to be just as busy as he was—or busier. Church and community meetings. Basketball games. Work trips. All good things, but I would be alone, never quite feeling as if I fit in at church or work or the Englisch community. Could I give and serve if I always felt on the outside? If I always felt unsatisfied?

After a while I fished my phone out of my sweatshirt pocket and called Amos. He didn't pick up, so I left a message, stammering that I just wanted to check in to see how he was doing instead of confessing how lonely I was.

He called me back a few minutes later, as I was turning on every light in the room. Without even saying hello, he said, "The funniest thing happened yesterday. Your Mamm called me."

"My Mamm?"

"That's right," he said. "What did you say to her?"

"About?"

"Arden."

I couldn't remember what I'd said, not exactly. "What did she say?"

"That she was sorry for not believing me all those years ago. That she hadn't considered that there could be another side of the story, not after Arden spoke his side first."

I grimaced. Mamm had done the same thing to me regarding the narrative Bishop Jacobs, Marie, and Arden spun.

"What did you say to Mamm?" I asked and then took a sip of my tea.

"That I accepted her apology. Then she asked me to come visit again and bring my daughter."

I nearly choked. "She knows about Becca?"

"Apparently so. She said Dat told her before he died."

"What else did he tell her?"

"That Arden wasn't always honest, that she should keep an eye on him."

"Wow."

"Yeah." We talked a little bit more about things back home, and then he asked how I was doing.

"Oh, fine. Just having a little bit of culture shock adjusting back to my Englisch life."

He chuckled. "I know what you mean. It was all better than what I remembered."

"For me too," I said. "Except for sitting at the kids' table."

He laughed. "I still have bruises on my knees."

"Me too," I said. He started to wrap up the conversation, but I stopped him. "Did you talk to Becca about coming out to Lancaster County for a visit?"

"I mentioned it," he said. "She's interested."

A lump began to form in my throat. "I really hope to meet her," I said.

"I'd like that," he answered. "I'll keep you posted."

I promised to call again soon, and then we said our good-byes. After I hung up, instead of feeling less lonely, I felt more so. A numbness spread through me, part of my grief for Dat most likely. But I was missing my Mamm for the first time in three years too. I thought of Ruby's love for her mother and her sorrow when she died. Would I ever have a chance to improve my relationship with my mother? I doubted it.

I finished my tea and went to bed early, trying to remember what I'd liked so much about my Englisch life before going home.

Friday morning Tom picked me up at seven a.m. to go to the Stoltz farm. We chatted on the way there, but it didn't feel as comfortable as it had before Dat died. Although Tom admired my Dat, his death wasn't weighing on him. I was still in mourning. He wasn't.

In the Englisch world I wore black all the time. It wasn't a sign of mourning, not like in the Amish. Actually, there seemed to be no sign of mourning in the Englisch world. And I'd noticed that people only took a few days off work when a parent or grandparent or other family member died—or in my case an entire week, which probably seemed excessive to most.

Jah, grief in an Amish community meant grieving with others. It meant never grieving alone.

As he drove, Tom grilled me about how he should approach the interview. I told him to be himself.

"I brought my camera," he said.

"You can't take photos of John."

He nodded. "But could I get one of his back, looking over his farm? Something like that?"

I shook my head. "But John did say you can take photos of his farm," I said. "Just don't photograph him. Not even his back." Tom could take a photo of Silas, because he hadn't joined the church yet, but I wasn't going to suggest it.

As we crossed into Lancaster County, my heart lifted with the sights of home. The green fields. The black soil. The dairy herds. But it was more than that. It was a sensation of home—a feeling of hope.

I breathed a prayer of gratitude.

"What are you smiling about?" Tom asked, his gaze on me for a moment.

"Nothing," I replied, glancing toward him. "Just how beautiful the countryside is."

He nodded in agreement, but didn't say anything more.

When we arrived at the Stoltz farm, Silas was nowhere in sight, and this time I didn't ask after him. Tom asked John question after question, but the man was much more reticent than he had been with me. Getting answers from him, beyond the basic facts, escaped Tom. I tried to encourage the conversation, asking more direct questions than Tom knew to ask as we walked around the farm, but John couldn't seem to be as open as he'd been with me alone.

Tom asked about taking a couple of photos of the farm, and John agreed the land was fine, but he didn't even want his yellow lab photographed.

I looked one last time for Silas but didn't see him. Perhaps John knew what I was doing because he said, "My new farmhand is working out well. In fact, he may be an answer to our prayers."

I smiled.

"And not just our immediate prayers," he added.

Now I was curious. "Oh?"

"Our prayers about what to do with the farm when we die."

I nearly choked. Surely they didn't plan to give their farm to Silas after only knowing him for five days.

"We're still thinking about it," John said. "We plan to live here . . . as long as we can. We'd charge him, of course, if he'd like to buy the property, in payments probably. But we'd make it affordable. It's an idea we're thinking about, talking about, and praying about." He sighed. "We'll see. I'm looking into drilling a new well on the other side of our property."

"That's great," I managed to say. It seemed as if Silas and whomever he chose to marry would soon be living on the Stoltzes' farm. God was providing for Silas in a way I'd always prayed he would. So why did I feel as if I'd just been kicked in the stomach?

I finally managed to sputter out what I'd been wanting to ask since we arrived. "Where *is* Silas?"

"Oh, he had some sort of personal business today. An Amish woman came by, with a driver, right before you arrived. I gave him the day off."

How curious. Could Aenti Suz have been mistaken and Gail and Silas reconciled after all? They were clearly going somewhere together. The courthouse to get a marriage license? No, he still needed to join the church. And he had a few classes to finish up first, but perhaps Bishop Jacobs would baptize Silas early. He'd taken the class before, with me. It wasn't as if he didn't know what he was getting into.

"Well," Tom said, probably bored with the conversation about Silas. He stuck out his hand. "It's certainly nice to meet you, Mr. Stoltz. Thank you again for being willing to be interviewed."

John nodded. "I just hope it helps someone else make a better decision than I did."

I thanked him too. "Please tell Mildred hello."

"I will," he said. "She's resting. It's not a good day for her, so far."

I felt nothing but kindness toward the man. Mildred was blessed to have a husband who loved her so well. I told him that he and Mildred were in my prayers and then said good-bye.

As Tom and I left the farm, I tried not to think of Silas and Gail marrying. But I couldn't help it. Sadness filled me as I did, and the harmonious feeling that had fallen on me earlier as we entered Lancaster County started to fade. I tried to pray, to regain the peace I'd felt, but I couldn't seem to form even a simple prayer.

Tom vented his frustration about the interview on the way back to Harrisburg. It hadn't gone as he'd hoped at all. "John didn't seem very friendly."

"He is," I said. "He just wasn't comfortable."

"With me?"

I nodded. "He wouldn't be with any Englischer."

"He was with you, though. I could sense the difference."

"Well . . ." I didn't bother to explain. He was actually friendlier with me than I'd expected, considering I'd left the Amish. The truth was, John Stoltz made me feel as if I'd never left, even though I was wearing Englisch clothes. He'd been nothing but kind to me. I leaned back in my seat, feeling frustrated with both Tom and myself.

Even though I'd been living Englisch for three years, there were things neither of us would ever understand about the other. In many cases it wouldn't matter, but I feared it might for us. But I couldn't verbalize what I was feeling to Tom.

Instead I asked, "Do you think you have enough for an article?"

"I hope so," Tom said.

We chatted more about work and then about church. Easter was coming up. My heart fell a little. I always loved Easter back home and would even help with the extra baking the week before. Then the remembrance of the Lord's death started off solemnly with fasting on Good Friday morning, which ended with dinner. On Saturday, friends and family stopped by to visit and we served the baked goods we'd prepared earlier. Sunday morning we ate hard-boiled eggs with breakfast, as a reminder of rebirth, and then celebrated the Lord's resurrection. We dyed eggs and then hid them after the noon meal. On Monday, we had another day of reflecting on Christ's sacrifice for us, and also on the salvation He offered.

Tom didn't ask me about Easter back home, but instead talked about the music program at church and then Easter with his family. "You're invited, of course," he said.

"Thank you." I smiled, but inside I felt only grief. I appreciated his family, I really did. But the ache for my own was stronger than it had been in the last three years.

My grief—and not just for Dat—overwhelmed me. "You know, I think I'll take the rest of the day off," I said.

"Really?" Tom turned toward downtown. "After taking a whole week?"

"Jah," I answered. This time the word didn't make me wince. "Please take me to my apartment."

He shook his head, just enough to appear patronizing, and then said, "If you insist."

"Jah," I answered again. "I do."

We rode for a moment in silence and then I said, "I think we should take a break."

"Jessica," he said. "What's going on?"

"I'm not sure." I fought back tears.

"I'm sorry," he said. "I should have been more understanding about you needing more time, to mourn your dad. . . ." His voice trailed off.

Too choked up to speak, I said nothing. It was more than that. I felt overcome with conflict. I hadn't felt such a lack of harmony in my life since I fled Lancaster County the first time.

But honestly, it was grief over Silas too. I thought of Ruby. My situation wasn't the same as hers, but why had I ever gotten involved with Tom when I still loved Silas? Denial was why. I'd convinced myself I no longer cared for Silas.

I couldn't keep denying it any longer. I'd never marry Silas. But I couldn't continue dating Tom, not when I felt this way about someone else.

Tom pulled into a parking space in front of my building. "I'll give you time, then we'll sort this out." He smiled kindly. Clearly he didn't think I was trying to break up with him. I'd have to figure out how to talk with him later.

I thanked him, and then as I started to get out of the car, he said, "I'll call you Sunday."

I almost laughed. *Time* was two days to him. Oh well. I'd have to find my words soon enough.

After a quick good-bye, I dug in my purse for my key as I headed to the outside door, pausing a moment. Tom couldn't give me what I needed. And neither could Silas. Nor my Amish community. They could add to my transformation, but only the Lord could change me and give me peace. *Help me to trust you,* I prayed as I unlocked the door. *To follow you. Use the conflict—this pain—to show me who I am, to show me how to serve you better, to strengthen me, to help me. Even if that*

means returning home—especially if it means returning home.
My knees grew weak. Was that the decision that I'd just made?
To go back home? Even though I had no future with Silas?

Honestly, the thought of returning felt scarier than leaving
had. *"Fear thou not; for I am with thee. . . ."*

Help me not to be afraid, I prayed.

I opened the door to the stairwell and paused. The hard
things in her life had shaped Ruby. My leaving Lancaster and
the change I'd gone through had convinced me that the place
I truly belonged was back on my ancestral land. Hopefully
Mamm—and ultimately Arden—would welcome me home.
For good.

As I stepped on the first stair, out of the corner of my eye,
I noticed a young woman dressed Plain come out of the coffee
shop. Then a man.

I froze. It was Silas. I took another look at the woman, expecting Gail. It wasn't. It was Leisel.

— 21 —

Leisel!" I blurted out as she rushed toward me. We hugged for a long moment. As she released me, she said, "We need to talk."

I peered over her shoulder and made eye contact with Silas. My heart began to race. "Has something happened to Mamm? Or Marie?" Tears stung my eyes. "Has Arden taken a turn for the worse?"

"No, everyone's fine," Leisel said. "But we have some information you need to know."

Relieved no one was hurt or dying, I said, "Come on up." I motioned for them to head up the stairs. "Third floor, at the end of the hall."

Once we were inside my apartment, I offered to make some tea.

Leisel shook her head and smiled. "We've been drinking coffee all morning. We thought we'd catch you before you went to work this morning. Then we stopped by your office and found out you'd gone to Lancaster County for an interview. Because your car was here, we decided to wait in the coffee shop."

Once we'd all sat down in my tiny living room, I asked, "What's going on?"

"Do you remember that older Englischman at Dat's service? The one in the rumpled suit?"

I nodded.

"It turns out he's a lawyer. He stopped by yesterday to speak with Mamm, and then the two of them went and talked to Arden." She explained that Dat had set up some sort of trust for the farm. "He specified that he wanted you and Arden to make all of the decisions concerning the property together, that you have to be in agreement or no changes as far as the use or sale of the land can be made."

"What?" That sounded like a nightmare—but also an answer to the prayer of my heart a few minutes ago.

"Jah," Leisel said, "so Arden can't sell off the woods without you agreeing to it."

Silas spoke up. "Or allow fracking on the property."

I turned toward him. "Did you know about Arden's plans all along? Were you the one who put the plans on the desk?"

He nodded, his eyes bright. "Jah."

Leisel stepped closer to me. "Mamm told us about the plans you showed her, that Arden contacted the company when Dat fell ill." She bit her lip and turned toward Silas again.

"I found the plans after you arrived," he said, "when I was looking for more cleaning forms in the office. I'm the one who left them out on the desk. So you'd find them."

I nodded. "I wondered when you later told me they were in the cabinet." I wrinkled my nose. "Is Dat's plan legit, though? Since I left the church? Won't Bishop Jacobs veto it?"

"No," Leisel said. "Mamm asked the lawyer the same thing. Apparently a legal document has more power than the bishop."

The Englisch girl inside of me believed her, but the Amish

girl had her doubts. Surely Arden and Bishop Jacobs could do something to overrule it.

But I knew Dat would have made certain his plan would work before having his lawyer draft the paperwork. From the grave, he was forcing two of his children to work out their differences, to push past the conflict, to put the good of the land before anything else. While he was alive, he'd been so careful not to meddle in the lives of his adult children, most likely praying we'd work out things on our own. But as he neared death, he'd come up with a plan to, hopefully, provide the opportunity for healing—and to save the farm.

"You'll cooperate, right?" Leisel said. "Dat was brilliant to do this. You should have seen the look on Milton's face when he figured out what was going on. He was so relieved."

My eyes widened. I thought Milton was on Arden's side, but perhaps not. He valued the land too. Dat had wanted the farm to be preserved for the next generation. He'd done what he could to make sure it would be.

"Will you go with me?" I asked Leisel. "To talk with the lawyer?"

It was Leisel's turn to blush. She shook her head. "I'm leaving."

"Leaving? What do you mean?"

"I'm headed to Pittsburgh. To nursing school—"

She was going to become a nurse. Part of me was happy for her, but mostly I felt alarmed.

"—I just received my acceptance. I start the end of August. But I'm going to find a job and get settled."

"Leisel," I said. "Why?"

She shook her head, a wry smile on her face. "Because it's what I need to do."

That was exactly what I'd said to her when I left three years before.

"What did Mamm say?"

Leisel eyes softened. "She cried. The timing is bad, I know."

"I see." My stomach dropped. Surely I'd encouraged her by my own leaving.

Silas shot Leisel a sympathetic look.

My stomach fell even further. Why was Silas with her? Had something happened this week? Surely he wasn't going with her. A wave of nausea swept over me.

"Where are your bags?" I glanced from Leisel to Silas as I spoke, looking around as if I might have overlooked a bag or two.

"My bag is in the coffee shop storeroom. The nice people there said I could keep it there until my friend arrives to give me a ride to Pittsburgh."

"Friend?"

She blushed. "I met him in my CNA class. But he really is just a friend. I have no intention of becoming involved with him."

"Why is he going to Pittsburgh?"

Her face turned a brighter shade of red. "He lives there. He started the nursing program last fall."

"Oh." So it seemed Silas wasn't going with her. How paranoid was I? More important, when would I stop caring about Silas?

I got over my distraction and realized Leisel had a relationship with this young man, whether it was romantic or not. My heart lurched. She'd never joined the church, so she wouldn't be shunned the same way I had, but I still didn't want her to move to Pittsburgh, to be so far away. To be on her own. Especially if I was going home.

No matter what, I needed to go back to the farm now, at least to fulfill my duty that Dat had conscripted me to do. And hopefully to stay. No matter what Leisel had decided.

I turned toward Silas. "What do I need to do now? As far as the farm."

"Meet with the lawyer, to start with," he said. "And then with Arden. He should know you plan to hold him accountable."

"What about Bishop Jacobs?"

"Meet with him too—immediately, before Arden slants all of this from his point of view."

I must have appeared terrified because Silas said, "I'll go with you to both meetings. I'll do whatever I can."

I couldn't help but think of Duncan telling Ruby, *"I'll do it for you."* But Silas was telling me, "I'll do it with you." That was even better.

My eyes met his in gratitude. "Denki," I said. But I still wasn't sure why Silas came with Leisel. "What about you?" I said to him. "What are your long-term plans?"

"John Stoltz has an idea, as far as his land."

I nodded. "He told me." Again, I felt the grief of losing Silas, but if I truly cared about his well-being as much as my own, then I'd want what was best for him. I sighed inside. That was what I wanted—God's best for all of us.

Silas glanced at Leisel. She pointed toward the door. "I'm going to go get my bag. My ride will be here in a few minutes. Come down and tell me good-bye." She quickly slipped out.

I turned toward Silas. "What's going on?"

"I do hope to buy John Stoltz's farm, although I'm afraid it's too early for him to consider such an arrangement. He doesn't know me yet."

"But he's impressed with you."

"Time will tell," Silas said. "But it gives me hope that perhaps I can have my own place someday."

I nodded. That's what I truly hoped for him too.

"And if everything works out with John and Mildred, I'll be able to care for my mother and support a family."

"So you'll join the church soon?"

He nodded.

I swallowed, trying to get rid of the growing lump in my throat, thinking about my earlier suspicion that he and Gail had gone to get a marriage license. I'd been wrong—but what if I wasn't? "The church. A farm. All of that will be nice for you . . . and Gail."

"Gail?"

"Jah . . ."

He shook his head. "I need to know what your intentions are."

"Mine?"

"Are you considering coming home? For more than to work with Arden on the direction of the farm?"

"Why are you asking?"

He stepped toward me. "So I know what I should do."

My heart skipped a beat.

"I regretted not leaving with you, not following you," he said. "Even more, I regretted not sticking up for you when it came to the bishop and Arden. I was trying so hard to act like an adult that I acted like a child."

He exhaled slowly. Thankfully he didn't seem to want a response from me, because I had no idea what to say.

Silas stepped closer. "I know you've been dating Tom, but I don't sense you're as committed to him as you indicated." He reached for my hand. I let him take it, and his warmth quickly spread through me. "I haven't stopped loving you, Jessie," Silas said. "I thought maybe I had—until I saw you that day, climbing out of your car. I want to join the church, to commit to God and our community. But I want nothing more than for you to come home, for us to commit together."

My eyes locked with Silas's as a knock fell on the open door. "Jessica?"

It was Tom.

I stepped away from Silas toward the door. But my thoughts weren't on Tom. They were on Ruby Bachmann. On the moment when she stepped away from Paul and took Duncan's hand.

"Oh," Tom said as I opened the door and he saw Silas. "I see they found you." He glanced around. "But at work they said there was an Amish girl too."

"Leisel. She's down in the coffee shop."

"Is everything all right?" Tom asked.

I nodded.

"Oh, good. I thought perhaps something had happened."

I shook my head. Too much had happened. I couldn't explain it all.

I turned toward Silas. "Could you go check on Leisel? I'll be right down."

Silas headed to the door as I took a deep breath. Tom had a right to know what my decision was, before even Silas did. "Thank you for coming to check. It was very kind of you." I sincerely meant it.

I met his gaze. "I'm going back to Lancaster, back to the farm."

A confused smile passed over his face. "For how long?"

"Indefinitely," I said. "I'll put in my resignation at work today."

"Jessica." He stepped toward me, extending his hand. I put both of mine behind my back.

A hint of anger flashed across his face. "This? After every-thing . . ."

He stopped himself. But I could fill in the blanks. *Everything he'd done for me.*

"I appreciate all of it," I said. "Honestly. But we're not meant for each other. My place is back home, and I know that now after this last week."

He nodded toward the street. "Is this because of Silas?"

"I'll be honest," I said. "I still have feelings for Silas. But I'll stay in Lancaster regardless of what the outcome is between us. I belong back home, with my family. It's the best place for me—spiritually and emotionally."

He shook his head a little, a frown on his face. "I didn't think you were one to give up."

"I'm not giving up," I said. "I'm embracing what God has for me. Even before Silas and Leisel came here today, I tried to tell you earlier, when you dropped me off, that things weren't working. I'm sorry I wasn't clearer."

He shook his head, as if I hadn't tried to tell him a thing. "I'm afraid you'll regret this," he said. "You have so much potential. You'll be back in a month."

All I could say was, "We'll see."

I stepped toward the door. "Thank you for coming to check on me. I really do appreciate it." I held the door as he stepped through. "And I'm thankful for everything you've done for me. You've been the friend I needed."

He shook his head. "I still think you'll absolutely regret this." But then he smiled a little and added, "You're welcome."

I walked Tom to his car and then told him a quick good-bye. I waited until he drove away, and then turned toward the coffee shop. Silas stood at the door, watching.

God? I prayed. *Is this where you're leading me?*

Silas held out his hand.

Before he could speak, I blurted out, "I'm going home for good. I'm rejoining the church. As far as us, I never stopped loving you either, but we need to start courting again. To make sure this is what you truly want, what God wants for both of us."

His eyes locked onto mine. "What about Tom?"

I held Silas's gaze. "I told him good-bye."

Silas wrapped his arm around me and pulled me close. For a moment I fell against him, as joyful as I'd been since the last time he'd hugged me. Then over his shoulder, I saw Leisel sitting at a table by the window, her bag at her feet and a big smile on her face.

But then she turned toward the window, waved, and jumped to her feet. Her bag in her hand, she exclaimed, "Nick's here."

Silas let me go as Leisel rushed past me. I grabbed her arm, "Don't go," I said. "I'll help you find a school closer to home."

She shook her head. "It's all been decided." She pulled a piece of paper from her pocket. "Here's my new address. And Nick's phone number, in case of an emergency."

I took the piece of paper. "Be wise," I said. "Don't forget what we were taught. . . ." Ruby's Mamm's word echoed in my mind. "Trust the Lord, Leisel," I said. "Pray that His will be done."

"I will," she promised, giving me a hug.

I followed her out the door. Nick drove an old Chevy pickup. He climbed out of the driver's seat, his hand extended, and introduced himself to me and then to Silas. "I'll be a good friend to Leisel," he said. He was tall and thin with a boyish charm. "I promise."

All I could do was take him at his word. I stood on the sidewalk and waved at Leisel as they left.

Once the pickup was out of sight, Silas asked, "What now?"

"I'll go send an e-mail to give my official two weeks' notice," I said. "And I'll give notice on my apartment. But then let's go home. We'll talk to the lawyer and Bishop Jacobs and then to Arden. I'll spend the weekend at the farm—and then go home for good once everything is settled here."

An hour later, as we crossed into Lancaster County, I thought of Ruby again. How did her story end? I shivered and glanced over at Silas.

More important, how in the world would ours? Driving with Silas in the car felt both familiar and foreign. My face grew warm as I realized he was staring. After all this time, his eyes still reflected me.

He reached out and took my free hand. We drove that way, my internal conflict finally gone. Harmony once again filled my soul, replacing the hollowness that had grown inside me for the last three years. Silas began singing "How Great Thou Art." I joined along, belting out "Consider all the woods Thy hands have made." God had definitely made my woods, but more important, my *world*. I was so grateful He'd created the same world for Silas—and put us in it, together.

Silas stayed by my side every inch of the way: through talking with Mamm, my appointment with the lawyer, our meeting with Bishop Jacobs, and then my talk with Arden. Step by step, together, we dealt with each person that weekend I was home.

And after two weeks back in Harrisburg, I packed up everything in my apartment and took the clothes, appliances, and lights I wouldn't be using to a thrift shop. I sold my phone and laptop, and once I'd moved home, sold my car too. Then I began the process of being reinstated in the church. It wasn't hard to give up my car or phone—but it was extremely difficult to give up my laptop. However, I'd never give up the knowledge I'd gained or my thirst for more. I spent time, as I could, at the library, continuing my research on farming and all sorts of other things, including our family history.

In time Marie seemed to forgive me for leaving—and returning. I feared she'd never forgive me for what she believed was my influence on Leisel. Still, we reached a truce, and although we didn't regain our friendship, we were able to be kind to each other. Gail, heartbroken that Silas really had ended their courtship, joined her family in Ohio and that, in time, decreased the conflict between Marie and me too.

I wouldn't agree to the fracking or selling off the woods, which at first riled Arden, but with my help the farmwork got done and profits began to rise. I had some help, though. Arden hired a young Mennonite man, Gordon Martin. He proved to be a hard worker—and also interested in Marie. Not surprisingly, she wouldn't have anything to do with him. If she had, I'm sure Arden would have fired Gordon immediately. Still, I thought it interesting that God would "test" Marie in such a way. There was a lot about Gordon to be attracted to—if one were a single young woman.

But, of course, I only had eyes for Silas.

Several times I asked Aenti Suz to tell me the rest of Ruby and Duncan's story, but she always had one excuse or another not to.

In early June, Silas and I both joined the church. The service happened to be at our farm on a gorgeous summer day. After the service and meal, as Aenti Suz and I cleaned up the last of the dishes after the others had left, I asked her again to tell me about Ruby.

This time she smiled, glanced around to make sure we were truly alone, and then said, "As I said, she left the church and married Duncan. Isabelle married a businessman in Lancaster and stayed in the county too. She and Ruby became as close as sisters. Zachary, your . . ." She sighed. "I can't keep track of how many greats he would be. Anyway, he married Lettie and they had one son and several daughters and stayed with the Amish, helping to rebuild the community after so many had left.

"Duncan inherited and farmed the Wallis place, and with Ruby's help earned a decent living. Sadly, they never had children."

"Oh," I said. That wasn't what I expected. "So their land was sold?"

Aenti shook her head. "No, they deeded it to Zachary's son when they gave up farming. The Wallis land is part of the Bachmann farm."

How had I missed that? "So the oak tree? The one that Ruby and Duncan met under? That's our oak tree?"

Aenti Suz nodded. "Jah, your and Silas's tree."

The lay of the land hadn't changed in all of these years. I started to laugh, but then thought of Ruby.

"Is she buried in our cemetery?"

"No, after she and Duncan deeded their place to their nephew, they moved to Philadelphia, to his parents' estate. Isabelle and her husband went with them. For the last years of their lives, Ruby and Isabelle were ladies of a fine home, together."

I smiled. "What about Hans and Daniel and their families? Did they stay in Canada?"

Aenti Suz cocked her head. "We're not sure. There was no traceable Amish community up there until the early 1800s. They either moved back to the states and settled somewhere else, perhaps Ohio, or assimilated in Canada."

"What about Paul?"

She answered, "I assumed he ended up wherever Hans and Daniel did."

"Was Ruby shunned?"

Aenti Suz shrugged. "I don't have details on that. Perhaps things were different back then or maybe just in their circumstances. Or maybe because Zachary had left to go off to war, he was more understanding of his sister." She smiled. "And perhaps he felt more tenderhearted, considering Ruby probably saved his life by rescuing him and then nursing him back to health. Over two thousand soldiers died at Valley Forge that winter."

I grimaced.

"Anyway," Aenti Suz said, "it seems she and Zachary maintained a good relationship, don't you think?"

I nodded. It didn't seem likely Duncan and Ruby would have left their property to Zachary's son if they hadn't.

Zachary made me think of Dat. Perhaps my father had been understanding of Amos and me because he'd considered leaving. And, in a sense, he had by going off to Vietnam, to a war zone. I knew grace often begat grace. I shivered, vowing to continue to show grace to Leisel.

I glanced out the kitchen window. Silas stood at the fence line with Arden and Milton, the oak tree behind him and beyond that the woods. Duncan and Ruby had given us so much.

My heart swelled. Silas must have seen me through the window because he waved.

"Go on out," Aenti Suz said. "I'll finish up."

"Denki," I said. We were having the Youngie singing in our shed that evening, the first Silas and I would attend as a courting couple—again. We needed to help Mamm and Marie finish setting up. But first, we had time for a walk through the field and a stop under our oak tree.

We weren't the first couple, and we surely wouldn't be the last, God willing, to court on the Bachmann farm. I wouldn't be the first daughter to leave the farm either and make a new life somewhere else, most likely at the Stoltz place. But I would be the first daughter to have a say in how the family managed the land—thanks to the trust of my father. It was his act of grace, inspired by a loving God, that brought me to a place of harmony in my heart again, and ultimately back home.

Acknowledgments

I'm thankful to my husband, Peter, for his encouragement, medical expertise, and help with research. And for keeping me calm as I rush to meet deadlines! (I couldn't do this without you.) I'm also grateful to our four children—Kaleb, Taylor, Hana, and Thao—who inspire me and also challenge me to see the world in deeper ways.

A bouquet of thanks to Marietta Couch, my dear friend, who has shared her Amish experiences with me and acts as a sounding board for my wild ideas. Any mistakes are mine and mine alone.

I'm indebted to Chip MacGregor, my agent, for his encouragement and ongoing belief in my ability to tell a good story.

I'm very thankful for all of the good people at Bethany House Publishers—editors, designers, marketers, publicists, salespeople, and everyone else who works on behalf of my books. What a great team! A special shout-out to Jennifer Veilleux and Dave Long, who guided me through this particular story.

I'm grateful for my father on earth, Bruce Egger, who passed away as I finished this book. Besides being a good man and father, he was also a good writer and an inspiration to my own storytelling. He taught me about the world and myself, up until the last day of his life. I'm so grateful he's now in heaven.

Most important, I'm thankful to my Father in heaven for His endless grace, mercy, and inspiration.

Leslie Gould is the #1 bestselling and award-winning author of twenty-six novels, including the COURTSHIPS OF LANCASTER COUNTY and NEIGHBORS OF LANCASTER COUNTY series. She holds an MFA in creative writing and teaches at the college level. She enjoys research trips, church history, and hiking, especially in the beautiful state of Oregon where she lives. She and her husband, Peter, are the parents of four children.

Sign Up for Leslie's Newsletter!

Keep up to date with Leslie's news on book releases and events by signing up for her email list at lesliegould.com.

More from Leslie Gould

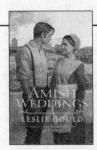

Rose Lehman has always known who she wants to marry: the bishop's son, Reuben. But then Trevor, a handsome Army man, visits Lancaster County, and Rose starts to question her plan. When the thrill of adventure fades, will Rose find happiness—or ruin her best chance at love?

Amish Weddings
NEIGHBORS OF LANCASTER COUNTY #3

You May Also Like . . .

Genealogist Nora Bradford has decided that focusing on her work is far safer than romance. But when a former Navy SEAL hires her to find his birth mother, their connection is undeniable. The trouble is that they seem to have met the right person at the worst possible time.

True to You by Becky Wade, A Bradford Sisters Romance
beckywade.com

When a British plane crashes in WWI German-occupied Brussels, English nurse Evelyn Marche must protect the injured soldier, who has top-secret orders and a target on his back.

High as the Heavens by Kate Breslin
katebreslin.com

In Scotland's Shetland Islands, a clan patriarch has died, and a dispute over the inheritance has frozen an entire community's assets. When a letter from the estate's solicitor finds American Loni Ford, she sets out on a journey to discover her roots—but is this dream too good to be true?

The Inheritance by Michael Phillips, Secrets of the Shetlands #1
fatheroftheinklings.com

Nurse practitioner Mia Robinson is done with dating. Instead, she's focused on caring for her teenage sister, Lucy—who, it turns out, is pregnant and plans to marry her boyfriend. Mia is determined to stop the wedding, but she's in for a surprise when she meets the best man.

The Two of Us by Victoria Bylin
victoriabylin.com

◊ BETHANYHOUSE